THE NEW HUGO WINNERS

Presented
by
ISAAC ASIMOV

D0709061

BAEN BOOKS

THE NEW HUGO WINNERS

Contents

The most prestigious awards in their field, the Science Fiction Achievement Awards were nicknamed in honor of Hugo Gernsback, the founding editor of the world's first science fiction magazine, Amazing Stories.

Initiated at the World Science Fiction Convention in Philadelphia in 1953, and a continuous event since 1955, the Hugos are presented in twelve categories: best Novel, Novella, Novelette, Short Story, Nonfiction Book, Professional Editor, Dramatic Presentation, Professional Artist, Fan Writer, Fan Artist, Semi-Professional Magazine, and Fanzine.

The winners are determined by members of the annual World Science Fiction Convention.

INTRODUCTION

Back in 1962 I published my very first science fiction anthology. It was *The Hugo Winners*, and the idea came first, I believe, to the science fiction writer Avram Davidson (who *was* a Hugo winner and saw no reason not to have his story anthologized). He suggested the notion to his agent, Robert P. Mills, who decided that the anthology would need an editor who was well known in the field but who had *not* won a Hugo, and he thought of me.

Why not? The stories had already been selected by the voting readers themselves, and even the order was prescribed. There would be very little work, and as everybody knows, I am dedicated to the principle of "very little work." So I did the anthology, and it was my very first.

In one way it was good, for in order to make the book my own by doing *something* to get credit for, I wrote a longish, chatty introduction and longish, chatty headnotes. That proved to be so much fun that I have seized ever since every possible occasion to talk to readers about myself and my stories.

I never lie to my readers, however, so I'm going to tell you that in another respect the anthology made me unhappy. I hated writing for permissions. I hated the arithmetic of dividing royalty checks and the time-consuming labor that involved mailing them out to various authors and agents. I hated the *bookkeeping*. So I didn't rush to do other anthologies, and over the next sixteen years I edited only eight altogether (virtually nothing, weighed against my usual scale of production of anything that interests me). What's more, two of them were additional Hugo Winner anthologies, for the world science fiction conventions did not cease and neither did the awarding of Hugos. Of course, having learned from my first attempt, I was shrewd enough to stick my publishers with the bookkeeping in the later anthologies, but I still didn't enjoy anthologizing and I still didn't rush to do it.

And yet I have done five of the Hugo Winner anthologies, and here, if you are interested (or even if you are not), are the statistics:

Hugo Winners (1962) 9 stories

Hugo Winners, Volume Two (1971) 14 stories

Hugo Winners, Volume Three (1977) 15 stories

Hugo Winners, Volume Four (1985) 13 stories

Hugo Winners, Volume Five (1986) 9 stories

The total is sixty stories, including every Hugo Winner (except the novels, of course) awarded between 1955 and 1982.

Frankly, I had had enough, and I rather made up my mind that I wouldn't do any more. I had aged a year or two in the quarter century since I had begun. I no longer knew, with any great intimacy, the flood of dazzling new writers who had entered the field and were garnering awards—not the way I knew the few old-timers who had shared the field with me when the world and we were young.

However, Martin H. Greenberg told me severely that I could not do that. The Hugo Winners volumes, he said, were important items to the lore and history of the field and transcended my personal desires for ease and comfort, so I would have to continue.

At this point, let me digress and tell you about Martin H. Greenberg. He is a tall, ferociously hardworking and intelligent academic. He's Dr. Greenberg, actually, and he is a professor of political science. He is also a lifelong science fiction reader, and back in the late 1970s he thought he would leaven his writings with some collections of science fiction that would illuminate his field of political science. So the time came when he wanted some stories of mine, and he wrote to ask about them.

Now you have to understand that Martin Greenberg is *not* a very uncommon name. As it happened, back in the early 1950s there had been a Martin Greenberg who was the owner of Gnome Press and who had published four of my very early books. What's more, he had published a couple of anthologies that had included a couple of my stories. The only trouble was that I had not seen eye-to-eye with Martin Greenberg, and we had broken off relations in a friendly way. (I never fight with anybody.) However, I didn't want to resume relations.

So I wrote a very cautious letter to this person who had written for anthology permissions, saying, "Before we discuss the granting of permissions, are you the Martin Greenberg who, back in the early 1950s, . . ."

He replied quickly, saying that he was only a grade-school boy in the early 1950s and that his name was Martin *Harry* Greenberg. To which I replied that of course he could have permission to anthologize my stories, but he had better use his middle name, or at least his middle initial, on his books.

As a result of this epistolary exchange, Marty and I (I called him "Marty the Other" for a few years) became close friends, and almost at once he suggested that I join him in an anthology. I discovered that Marty loved writing for permissions, adored figuring out who gets what out of the payments, grew ecstatic over the process of mailing out checks to all and sundry. He would do *all* of that, and gloat over it.

Well!

Our first anthology came out in 1978, and I have now done well over a hundred, almost all of them with Marty, and usually with a third person involved as well (mostly Charles G. Waugh, a professor of psychology in Maine). Marty doesn't work exclusively with me, and he has put out well over three hundred anthologies. He is undoubtedly the most prolific (and the *best*) anthologist who has ever lived—and I mean in any field, not just science fiction. Right now, I think that he may be the outstanding personality in the field who is not and has never been an actual science fiction writer. He wins awards, he gets the nod as guest of honor now and then, and, in general, is loved by one and all.

So you can well imagine that when Marty views with concern and disapproval my intention of retiring from the Hugo Winners anthology business, and gives me all that high-flown malarkey about serving the field and the anthologies' being historical monuments, I am forced to listen and even to get to be a little ashamed of myself.

However, neither am I an utter idiot. I looked him right in the eye and said, "All right, Marty. I'll do it. I'll prepare the Hugo Winners' sixth anthology. But you'll have to do it with me."

I insisted, and here we are, together again—and we have a fair division of labor. I write the introduction. I write the headnotes. He does the work. It couldn't be better.

Besides, he is twenty-one years younger than I am. If things go as they ought to go, he will be able to carry on these volumes after I have departed to the great word processor in the sky (it used to be a typewriter, as I recall). And he can train others, who can train others, so that for as long as Earth and the human species lasts, volumes of Hugo Winners will come out periodically.

It might, of course, be a publishing problem to make readers understand that volume 125,874 is a new volume and not a reprint of the very similarly titled volume 125,873, but that will have to be dealt with after my time, I think.

—Isaac Asimov

1983
Forty-first Convention
Baltimore

When I first entered the science fiction writing field, it was largely the domain of young men. The sixty stories in the first five volumes of this series of Hugo Winners were written by thirty-four writers, of whom only six were women: Anne McCaffrey, Ursula K. Le Guin (who appeared twice), Alice Sheldon (who wrote under the pseudonym of James Tiptree, Jr., and who also appeared twice), Jeanne Robinson (in collaboration with her husband, Spider Robinson), Joan D. Vinge, and C. J. Cherryh.

Yet among the nine stories in this sixth volume, three women are represented, one of them twice. Considering that women writers are, as nearly as I can tell, still in a minority in the field, that speaks all the more highly for their quality.

And you'll see what I mean instantly if you read "Souls" by Joanna Russ. It is a true tour de force. It has to hold the science fiction reader tightly bound to the pages of the tale, even though it seems almost all the way through to be a piece of historical fiction, and with strong religious overtones. Don't get me wrong; it's a very good piece of historical fiction, and yet it is not the sort of thing you would expect to seize a science fiction reader's attention and extort from him or her a Hugo vote. Yet it does, and if you haven't read it before, you will now have the pleasure of seeing why.

I hate to try to analyze a story, because I'm never sure that I'm qualified to do so. (I can't even figure out what's what about my own stories.) Still, I can't help but point out that there seems to me to be something strongly Shavian about this story. As in the case of George Bernard Shaw's plays, we are treated primarily to intricate conversation in which the reader is forced to look at the world, and at the men and women in it, with new eyes. It is a story in which neither an abbess nor a Viking raider speaks as you would expect, and everything they say is interesting.

It makes me feel my own deficiencies. My stories tend to be told very largely through dialog (and the reviewers get pettish over the fact sometimes, though the readers don't seem to), but my dialog is much more prosaic than Joanna's is. Too bad for me.

Incidentally, women often complain that men, in their writing, rarely manage to have strong women but are satisfied with giving them supporting roles. This is changing, I think, but if you want an example of a strong woman, just consider Abbess Radegunde.

—Isaac Asimov

Souls

by Joanna Russ

Deprived of other Banquet
I entertained myself—

—Emily Dickinson

This is the tale of the Abbess Radegunde and what happened
when the Norsemen came. I tell it not as it was told to me but as I
saw it, for I was a child then and the Abbess had made a pet and
errand boy of me, although the stern old Wardress, Cunigunt, who
had outlived the previous Abbess, said I was more in the Abbey than
out of it and a scandal. But the Abbess would only say mildly, "Dear
Cunigunt, a scandal at the age of seven?" which was turning it off
with a joke, for she knew how harsh and disliking my new stepmother was to me and my father did not care and I with no sisters
or brothers. You must understand that joking and calling people
"dear" and "my dear" was only her manner; she was in every way
an unusual woman. The previous Abbess, Herrade, had found that
Radegunde, who had been given to her to be fostered, had great gifts
and so sent the child south to be taught, and that has never happened here before. The story has it that the Abbess Herrade found
Radegunde seeming to read the great illuminated book in the Abbess's study; the child had somehow pulled it off its stand and was
sitting on the floor with the volume in her lap, sucking her thumb,
and turning the pages with her other hand just as if she were
reading.

"Little two-years," said the Abbess Herrade, who was a kind
woman, "what are you doing?" She thought it amusing, I suppose,
that Radegunde should pretend to read this great book, the largest
and finest in the Abbey, which had many, many books more than
any other nunnery or monastery I have ever heard of: a full forty
then, as I remember. And then little Radegunde was doing the book
no harm.

"Reading, Mother," said the little girl.

12

"Oh, reading?" said the Abbess, smiling. "Then tell me what you are reading," and she pointed to the page.

"This," said Radegunde, "is a great *D* with flowers and other beautiful things about it, which is to show that *Dominus*, our Lord God, is the greatest thing and the most beautiful and makes everything to grow and be beautiful, and then it goes on to say *Domine nobis pacem*, which means *Give peace to us, O Lord.*"

Then the Abbess began to be frightened but she said only, "Who showed you this?" thinking that Radegunde had heard someone read and tell the words or had been pestering the nuns on the sly.

"No one," said the child. "Shall I go on?" and she read page after page of the Latin, in each case telling what the words meant.

There is more to the story, but I will say only that after many prayers the Abbess Herrade sent her foster daughter far southwards, even to Poitiers, where Saint Radegunde had ruled an Abbey before, and some say even to Rome, and in these places Radegunde was taught all learning, for all learning there is in the world remains in these places. Radegunde came back a grown woman and nursed the Abbess through her last illness and then became Abbess in her turn. They say that the great folk of the Church down there in the south wanted to keep her because she was such a prodigy of female piety and learning, there where life is safe and comfortable and less rude than it is here, but she said that the gray skies and flooding winters of her birthplace called to her very soul. She often told me the story when I was a child: how headstrong she had been and how defiant, and how she had sickened so desperately for her native land that they had sent her back, deciding that a rude life in the mud of a northern village would be a good cure for such a rebellious soul as hers.

"And so it was," she would say, patting my cheek or tweaking my ear. "See how humble I am now?" For you understand, all this about her rebellious girlhood, twenty years back, was a kind of joke between us. "Don't you do it," she would tell me and we would laugh together, I so heartily at the very idea of my being a pious monk full of learning that I would hold my sides and be unable to speak.

She was kind to everyone. She knew all the languages, not only ours, but the Irish too and the tongues folk speak to the north and south, and Latin and Greek also, and all the other languages in the world, both to read and write. She knew how to cure sickness, both the old women's way with herbs or leeches and out of books also. And never was there a more pious woman! Some speak ill of her now she's gone and say she was too merry to be a good Abbess, but she would say, "Merriment is God's flowers," and when the winter wind blew her headdress awry and showed the gray hair—which happened once; I was there and saw the shocked faces of the Sisters with her—she merely tapped the band back into place, smiling and saying, "Impudent wind! Thou showest thou hast power which is more than our silly human power, for it is from God"—and this quite satisfied the girls with her.

No one ever saw her angry. She was impatient sometimes, but in a kindly way, as if her mind were elsewhere. It was in Heaven, I used to think, for I have seen her pray for hours or sink to her knees—right in the marsh!—to see the wild duck fly south, her hands clasped and a kind of wild joy on her face, only to rise a moment later, looking at the mud on her habit and crying half ruefully, half in laughter, "Oh, what will Sister Laundress say to me? I am hopeless! Dear child, tell no one; I will say I fell," and then she would clap her hand to her mouth, turning red and laughing even harder, saying, "I *am* hopeless, telling lies!"

The town thought her a saint, of course. We were all happy then, or so it seems to me now, and all lucky and well, with this happiness of having her amongst us burning and blooming in our midst like a great fire around which we could all warm ourselves, even those who didn't know why life seemed so good. There was less illness; the food was better; the very weather stayed mild; and people did not quarrel as they had before her time and do again now. Nor do I think, considering what happened at the end, that all this was nothing but the fancy of a boy who's found his mother, for that's what she was to me; I brought her all the gossip and ran errands when I could, and she called me Boy News in Latin; I was happier than I have ever been.

And then one day those terrible, beaked prows appeared in our river.

I was with her when the warning came, in the main room of the Abbey tower just after the first fire of the year had been lit in the great hearth; we thought ourselves safe, for they had never been seen so far south and it was too late in the year for any sensible shipman to be in our waters. The Abbey was host to three Irish priests who turned pale when young Sister Sibihd burst in with the news, crying and wringing her hands; one of the brothers exclaimed a thing in Latin which means "God protect us!" for they had been telling us stories of the terrible sack of the monastery of Saint Columbanus and how everyone had run away with the precious manuscripts or had hidden in the woods, and that was how Father Cairbre and the two others had decided to go "walk the world," for this (the Abbess had been telling it all to me, for I had no Latin) is what the Irish say when they leave their native land to travel elsewhere.

"God protects our souls, not our bodies," said the Abbess Radegunde briskly. She had been talking with the priests in their own language or in the Latin, but this she said in ours so even the women workers from the village would understand. Then she said, "Father Cairbre, take your friends and the younger Sisters to the underground passages; Sister Diemud, open the gates to the villagers; half of them will be trying to get behind the Abbey walls and the others will be fleeing to the marsh. You, Boy News, down to the cellars with the girls." But I did not go and she never saw it; she was up and looking out one of the window slits instantly. So was I. I had always thought the Norsemen's big ships came right up on land—on legs, I supposed—and was disappointed to see that after they came up our river they stayed in the water like other ships and the men were coming ashore in little boats, which they were busy pulling up on shore through the sand and mud. Then the Abbess repeated her order—"Quickly! Quickly!"—and before anyone knew what had happened, she was gone from the room. I watched from the tower window; in the turmoil nobody bothered about me. Below, the Abbey grounds and gardens were packed with folk, all stepping on the herb plots and the Abbess's paestum roses, and great logs were being dragged to bar the door set in the stone walls around the Abbey, not high walls, to tell truth, and Radegunde was going quickly through the crowd: Do this! Do that! Stay, thou! Go, thou! and like things.

Then she reached the door and motioned Sister Oddha, the doorkeeper, aside—the old Sister actually fell to her knees in entreaty—and all this, you must understand, was wonderfully pleasant to me. I had no more idea of danger than a puppy. There was some tumult by the door—I think the men with the logs were trying to get in her way—and Abbess Radegunde took out from the neck of her habit her silver crucifix, brought all the way from Rome, and shook it impatiently at those who would keep her in. So of course they let her through at once.

I settled into my corner of the window, waiting for the Abbess's crucifix to bring down God's lightning on those tall, fair men who defied Our Savior and the law and were supposed to wear animal horns on their heads, though these did not (and I found out later that's just a story; that is not what the Norse do). I did hope that the Abbess, or Our Lord, would wait just a little while before destroying them, for I wanted to get a good look at them before they all died, you understand. I was somewhat disappointed, as they seemed to be wearing breeches with leggings under them and tunics on top, like ordinary folk, and cloaks also, though some did carry swords and axes and there were round shields piled on the beach at one place. But the long hair they had was fine, and the bright colors of their clothes, and the monsters growing out of the heads of the ships were splendid and very frightening, even though one could see that they were only painted, like the pictures in the Abbess's books.

I decided that God had provided me with enough edification and could now strike down the impious strangers.

But He did not.

Instead the Abbess walked alone toward these fierce men, over the stony riverbank, as calmly as if she were on a picnic with her girls. She was singing a little song, a pretty tune that I repeated many years later, and a well-traveled man said it was a Norse cradle-song. I didn't know that then, but only that the terrible, fair men, who had looked up in surprise at seeing one lone woman come out of the Abbey (which was barred behind her; I could see that), now began a sort of whispering astonishment among themselves. I saw the Abbess's gaze go quickly from one to the other—we often said that she could tell what was hidden in the soul from one look at the face—and then she picked the skirt of her habit up with one hand and daintily went among the rocks to one of the men, one older than the others, as it proved later, though I could not see so well at the time—and said to him, in his own language:

"Welcome, Thorvald Einarsson, and what do you, good farmer, so far from your own place, with the harvest ripe and the great autumn storms coming on over the sea?" (You may wonder how I knew what she said when I had no Norse; the truth is that Father

Cairbre, who had not gone to the cellars, after all, was looking out the top of the window while I was barely able to peep out the bottom, and he repeated everything that was said for the folk in the room, who all kept very quiet.)

Now you could see that the pirates were dumbfounded to hear her speak their own language and even more so that she called one by his name; some stepped backwards and made strange signs in the air and others unsheathed axes or swords and came running toward the Abbess. But at this Thorvald Einarsson put up his hand for them to stop and laughed heartily.

"Think!" he said. "There's no magic here, only cleverness—what pair of ears could miss my name with the lot of you brawling out 'Thorvald Einarsson, help me with this oar'; 'Thorvald Einarsson, my leggings are wet to the knees'; 'Thorvald Einarsson, this stream is as cold as a Fimbul-winter!' "

The Abbess Radegunde nodded and smiled. Then she sat down plump on the riverbank. She scratched behind one ear, as I had often seen her do when she was deep in thought. Then she said (and I am sure that this talk was carried on in a loud voice so that we in the Abbey could hear it):

"Good friend Thorvald, you are as clever as the tale I heard of you from your sister's son, Ranulf, from whom I learned the Norse when I was in Rome, and to show you it was he, he always swore by his gray horse, Lamefoot, and he had a difficulty in his speech; he could not say the sounds as we do and so spoke of you always as 'Torvald.' Is not that so?"

I did not realize it then, being only a child, but the Abbess was—by this speech—claiming hospitality from the man and had also picked by chance or inspiration the cleverest among these thieves, for his next words were:

"I am not the leader. There are no leaders here."

He was warning her that they were not his men to control, you see. So she scratched behind her ear again and got up. Then she began to wander, as if she did not know what to do, from one to the other of these uneasy folk—for some backed off and made signs at her still, and some took out their knives—singing her little tune again and walking slowly, more bent over and older and infirm-looking than we had ever seen her, one helpless little woman in black before all those fierce men. One wild young pirate snatched the headdress from her as she passed, leaving her short gray hair bare to the wind; the others laughed and he that had done it cried out:

"Grandmother, are you not ashamed?"

"Why, good friend, of what?" said she mildly.

"Thou art married to thy Christ," he said, holding the head covering behind his back, "but this bridegroom of thine cannot even defend thee against the shame of having thy head uncovered! Now if thou wert married to me—"

There was much laughter. The Abbess Radegunde waited until it was over. Then she scratched her bare head and made as if to turn away, but suddenly she turned back upon him with the age and infirmity dropping from her as if they had been a cloak, seeming taller and very grand, as if lit from within by some great fire. She looked directly into his face. This thing she did was something we had all seen, of course, but they had not, nor had they heard that great, grand voice with which she sometimes read the Scriptures to us or talked with us of the wrath of God. I think the young man was frightened, for all his daring. And I know now what I did not then: that the Norse admire courage above all things and that—to be blunt—everyone likes a good story, especially if it happens right in front of your eyes.

"Grandson!"—and her voice tolled like the great bell of God; I think folk must have heard her all the way to the marsh!—"Little grandchild, thinkest thou that the Creator of the World who made the stars and the moon and the sun and our bodies, too, and the change of the seasons and the very earth we stand on—yea, even into the shit in thy belly!—thinkest thou that such a being has a big house in the sky where he keeps his wives and goes in to fuck them as thou wouldst thyself or like the King of Turkey? Do not dishonor the wit of the mother who bore thee! We are the servants of God, not his wives, and if we tell our silly girls they are married to the Christus, it is to make them understand that they must not run off and marry Otto Farmer or Ekkehard Blacksmith, but stick to their work, as they promised. If I told them they were married to an Idea, they would not understand me, and neither dost thou."

(Here Father Cairbre, above me in the window, muttered in a protesting way about something.)

Then the Abbess snatched the silver cross from around her neck and put it into the boy's hand, saying: "Give this to thy mother with my pity. She must pull out her hair over such a child."

But he let it fall to the ground. He was red in the face and breathing hard.

"Take it up," she said more kindly, "take it up, boy; it will not hurt thee and there's no magic in it. It's only pure silver and good workmanship; it will make thee rich." When she saw that he would not—his hand went to his knife—she *tched* to herself in a motherly way (or I believe she did, for she waved one hand back and forth as she always did when she made that sound) and got down on her knees—with more difficulty than was truth, I think—saying loudly, "I will stoop, then; I will stoop," and got up; holding it out to him, saying, "Take. Two sticks tied with a cord would serve me as well."

The boy cried, his voice breaking, "My mother is dead and thou art a witch!" and in an instant he had one arm around the Abbess's neck and with the other his knife at her throat. The man Thorvald Einarsson roared "Thorfinn!" but the Abbess only said clearly, "Let him be. I have shamed this man but did not mean to. He is right to be angry."

The boy released her and turned his back. I remember wondering if these strangers could weep. Later I heard—and I swear that the Abbess must have somehow known this or felt it, for although she was no witch, she could probe a man until she found the sore places in him and that very quickly—that this boy's mother had been known for an adulteress and that no man would own him as a son. It is one thing among those people for a man to have what the Abbess called a concubine and they do not hold the children of such in scorn as we do, but it is a different thing when a married woman has more than one man. Such was Thorfinn's case; I suppose that was what had sent him *viking*. But all this came later; what I saw then—with my nose barely above the window slit—was that the Abbess slipped her crucifix over the hilt of the boy's sword; she really wished him to have it, you see—and then walked to a place near the walls of the Abbey but far from the Norsemen. I think she meant them to come to her. I saw her pick up her skirts like a peasant woman, sit down with legs crossed, and say in a loud voice:

"Come! Who will bargain with me?"

A few strolled over, laughing, and sat down with her.

"All!" she said, gesturing them closer.

"And why should we all come?" said one who was furthest away.

"Because you will miss a bargain," said the Abbess.

"Why should we bargain when we can take?" said another.

"Because you will only get half," said the Abbess. "The rest you will not find."

"We will ransack the Abbey," said a third.

"Half the treasure is not in the Abbey," said she.

"And where is it then?"

She tapped her forehead. They were drifting over by twos and threes. I have heard since that the Norse love riddles and this was a sort of riddle; she was giving them good fun.

"If it is in your head," said the man Thorvald, who was standing behind the others, arms crossed, "we can get it out, can we not?" And he tapped the hilt of his knife.

"If you frighten me, I shall become confused and remember nothing," said the Abbess calmly. "Besides, do you wish to play that old game? You saw how well it worked the last time. I am surprised at you, Ranulf mother's-brother."

"I will bargain then," said the man Thorvald, smiling.

"And the rest of you?" said Radegunde. "It must be all or none; decide for yourselves whether you wish to save yourselves trouble and danger and be rich," and she deliberately turned her back on them. The men moved down to the river's edge and began to talk among themselves, dropping their voices so that we could not hear them any more. Father Cairbre, who was old and shortsighted, cried, "I cannot hear them. What are they doing?" and I cleverly said, "I have good eyes, Father Cairbre," and he held me up to see. So it was just at the time that the Abbess Radegunde was facing the Abbey tower that I appeared in the window. She clapped one hand across her mouth. Then she walked to the gate and called (in a voice I had learned not to disregard; it had often gotten me a smacked bottom), "Boy News, down! Come down to me here *at once!* And bring Father Cairbre with you."

I was overjoyed. I had no idea that she might want to protect me if anything went wrong. My only thought was that I was going to see it all from wonderfully close by. So I wormed my way, half suffo-cated, through the folk in the tower room, stepping on feet and skirts, and having to say every few seconds, "But I *have* to! The Abbess wants me," and meanwhile she was calling outside like an

Empress, "Let that boy through! Make a place for that boy! Let the Irish priest through!" until I crept and pushed and complained my way to the very wall itself—no one was going to open the gate for us, of course—and there was a great fuss and finally someone brought a ladder. I was over at once, but the old priest took a longer time, although it was a low wall, as I've said, the builders having been somewhat of two minds about making the Abbey into a true fortress.

Once outside it was lovely, away from all that crowd, and I ran, gloriously pleased, to the Abbess, who said only, "Stay by me, whatever happens," and immediately turned her attention away from me. It had taken so long to get Father Cairbre outside the walls that the tall, foreign men had finished their talking and were coming back—all twenty or thirty of them—toward the Abbey and the Abbess Radegunde, and most especially of all, me. I could see Father Cairbre tremble. They did look grim, close by, with their long, wild hair and the brightness of their strange clothes. I remember that they smelled different from us, but cannot remember how after all these years. Then the Abbess spoke to them in that outlandish language of theirs, so strangely light and lilting to hear from their bearded lips, and then she said something in Latin to Father Cairbre, and he said, with a shake in his voice:

"This is the priest, Father Cairbre, who will say our bargains aloud in our own tongue so that my people may hear. I cannot deal behind their backs. And this is my foster baby, who is very dear to me and who is now having his curiosity rather too much satisfied, I think." (I was trying to stand tall like a man but had one hand secretly holding on to her skirt; so that was what the foreign men had chuckled at!) The talk went on, but I will tell it as if I had understood the Norse, for to repeat everything twice would be tedious.

The Abbess Radegunde said, "Will you bargain?"

There was a general nodding of heads, with a look of: After all, why not?

"And who will speak for you?" said she.

A man stepped forward; I recognized Thorvald Einarsson.

"Ah, yes," said the Abbess dryly. "The company that has no leaders. Is this leaderless company agreed? Will it abide by its word? I want no treachery-planners, no Breakwords here!"

There was a general mutter at this. The Thorvald man (he *was* big, close up!) said mildly, "I sail with none such. Let's begin."

We all sat down.

"Now," said Thorvald Einarsson, raising his eyebrows, "according to my knowledge of this thing, you begin. And according to my knowledge, you will begin by saying that you are very poor."

"But, no," said the Abbess, "we are rich." Father Cairbre groaned. A groan answered him from behind the Abbey walls. Only the Abbess and Thorvald Einarsson seemed unmoved; it was as if these two were joking in some way that no one else understood. The Abbess went on, saying, "We are very rich. Within is much silver, much gold, many pearls, and much embroidered cloth, much fine-woven cloth, much carved and painted wood, and many books with gold upon their pages and jewels set into their covers. All this is yours. But we have more and better: herbs and medicines, ways to keep food from spoiling, the knowledge of how to cure the sick; all this is yours. And we have more and better even than this: we have the knowledge of Christ and the perfect understanding of the soul, which is yours, too, anytime you wish; you have only to accept it."

Thorvald Einarsson held up his hand. "We will stop with the first," he said, "and perhaps a little of the second. That is more practical."

"And foolish," said the Abbess politely, "in the usual way." And again I had the odd feeling that these two were sharing a joke no one else even saw. She added, "There is one thing you may not have, and that is the most precious of all."

Thorvald Einarsson looked inquiring.

"*My people.* Their safety is dearer to me than myself. They are not to be touched, not a hair on their heads, not for any reason. Think: you can fight your way into the Abbey easily enough, but the folk in there are very frightened of you, and some of the men are armed. Even a good fighter is cumbered in a crowd. You will slip and fall upon one another without meaning to or knowing that you do so. Heed my counsel. Why play butcher when you can have treasure poured into your laps like kings, without work? And after that there will be as much again, when I lead you to the hidden places. An Earl's mountain of treasure. Think of it! And to give all this up for slaves, half of whom will get sick and die before you get them home—and will need to be fed if they are to be any good. Shame on you for bad advice-takers! Imagine what you will say to your wives and families: Here are a few miserable bolts of cloth with blood spots that won't come out, here are some pearls and jewels smashed to powder in the fighting, here is a torn piece of embroidery which was whole until someone stepped on it in the battle, and I had slaves but they died of illness and I fucked a pretty young nun and meant to bring her back, but she leapt into the sea. And, oh, yes, there was twice as much again and all of it whole but we decided not to take that. Too much trouble, you see."

This was a lively story and the Norsemen enjoyed it. Radegunde held up her hand.

"People!" she called in German, adding, "Sea-rovers, hear what I say; I will repeat it for you in your tongue." (And so she did.) *"People, if the Norsemen fight us, do not defend yourselves but smash everything! Wives, take your cooking knives and shred the valuable cloth to pieces! Men, with your axes and hammers hew the altars and the carved wood to fragments! All, grind the pearls and smash the jewels against the stone floors! Break the bottles of wine! Pound the gold and silver to shapelessness! Tear to pieces the illuminated books! Tear down the hangings and burn them!*

"But" (she added, her voice suddenly mild) "if these wise men will accept our gifts, let us heap untouched and spotless at their feet all that we have and hold nothing back, so that their kinsfolk will marvel and wonder at the shining and glistering of the wealth they bring back, though it leave us nothing but our bare stone walls."

If anyone had ever doubted that the Abbess Radegunde was inspired by God, their doubts must have vanished away, for who could resist the fiery vigor of her first speech or the beneficent unction of her second? The Norsemen sat there with their mouths open. I saw tears on Father Cairbre's cheeks. Then Thorvald said, "Abbess—"

He stopped. He tried again but again stopped. Then he shook himself, as a man who has been under a spell, and said:

"Abbess, my men have been without women for a long time."

Radegunde looked surprised. She looked as if she could not believe what she had heard. She looked the pirate up and down, as if puzzled, and then walked around him as if taking his measure. She did this several times, looking at every part of his big body as if she were summing him up while he got redder and redder. Then she backed off and surveyed him again, and with her arms akimbo like a peasant, announced very loudly in both Norse and German:

"What! Have they lost the use of their hands?"

It was irresistible, in its way. The Norse laughed. Our people laughed. Even Thorvald laughed. I did, too, though I was not sure what everyone was laughing about. The laughter would die down and then begin again behind the Abbey walls, helplessly, and again die down and again begin. The Abbess waited until the Norsemen had stopped laughing and then called for silence in German until there were only a few snickers here and there. She then said:

"These good men—Father Cairbre, tell the people—these good men will forgive my silly joke. I meant no scandal, truly, and no harm, but laughter is good; it settles the body's waters, as the physicians say. And my people know that I am not always as solemn and good as I ought to be. Indeed I am a very great sinner and scandal-maker. Thorvald Einarsson, do we do business?"

The big man—who had not been so pleased as the others, I can tell you!—looked at his men and seemed to see what he needed to know. He said, "I go in with five men to see what you have. Then we let the poor folk on the grounds go, but not those inside the Abbey. Then we search again. The gates will be locked and guarded by the rest of us; if there's any treachery, the bargain's off."

"Then I will go with you," said Radegunde. "That is very just and my presence will calm the people. To see us together will assure them that no harm is meant. You are a good man, Torvald—forgive me; I call you as your nephew did so often. Come, Boy News, hold on to me."

"Open the gates!" she called then. "All is safe!" and with the five men (one of whom was that young Thorfinn who had hated her so) we waited while the great logs were pulled back. There was little space within, but the people shrank back at the sight of those fierce warriors and opened a place for us.

I looked back and the Norsemen had come in and were standing just inside the walls, on either side of the gate, with their swords out and their shields up. The crowd parted for us more slowly as we reached the main tower, with the Abbess repeating constantly, "Be calm, people, be calm. All is well," and deftly speaking by name to this one or that. It was much harder when the people gasped upon hearing the big logs pushed shut with a noise like thunder, and it was very close on the stairs; I heard her say something like an apology in the queer foreign tongue. Something that probably meant, "I'm sorry that we must wait." It seemed an age until the stairs were even partly clear and I saw what the Abbess had meant by the cumbering of a crowd; a man might swing a weapon in the press of people, but not very far, and it was more likely he would simply fall over someone and crack his head. We gained the great room with the big crucifix of painted wood and the little one of pearls and gold, and the scarlet hangings worked in gold thread that I had played robbers behind so often before I learned what real robbers were: these tall, frightening men whose eyes glistened with greed at what I had fancied every village had. Most of the Sisters had stayed in the great room, but somehow it was not so crowded, as the folk had huddled back against the walls when the Norsemen came in. The youngest girls were all in a corner, terrified—one could smell it, as one can in people—and when that young Thorfinn went for the little gold-and-pearl cross, Sister Sibihd cried in a high, cracked voice, "It is the body of our Christ!" and leapt up, snatching it from the wall before he could get to it.

"Sibihd!" exclaimed the Abbess, in as sharp a voice as I had ever heard her use. "Put that back or you will feel the weight of my hand, I tell you!"

Now it is odd, is it not, that a young woman desperate enough not to care about death at the hands of a Norse pirate should nonetheless be frightened away at the threat of getting a few slaps from her Abbess? But folk are like that. Sister Sibihd returned the cross to its place (from whence young Thorfinn took it) and fell back among the nuns, sobbing, "He desecrates our Lord God!"

"Foolish girl!" snapped the Abbess. "God only can consecrate or desecrate; man cannot. That is a piece of metal."

Thorvald said something sharp to Thorfinn, who slowly put the cross back on its hook with a sulky look which said, plainer than words: Nobody gives me what I want. Nothing else went wrong in the big room or the Abbess's study or the storerooms, or out in the kitchens. The Norsemen were silent and kept their hands on their swords, but the Abbess kept talking in a calm way in both tongues; to our folk she said, "See? It is all right but everyone must keep still. God will protect us." Her face was steady and clear, and I believed her a saint, for she had saved Sister Sibihd and the rest of us.

But this peacefulness did not last, of course. Something had to go wrong in all that press of people; to this day I do not know what. We were in a corner of the long refectory, which is the place where the

Sisters or Brothers eat in an Abbey, when something pushed me into the wall and I fell, almost suffocated by the Abbess's lying on top of me. My head was ringing and on all sides there was a terrible roaring sound with curses and screams, a dreadful tumult as if the walls had come apart and were falling on everyone. I could hear the Abbess whispering something in Latin over and over in my ear. There were dull, ripe sounds, worse than the rest, which I know now to have been the noise steel makes when it is thrust into bodies. This all seemed to go on forever and then it seemed to me that the floor was wet. Then all became quiet. I felt the Abbess Radegunde get off me. She said:

"So this is how you wash your floors up North." When I lifted my head from the rushes and saw what she meant, I was very sick into the corner. Then she picked me up in her arms and held my face against her bosom so that I would not see, but it was no use; I had already seen: all the people lying sprawled on the floor with their bellies coming out, like heaps of dead fish, old Walafrid with an ax handle standing out of his chest—he was sitting up with his eyes shut in a press of bodies that gave him no room to lie down—and the young beekeeper, Uta, from the village, who had been so merry, lying on her back with her long braids and her gown all dabbled in red dye and a great stain of it on her belly. She was breathing fast and her eyes were wide open. As we passed her, the noise of her breathing ceased.

The Abbess said mildly, "Thy people are thorough housekeepers, Earl Split-gut."

Thorvald Einarsson roared something at us, and the Abbess replied softly, "Forgive me, good friend. You protected me and the boy and I am grateful. But nothing betrays a man's knowledge of the German like a word that bites, is it not so? And I had to be sure."

It came to me then that she had called him "Torvald" and reminded him of his sister's son so that he would feel he must protect us if anything went wrong. But now she would make him angry, I thought, and I shut my eyes tight. Instead he laughed and said in odd, light German, "I did no housekeeping but to stand over you and your pet. Are you not grateful?"

"Oh, very, thank you," said the Abbess with such warmth as she might show to a Sister who had brought her a rose from the garden, or another who copied her work well, or when I told her news, or if Ita the cook made a good soup. But he did not know that the warmth was for everyone and so seemed satisfied. By now we were in the garden and the air was less foul; she put me down, although my limbs were shaking, and I clung to her gown, crumpled, stiff, and blood-reeking though it was. She said, "Oh my God, what a deal of washing hast Thou given us!" She started to walk toward the gate, and Thorvald Einarsson took a step toward her. She said, without turning around: "Do not insist, Thorvald, there is no reason to lock me up. I am forty years old and not likely to be running away into the swamp, what with my rheumatism and the pain in my knees and the folk needing me as they do."

There was a moment's silence. I could see something odd come into the big man's face. He said quietly:

"I did not speak, Abbess."

She turned, surprised. "But you did. I heard you."

He said strangely, "I did not."

Children can guess sometimes what is wrong and what to do about it without knowing how; I remember saying, very quickly, "Oh, she does that sometimes. My stepmother says old age has addled her wits," and then, "Abbess, may I go to my stepmother and my father?"

"Yes, of course," she said, "run along, Boy News—" and then stopped, looking into the air as if seeing in it something we could not. Then she said very gently, "No, my dear, you had better stay here with me," and I knew, as surely as if I had seen it with my own eyes, that I was not to go to my stepmother or my father because both were dead.

She did things like that, too, sometimes.

For a while it seemed that everyone was dead. I did not feel grieved or frightened in the least, but I think I must have been, for I had only one idea in my head: that if I let the Abbess out of my sight, I would die. So I followed her everywhere. She was let to move about and comfort people, especially the mad Sibihd, who would do nothing but rock and wail, but toward nightfall, when the Abbey had been stripped of its treasures, Thorvald Einarsson put her and me in her study, now bare of its grand furniture, on a straw pallet on the floor, and bolted the door on the outside. She said:

"Boy News, would you like to go to Constantinople, where the

Turkish Sultan is, and the domes of gold and all the splendid pagans? For that is where this man will take me to sell me."

"Oh, yes!" said I, and then: "But will he take me, too?"

"Of course," said the Abbess, and so it was settled. Then in came Thorvald Einarsson, saying:

"Thorfinn is asking for you." I found out later that they were waiting for him to die; none other of the Norse had been wounded, but a farmer had crushed Thorfinn's chest with an ax, and he was expected to die before morning. The Abbess said:

"Is that a good reason to go?" She added, "I mean that he hates me; will not his anger at my presence make him worse?"

Thorvald said slowly, "The folks here say you can sit by the sick and heal them. Can you do that?"

"To my own knowledge, not at all," said the Abbess Radegunde, "but if they believe so, perhaps that calms them and makes them better. Christians are quite as foolish as other people, you know. I will come if you want," and though I saw that she was pale with tiredness, she got to her feet. I should say that she was in a plain, brown gown taken from one of the peasant women because her own was being washed clean, but to me she had the same majesty as always. And for him, too, I think.

Thorvald said, "Will you pray for him or damn him?"

She said, "I do not pray, Thorvald, and I never damn anybody; I merely sit." She added, "Oh, let him; he'll scream your ears off if you don't," and this meant me, for I was ready to yell for my life if they tried to keep me from her.

They had put Thorfinn in the chapel, a little stone room with nothing left in it now but a plain wooden cross, not worth carrying off. He was lying, his eyes closed, on the stone altar with furs under him, and his face was gray. Every time he breathed, there was a bubbling sound, a little, thin, reedy sound; and as I crept closer, I saw why, for in the young man's chest was a great red hole with sharp pink things sticking out of it, all crushed, and in the hole one could see something jump and fall, jump and fall, over and over again. It was his heart beating. Blood kept coming from his lips in a froth. I do not know, of course, what either said, for they spoke in the Norse, but I saw what they did and heard much of it talked of between the Abbess and Thorvald Einarsson later. So I will tell it as if I knew.

The first thing Abbess did was to stop suddenly on the threshold and raise both hands to her mouth as if in horror. Then she cried furiously to the two guards:

"Do you wish to kill your comrade with the cold and damp? Is this how you treat one another? Get fire in here and some woollen cloth to put over him! No, not more skins, you idiots, *wool* to mold to his body and take up the wet. Run now!"

One said sullenly, "We don't take orders from you, Grandma."

"Oh, no?" said she. "Then I shall strip this wool dress from my old body and put it over that boy and then sit here all night in my flabby, naked skin! What will this child's soul say when it enters the Valhall? That his friends would not give up a little of their booty so that he might fight for life? Is this your fellowship? Do it, or I will strip myself and shame you both for the rest of your lives!"

"Well, take it from his share," said the one in a low voice, and the other ran out. Soon there was a fire on the hearth and russet-colored woollen cloth—"From my own share," said one of them loudly, though it was a color the least costly, not like blue or red—and the Abbess laid it loosely over the boy, carefully putting it close to his sides but not moving him. He did not look to be in any pain, but his color got no better. But then he opened his eyes and said in such a little voice as a ghost might have, a whisper as thin and reedy and bubbling as his breath:

"You . . . old witch. But I beat you . . . in the end."

"Did you, my dear?" said the Abbess. "How?"

"Treasure," he said, "for my kinfolk. And I lived as a man at last. Fought . . . and had a woman . . . the one here with the big breasts, Sibihd. . . . Whether she liked it or not. That was good."

"Yes, Sibihd," said the Abbess mildly. "Sibihd has gone mad. She hears no one and speaks to no one. She only sits and rocks and moans and soils herself and will not feed herself, although if one puts food in her mouth with a spoon, she will swallow."

The boy tried to frown. "Stupid," he said at last. "Stupid nuns. The beasts do it."

"Do they?" said the Abbess, as if this were a new idea to her. "Now that is very odd. For never yet heard I of a gander that blacked the goose's eye or hit her over the head with a stone or stuck a knife in her entrails when he was through. When God puts it into their hearts to desire one another, she squats and he comes running. And

a bitch in heat will jump through the window if you lock the door.
Poor fools! Why didn't you camp three hours downriver and wait?
In a week half the young married women in the village would have
been slipping away at night to see what the foreigners were like. Yes,
and some unmarried ones, and some of my own girls, too. But you
couldn't wait, could you?"

"No," said the boy, with the ghost of a brag. "Better . . . this
way."

"*This* way," said she. "Oh, yes, my dear, old Granny knows about
this way! Pleasure for the count of three or four, and the rest of it as
much joy as rolling a stone uphill."

He smiled a ghostly smile. "You're a whore, Grandma."

She began to stroke his forehead. "No, Grandbaby," she said,
"but all Latin is not the Church Fathers, you know, great as they are.
One can find a great deal in those strange books written by the ones
who died centuries before our Lord was born. Listen," and she
leaned closer to him and said quietly:

> "Syrian dancing girl, how subtly
>   you sway those sensuous limbs,
> Half-drunk in the smoky tavern,
>   lascivious and wanton,
> Your long hair bound back in the
>   Greek way, clashing the castanets
>   in your hands—"

The boy was too weak to do anything but look astonished. Then
she said this:

> "I love you so that anyone permitted to sit near you and talk
> to you seems to me like a god; when I am near you my spirit
> is broken, my heart shakes, my voice dies, and I can't even
> speak. Under my skin I flame up all over and I can't see; there's
> thunder in my ears and I break out in a sweat, as if from fever;
> I turn paler than cut grass and feel that I am utterly changed;
> I feel that Death has come near me."

He said, as if frightened, "Nobody feels like that."
"They do," she said.
He said, in feeble alarm, "You're trying to kill me!"

She said, "No, my dear. I simply don't want you to die a virgin."

It was odd, his saying those things and yet holding on to her hand where he had got at it through the woollen cloth; she stroked his head and he whispered, "Save me, old witch."

"I'll do my best," she said. "You shall do your best by not talking and I by not tormenting you anymore, and we'll both try to sleep."

"Pray," said the boy.

"Very well," said she, "but I'll need a chair," and the guards—seeing I suppose, that he was holding her hand—brought in one of the great wooden chairs from the Abbey, which were too plain and heavy to carry off, I think. Then the Abbess Radegunde sat in the chair and closed her eyes. Thorfinn seemed to fall asleep. I crept nearer her on the floor and must have fallen asleep myself almost at once, for the next thing I knew a gray light filled the chapel, the fire had gone out, and someone was shaking Radegunde, who still slept in her chair, her head leaning to one side. It was Thorvald Einarsson and he was shouting with excitement in his strange German, "Woman, how did you do it! How did you do it!"

"Do what?" said the Abbess thickly. "Is he dead?"

"Dead?" exclaimed the Norseman. "He is healed! Healed! The lung is whole and all is closed up about the heart and the shattered pieces of the ribs are grown together! Even the muscles of the chest are beginning to heal!"

"That's good," said the Abbess, still half asleep. "Let me be."

Thorvald shook her again. She said again. "Oh, let me sleep." This time he hauled her to her feet and she shrieked, "My back, my back! Oh, the saints, my rheumatism!" and at the same time a sick voice from under the russet woollens—a sick voice but a man's voice, not a ghost's—said something in Norse.

"Yes, I hear you," said the Abbess. "You must become a follower of the White Christ right away, this very minute. But *Dominus noster*, please do You put it into these brawny heads that I must have a tub of hot water with pennyroyal in it? I am too old to sleep all night in a chair, and I am one ache from head to foot."

Thorfinn got louder.

"Tell him," said the Abbess Radegunde to Thorvald in German, "that I will not baptize him and I will not shrive him until he is a different man. All that child wants is someone more powerful than your Odin god or your Thor god to pull him out of the next scrape

he gets into. Ask him: Will he adopt Sibihd as his sister: Will he clean
her when she soils herself and feed her and sit with his arm about
her, talking to her gently and lovingly until she is well again? The
Christ does not wipe out our sins only to have us commit them all
over again, and that is what he wants and what you all want, a God
that gives and gives and gives, but God does not give; He takes and
takes and takes. He takes away everything that is not God until there
is nothing left but God, and none of you will understand that! There
is no remission of sins; there is only change, and Thorfinn must
change before God will have him."

"Abbess, you are eloquent," said Thorvald, smiling, "but why do
you not tell him all this yourself?"

"Because I ache so!" said Radegunde; "Oh, do get me into some
hot water!" and Thorvald half led and half supported her as she
hobbled out. That morning, after she had had her soak—when I
cried, they let me stay just outside the door—she undertook to cure
Sibihd, first by rocking her in her arms and talking to her, telling her
she was safe now, and promising that the Norsemen would go soon,
and then when Sibihd became quieter, leading her out into the
woods with Thorvald as a bodyguard to see that we did not run
away, and little, dark Sister Hedwic, who had stayed with Sibihd
and cared for her. The Abbess would walk for a while in the mild
autumn sunshine, and then she would direct Sibihd's face upwards
by touching her gently under the chin and say, "See? There is God's
sky still," and then, "Look, there are God's trees; they have not
changed," and tell her that the world was just the same and God still
kindly to folk, only a few more souls had joined the Blessed and were
happier waiting for us in Heaven than we could ever be, or even
imagine being, on the poor earth. Sister Hedwic kept hold of Sibihd's hand. No one paid more attention to me than if I had been a
dog, but every time poor Sister Sibihd saw Thorvald she would
shrink away, and you could see that Hedwic could not bear to look
at him at all; every time he came in her sight she turned her face
aside, shut her eyes hard, and bit her lower lip. It was a quiet, almost
warm day, as autumn can be sometimes, and the Abbess found a
few little blue late flowers growing in a sheltered place against a log
and put them into Sibihd's hand, speaking of how beautifully and
cunningly God had made all things. Sister Sibihd had enough wit to

hold on to the flowers, but her eyes stared and she would have stumbled and fallen if Hedwic had not led her.

Sister Hedwic said timidly, "Perhaps she suffers because she has been defiled, Abbess," and then looked ashamed. For a moment the Abbess looked shrewdly at young Sister Hedwic and then at the mad Sibihd. Then she said:

"Dear daughter Sibihd and dear daughter Hedwic, I am now going to tell you something about myself that I have never told to a single living soul but my confessor. Do you know that as a young woman I studied at Avignon and from there was sent to Rome, so that I might gather much learning? Well, in Avignon I read mightily our Christian Fathers but also in the pagan poets, for as it has been said by Ermenrich of Ellwangen: As dung spread upon a field enriches it to good harvest, thus one cannot produce divine eloquence without the filthy writings of the pagan poets. This is true but perilous, only I thought not so, for I was very proud and fancied that if the pagan poems of love left me unmoved, that was because I had the gift of chastity right from God Himself, and I scorned sensual pleasures and those tempted by them. I had forgotten, you see, that chastity is not given once and for all like a wedding ring that is put on never to be taken off, but is a garden which each day must be weeded, watered, and trimmed anew, or soon there will be only brambles and wilderness.

"As I have seen, the words of the poets did not tempt me, for words are only marks on the page with no life save what we give them. But in Rome there were not only the old books, daughters, but something much worse.

"There were statues. Now you must understand that these are not such as you can imagine from our books, like Saint John or the Virgin; the ancients wrought so cunningly in stone that it is like magic; one stands before the marble holding one's breath, waiting for it to move and speak. They are not statues at all but beautiful, naked men and women. It is a city of sea gods pouring water, daughter Sibihd and daughter Hedwic, of athletes about to throw the discus, and runners and wrestlers and young emperors, and the favorites of kings; but they do not walk the streets like real men, for they are all of stone.

"There was one Apollo, all naked, which I knew I should not look on but which I always made some excuse to my companions to pass by, and this statue, although three miles distant from my dwelling, drew me as if by magic. Oh, he was fair to look on! Fairer than any youth alive now in Germany, or in the world, I think. And then all the old loves of the pagan poets came back to me: Dido and Aeneas, the taking of Venus by Mars, the love of the moon, Diana, for the shepherd boy—and I thought that if my statue could only come to life, he would utter honeyed love words from the old poets and would be wise and brave, too, and what woman could resist him?"

Here she stopped and looked at Sister Sibihd but Sibihd only stared on, holding the little blue flowers. It was Sister Hedwic who cried, one hand pressed to her heart:

"Did you pray, Abbess?"

"I did," said Radegunde solemnly, "and yet my prayers kept becoming something else. I would pray to be delivered from the temptation that was in the statue, and then, of course, I would have to think of the statue itself, and then I would tell myself that I must run, like the nymph Daphne, to be armored and sheltered within a laurel tree, but my feet seemed to be already rooted to the ground, and then at the last minute I would flee and be back at my prayers again. But it grew harder each time, and at last the day came when I did not flee."

"Abbess, you?" cried Hedwic, with a gasp. Thorvald, keeping his watch a little way from us, looked surprised. I was very pleased—I loved to see the Abbess astonish people; it was one of her gifts—and at seven I had not knowledge of lust except that my little thing felt good sometimes when I handled it to make water, and what had that to do with statues coming to life or women turning into laurel trees? I was more interested in mad Sibihd, the way children are; I did not know what she might do, or if I should be afraid of her, or if I should go mad myself, what it would be like. But the Abbess was laughing gently at Hedwic's amazement.

"Why not me?" said the Abbess. "I was young and healthy and had no special grace from God any more than the hens or the cows do! Indeed, I burned so with desire for that handsome young hero—for so I had made him in my mind, as a woman might do with a man she had seen a few times on the street—that thoughts of him tormented me waking and sleeping. It seemed to me that because of my vows I could not give myself to this Apollo of my own free will.

So I would dream that he took me against my will, and, oh, what an exquisite pleasure that was!"

Here Hedwic's blood came all to her face and she covered it with her hands. I could see Thorvald grinning, back where he watched us.

"And then," said the Abbess, as if she had not seen either of them, "a terrible fear came to my heart that God might punish me by sending a ravisher who would use me unlawfully, as I had dreamed my Apollo did, and that I would not even wish to resist him and would feel the pleasures of a base lust and would know myself a whore and a false nun forever after. This fear both tormented and drew me. I began to steal looks at young men in the streets, not letting the other Sisters see me do it, thinking: Will it be he? Or he? Or he?

"And then it happened. I had lingered behind the others at a melon seller's, thinking of no Apollos or handsome heroes but only of the convent's dinner, when I saw my companions disappearing around a corner. I hastened to catch up with them—and made a wrong turning—and was suddenly lost in a narrow street—and at that very moment a young fellow took hold of my habit and threw me to the ground! You may wonder why he should do such a mad thing, but as I found out afterwards, there are prostitutes in Rome who affect our way of dress to please the appetites of certain men who are depraved enough to—well, really, I do not know how to say it! Seeing me alone, he had thought I was one of them and would be glad of a customer and a bit of play. So there was a reason for it.

"Well, there I was on my back with this young fellow, sent as a vengeance by God, as I thought, trying to do exactly what I had dreamed, night after night, that my statue should do. And do you know, it was nothing in the least like my dream! The stones at my back hurt me, for one thing. And instead of melting with delight, I was screaming my head off in terror and kicking at him as he tried to pull up my skirts, and praying to God that this insane man might not break any of my bones in his rage!

"My screams brought a crowd of people and he went running. So I got off with nothing worse than a bruised back and a sprained knee. But the strangest thing of all was that while I was cured forever of lusting after my Apollo, instead I began to be tormented by a new fear—that I had lusted after *him*, that foolish young man with the foul breath and the one tooth missing!—and I felt strange creepings and crawlings over my body that were half like desire and half like fear and half like disgust and shame with all sorts of other things mixed in—I know that is too many halves but it is how I felt—and nothing at all like the burning desire I had felt for my Apollo. I went to see the statue once more before I left Rome, and it seemed to look at me sadly, as if to say: Don't blame me, poor girl; I'm only a piece of stone. And that was the last time I was so proud as to believe that God had singled me out for a special gift, like chastity—or a special sin, either—or that being thrown down on the ground and hurt had anything to do with any sin of mine, no matter how I mixed the two together in my mind. I dare say you did not find it a great pleasure yesterday, did you?"

Hedwic shook her head. She was crying quietly. She said, "Thank you, Abbess," and the Abbess embraced her. They both seemed happier, but then all of a sudden Sibihd muttered something, so low that one could not hear her.

"The—" she whispered and then she brought it out but still in a whisper: "The blood."

"What, dear, your blood?" said Radegunde.

"No, Mother," said Sibihd, beginning to tremble, "the blood. All over us. Walafrid and—and Uta—and Sister Hildegarde—and everyone broken and spilled out like a dish! And none of us had done anything but I could smell it all over me and the children screaming because they were being trampled down, and those demons come up from Hell though we had done nothing and—and—I understand, Mother, about the rest, but I will never, ever forget it, oh Christus, it is all around me now, oh, Mother, the *blood!*"

Then Sister Sibihd dropped to her knees on the fallen leaves and began to scream, not covering her face as Sister Hedwic had done, but staring ahead with her wide eyes as if she were blind or could see something we could not. The Abbess knelt down and embraced her, rocking her back and forth, saying, "Yes, yes, dear, but we are here; we are here now; that is gone now," but Sibihd continued to scream, covering her ears as if the scream were someone else's and she could hide herself from it.

Thorvald said, looking, I thought, a little uncomfortable, "Cannot your Christ cure this?"

"No," said the Abbess. "Only by undoing the past. And that is the one thing He never does, it seems. She is in Hell now and must go back there many times before she can forget."

"She would make a bad slave," said the Norseman, with a glance at Sister Sibihd, who had fallen silent and was staring ahead of her again. "You need not fear that anyone will want her."

"God," said the Abbess Radegunde calmly, "is merciful."

Thorvald Einarsson said, "Abbess, I am not a bad man."

"For a good man," said the Abbess Radegunde, "you keep surprisingly bad company."

He said angrily, "I did not choose my shipmates. I have had bad luck!"

"Ours has," said the Abbess, "been worse, I think."

"Luck is luck," said Thorvald, clenching his fists. "It comes to some folk and not to others."

"As you came to us," said the Abbess mildly. "Yes, yes, I see, Thorvald Einarsson; one may say that luck is Thor's doing or Odin's doing, but you must know that our bad luck is your own doing and not some god's. You are our bad luck, Thorvald Einarsson. It's true that you're not as wicked as your friends, for they kill for pleasure and you do it without feeling, as a business, the way one hews down grain. Perhaps you have seen today some of the grain you have cut. If you had a man's soul, you would not have gone *viking*, luck or no luck, and if your soul were bigger still, you would have tried to stop your shipmates, just as I talk honestly to you now, despite your anger, and just as Christus himself told the truth and was nailed on the cross. If you were a beast you could not break God's law, and if you were a man you would not, but you are neither, and that makes you a kind of monster that spoils everything it touches and never knows the reason, and that is why I will never forgive you until you become a man, a true man with a true soul. As for your friends—"

Here Thorvald Einarsson struck the Abbess on the face with his open hand and knocked her down. I heard Sister Hedwic gasp in horror and behind us Sister Sibihd began to moan. But the Abbess only sat there, rubbing her jaw and smiling a little. Then she said:

"Oh, dear, have I been at it again? I am ashamed of myself. You are quite right to be angry, Torvald; no one can stand me when I go on in that way, least of all myself; it is such a bore. Still, I cannot seem to stop it; I am too used to being the Abbess Radegunde, that is clear. I promise never to torment you again, but you, Thorvald, must never strike me again, because you will be very sorry if you do."

He took a step forward.

"No, no, my dear man," the Abbess said merrily, "I mean no threat—how could I threaten you?—I mean only that I will never tell you any jokes, my spirits will droop, and I will become as dull as any other woman. Confess it now: I am the most interesting thing that has happened to you in years and I have entertained you better, sharp tongue and all, than all the *skalds* at the Court of Norway. And I know more tales and stories than they do—more than anyone in the whole world—for I make new ones when the old ones wear out.

"Shall I tell you a story now?"

"About your Christ?" said he, the anger still in his face.

"No," said she, "about living men and women. Tell me, Torvald, what do you men want from us women?"

"To be talked to death," said he, and I could see there was some anger in him still, but he was turning it to play also.

The Abbess laughed in delight. "Very witty!" she said, springing to her feet and brushing the leaves off her skirt. "You are a very clever man, Torvald. I beg your pardon, Thorvald. I keep forgetting. But as to what men want from women, if you asked the young men, they would only wink and dig one another in the ribs, but that is only how they deceive themselves. That is only body calling to body. They want something quite different and they want it so much that it frightens them. So they pretend it is anything and everything else: pleasure, comfort, a servant in the home. Do you know what it is that they want?"

"What?" said Thorvald.

"The mother," said Radegunde, "as women do, too; we all want the mother. When I walked before you on the riverbank yesterday, I was playing the mother. Now you did nothing, for you are no young fool, but I knew that sooner or later one of you, so tormented by his longing that he would hate me for it, would reveal himself. And so he did: Thorfinn, with his thoughts all mixed up between witches and grannies and what not. I knew I could frighten him, and through him, most of you. That was the beginning of my bargaining. You Norse have too much of the father in your country and not enough mother; that is why you die so well and kill other folk so well—and live so very, very badly."

"You are doing it again," said Thorvald, but I think he wanted to listen all the same.

"Your pardon, friend," said the Abbess. "You are brave men; I don't deny it. But I know your *sagas* and they are all about fighting and dying and afterwards not Heavenly happiness but the end of the world: everything, even the gods, eaten by the Fenris Wolf and the Midgaard snake! What a pity, to die bravely only because life is not worth living! The Irish know better. The pagan Irish were heroes, with their Queens leading them to battle as often as not, and Father Cairbre, God rest his soul, was complaining only two days ago that the common Irish folk were blasphemously making a goddess out of God's mother, for do they build shrines to Christ or Our Lord or pray to them? No! It is Our Lady of the Rocks and Our Lady of the Sea and Our Lady of the Grove and Our Lady of this or that from one end of the land to the other. And even here it is only the Abbey folk who speak of God the Father and of Christ. In the village if one is sick or another in trouble it is: Holy Mother, save me! and: *Miriam Virginem*, intercede for me, and: Blessed Virgin, blind my husband's eyes! and: Our Lady, preserve my crops, and so on, men and women both. We all need the mother."

"You, too?"

"More than most," said the Abbess.

"And I?"

"Oh, no," said the Abbess, stopping suddenly, for we had all been walking back toward the village as she spoke. "No, and that is what drew me to you at once. I saw it in you and knew you were the leader. It is followers who make leaders, you know, and your shipmates have made you leader, whether you know it or not. What you want is—how shall I say it? You are a clever man, Thorvald, perhaps the cleverest man I have ever met, more even than the scholars I knew in my youth. But your cleverness has had no food. It is a cleverness of the world and not of books. You want to travel and know about folk and their customs, and what strange places are like, and what has happened to men and women in the past. If you take me to Constantinople, it will not be to get a price for me but merely to go there; you went seafaring because this longing itched at you until you could bear it not a year more; I know that."

"Then you are a witch," said he, and he was not smiling.

"No, I only saw what was in your face when you spoke of that city," said she. "Also there is gossip that you spent much time in

Göteborg as a young man, idling and marveling at the ships and markets when you should have been at your farm."

She said, "Thorvald, I can feed that cleverness. I am the wisest woman in the world. I know everything—everything! I know more than my teachers; I make it up or it comes to me, I don't know how, but it is real—real!—and I know more than anyone. Take me from here, as your slave if you wish but as your friend also, and let us go to Constantinople and see the domes of gold, and the walls all inlaid with gold, and the people so wealthy you cannot imagine it, and the whole city so gilded it seems to be on fire, pictures as high as a wall, set right in the wall and all made of jewels so there is nothing else like them, redder than the reddest rose, greener than the grass, and with a blue that makes the sky pale!"

"You are indeed a witch," said he, "and not the Abbess Radegunde."

She said slowly, "I think I am forgetting how to be the Abbess Radegunde."

"Then you will not care about them anymore," said he, and pointed to Sister Hedwic, who was still leading the stumbling Sister Sibihd.

The Abbess's face was still and mild. She said, "I care. Do not strike me, Thorvald, not ever again, and I will be a good friend to you. Try to control the worst of your men and leave as many of my people free as you can—I know them and will tell you which can be taken away with the least hurt to themselves or others—and I will feed that curiosity and cleverness of yours until you will not recognize this old world anymore for the sheer wonder and awe of it; I swear this on my life."

"Done," said he, adding, "but with my luck, your life is somewhere else, locked in a box on top of a mountain, like the troll's in the story, or you will die of old age while we are still at sea."

"Nonsense," she said, "I am a healthy, mortal woman with all my teeth, and I mean to gather many wrinkles yet."

He put his hand out and she took it; then he said, shaking his head in wonder, "If I sold you in Constantinople, within a year you would become Queen of the place!"

The Abbess laughed merrily and I cried in fear, "Me, too! Take me too!" and she said, "Oh, yes, we must not forget little Boy News," and lifted me into her arms.

The frightening, tall man, with his face close to mine, said in his strange, singsong German:

"Boy, would you like to see the whales leaping in the open sea and the seals barking on the rocks? And cliffs so high that a giant could stretch his arms up and not reach their tops? And the sun shining at midnight?"

"Yes!" said I.

"But you will be a slave," he said, "and may be ill treated and will always have to do as you are bid. Would you like that?"

"No!" I cried lustily, from the safety of the Abbess's arms, "I'll fight!"

He laughed a mighty, roaring laugh and tousled my head—rather too hard, I thought—and said, "I will not be a bad master, for I am named for Thor Red-beard and he is strong and quick to fight but good-natured, too, and so am I," and the Abbess put me down, and so we walked back to the village, Thorvald and the Abbess Radegunde talking of the glories of this world and Sister Hedwic saying softly, "She is a saint, our Abbess, a saint, to sacrifice herself for the good of the people," and all the time behind us, like a memory, came the low, witless sobbing of Sister Sibihd, who was in Hell.

When we got back we found that Thorfinn was better and the Norsemen were to leave in the morning. Thorvald had a second pallet brought into the Abbess's study and slept on the floor with us that night. You might think his men would laugh at this, for the Abbess was an old woman, but I think he had been with one of the young ones before he came to us. He had that look about him. There was no bedding for the Abbess but an old brown cloak with holes in it, and she and I were wrapped in it when he came in and threw himself down, whistling, on the other pallet. Then he said:

"Tomorrow, before we sail, you will show me the old Abbess's treasure."

"No," said she. "That agreement was broken."

He had been playing with his knife and now ran his thumb along the edge of it. "I can make you do it."

"No," said she patiently, "and now I am going to sleep."

"So you make light of death?" he said. "Good! That is what a brave woman should do, as the *skalds* sing, and not move even when the keen sword cuts off her eyelashes. But what if I put this knife here not to your throat but to your little boy's? You would tell me then quick enough!"

The Abbess turned away from him, yawning and saying, "No, Thorvald, because you would not. And if you did, I would despise you for a cowardly oath breaker and not tell you for that reason. Good night."

He laughed and whistled again for a bit. Then he said:

"Was all that true?"

"All what?" said the Abbess. "Oh, about the statue. Yes, but there was no ravisher. I put him in the tale for poor Sister Hedwic."

Thorvald snorted, as if in disappointment. "Tale? You tell lies, Abbess!"

The Abbess drew the old brown cloak over her head and closed her eyes. "It helped her."

Then there was a silence, but the big Norseman did not seem able to lie still. He shifted his body again as if the straw bothered him, and again turned over. He finally burst out, "But what happened!"

She sat up. Then she shut her eyes. She said, "Maybe it does not come into your man's thoughts that an old woman gets tired and that the work of dealing with folk is hard work, or even that it is work at all. Well!

"Nothing 'happened,' Thorvald. Must something happen only if this one fucks that one or one bangs in another's head? I desired my statue to the point of such foolishness that I determined to find a real, human lover, but when I raised my eyes from my fancies to the real, human men of Rome and unstopped my ears to listen to their talk, I realized that the thing was completely and eternally impossible. Oh, those younger sons with their skulking, jealous hatred of the rich, and the rich ones with their noses in the air because they thought themselves of such great consequence because of their silly money, and the timidity of the priests to their superiors, and their superiors' pride, and the artisans' hatred of the peasants, and the peasants being worked like animals from morning until night, and half the men I saw beating their wives and the other half out to cheat some poor girl of her money or her virginity or both—this was enough to put out any fire! And the women doing less harm only because they had less power to do harm, or so it seemed to me then. So I put all away, as one does with any disappointment. Men are not such bad folk when one stops expecting them to be gods, but they are not for me. If that state is chastity, then a weak stomach is temperance, I think. But whatever it is, I have it, and that's the end of the matter."

"*All* men?" said Thorvald Einarsson with his head to one side, and it came to me that he had been drinking, though he seemed sober.

"Thorvald," said the Abbess, "what you want with this middle-aged wreck of a body I cannot imagine, but if you lust after my wrinkles and flabby breasts and lean, withered flanks, do whatever you want quickly and then, for Heaven's sake, let me sleep. I am tired to death."

He said in a low voice, "I need to have power over you."

She spread her hands in a helpless gesture. "Oh, Thorvald, Thorvald, I am a weak little woman over forty years old! Where is the power? All I can do is talk!"

He said, "That's it. That's how you do it. You talk and talk and talk and everyone does just as you please; I have seen it!"

The Abbess said, looking sharply at him, "Very well. If you must. *But if I were you, Norseman, I would as soon bed my own mother.* Remember that as you pull my skirts up."

That stopped him. He swore under his breath, turning over on his side, away from us. Then he thrust his knife into the edge of his pallet, time after time. Then he put the knife under the rolled-up cloth he was using as a pillow. We had no pillow and so I tried to make mine out of the edge of the cloak and failed. Then I thought that the Norseman was afraid of God working in Radegunde, and then I thought of Sister Hedwic's changing color and wondered why. And then I thought of the leaping whales and the seals, which must be like great dogs because of the barking, and then the seals jumped on land and ran to my pallet and lapped at me with great, icy tongues of water so that I shivered and jumped, and then I woke up.

The Abbess Radegunde had left the pallet—it was her warmth I had missed—and was walking about the room. She would step and pause, her skirts making a small noise as she did so. She was careful not to touch the sleeping Thorvald. There was a dim light in the room from the embers that still glowed under the ashes in the hearth, but no light came from between the shutters of the study window, now shut against the cold. I saw the Abbess kneel under the plain wooden cross which hung on the study wall and heard her say a few words in Latin; I thought she was praying. But then she said in a low voice:

"Do not call upon Apollo and the Muses, for they are deaf things and vain. But so are you, Pierced Man, deaf and vain."

Then she got up and began to pace again. Thinking of it now frightens me, for it was the middle of the night and no one to hear her—except me, but she thought I was asleep—and yet she went on and on in that low, even voice as if it were broad day and she were explaining something to someone, as if things that had been in her thoughts for years must finally come out. But I did not find anything alarming in it then, for I thought that perhaps all Abbesses had to do such things, and besides she did not seem angry or hurried or afraid; she sounded as calm as if she were discussing the profits from the Abbey's beekeeping—which I had heard her do—or the accounts for the wine cellars—which I had also heard—and there was nothing alarming in that. So I listened as she continued walking about the room in the dark. She said:

"Talk, talk, talk, and always to myself. But one can't abandon the kittens and puppies; that would be cruel. And being the Abbess Radegunde at least gives one something to do. But I am so sick of the good Abbess Radegunde; I have put on Radegunde every morning of my life as easily as I put on my smock, and then I have had to hear the stupid creature praised all day!—sainted Radegunde, just Radegunde who is never angry or greedy or jealous, kindly Radegunde who sacrifices herself for others, and always the talk, talk, talk, bubbling and boiling in my head with no one to hear or understand, and no one to answer. No, not even in the south, only a line here, or a line there, and all written by the dead. Did they feel as I do? That the world is a giant nursery full of squabbles over toys and the babes thinking me some kind of goddess because I'm not greedy for their dolls or bits of straw or their horses made of tied-together sticks?

"Poor people, if only they knew! It's so easy to be temperate when one enjoys nothing, so easy to be kind when one loves nothing, so easy to be fearless when one's life is no better than one's death. And so easy to scheme when the success doesn't matter.

"Would they be surprised, I wonder, to find out what my real thoughts were when Thorfinn's knife was at my throat? Curiosity!

But he would not do it, of course; he does everything for show. And they would think I was twice holy, not to care about death.

"Then why not kill yourself, impious Sister Radegunde? Is it your religion which stops you? Oh, you mean the holy wells, and the holy trees, and the blessed saints with their blessed relics, and the stupidity that shamed Sister Hedwic, and the promises of safety that drove poor Sibihd mad when the blessed body of her Lord did not protect her and the blessed love of the blessed Mary turned away the sharp point of not one knife? Trash! Idle leaves and sticks, reeds and rushes, filth we sweep off our floors when it grows too thick. As if holiness had anything to do with all of that. As if every place were not as holy as every other and every thing as holy as every other, from the shit in Thorfinn's bowels to the rocks on the ground. As if all places and things were not clouds placed in front of our weak eyes, to keep us from being blinded by that glory, that eternal shining, that blazing all about us, the torrent of light that is everything and is in everything! That is what keeps me from the river, but it never speaks to me or tells me what to do, and to it good and evil are the same—no, it is something else than good or evil; it *is*, only—so it is not God. That I know.

"So, people, is your Radegunde a witch or a demon? Is she full of pride or is Radegunde abject? Perhaps she is a witch. Once, long ago, I confessed to old Gerbertus that I could see things that were far away merely by closing my eyes, and I proved it to him, too, and he wept over me and gave me much penance, crying, 'If it come of itself it may be a gift of God, daughter, but it is more likely the work of a demon, so do not do it!' And then we prayed and I told him the power had left me, to make the poor old puppy less troubled in its mind, but that was not true, of course. I could still see Turkey as easily as I could see him, and places far beyond: the squat, wild men of the plains on their ponies, and the strange, tall people beyond that with their great cities and odd eyes, as if one pulled one's eyelid up on a slant, and then the seas with the great, wild lands and the cities more full of gold than Constantinople, and water again until one comes back home, for the world's a ball, as the ancients said.

"But I did stop somehow, over the years. Radegunde never had time, I suppose. Besides, when I opened that door it was only pictures, as in a book, and all to no purpose, and after a while I had seen them all and no longer cared for them. It is the other door that draws me, when it opens itself but a crack and strange things peep through, like Ranulf sister's son and the name of his horse. That door is good but very heavy; it always swings back after a little. I shall have to be on my deathbed to open it all the way, I think.

"The fox is asleep. He is the cleverest yet; there is something in him so that at times one can almost talk to him. But still a fox, for the most part. Perhaps in time . . .

"But let me see; yes, he is asleep. And the Sibihd puppy is asleep, though it will be having a bad dream soon, I think, and the Thorfinn kitten is asleep, as full of fright as when it wakes, with its claws going in and out, in and out, lest something strangle it in its sleep."

Then the Abbess fell silent and moved to the shuttered window as if she were looking out, so I thought that she was indeed looking out—but not with her eyes—at all the sleeping folk, and this was something she had done every night of her life to see if they were safe and sound. But would she not know that I was awake? Should I not try very hard to get to sleep before she caught me? Then it seemed to me that she smiled in the dark, although I could not see it. She said in that same low, even voice: "Sleep or wake, Boy News; it is all one to me. Thou hast heard nothing of any importance, only the silly Abbess talking to herself, only Radegunde saying good-bye to Radegunde, only Radegunde going away—don't cry, Boy News; I am still here—but there: Radegunde has gone. This Norseman and I are alike in one way: our minds are like great houses with many of the rooms locked shut. We crowd in a miserable, huddled few, like poor folk, when we might move freely among them all, as gracious as princes. It is fate that locked away so much of the Norseman—see, Boy News, I do not say his name, not even softly, for that wakes folks—but I wonder if the one who bolted me in was not Radegunde herself, she and old Gerbertus—whom I partly believed—they and the years and years of having to be Radegunde and do the things Radegunde did and pretend to have the thoughts Radegunde had and the endless, endless lies Radegunde must tell everyone, and Radegunde's utter and unbearable loneliness."

She fell silent again. I wondered at the Abbess's talk this time: saying she was not there when she was, and about living locked up in small rooms—for surely the Abbey was the most splendid house in all the world, and the biggest—and how could she be

lonely when all the folk loved her? But then she said in a voice so
low that I could hardly hear it:

"Poor Radegunde! So weary of the lies she tells and the fooling of
men and women with the collars around their necks and bribes of
food for good behavior and a careful twitch of the leash that they do
not even see or feel. And with the Norseman it will be all the same:
lies and flattery and all of it work that never ends and no one ever
even sees, so that finally Radegunde will lie down like an ape in a
cage, weak and sick from hunger, and will never get up.

"Let her die now. There: Radegunde is dead. Radegunde is gone.
Perhaps the door was heavy only because she was on the other side
of it, pushing against me. Perhaps it will open all the way now. I
have looked in all directions: to the east, to the north and south, and
to the west, but there is one place I have never looked and now I will:
away from the ball, straight out. Let us see—"

She stopped speaking all of a sudden. I had been falling asleep but
this silence woke me. Then I heard the Abbess gasp terribly, like one
mortally stricken, and then she said in a whisper so keen and
thrilling that it made the hair stand up on my head: *Where art thou?*
The next moment she had torn the shutters open and was crying out
with all her voice: *Help me! Find me! Oh, come, come, come, or I die!*

This waked Thorvald. With some Norse oath he stumbled up and
flung on his sword belt and then put his hand to his dagger; I had
noticed this thing with the dagger was a thing Norsemen liked to do.
The Abbess was silent. He let out his breath in an oof! and went to
light the tallow dip at the live embers under the hearth ashes; when
the dip had smoked up, he put it on its shelf on the wall.

He said in German, "What the devil, woman! What has happened?"

She turned around. She looked as if she could not see us, as if she
had been dazed by a joy too big to hold, like one who has looked into
the sun and is still dazzled by it so that everything seems changed,
and the world seems all God's and everything in it like Heaven. She
said softly, with her arms around herself, hugging herself: "My
people. The real people."

"What are you talking of!" said he.

She seemed to see him then, but only as Sibihd had beheld us; I
do not mean in horror as Sibihd had, but beholding through something else, like someone who comes from a vision of bliss which still

lingers about her. She said in the same soft voice, "They are coming for me, Thorvald. Is it not wonderful? I knew all this year that something would happen, but I did not know it would be the one thing I wanted in all the world."

He grasped his hair. *"Who* is coming?"

"My people," she said, laughing softly. "Do you not feel them? I do. We must wait three days for they come from very far away. But then—oh, you will see!"

He said, "You've been dreaming. We sail tomorrow."

"Oh, no," said the Abbess simply, "you cannot do that for it would not be right. They told me to wait; they said if I went away, they might not find me."

He said slowly, "You've gone mad. Or it's a trick."

"Oh, no, Thorvald," said she. "How could I trick you? I am your friend. And you will wait these three days, will you not, because you are my friend also."

"You're mad," he said, and started for the door of the study, but she stepped in front of him and threw herself on her knees. All her cunning seemed to have deserted her; or perhaps it was Radegunde who had been the cunning one. This one was like a child. She clasped her hands and tears came out of her eyes; she begged him, saying:

"Such a little thing, Thorvald, only three days! And if they do not come, why then we will go anywhere you like, but if they do come you will not regret it, I promise you; they are not like the folk here and that place is like nothing here. It is what the soul craves, Thorvald!"

He said, "Get up, woman, for God's sake!"

She said, smiling in a sly, frightened way through her blubbered face, "If you let me stay, I will show you the old Abbess's buried treasure, Thorvald."

He stepped back, the anger clear in him. "So this is the brave old witch who cares nothing for death!" he said. Then he made for the door, but she was up again, as quick as a snake, and had flung herself across it.

She said, still with that strange innocence, "Do not strike me. Do not push me. I am your friend!"

He said, "You mean that you lead me by a string around the neck, like a goose. Well, I am tired of that!"

"But I cannot do that anymore," said the Abbess breathlessly, "not since the door opened. I am not able now." He raised his arm to strike her and she cowered, wailing, "Do not strike me! Do not push me! Do not, Thorvald!"

He said, "Out of my way then, old witch!"

She began to cry in sobs and gulps. She said, "One is here but another will come! One is buried but another will rise! She will come, Thorvald!" and then in a low, quick voice, "Do not push open this last door. There is one behind it who is evil and I am afraid"—but one could see that he was angry and disappointed and would not listen. He struck her for the second time and again she fell, but with a desperate cry, covering her face with her hands. He unbolted the door and stepped over her and I heard his footsteps go down the corridor. I could see the Abbess clearly—at that time I did not wonder how this could be, with the shadows from the tallow dip half hiding everything in their drunken dance—but I saw every line in her face as if it had been full day, and in that light I saw Radegunde go away from us at last.

Have you ever been at some great King's court or some Earl's and heard the storytellers? There are those so skilled in the art that they not only speak for you what the person in the tale said and did, but they also make an action with their faces and bodies as if they truly were that man or woman, so that it is a great surprise to you when the tale ceases, for you almost believe that you have seen the tale happen in front of your very eyes, and it is as if a real man or woman had suddenly ceased to exist, for you forget that all this was only a teller and a tale.

So it was with the woman who had been Radegunde. She did not change; it was still Radegunde's gray hairs and wrinkled face and old body in the peasant woman's brown dress, and yet at the same time it was a stranger who stepped out of the Abbess Radegunde as out of a gown dropped to the floor. This stranger was without feeling, though Radegunde's tears still stood on her cheeks, and there was no kindness or joy in her. She got up without taking care of her dress where the dirty rushes stuck to it; it was as if the dress were an accident and did not concern her. She said in a voice I had never heard before, one with no feeling in it, as if I did not concern her, or Thorvald Einarsson either, as if neither of us were worth a second glance:

"Thorvald, turn around."

Far up in the hall something stirred.

"Now come back. This way."

There were footsteps, coming closer. Then the big Norseman walked clumsily into the room—jerk! jerk! jerk! at every step as if he were being pulled by a rope. Sweat beaded his face. He said, "You—how?"

"By my nature," she said. "Put up your right arm, fox. Now the left. Now both down. Good."

"You—troll!" he said.

"That is so," she said. "Now listen to me, you. There's a man inside you but he's not worth getting at; I tried moments ago when I was new-hatched and he's buried too deep, but now I have grown beak and claws and care nothing for him. It's almost dawn and your boys are stirring; you will go out and tell them that we must stay here another three days. You are weatherwise; make up some story they will believe. And don't try to tell anyone what happened here tonight; you will find that you cannot."

"Folk—come," said he, trying to turn his head, but the effort only made him sweat.

She raised her eyebrows. "Why should they? No one has heard anything. Nothing has happened. You will go out and be as you always are and I will play Radegunde. For three days only. Then you are free."

He did not move. One could see that to remain still was very hard for him; the sweat poured and he strained until every muscle stood out. She said:

"Fox, don't hurt yourself. And don't push me; I am not fond of you. My hand is light upon you only because you still seem to me a little less unhuman than the rest; do not force me to make it heavier. To be plain: I have just broken Thorfinn's neck, for I find that the change improves him. Do not make me do the same to you."

"No worse—than death," Thorvald brought out.

"Ah, no?" said she, and in a moment he was screaming and clawing at his eyes. She said, "Open them, open them; your sight is back," and then, "I do not wish to bother myself thinking up worse things, like worms in your guts. Or do you wish dead sons and a dead wife? Now go.

"*As you always do*," she added sharply, and the big man turned and walked out. One could not have told from looking at him that anything was wrong.

I had not been sorry to see such a bad man punished, one whose friends had killed our folk and would have taken us for slaves—and yet I was sorry, too, in a way, because of the seals barking and the whales—and he *was* splendid, after a fashion—and yet truly I forgot all about that the moment he was gone, for I was terrified of this strange person or demon or whatever it was, for I knew that whoever was in the room with me was not the Abbess Radegunde. I knew also that it could tell where I was and what I was doing, even if I made no sound, and was in a terrible riddle as to what I ought to do when soft fingers touched my face. It was the demon, reaching swiftly and silently behind her.

And do you know, all of a sudden everything was all right! I don't mean that she was the Abbess again—I still had very serious suspicions about that—but all at once I felt light as air and nothing seemed to matter very much because my stomach was full of bubbles of happiness, just as if I had been drunk, only nicer. If the Abbess Radegunde were really a demon, what a joke that was on her people! And she did not, now that I came to think of it, seem a bad sort of demon, more the frightening kind than the killing kind, except for Thorfinn, of course, but then Thorfinn had been a very wicked man. And did not the angels of the Lord smite down the wicked? So perhaps the Abbess was an angel of the Lord and not a demon, but if she were truly an angel, why had she not smitten the Norsemen down when they first came and so saved all our folk? And then I thought that whether angel or demon, she was no longer the Abbess and would love me no longer, and if I had not been so full of the silly happiness which kept tickling about inside me, this thought would have made me weep.

I said, "Will the bad Thorvald get free, demon?"

"No," she said. "Not even if I sleep."

I thought: *But she does not love me.*

"I love thee," said the strange voice, but it was not the Abbess Radegunde's and so was without meaning, but again those soft fingers touched me and there was some kindness in them, even if it was a stranger's kindness.

Sleep, they said.

So I did.

The next three days I had much secret mirth to see the folk bow down to the demon and kiss its hands and weep over it because it had sold itself to ransom them. That is what Sister Hedwic told them. Young Thorfinn had gone out in the night to piss and had fallen over a stone in the dark and broken his neck, which secretly rejoiced our folk, but his comrades did not seem to mind much either, save for one young fellow who had been Thorfinn's friend, I think, and so went about with a long face. Thorvald locked me up in the Abbess's study with the demon every night and went out—or so folk said—to one of the young women, but on those nights the demon was silent, and I lay there with the secret tickle of merriment in my stomach, caring about nothing.

On the third morning I woke sober. The demon—or the Abbess— for in the day she was so like the Abbess Radegunde that I wondered—took my hand and walked us up to Thorvald, who was out picking the people to go aboard the Norseman's boats at the riverbank to be slaves. Folk were standing about weeping and wringing their hands; I thought this strange because of the Abbess's promise to pick those whose going would hurt least, but I know now that least is not none. The weather was bad, cold rain out of mist, and some of Thorvald's companions were speaking sourly to him in the Norse, but he talked them down—bluff and hearty—as if making light of the weather. The demon stood by him and said, in German, in a low voice so that none might hear: "You will say we go to find the Abbess's treasure and then you will go with us into the woods."

He spoke to his fellows in Norse and they frowned, but the end of it was that two must come with us, for the demon said it was such a treasure as three might carry. The demon had the voice and manner of the Abbess Radegunde, all smiles, so they were fooled. Thus we started out into the trees behind the village, with the rain worse and the ground beginning to soften underfoot. As soon as the village was out of sight, the two Norsemen fell behind, but Thorvald did not seem to notice this; I looked back and saw the first man standing in the mud with one foot up, like a goose, and the second with his head lifted and his mouth open so that the rain fell in it. We walked on, the earth sucking at our shoes and all of us getting wet: Thorvald's hair stuck fast against his face, and the demon's old brown cloak clinging to its body. Then suddenly the demon began to breathe harshly and it put its hand to its side with a cry. Its cloak fell off and it stumbled before us between the wet trees, not weeping but breathing hard. Then I saw, ahead of us through the pelting rain, a kind of shining among the bare tree trunks, and as we came nearer the shining became more clear until it was very plain to see, not a blazing thing like a fire at night but a mild and even brightness as though the sunlight were coming through the clouds pleasantly but without strength, as it often does at the beginning of the year.

And then there were folk inside the brightness, both men and women, all dressed in white, and they held out their arms to us, and the demon ran to them, crying out loudly and weeping but paying no mind to the tree branches which struck it across the face and body. Sometimes it fell but it quickly got up again. When it reached the strange folk they embraced it, and I thought that the filth and mud of its gown would stain their white clothing, but the foulness dropped off and would not cling to those clean garments. None of the strange folk spoke a word, nor did the Abbess—I knew then that she was no demon, whatever she was—but I felt them talk to one another, as if in my mind, although I know not how this could be nor the sense of what they said. An odd thing was that as I came closer I could see they were not standing on the ground, as in the way of nature, but higher up, inside the shining, and that their white robes were nothing at all like ours, for they clung to the body so that one might see the people's legs all the way up to the place where the legs joined, even the women's. And some of the folk were like us, but most had a darker color, and some looked as if they had been smeared with soot—there are such persons in the far parts of the world, you know, as I found out later; it is their own natural color—and there were some with the odd eyes the Abbess had spoken of—but the oddest thing of all I will not tell you now. When the Abbess had embraced and kissed them all and all had wept, she turned and looked down upon us: Thorvald standing there as if held by a rope and I, who had lost my fear and had crept close in pure awe, for there was such a joy about these people, like the light about them, mild as spring light and yet as strong as in a spring where the winter has gone forever.

"Come to me, Thorvald," said the Abbess, and one could not see from her face if she loved or hated him. He moved closer—jerk! jerk!—and she reached down and touched his forehead with her fingertips, at which one side of his lip lifted, as a dog's does when it snarls.

"As thou knowest," said the Abbess quietly, "I hate thee and would be revenged upon thee. Thus I swore to myself three days ago, and such vows are not lightly broken."

I saw him snarl and he turned his eyes from her.

"I must go soon," said the Abbess, unmoved, "for I could stay here long years only as Radegunde, and Radegunde is no more; none of us can remain here long as our proper selves or even in our true bodies, for if we do we go mad like Sibihd or walk into the river and drown or stop our own hearts, so miserable, wicked, and brutish does your world seem to us. Nor may we come in large companies, for we are few and our strength is not great and we have much to learn and study of thy folk so that we may teach and help without marring all in our ignorance. And ignorant or wise, we can do naught except thy folk aid us.

"Here is my revenge," said the Abbess, and he seemed to writhe under the touch of her fingers, for all they were so light. "Henceforth be not Thorvald Farmer nor yet Thorvald Seafarer but Thorvald Peacemaker, Thorvald War-hater, put into anguish by bloodshed and agonized at cruelty. I cannot make long thy life—that gift is beyond me—but I give thee this: to the end of thy days, long or short, thou wilt know the Presence about thee always, as I do, and thou wilt know that it is neither good nor evil, as I do, and this knowing will trouble and frighten thee always, as it does me, and so about this one thing, as about many another, Thorvald Peacemaker will never have peace.

"Now, Thorvald, go back to the village and tell thy comrades I was assumed into the company of the saints, straight up to Heaven. Thou mayst believe it, if thou wilt. That is all my revenge."

Then she took away her hand, and he turned and walked from us like a man in a dream, holding out his hands as if to feel the rain and stumbling now and again, as one who wakes from a vision.

Then I began to grieve, for I knew she would be going away with the strange people, and it was to me as if all the love and care and light in the world were leaving me. I crept close to her, meaning to spring secretly onto the shining place and so go away with them, but she spied me and said, "Silly Radulphus, you cannot," and that *you* hurt me more than anything else so I began to bawl.

"Child," said the Abbess, "come to me," and loudly weeping I leaned against her knees. I felt the shining around me, all bright and good and warm, that wiped away all grief, and then the Abbess's touch on my hair.

She said, "Remember me. And be . . . content."

I nodded, wishing I dared to look up at her face, but when I did, she had already gone with her friends. Not up into the sky, you understand, but as if they moved very swiftly backwards among the trees—although the trees were still behind them somehow—and as they moved, the shining and the people faded away into the rain until there was nothing left.

Then there was no rain. I do not mean that the clouds parted or the sun came out; I mean that one moment it was raining and cold and the next the sky was clear blue from side to side, and it was splendid, sunny, breezy, bright, sailing weather. I had the oddest thought that the strange folk were not agreed about doing such a big miracle—and it was hard for them, too—but they had decided that no one would believe this more than all the other miracles folk speak of, I suppose. And it would surely make Thorvald's lot easier when he came back with wild words about saints and Heaven, as indeed it did, later.

Well, that is the tale, really. She said to me "Be content" and so I am; they call me Radulf the Happy now. I have had my share of trouble and sickness, but always somewhere in me there is a little spot of warmth and joy to make it all easier, like a traveler's fire burning out in the wilderness on a cold night. When I am in real sorrow or distress, I remember her fingers touching my hair and that takes part of the pain away, somehow. So perhaps I got the best gift, after all. And she said also, "Remember me," and thus I have, every little thing, although it all happened when I was the age my own grandson is now, and that is how I can tell you this tale today.

And the rest? Three days after the Norsemen left, Sibihd got back her wits and no one knew how, though I think I do! And as for Thorvald Einarsson, I have heard that after his wife died in Norway he went to England and ended his days there as a monk, but whether this story be true or not I do not know.

I know this: they may call me Happy Radulf all they like, but there is much that troubles me. Was the Abbess Radegunde a demon, as the new priest says? I cannot believe this, although he called half her sayings nonsense and the other half blasphemy when I asked him.

Father Cairbre, before the Norse killed him, told us stories about the Sidhe, that is, the Irish fairy people, who leave changelings in human cradles; and for a while it seemed to me that Radegunde must be a woman of the Sidhe when I remembered that she could read Latin at the age of two and was such a marvel of learning when so young, for the changelings the fairies leave are not their own children, you understand, but one of the fairy folk themselves, who are hundreds upon hundreds of years old, and the other fairy folk always come back for their own in the end. And yet this could not have been, for Father Cairbre said also that the Sidhe are wanton and cruel and without souls, and neither the Abbess Radegunde nor the people who came for her were one blessed bit like that, although she did break Thorfinn's neck—but then it may be that Thorfinn broke his own neck by chance, just as we all thought at the time, and she told this to Thorvald afterwards, as if she had done it herself, only to frighten him. She had more of a soul with a soul's griefs and joys than most of us, no matter what the new priest says. He never saw her or felt her sorrow and lonesomeness, or heard her talk of the blazing light all around us—and what can that be but God Himself? Even though she did call the crucifix a deaf thing and vain, she must have meant not Christ, you see, but only the piece of wood itself, for she was always telling the Sisters that Christ was in Heaven and not on the wall. And if she said the light was not good or evil, well, there is a traveling Irish scholar who told me of a holy Christian monk named Augustinus who tells us that all which is, is good, and evil is only a lack of the good, like an empty place not filled up. And if the Abbess truly said there was no God, I say it was the sin of despair, and even saints may sin, if only they repent, which I believe she did at the end.

So I tell myself, and yet I know the Abbess Radegunde was no saint, for are the saints few and weak, as she said? Surely not! And then there is a thing I held back in my telling, a small thing, and it will make you laugh and perhaps means nothing one way or the other, but it is this:

Are the saints bald?

These folk in white had young faces but they were like eggs; there was not a stitch of hair on their domes! Well, God may shave His saints if He pleases, I suppose.

But I know she was no saint. And then I believe that she did kill Thorfinn and the light was not God and she not even a Christian or maybe even human, and I remember how Radegunde was to her only a gown to step out of at will, and how she truly hated and scorned Thorvald until she was happy and safe with her own people. Or perhaps it was like her talk about living in a house with the rooms shut up; when she stopped being Radegunde, first one part of her came back and then the other—the joyful part that could not lie or plan and then the angry part—and then they were all together when she was back among her own folk. And then I give up trying to weigh this matter and go back to warm my soul at the little fire she lit in me, that one warm, bright place in the wide and windy dark.

But something troubles me even there and will not be put to rest by the memory of the Abbess's touch on my hair. As I grow older it troubles me more and more. It was the very last thing she said to me, which I have not told you but will now. When she had given me the gift of contentment, I became so happy that I said, "Abbess, you said you would be revenged on Thorvald, but all you did was change him into a good man. That is no revenge!"

What this saying did to her astonished me, for all the color went out of her face and left it gray. She looked suddenly old, like a death's-head, even standing there among her own true folk with love and joy coming from them so strongly that I myself might feel it. She said, "I did not change him. I lent him my eyes, that is all." Then she looked beyond me, as if at our village, at the Norsemen loading their boats with weeping slaves, at all the villages of Germany and England and France where the poor folk sweat from dawn to dark so that the great lords may do battle with one another, at castles under siege with the starving folk within eating mice and rats and sometimes one another, at the women carried off or raped or beaten, at the mothers wailing for their little ones, and beyond this at the great wide world itself with all its battles which I had used to think so grand, and the misery and greediness and fear and jealousy and hatred of folk one for the other, save—perhaps—for a few small bands of savages, but they were so far from us that one could scarcely see them. She said: *No revenge? Thinkest thou so, boy?* And then she said as one who believes absolutely, as one who has seen all the folk at their living and dying, not for one year but for many, not in one place but in all places, as one who knows it all over the whole wide earth:

Think again . . .

I have just met Connie Willis at a banquet. Her daughter was with her, and it was amazing to see them together. Each of them is taller than I am (I'm afraid I'm only of average height for a man), and they looked so nearly alike that if I stood off at a distance and crossed my eyes so as to make their images merge, I felt they might make a four-dimensional, hyperstereoscopic whole.

Since Connie began writing she has been piling up awards at a fearful— well, no, that isn't the adjective—at a gratifying rate. This is her first appearance in the Hugo winners volumes and, as in the case of Joanna Russ's story, hers is quasi-historical.

It opens up a thought, though, this use of time travel to save antiquities. Here's a suggestion—

In 438 B.C., at the height of Athens' Golden Age, the sculptor Phidias completed the construction of the Temple to Athena on the Acropolis. It is popularly called the Parthenon, from the Greek word for "virgin," because Athena was a virgin goddess.

Now imagine that 2,125 years have passed. Over twenty-one centuries of vicissitudes have taken place. Athens has been taken by Sparta, by Alexander the Great, by a variety of Macedonian and Roman generals. The Goths have taken it; the Crusaders have taken it; the Turks have taken it. Through all those years replete with disasters, the Parthenon has stood on the Acropolis, its beauty undiminished by age and time (and there are many who consider it to have been, for proportion and good taste, the most beautiful building ever built).

The year is now A.D. 1687. The Turks and the Venetians have been fighting, on and off, for a couple of centuries, and the Venetians are putting on their last successful aggressive enterprise. They have invaded southern Greece and are bombarding Athens (which is a crime in itself).

The Turks are, of course, defending vigorously, and having stocked Athens against a siege, have stored gunpowder in the Parthenon (a crime of enormous proportions).

The Venetian cannonballs are flying. One hits the Parthenon and sets off the gunpowder. In one minute, the Parthenon is in ruins, with its roof blown off—as we see it, today.

Now who will volunteer to go back three centuries to Athens and save the Parthenon? And how can that possibly be done?

But that's one of the great joys of science fiction. It gives rise to thoughts you won't get out of ordinary tales.

—Isaac Asimov

Fire Watch

by Connie Willis

History hath triumphed over time, which besides it nothing but eternity hath triumphed over.

—Sir Walter Raleigh

September 20—Of course the first thing I looked for was the fire watch stone. And of course it wasn't there yet. It wasn't dedicated until 1951, accompanying speech by the Very Reverend Dean Walter Matthews, and this is only 1940. I knew that. I went to see the fire watch stone only yesterday, with some kind of misplaced notion that seeing the scene of the crime would somehow help. It didn't.

The only things that would have helped were a crash course in London during the Blitz and a little more time. I had not gotten either.

"Traveling in time is not like taking the tube, Mr. Bartholomew," the esteemed Dunworthy had said, blinking at me through those antique spectacles of his. "Either you report on the twentieth or you don't go at all."

"But I'm not ready," I'd said. "Look, it took me four years to get ready to travel with St. Paul. *St. Paul.* Not St. Paul's. You can't expect me to get ready for London in the Blitz in two days."

"Yes," Dunworthy had said. "We can." End of conversation.

"Two days!" I had shouted at my roommate Kivrin. "All because some computer adds an *'s*. And the esteemed Dunworthy doesn't even bat an eye when I tell him. 'Time travel is not like taking the tube, young man,' he says. 'I'd suggest you get ready. You're leaving day after tomorrow.' The man's a total incompetent."

"No," she said. "He isn't. He's the best there is. He wrote the book on St. Paul's. Maybe you should listen to what he says."

I had expected Kivrin to be at least a little sympathetic. She had been practically hysterical when she got her practicum changed from fifteenth- to fourteenth-century England, and how did either century qualify as a practicum? Even counting infectious diseases

59

they couldn't have been more than a five. The Blitz is an eight, and St. Paul's itself is, with my luck, a ten.

"You think I should go see Dunworthy again?" I said.

"Yes."

"And then what? I've got two days. I don't know the money, the language, the history. Nothing."

"He's a good man," Kivrin said. "I think you'd better listen to him while you can." Good old Kivrin. Always the sympathetic ear.

The good man was responsible for my standing just inside the propped-open west doors, gawking like the country boy I was supposed to be, looking for a stone that wasn't there. Thanks to the good man, I was about as unprepared for my practicum as it was possible for him to make me.

I couldn't see more than a few feet into the church. I could see a candle gleaming feebly a long way off and a closer blur of white moving toward me. A verger, or possibly the Very Reverend Dean himself. I pulled out the letter from my clergyman uncle in Wales that was supposed to gain me access to the dean, and patted my back pocket to make sure I hadn't lost the microfiche *Oxford English Dictionary, Revised, with Historical Supplements* I'd smuggled out of the Bodleian. I couldn't pull it out in the middle of the conversation, but with luck I could muddle through the first encounter by context and look up the words I didn't know later.

"Are you from the ayarpee?" he said. He was no older than I am, a head shorter and much thinner. Almost ascetic looking. He reminded me of Kivrin. He was not wearing white, but clutching it to his chest. In other circumstances I would have thought it was a pillow. In other circumstances I would know what was being said to me, but there had been no time to unlearn sub-Mediterranean Latin and Jewish law and learn Cockney and air raid procedures. Two days, and the esteemed Dunworthy, who wanted to talk about the sacred burdens of the historian instead of telling me what the ayarpee was.

"Are you?" he demanded again.

I considered whipping out the OED after all on the grounds that Wales was a foreign country, but I didn't think they had microfilm in 1940. Ayarpee. It could be anything, including a nickname for the fire watch, in which case the impulse to say no was not safe at all. "No," I said.

He lunged suddenly toward and past me and peered out the open doors. "Damn," he said, coming back to me. "Where are they then? Bunch of lazy bourgeois tarts!" And so much for getting by on context.

He looked at me closely, suspiciously, as if he thought I was only pretending not to be with the ayarpee. "The church is closed," he said finally.

I held up the envelope and said, "My name's Bartholomew. Is Dean Matthews in?"

He looked out the door a moment longer as if he expected the lazy bourgeois tarts at any moment and intended to attack them with the white bundle; then he turned and said, as if he were guiding a tour, "This way, please," and took off into the gloom.

He led me to the right and down the south aisle of the nave. Thank God I had memorized the floor plan or at that moment, heading into total darkness, led by a raving verger, the whole bizarre metaphor of my situation would have been enough to send me out the west doors and back to St. John's Wood. It helped a little to know where I was. We should have been passing number twenty-six: Hunt's painting of *The Light of the World*—Jesus with his lantern—but it was too dark to see it. We could have used the lantern ourselves.

He stopped abruptly ahead of me, still raving. "We weren't asking for the bloody Savoy, just a few cots. Nelson's better off than we are—at least he's got a pillow provided." He brandished the white bundle like a torch in the darkness. It was a pillow after all. "We asked for them over a fortnight ago, and here we still are, sleeping on the bleeding generals from Trafalgar because those bitches want to play tea and crumpets with the Tommies at Victoria and the hell with us!"

He didn't seem to expect me to answer his outburst, which was good, because I had understood perhaps one key word in three. He stomped on ahead, moving out of sight of the one pathetic altar candle and stopping again at a black hole. Number twenty-five: stairs to the Whispering Gallery, the Dome, the library (not open to the public). Up the stairs, down a hall, stop again at a medieval door and knock. "I've got to go wait for them," he said. "If I'm not there they'll likely take them over to the Abbey. Tell the Dean to ring them up again, will you?" and he took off down the stone steps, still holding his pillow like a shield against him.

He had knocked, but the door was at least a foot of solid oak, and it was obvious the Very Reverend Dean had not heard. I was going to have to knock again. Yes, well, and the man holding the pinpoint had to let go of it, too, but even knowing it will all be over in a moment and you won't feel a thing doesn't make it any easier to say, "Now!" So I stood in front of the door, cursing the history department and the esteemed Dunworthy and the computer that had made the mistake and brought me here to this dark door with only a letter from a fictitious uncle that I trusted no more than I trusted the rest of them.

Even the old reliable Bodleian had let me down. The batch of research stuff I cross-ordered through Balliol and the main terminal is probably sitting in my room right now, a century out of reach. And Kivrin, who had already done her practicum and should have been bursting with advice, walked around as silent as a saint until I begged her to help me.

"Did you go to see Dunworthy?" she said.

"Yes. You want to know what priceless bit of information he had for me? 'Silence and humility are the sacred burdens of the historian.' He also told me I would love St. Paul's. Golden gems from the Master. Unfortunately, what I need to know are the times and places of the bombs so one doesn't fall on me." I flopped down on the bed. "Any suggestions?"

"How good are you at memory retrieval?" she said.

I sat up. "I'm pretty good. You think I should assimilate?"

"There isn't time for that," she said. "I think you should put everything you can directly into long-term."

"You mean endorphins?" I said.

The biggest problem with using memory-assistance drugs to put information into your long-term memory is that it never sits, even for a microsecond, in your short-term memory, and that makes retrieval complicated, not to mention unnerving. It gives you the most unsettling sense of déjà vu to suddenly know something you're positive you've never seen or heard before.

The main problem, though, is not eerie sensations but retrieval. Nobody knows exactly how the brain gets what it wants out of storage, but short-term is definitely involved. That brief, sometimes miscroscopic, time information spends in short-term is apparently used for something besides tip-of-the-tongue availability. The whole complex sort-and-file process of retrieval is apparently centered in short-term, and without it, and without the help of the drugs that put it there or artificial substitutes, information can be impossible to retrieve. I'd used endorphins for examinations and never had any difficulty with retrieval, and it looked like it was the only way to store all the information I needed in anything approaching the time I had left, but it also meant that I would *never* have known any of the things I needed to know, even for long enough to have forgotten them. If and when I could retrieve the information, I would know it. Till then I was as ignorant of it as if it were not stored in some cobwebbed corner of my mind at all.

"You can retrieve without artificials, can't you?" Kivrin said, looking skeptical.

"I guess I'll have to."

"Under stress? Without sleep? Low body endorphin levels?" What exactly had her practicum been? She had never said a word about it, and undergraduates are not supposed to ask. Stress factors in the Middle Ages? I thought everybody slept through them.

"I hope so," I said. "Anyway, I'm willing to try this idea if you think it will help."

She looked at me with that martyred expression and said, "Nothing will help." Thank you, St. Kivrin of Balliol.

But I tried it anyway. It was better than sitting in Dunworthy's rooms having him blink at me through his historically accurate eyeglasses and tell me I was going to love St. Paul's. When my Bodleian requests didn't come, I overloaded my credit and bought out Blackwell's. Tapes on World War II, Celtic literature, history of mass transit, tourist guidebooks, everything I could think of. Then I rented a high-speed recorder and shot up. When I came out of it, I was so panicked by the feeling of not knowing any more than I had when I started that I took the tube to London and raced up Ludgate Hill to see if the fire watch stone would trigger any memories. It didn't.

"Your endorphin levels aren't back to normal yet," I told myself and tried to relax, but that was impossible with the prospect of the practicum looming up before me. And those are real bullets, kid. Just because you're a history major doing his practicum doesn't mean you can't get killed. I read history books all the way home on the tube and right up until Dunworthy's flunkies came to take me to St. John's Wood this morning.

Then I jammed the microfiche OED in my back pocket and went off feeling as if I would have to survive by my native wit and hoping I could get hold of artificials in 1940. Surely I could get through the first day without mishap, I thought, and now here I was, stopped cold by almost the first word that was spoken to me.

Well, not quite. In spite of Kivrin's advice that I not put anything in short-term, I'd memorized the British money, a map of the tube system, a map of my own Oxford. It had gotten me this far. Surely I would be able to deal with the Dean.

Just as I had almost gotten up the courage to knock, he opened the door, and as with the pinpoint, it really was over quickly and without pain. I handed him my letter and he shook my hand and said something understandable like, "Glad to have another man, Bartholomew." He looked strained and tired and as if he might collapse if I told him the Blitz had just started. I know, I know: Keep your mouth shut. The sacred silence, etc.

He said, "We'll get Langby to show you round, shall we?" I assumed that was my Verger of the Pillow, and I was right. He met us at the foot of the stairs, puffing a little but jubilant.

"The cots came," he said to Dean Matthews. "You'd have thought they were doing us a favor. All high heels and hoity-toity. 'You made us miss our tea, luv,' one of them said to me. 'Yes, well, and a good thing, too,' I said. 'You look as if you could stand to lose a stone or two.' "

Even Dean Matthews looked as though he did not completely understand him. He said, "Did you set them up in the crypt?" and then introduced us. "Mr. Bartholomew's just got in from Wales," he said. "He's come to join our volunteers." Volunteers, not fire watch.

Langby showed me around, pointing out various dimnesses in the general gloom and then dragged me down to see the ten folding canvas cots set up among the tombs in the crypt, and also, in passing, Lord Nelson's black marble sarcophagus. He told me I don't have to stand a watch the first night and suggested I go to bed, since sleep is the most precious commodity in the raids. I could well believe it. He was clutching that silly pillow to his breast like his beloved.

"Do you hear the sirens down here?" I asked, wondering if he buried his head in it.

He looked around at the low stone ceilings. "Some do, some don't. Brinton has to have his Horlich's. Bence-Jones would sleep if the roof fell in on him. I have to have a pillow. The important thing is to get your eight in no matter what. If you don't, you turn into one of the walking dead. And then you get killed."

On that cheering note he went off to post the watches for tonight, leaving his pillow on one of the cots with orders for me to let nobody touch it. So here I sit, waiting for my first air raid siren and trying to get all this down before I turn into one of the walking or non-walking dead.

I've used the stolen OED to decipher a little Langby. Middling success. A tart is either a pastry or a prostitute (I assume the latter, although I was wrong about the pillow). Bourgeois is a catchall term for all the faults of the middle class. A Tommy's a soldier. Ayarpee I could not find under any spelling and I had nearly given up when something in long-term about the use of acronyms and abbreviations in wartime popped forward (bless you, St. Kivrin) and I realized it must be an abbreviation. ARP. Air Raid Precautions. Of course. Where else would you get the bleeding cots from?

September 21—Now that I'm past the first shock of being here, I realize that the history department neglected to tell me what I'm suppose to do in the three-odd months of this practicum. They handed me this journal, the letter from my uncle, and ten pounds in pre-war money and sent me packing into the past. The ten pounds (already depleted by train and tube fares) is supposed to last me until the end of December and get me back to St. John's Wood for pickup when the second letter calling me back to Wales to sick uncle's bedside comes. Till then I live here in the crypt with Nelson, who, Langby tells me, is pickled in alcohol inside his coffin. If we take a direct hit, will he burn like a torch or simply trickle out in a decaying stream onto the crypt floor, I wonder. Board is provided by a gas ring, over which are cooked wretched tea and indescribable kippers. To pay for all this luxury I am to stand on the roofs of St. Paul's and put out incendiaries.

I must also accomplish the purpose of this practicum, whatever it

may be. Right now the only purpose I care about is staying alive until
the second letter from uncle arrives and I can go home.

I am doing make-work until Langby has time to "show me the
ropes." I've cleaned the skillet they cook the foul little fishes in,
stacked wooden folding chairs at the altar end of the crypt (flat
instead of standing because they tend to collapse like bombs in the
middle of the night), and tried to sleep.

I am apparently not one of the lucky ones who can sleep through
the raids. I spent most of the night wondering what St. Paul's risk
rating is. Practica have to be at least a six. Last night I was convinced
this was a ten, with the crypt as ground zero, and that I might as well
have applied for Denver.

The most interesting thing that's happened so far is that I've seen
a cat. I am fascinated, but trying not to appear so, since they seem
commonplace here.

September 22—Still in the crypt. Langby comes dashing through
periodically cursing various government agencies (all abbreviated)
and promising to take me up on the roofs. In the meantime I've run
out of make-work and taught myself to work a stirrup pump. Kivrin
was overly concerned about my memory retrieval abilities. I have
not had any trouble so far. Quite the opposite. I called up fire-
fighting information and got the whole manual with pictures, including instructions on the use of the stirrup pump. If the kippers
set Lord Nelson on fire, I shall be a hero.

Excitement last night. The sirens went early and some of the chars
who clean offices in the City sheltered in the crypt with us. One of
them woke me out of a sound sleep, going like an air raid siren.
Seems she'd seen a mouse. We had to go whacking at tombs and
under the cots with a rubber boot to persuade her it was gone.
Obviously what the history department had in mind: murdering
mice.

September 24—Langby took me on rounds. Into the choir, where I
had to learn the stirrup pump all over again, assigned rubber boots
and a tin helmet. Langby says Commander Allen is getting us
asbestos firemen's coats, but hasn't yet, so it's my own wool coat and
muffler and very cold on the roofs even in September. It feels like
November and looks it, too, bleak and cheerless with no sun. Up to

the dome and onto the roofs, which should be flat but in fact are littered with towers, pinnacles, gutters, statues, all designed expressly to catch and hold incendiaries out of reach. Shown how to smother an incendiary with sand before it burns through the roof and sets the church on fire. Shown the ropes (literally) lying in a heap at the base of the dome in case somebody has to go up one of the west towers or over the top of the dome. Back inside and down to the Whispering Gallery.

Langby kept up a running commentary through the whole tour, part practical instruction, part church history. Before we went up into the Gallery he dragged me over to the south door to tell me how Christopher Wren stood in the smoking rubble of Old St. Paul's and asked a workman to bring him a stone from the graveyard to mark the cornerstone. On the stone was written in Latin, "I shall rise again," and Wren was so impressed by the irony that he had the word inscribed above the door. Langby looked as smug as if he had not told me a story every first-year history student knows, but I suppose without the impact of the fire watch stone, the other is just a nice story.

Langby raced me up the steps and onto the narrow balcony circling the Whispering Gallery. He was already halfway around to the other side, shouting dimensions and acoustics at me. He stopped facing the wall opposite and said softly, "You can hear me whispering because of the shape of the dome. The sound waves are reinforced around the perimeter of the dome. It sounds like the very crack of doom up here during a raid. The dome is one hundred and seven feet across. It is eighty feet above the nave."

I looked down. The railing went out from under me and the black-and-white marble floor came up with dizzying speed. I hung on to something in front of me and dropped to my knees, staggered and sick at heart. The sun had come out, and all of St. Paul's seemed drenched in gold. Even the carved wood of the choir, the white stone pillars, the leaden pipes of the organ, all of it golden, golden.

Langby was beside me, trying to pull me free. "Bartholomew," he shouted, "what's wrong? For God's sake, man."

I knew I must tell him that if I let go, St. Paul's and all the past would fall in on me, and that I must not let that happen because I was an historian. I said something, but it was not what I intended because Langby merely tightened his grip. He hauled me violently free of the railing and back onto the stairway, then let me collapse limply on the steps and stood back from me, not speaking.

"I don't know what happened in there," I said. "I've never been afraid of heights before."

"You're shaking," he said sharply. "You'd better lie down." He led me back to the crypt.

September 25—Memory retrieval: ARP manual. Symptoms of bombing victims. Stage one—shock; stupefaction; unawareness of injuries; words may not make sense except to victim. Stage two—shivering; nausea; injuries, losses felt; return to reality. Stage three—talkativeness that cannnot be controlled; desire to explain shock behavior to rescuers.

Langby must surely recognize the symptoms, but how does he account for the fact there was no bomb? I can hardly explain my shock behavior to him, and it isn't just the sacred silence of the historian that stops me.

He has not said anything, in fact assigned me my first watches for tomorrow night as if nothing had happened, and he seems no more preoccupied than anyone else. Everyone I've met so far is jittery (one thing I had in short-term was how calm everyone was during the raids) and the raids have not come near us since I got here. They've been mostly over the East End and the docks.

There was a reference tonight to a UXB, and I have been thinking about the Dean's manner and the church being closed when I'm almost sure I remember reading it was open through the entire Blitz. As soon as I get a chance, I'll try to retrieve the events of September. As to retrieving anything else, I don't see how I can hope to remember the right information until I know what it is I am supposed to do here, if anything.

There are no guidelines for historians, and no restrictions either. I could tell everyone I'm from the future if I thought they would believe me. I could murder Hitler if I could get to Germany. Or could I? Time paradox talk abounds in the history department, and the graduate students back from their practica don't say a word one way or the other. Is there a tough, immutable past? Or is there a new past every day and do we, the historians, make it? And what are the consequences of what we do, if there are consequences? And how do we dare do anything without knowing them? Must we interfere

boldly, hoping we do not bring about all our downfalls? Or must we
do nothing at all, not interfere, stand by and watch St. Paul's burn
to the ground if need be so that we don't change the future?

All those are fine questions for a late-night study session. They do
not matter here. I could no more let St. Paul's burn down than I could
kill Hitler. No, that is not true. I found that out yesterday in the
Whispering Gallery. I could kill Hitler if I caught him setting fire to
St. Paul's.

September 26—I met a young woman today. Dean Matthews has
opened the church, so the watch have been doing duties as chars
and people have started coming in again. The young woman reminded me of Kivrin, though Kivrin is a good deal taller and would
never frizz her hair like that. She looked as if she had been crying.
Kivrin has looked like that since she got back from her practicum.
The Middle Ages were too much for her. I wonder how she would
have coped with this. By pouring out her fears to the local priest, no
doubt, as I sincerely hoped her look-alike was not going to do.

"May I help you?" I said, not wanting in the least to help. "I'm a
volunteer."

She looked distressed. "You're not paid?" she said, and wiped at
her reddened nose with a handkerchief. "I read about St. Paul's and
the fire watch and all, and I thought perhaps there's a position there
for me. In the canteen, like, or something. A paying position." There
were tears in her red-rimmed eyes.

"I'm afraid we don't have a canteen," I said as kindly as I could,
considering how impatient Kivrin always makes me, "and it's not
actually a real shelter. Some of the watch sleep in the crypt. I'm afraid
we're all volunteers, though."

"That won't do, then," she said. She dabbed at her eyes with the
handkerchief. "I love St. Paul's, but I can't take on volunteer work,
not with my little brother Tom back from the country." I was not
reading this situation properly. For all the outward signs of distress
she sounded quite cheerful and no closer to tears than when she had
come in. "I've got to get us a proper place to stay. With Tom back,
we can't go on sleeping in the tubes."

A sudden feeling of dread, the kind of sharp pain you get sometimes from involuntary retrieval, went over me. "The tubes?" I said,
trying to get at the memory.

"Marble Arch, usually," she went on. "My brother Tom saves us a place early and I go . . ." She stopped, held the handkerchief close to her nose, and exploded into it. "I'm sorry," she said, "this awful cold!"

Red nose, watering eyes, sneezing. Respiratory infection. It was a wonder I hadn't told her not to cry. It's only by luck that I haven't made some unforgivable mistake so far, and this is not because I can't get at the long-term memory. I don't have half the information I need even stored: cats and colds and the way St. Paul's looks in full sun. It's only a matter of time before I am stopped cold by something I do not know. Nevertheless, I am going to try for retrieval tonight after I come off watch. At least I can find out whether and when something is going to fall on me.

I have seen the cat once or twice. He is coal-black with a white patch on his throat that looks as if it were painted on for the blackout.

September 27—I have just come down from the roofs. I am still shaking.

Early in the raid the bombing was mostly over the East End. The view was incredible. Searchlights everywhere, the sky pink from the fires and reflecting in the Thames, the exploding shells sparkling like fireworks. There was a constant, deafening thunder broken by the occasional droning of the planes high overhead, then the repeating stutter of the ack-ack guns.

About midnight the bombs began falling quite near with a horrible sound like a train running over me. It took every bit of will I had to keep from flinging myself flat on the roof, but Langby was watching. I didn't want to give him the satisfaction of watching a repeat performance of my behavior in the dome. I kept my head up and my sand bucket firmly in hand and felt quite proud of myself.

The bombs stopped roaring past about three, and there was a lull of about half an hour, and then a clatter like hail on the roofs. Everybody except Langby dived for shovels and stirrup pumps. He was watching me. And I was watching the incendiary.

It had fallen only a few meters from me, behind the clock tower. It was much smaller than I had imagined, only about thirty centimeters long. It was sputtering violently, throwing greenish-white fire almost to where I was standing. In a minute it would simmer down into a molten mass and begin to burn through the roof. Flames and the frantic shouts of firemen, and then the white rubble stretching for miles, and nothing, nothing left, not even the fire watch stone.

It was the Whispering Gallery all over again. I felt that I had said something, and when I looked at Langby's face he was smiling crookedly.

"St. Paul's will burn down," I said. "There won't be anything left."

"Yes," Langby said. "That's the idea, isn't it? Burn St. Paul's to the ground? Isn't that the plan?"

"Whose plan?" I said stupidly.

"Hitler's, of course," Langby said. "Who did you think I meant?" and, almost casually, picked up his stirrup pump.

The page of the ARP manual flashed suddenly before me. I poured the bucket of sand around the still-sputtering bomb, snatched up another bucket and dumped that on top of it. Black smoke billowed up in such a cloud that I could hardly find my shovel. I felt for the smothered bomb with the tip of it and scooped it into the empty bucket, then shoveled the sand in on top of it. Tears were streaming down my face from the acrid smoke. I turned to wipe them on my sleeve and saw Langby.

He had not made a move to help me. He smiled. "It's not a bad plan, actually. But of course we won't let it happen. That's what the fire watch is here for. To see that it doesn't happen. Right, Bartholomew?"

I know now what the purpose of my practicum is. I must stop Langby from burning down St. Paul's.

September 28—I try to tell myself I was mistaken about Langby last night, that I misunderstood what he said. Why would he want to burn down St. Paul's unless he is a Nazi spy? How can a Nazi spy have gotten on the fire watch? I think about my faked letter of introduction and shudder.

How can I find out? If I set him some test, some fatal thing that only a loyal Englishman in 1940 would know, I fear I am the one who would be caught out. I *must* get my retrieval working properly.

Until then, I shall watch Langby. For the time being at least that should be easy. Langby has just posted the watches for the next two weeks. We stand every one together.

*   *   *

September 30—I know what happened in September. Langby told me.

Last night in the choir, putting on our coats and boots, he said, "They've already tried once, you know."

I had no idea what he meant. I felt as helpless as that first day when he asked me if I was from the ayarpee.

"The plan to destroy St. Paul's. They've already tried once. The tenth of September. A high explosive bomb. But of course you didn't know about that. You were in Wales."

I was not even listening. The minute he had said "high explosive bomb" I had remembered it all. It had burrowed in under the road and lodged on the foundations. The bomb squad had tried to defuse it, but there was a leaking gas main. They decided to evacuate St. Paul's, but Dean Matthews refused to leave, and they got it out after all and exploded it in Barking Marshes. Instant and complete retrieval.

"The bomb squad saved her that time," Langby was saying. "It seems there's always somebody about."

"Yes," I said, "there is," and walked away from him.

October 1—I thought last night's retrieval of the events of September tenth meant some sort of breakthrough, but I have been lying here on my cot most of the night trying for Nazi spies in St. Paul's and getting nothing. Do I have to know exactly what I'm looking for before I can remember it? What good does that do me?

Maybe Langby is not a Nazi spy. Then what is he? An arsonist? A madman? The crypt is hardly conducive to thought, being not at all as silent as a tomb. The chars talk most of the night and the sound of the bombs is muffled, which somehow makes it worse. I find myself straining to hear them. When I did get to sleep this morning, I dreamed about one of the tube shelters being hit, broken mains, drowning people.

October 4—I tried to catch the cat today. I had some idea of persuading it to dispatch the mouse that has been terrifying the chars. I also wanted to see one up close. I took the water bucket I had used with the stirrup pump last night to put out some burning shrapnel from one of the antiaircraft guns. It still had a bit of water in it, but not enough to drown the cat, and my plan was to clamp the bucket over him, reach under, and pick him up, then carry him down to the crypt and point him at the mouse. I did not even come close to him.

I swung the bucket, and as I did so, perhaps an inch of water splashed out. I thought I remembered that the cat was a domesticated animal, but I must have been wrong about that. The cat's wide complacent face pulled back into a skull-like mask that was absolutely terrifying, vicious claws extended from what I had thought were harmless paws, and the cat let out a sound to top the chars.

In my surprise I dropped the bucket and it rolled against one of the pillars. The cat disappeared. Behind me, Langby said, "That's no way to catch a cat."

"Obviously," I said, and bent to retrieve the bucket.

"Cats hate water," he said, still in that expressionless voice.

"Oh," I said, and started in front of him to take the bucket back to the choir. "I didn't know that."

"Everybody knows it. Even the stupid Welsh."

October 8—We have been standing double watches for a week—bomber's moon. Langby didn't show up on the roofs, so I went looking for him in the church. I found him standing by the west doors talking to an old man. The man had a newspaper tucked under his arm and he handed it to Langby, but Langby gave it back to him. When the man saw me, he ducked out. Langby said, "Tourist. Wanted to know where the Windmill Theatre is. Read in the paper the girls are starkers."

I know I looked as if I didn't believe him because he said, "You look rotten, old man. Not getting enough sleep, are you? I'll get somebody to take the first watch for you tonight."

"No," I said coldly. "I'll stand my own watch. I like being on the roofs," and added silently, *where I can watch you.*

He shrugged and said, "I suppose it's better than being down in the crypt. At least on the roofs you can hear the one that gets you."

October 10—I thought the double watches might be good for me, take my mind off my inability to retrieve. The watched-pot idea. Actually, it sometimes works. A few hours of thinking about something else, or a good night's sleep, and the fact pops forward without any prompting, without any artificials.

The good night's sleep is out of the question. Not only do the chars talk constantly, but the cat has moved into the crypt and sidles up to everyone, making siren noises and begging for kippers. I am moving my cot out of the transept and over by Nelson before I go on watch. He may be pickled, but he keeps his mouth shut.

October 11—I dreamed Trafalgar, ships' guns and smoke and falling plaster and Langby shouting my name. My first waking thought was that the folding chairs had gone off. I could not see for all the smoke.

"I'm coming," I said, limping toward Langby and pulling on my boots. There was a heap of plaster and tangled folding chairs in the transept. Langby was digging in it. "Bartholomew!" he shouted, flinging a chunk of plaster aside. "Bartholomew!"

I still had the idea it was smoke. I ran back for the stirrup pump and then knelt beside him and began pulling on a splintered chair back. It resisted, and it came to me suddenly. There is a body under here. I will reach for a piece of the ceiling and find it is a hand. I leaned back on my heels, determined not to be sick, then went at the pile again.

Langby was going far too fast, jabbing with a chair leg. I grabbed his hand to stop him, and he struggled against me as if I were a piece of rubble to be thrown aside. He picked up a large flat square of plaster, and under it was the floor. I turned and looked behind me. Both chars huddled in the recess by the altar. "Who are you looking for?" I said, keeping hold of Langby's arm.

"Bartholomew," he said, and swept the rubble aside, his hands bleeding through the coating of smoky dust.

"I'm here," I said. "I'm all right." I choked on the white dust. "I moved my cot out of the transept."

He turned sharply to the chars and then said quite calmly, "What's under here?"

"Only the gas ring," one of them said timidly from the shadowed recess, "and Mrs. Galbraith's pocketbook." He dug through the mess until he had found them both. The gas ring was leaking at a merry rate, though the flame had gone out.

"You've saved St. Paul's and me after all," I said, standing there in my underwear and boots, holding the useless stirrup pump. "We might all have been asphyxiated."

He stood up. "I shouldn't have saved you," he said.

Stage one: shock, stupefaction, unawareness of injuries, words may not make sense except to victim. He would not know his hand was bleeding yet. He would not remember what he had said. He had said he shouldn't have saved my life.

"I shouldn't have saved you," he repeated. "I have my duty to think of."

"You're bleeding," I said sharply. "You'd better lie down." I sounded just like Langby in the gallery.

October 13—It was a high-explosive bomb. It blew a hole in the Choir, and some of the marble statuary is broken, but the ceiling of the crypt did not collapse, which is what I thought at first. It only jarred some plaster loose.

I do not think Langby has any idea what he said. That should give me some sort of advantage, now that I am sure where the danger lies, now that I am sure it will not come crashing down from some other direction. But what good is all this knowing, when I do not know what he will do? Or when?

Surely I have the facts of yesterday's bomb in long-term, but even falling plaster did not jar them loose this time. I am not even trying for retrieval, now. I lie in the darkness waiting for the roof to fall in on me. And remembering how Langby saved my life.

October 15—The girl came in again today. She still has the cold, but she has gotten her paying position. It was a joy to see her. She was wearing a smart uniform and open-toed shoes, and her hair was in an elaborate frizz around her face. We are still cleaning up the mess from the bomb, and Langby was out with Allen getting wood to board up the Choir, so I let the girl chatter at me while I swept. The dust made her sneeze, but at least this time I knew what she was doing.

She told me her name is Enola and that she's working for the WVS, running one of the mobile canteens that are sent to the fires. She came, of all things, to thank me for the job. She said that after she told the WVS that there was no proper shelter with a canteen for St. Paul's, they gave her a run in the City. "So I'll just pop in when I'm close and let you know how I'm making out, won't I just?"

She and her brother Tom are still sleeping in the tubes. I asked her if that was safe and she said probably not, but at least down there you couldn't hear the one that got you and that was a blessing.

October 18—I am so tired I can hardly write this. Nine incendiaries tonight and a land mine that looked as though it was going to catch on the dome till the wind drifted its parachute away from the church. I put out two of the incendiaries. I have done that at least twenty times since I got here and helped with dozens of others, and still it is not enough. One incendiary, one moment of not watching Langby, could undo it all.

I know that is partly why I feel so tired. I wear myself out every night trying to do my job and watch Langby, making sure none of the incendiaries falls without my seeing it. Then I go back to the crypt and wear myself out trying to retrieve something, anything, about spies, fires, St. Paul's in the fall of 1940, anything. It haunts me that I am not doing enough, but I do not know what else to do. Without the retrieval, I am as helpless as these poor people here, with no idea what will happen tomorrow.

If I have to, I will go on doing this till I am called home. He cannot burn down St. Paul's so long as I am here to put out the incendiaries. "I have my duty," Langby said in the crypt.

And I have mine.

October 21—It's been nearly two weeks since the blast and I just now realized we haven't seen the cat since. He wasn't in the mess in the crypt. Even after Langby and I were sure there was no one in there, we sifted through the stuff twice more. He could have been in the Choir, though.

Old Bence-Jones says not to worry. "He's all right," he said. "The Jerries could bomb London right down to the ground and the cats would waltz out to greet them. You know why? They don't love anybody. That's what gets half of us killed. Old lady out in Stepney got killed the other night trying to save her cat. Bloody cat was in the Anderson."

"Then where is he?"

"Someplace safe, you can bet on that. If he's not around St. Paul's, it means we're for it. That old saw about the rats deserting a sinking ship, that's a mistake, that is. It's cats, not rats."

*   *   *

October 25—Langby's tourist showed up again. He cannot still be looking for the Windmill Theatre. He had a newspaper under his arm again today, and he asked for Langby, but Langby was across town with Allen, trying to get the asbestos firemen's coats. I saw the name of the paper. It was *The Worker*. A Nazi newspaper?

November 2—I've been up on the roofs for a week straight, helping some incompetent workmen patch the hole the bomb made. They're doing a terrible job. There's still a great gap on one side a man could fall into, but they insist it'll be all right because, after all, you wouldn't fall clear through but only as far as the ceiling, and "the fall can't kill you." They don't seem to understand it's a perfect hiding place for an incendiary.

And that is all Langby needs. He does not even have to set a fire to destroy St. Paul's. All he needs to do is let one burn uncaught until it is too late.

I could not get anywhere with the workmen. I went down into the church to complain to Matthews, and saw Langby and his tourist behind a pillar, close to one of the windows. Langby was holding a newspaper and talking to the man. When I came down from the library an hour later, they were still there. So is the gap. Matthews says we'll put planks across it and hope for the best.

November 5—I have given up trying to retrieve. I am so far behind on my sleep I can't even retrieve information on a newspaper whose name I already know. Double watches the permanent thing now. Our chars have abandoned us altogether (like the cat), so the crypt is quiet, but I cannot sleep.

If I do manage to doze off, I dream. Yesterday I dreamed Kivrin was on the roofs, dressed like a saint. "What was the secret of your practicum?" I said. "What were you supposed to find out?"

She wiped her nose with a handkerchief and said, "Two things. One, that silence and humility are the sacred burdens of the historian. Two"—she stopped and sneezed into the handkerchief—"don't sleep in the tubes."

My only hope is to get hold of an artificial and induce a trance. That's a problem. I'm positive it's too early for chemical endorphins and probably hallucinogens Alcohol is definitely available, but I need something more concentrated than ale, the only alcohol I know by name. I do not dare ask the watch. Langby is suspicious enough of me already. It's back to the OED, to look up a word I don't know.

November 11—The cat's back. Langby was out with Allen again, still trying for the asbestos coats, so I thought it was safe to leave St. Paul's. I went to the grocer's for supplies, and hopefully an artificial. It was late, and the sirens sounded before I had even gotten to Cheapside, but the raids do not usually start until after dark. It took a while to get all the groceries and to get up my courage to ask whether he had any alcohol—he told me to go to a pub—and when I came out of the shop, it was as if I had pitched suddenly into a hole.

I had no idea where St. Paul's lay, or the street, or the shop I had just come from. I stood on what was no longer the sidewalk, clutching my brown-paper parcel of kippers and bread with a hand I could not have seen if I held it up before my face. I reached up to wrap my muffler closer about my neck and prayed for my eyes to adjust, but there was no reduced light to adjust to. I would have been glad of the moon, for all St. Paul's watch cursed it and called it a fifth columnist. Or a bus, with its shuttered headlights giving just enough light to orient myself by. Or a searchlight. Or the kickback flare of an ack-ack gun. Anything.

Just then I did see a bus, two narrow yellow slits a long way off. I started toward it and nearly pitched off the curb. Which meant the bus was sideways in the street, which meant it was not a bus. A cat meowed, quite near, and rubbed against my leg. I looked down into the yellow lights I had thought belonged to the bus. His eyes were picking up light from somewhere, though I would have sworn there was not a light for miles, and reflecting it flatly up at me.

"A warden'll get you for those lights, old Tom," I said, and then as a plane droned overhead, "Or a Jerry."

The word exploded suddenly into light, the searchlights and a glow along the Thames seeming to happen almost simultaneously, lighting my way home.

"Come to fetch me, did you, old Tom?" I said gaily. "Where've you been? Knew we were out of kippers, didn't you? I call that loyalty." I talked to him all the way home and gave him half a tin of the kippers for saving my life. Bence-Jones said he smelled the milk at the grocer's.

*   *   *

November 13—I dreamed I was lost in the blackout. I could not see my hands in front of my face, and Dunworthy came and shone a pocket torch at me, but I could only see where I had come from and not where I was going.

"What good is that to them?" I said. "They need a light to show them where they're going."

"Even the light from the Thames? Even the light from the fires and the ack-ack guns?" Dunworthy said.

"Yes. Anything is better than this awful darkness." So he came closer to give me the pocket torch. It was not a pocket torch, after all, but Christ's lantern from the Hunt picture in the south nave. I shone it on the curb before me so I could find my way home, but it shone instead on the fire watch stone and I hastily put the light out.

November 20—I tried to talk to Langby today. "I've seen you talking to the old gentleman," I said. It sounded like an accusation. I meant it to. I wanted him to think it was and stop whatever he was planning.

"Reading," he said. "Not talking." He was putting things in order in the choir, piling up sandbags.

"I've seen you reading then," I said belligerently, and he dropped a sandbag and straightened.

"What of it?" he said. "It's a free country. I can read to an old man if I want, same as you can talk to that little WVS tart."

"What do you read?" I said.

"Whatever he wants. He's an old man. He used to come home from his job, have a bit of brandy and listen to his wife read the papers to him. She got killed in one of the raids. Now I read to him. I don't see what business it is of yours."

It sounded true. It didn't have the careful casualness of a lie, and I almost believed him, except that I had heard the tone of truth from him before. In the crypt. After the bomb.

"I thought he was a tourist looking for the Windmill," I said.

He looked blank only a second, and then he said, "Oh, yes, that. He came in with the paper and asked me to tell him where it was. I looked it up to find the address. Clever, that. I didn't guess he couldn't read it for himself." But it was enough. I knew that he was lying.

He heaved a sandbag almost at my feet. "Of course you wouldn't understand a thing like that, would you? A simple act of human kindness?"

"No," I said coldly. "I wouldn't."

None of this proves anything. He gave away nothing, except perhaps the name of an artificial, and I can hardly go to Dean Matthews and accuse Langby of reading aloud.

I waited till he had finished in the choir and gone down to the crypt. Then I lugged one of the sandbags up to the roof and over to the chasm. The planking has held so far, but everyone walks gingerly around it, as if it were a grave. I cut the sandbag open and spilled the loose sand into the bottom. If it has occurred to Langby that this is the perfect spot for an incendiary, perhaps the sand will smother it.

November 21—I gave Enola some of "uncle's" money today and asked her to get me the brandy. She was more reluctant than I thought she'd be, so there must be societal complications I am not aware of, but she agreed.

I don't know what she came for. She started to tell me about her brother and some prank he'd pulled in the tubes that got him in trouble with the guard, but after I asked her about the brandy, she left without finishing the story.

November 25—Enola came today, but without bringing the brandy. She is going to Bath for the holidays to see her aunt. At least she will be away from the raids for a while. I will not have to worry about her. She finished the story of her brother and told me she hopes to persuade this aunt to take Tom for the duration of the Blitz but is not at all sure the aunt will be willing.

Young Tom is apparently not so much an engaging scapegrace as a near criminal. He has been caught twice picking pockets in the Bank tube shelter, and they have had to go back to Marble Arch. I comforted her as best I could, told her all boys were bad at one time or another. What I really wanted to say was that she needn't worry at all, that young Tom strikes me as a true survivor type, like my own tom, like Langby, totally unconcerned with anybody but himself, well equipped to survive the Blitz and rise to prominence in the future.

Then I asked her whether she had gotten the brandy.

She looked down at her open-toed shoes and muttered unhappily, "I thought you'd forgotten all about that."

I made up some story about the watch taking turns buying a bottle, and she seemed less unhappy, but I am not convinced she will not use this trip to Bath as an excuse to do nothing. I will have to leave St. Paul's and buy it myself, and I don't dare leave Langby alone in the church. I made her promise to bring the brandy today before she leaves. But she is still not back, and the sirens have already gone.

November 26—No Enola, and she said their train left at noon. I suppose I should be grateful that at least she is safely out of London. Maybe in Bath she will be able to get over her cold.

Tonight one of the ARP girls breezed in to borrow half our cots and tell us about a mess over in the East End where a surface shelter was hit. Four dead, twelve wounded. "At least it wasn't one of the tube shelters!" she said. "Then you'd see a real mess, wouldn't you?"

November 30—I dreamed I took the cat to St. John's Wood.

"Is this a rescue mission?" Dunworthy said.

"No, sir," I said proudly. "I know what I was supposed to find in my practicum. The perfect survivor. Tough and resourceful and selfish. This is the only one I could find. I had to kill Langby, you know, to keep him from burning down St. Paul's. Enola's brother has gone to Bath, and the others will never make it. Enola wears open-toed shoes in the winter and sleeps in the tubes and puts her hair up on metal pins so it will curl. She cannot possibly survive the Blitz."

Dunworthy said, "Perhaps you should have rescued her instead. What did you say her name was?"

"Kivrin," I said, and woke up cold and shivering.

December 5—I dreamed Langby had the pinpoint bomb. He carried it under his arm like a brown paper parcel, coming out of St. Paul's Station and around Ludgate Hill to the west doors.

"This is not fair," I said, barring his way with my arm. "There is no fire watch on duty."

He clutched the bomb to his chest like a pillow. "That is your fault," he said, and before I could get to my stirrup pump and bucket, he tossed it in the door.

The pinpoint was not even invented until the end of the twentieth century, and it was another ten years before the dispossessed communists got hold of it and turned it into something that could be carried under your arm. A parcel that could blow a quarter mile of the City into oblivion. Thank God that is one dream that cannot come true.

It was a sunlit morning in the dream, and this morning when I came off watch the sun was shining for the first time in weeks. I went down to the crypt and then came up again, making the rounds of the roofs twice more, then the steps and the grounds and all the treacherous alleyways between where an incendiary could be missed. I felt better after that, but when I got to sleep I dreamed again, this time of fire and Langby watching it, smiling.

December 15—I found the cat this morning. Heavy raids last night, but most of them over toward Canning Town and nothing on the roofs to speak of. Nevertheless the cat was quite dead. I found him lying on the steps this morning when I made my own, private rounds. Concussion. There was not a mark on him anywhere except the white blackout patch on his throat, but when I picked him up, he was all jelly under the skin.

I could not think what to do with him. I thought for one mad moment of asking Matthews if I could bury him in the crypt. Honorable death in war or something. Trafalgar, Waterloo, London, lied in battle. I ended by wrapping him in my muffler and taking him down Ludgate Hill to a building that had been bombed out and burying him in the rubble. It will do no good. The rubble will be no protection from dogs or rats, and I shall never get another muffler. I have gone through nearly all of uncle's money.

I should not be sitting here. I haven't checked the alleyways or the rest of the steps, and there might be a dud or a delayed incendiary or something that I missed.

When I came here, I thought of myself as the noble rescuer, the savior of the past. I am not doing very well at the job. At least Enola is out of it. I wish there were some way I could send St. Paul's to Bath for safekeeping. There were hardly any raids last night. Bence-Jones said cats can survive anything. What if he was coming to get me, to show me the way home? All the bombs were over Canning Town.

December 16—Enola has been back a week. Seeing her, standing on the west steps where I found the cat, sleeping in Marble Arch and not safe at all, was more than I could absorb. "I thought you were in Bath," I said stupidly.

"My aunt said she'd take Tom but not me as well. She's got a houseful of evacuation children, and what a noisy lot. Where is your muffler?" she said. "It's dreadful cold up here on the hill."

"I . . ." I said, unable to answer. "I lost it."

"You'll never get another one," she said. "They're going to start rationing clothes. And wool, too. You'll never get another one like that."

"I know," I said, blinking at her.

"Good things just thrown away," she said. "It's absolutely criminal, that's what it is."

I don't think I said anything to that, just turned and walked away with my head down, looking for bombs and dead animals.

December 20—Langby isn't a Nazi. He's a communist. I can hardly write this. A communist.

One of the chars found *The Worker* wedged behind a pillar and brought it down to the crypt as we were coming off the first watch.

"Bloody communists," Bence-Jones said. "Helping Hitler, they are. Talking against the king, stirring up trouble in the shelters. Traitors, that's what they are."

"They love England same as you," the char said.

"They don't love nobody but themselves, bloody selfish lot. I wouldn't be surprised to hear they were ringing Hitler up on the telephone," Bence-Jones said. " ' 'Ello, Adolf, here's where to drop the bombs.' "

The kettle on the gas ring whistled. The char stood up and poured the hot water into a chipped teapot, then sat back down. "Just because they speak their minds don't mean they'd burn down old St. Paul's, does it now?"

"Of course not," Langby said, coming down the stairs. He sat down and pulled off his boots, stretching his feet in their wool socks. "Who wouldn't burn down St. Paul's?"

"The communists," Bence-Jones said, looking straight at him, and
I wondered if he suspected Langby too.

Langby never batted an eye. "I wouldn't worry about them if I
were you," he said. "It's the Jerries that are doing their bloody best
to burn her down tonight. Six incendiaries so far, and one almost
went into that great hole over the choir." He held out his cup to the
char, and she poured him a cup of tea.

I wanted to kill him, smashing him to dust and rubble on the floor
of the crypt while Bence-Jones and the char looked on in helpless
surprise, shouting warnings to them and the rest of the watch. "Do
you know what the communists did?" I wanted to shout. "Do you?
We have to stop him." I even stood up and started toward him as
he sat with his feet stretched out before him and his asbestos coat still
over his shoulders.

And then the thought of the Gallery drenched in gold, the communist coming out of the tube station with the package so casually
under his arm, made me sick with the same staggering vertigo of
guilt and helplessness, and I sat back down on the edge of my cot
and tried to think what to do.

They do not realize the danger. Even Bence-Jones, for all his talk
of traitors, thinks they are capable only of talking against the king.
They do not know, cannot know, what the communists will become.
Stalin is an ally. Communists mean Russia. They have never heard
of Karinsky or the New Russia or any of the things that will make
"communist" into a synonym for "monster." They will never know
it. By the time the communists become what they became, there will
be no fire watch. Only I know what it means to hear the name
"communist" uttered here, so carelessly, in St. Paul's.

A communist. I should have known. I should have known.

December 22—Double watches again. I have not had any sleep and
I am getting very unsteady on my feet. I nearly pitched into the
chasm this morning, only saved myself by dropping to my knees.
My endorphin levels are fluctuating wildly, and I know I must get
some sleep soon or I will become one of Langby's walking dead, but
I am afraid to leave him alone on the roofs, alone in the church with
his communist party leader, alone anywhere. I have taken to watching him when he sleeps.

If I could just get hold of an artificial, I think I could induce a trance, in spite of my poor condition. But I cannot even go out to a pub. Langby is on the roofs constantly, waiting for his chance. When Enola comes again I must convince her to get the brandy for me. There are only a few days left.

December 28—Enola came this morning while I was on the west porch, picking up the Christmas tree. It has been knocked over three nights running by concussion. I righted the tree and was bending down to pick up the scattered tinsel when Enola appeared suddenly out of the fog like some cheerful saint. She stooped quickly and kissed me on the cheek. Then she straightened up, her nose red from her perennial cold, and handed me a box wrapped in colored paper.

"Merry Christmas," she said. "Go on then, open it. It's a gift."

My reflexes are almost totally gone. I knew the box was far too shallow for a bottle of brandy. Nevertheless, I believed she had remembered, had brought me my salvation. "You darling," I said, and tore it open.

It was a muffler. Gray wool. I stared at it for fully half a minute without realizing what it was. "Where's the brandy?" I said.

She looked shocked. Her nose got redder and her eyes started to blur. "You need this more. You haven't any clothing coupons and you have to be outside all the time. It's been so dreadful cold."

"I *needed* the brandy," I said angrily.

"I was only trying to be kind," she started, and I cut her off.

"Kind?" I said. "I asked you for brandy. I don't recall ever saying I needed a muffler." I shoved it back at her and began untangling a string of colored lights that had shattered when the tree fell.

She got that same holy martyr look Kivrin is so wonderful at. "I worry about you all the time up here," she said in a rush. "They're *trying* for St. Paul's, you know. And it's so close to the river. I didn't think you should be drinking. I—it's a crime when they're trying so hard to kill us all that you won't take care of yourself. It's like you're in it with them. I worry someday I'll come up to St. Paul's and you won't be here."

"Well, and what exactly am I supposed to do with a muffler? Hold it over my head when they drop the bombs?"

She turned and ran, disappearing into the gray fog before she had gone down two steps. I started after her, still holding the string of broken lights, tripped over it, and fell almost all the way to the bottom of the steps.

Langby picked me up. "You're off watches," he said grimly.

"You can't do that," I said.

"Oh, yes, I can. I don't want any walking dead on the roofs with me."

I let him lead me down here to the crypt, make me a cup of tea, put me to bed, all very solicitous. No indication that this is what he has been waiting for. I will lie here till the sirens go. Once I am on the roofs he will not be able to send me back without seeming suspicious. Do you know what he said before he left, asbestos coat and rubber boots, the dedicated fire watcher? "I want you to get some sleep." As if I could sleep with Langby on the roofs. I would be burned alive.

December 30—The sirens woke me, and old Bence-Jones said, "That should have done you some good. You've slept the clock round."

"What day is it?" I said, going for my boots.

"The twenty-ninth," he said, and as I dived for the door, "no need to hurry. They're late tonight. Maybe they won't come at all. That'd be a blessing, that would. The tide's out."

I stopped by the door to the stairs, holding on to the cool stone. "Is St. Paul's all right?"

"She's still standing," he said. "Have a bad dream?"

"Yes," I said, remembering the bad dreams of all the past weeks— the dead cat in my arms in St. John's Wood, Langby with his parcel and his *Worker* under his arm, the fire watch stone garishly lit by Christ's lantern. Then I remembered I had not dreamed at all. I had slept the kind of sleep I had prayed for, the kind of sleep that would help me remember.

Then I remembered. Not St. Paul's, burned to the ground by communists. A headline from the dailies. "Marble Arch hit. Eighteen killed by blast." The date was not clear except for the year. Nineteen forty. There were exactly two more days left in 1940. I grabbed my coat and muffler and ran up the stairs and across the marble floor.

"Where the hell do you think you're going?" Langby shouted to me. I couldn't see him.

"I have to save Enola," I said, and my voice echoed in the dark sanctuary. "They're going to bomb Marble Arch."

"You can't leave now," he shouted after me, standing where the fire watch stone would be. "The tide's out. You dirty—"

I didn't hear the rest of it. I had already flung myself down the steps and into a taxi. It took almost all the money I had, the money I had so carefully hoarded for the trip back to St. John's Wood. Shelling started while we were still in Oxford Street, and the driver refused to go any further. He let me out into pitch blackness, and I saw I would never make it in time.

Blast. Enola crumpled on the stairway down to the tube, her open-toed shoes still on her feet, not a mark on her. And when I try to lift her, jelly under the skin. I would have to wrap her in the muffler she gave me, because I was too late. I had gone back a hundred years to be too late to save her.

I ran the last blocks, guided by the gun emplacement that had to be in Hyde Park, and skidded down the steps into Marble Arch. The woman in the ticket booth took my last shilling for a ticket to St. Paul's Station. I stuck it in my pocket and raced toward the stairs.

"No running," she said placidly. "To your left, please." The door to the right was blocked off by wooden barricades, the metal gates beyond pulled to and chained. The board with names on it for the stations was x-ed with tape, and a new sign that read ALL TRAINS was nailed to the barricade, pointing left.

Enola was not on the stopped escalators or sitting against the wall in the hallway. I came to the first stairway and could not get through. A family had set out, just where I wanted to step, a communal tea of bread and butter, a little pot of jam sealed with waxed paper, and a kettle on a ring like the one Langby and I had rescued out of the rubble, all of it spread on a cloth embroidered at the corners with flowers. I stood staring down at the layered tea, spread like a waterfall down the steps.

"I—Marble Arch—" I said. Another twenty killed by flying tiles. "You shouldn't be here."

"We've as much right as anyone," the man said belligerently, "and who are you to tell us to move on?"

A woman lifting saucers out of a cardboard box looked up at me, frightened. The kettle began to whistle.

"It's you that should move on," the man said. "Go on then." He stood off to one side so I could pass. I edged past the embroidered cloth apologetically.

"I'm sorry," I said. "I'm looking for someone. On the platform."

"You'll never find her in there, mate, it's hell in there," the man said, thumbing in that direction. I hurried past him, nearly stepping on the tea cloth, and rounded the corner into hell.

It was not hell. Shopgirls folded coats and leaned back against them, cheerful or sullen or disagreeable, but certainly not damned. Two boys scuffled for a shilling and lost it on the tracks. They bent over the edge, debating whether to go after it, and the station guard yelled to them to back away. A train rumbled through, full of people. A mosquito landed on the guard's hand and he reached out to slap it and missed. The boys laughed. And behind and before them, stretching in all directions down the deadly tile curves of the tunnel like casualties, backed into the entranceways and onto the stairs, were people. Hundreds and hundreds of people.

I stumbled back onto the stairs, knocking over a teacup. It spilled like a flood across the cloth.

"I told you, mate," the man said cheerfully. "It's hell in there, ain't it? And worse below."

"Hell," I said. "Yes." I would never find her. I would never save her. I looked at the woman mopping up the tea, and it came to me that I could not save her either. Enola or the cat or any of them, lost here in the endless stairways and cul-de-sacs of time. They were already dead a hundred years, past saving. The past is beyond saving. Surely that was the lesson the history department sent me all this way to learn. Well, fine, I've learned it. Can I go home now?

Of course not, dear boy. You have foolishly spent all your money on taxicabs and brandy, and tonight is the night the Germans burn the City. (Now it is too late, I remember it all. Twenty-eight incendiaries on the roofs.) Langby must have his chance, and you must learn the hardest lesson of all and the one you should have known from the beginning. You cannot save St. Paul's.

I went back out onto the platform and stood behind the yellow line until a train pulled up. I took my ticket out and held it in my hand all the way to St. Paul's Station. When I got there, smoke billowed toward me like an easy spray of water. I could not see St. Paul's.

"The tide's out," a woman said in a voice devoid of hope, and I went down in a snake pit of limp cloth hoses. My hands came up covered with rank-smelling mud, and I understood finally (and too late) the significance of the tide. There was no water to fight the fires.

A policeman barred my way and I stood helplessly before him with no idea what to say. "No civilians allowed here," he said. "St. Paul's is for it." The smoke billowed like a thundercloud, alive with sparks, and the dome rose golden above it.

"I'm fire watch," I said, and his arm fell away, and then I was on the roofs.

My endorphin levels must have been going up and down like an air raid siren. I do not have any short-term from then on, just moments that do not fit together: the people in the church when we brought Langby down, huddled in a corner playing cards, the whirlwind of burning scraps of wood in the dome, the ambulance driver who wore open-toed shoes like Enola and smeared salve on my burned hands. And in the center, the one clear moment when I went after Langby on a rope and saved his life.

I stood by the dome, blinking against the smoke. The City was on fire and it seemed as if St. Paul's would ignite from the heat, would crumble from the noise alone. Bence-Jones was by the northwest tower, hitting at an incendiary with a spade. Langby was too close to the patched place where the bomb had gone through, looking toward me. An incendiary clattered behind him. I turned to grab a shovel, and when I turned back, he was gone.

"Langby!" I shouted, and could not hear my own voice. He had fallen into the chasm and nobody saw him or the incendiary. Except me. I do not remember how I got across the roof. I think I called for a rope. I got a rope. I tied it around my waist, gave the ends of it into the hands of the fire watch, and went over the side. The fires lit the walls of the hole almost all the way to the bottom. Below me I could see a pile of whitish rubble. He's under there, I thought, and jumped free of the wall. The space was so narrow there was nowhere to throw the rubble. I was afraid I would inadvertently stone him, and I tried to toss the pieces of planking and plaster over my shoulder, but there was barely room to turn. For one awful moment I thought he might not be there at all, that the pieces of splintered wood would brush away to reveal empty pavement, as they had in the crypt.

I was numbed by the indignity of crawling over him. If he was dead I did not think I could bear the shame of stepping on his helpless body. Then his hand came up like a ghost's and grabbed my ankle, and within seconds I had whirled and had his head free.

He was the ghastly white that no longer frightens me. "I put the bomb out," he said. I stared at him, so overwhelmed with relief I could not speak. For one hysterical moment I thought I would even laugh, I was so glad to see him. I finally realized what it was I was supposed to say.

"Are you all right?" I said.

"Yes," he said, and tried to raise himself on one elbow. "So much the worse for you."

He could not get up. He grunted with pain when he tried to shift his weight to his right side and lay back, the uneven rubble crunching sickeningly under him. I tried to lift him gently so I could see where he was hurt. He must have fallen on something.

"It's no use," he said, breathing hard. "I put it out."

I spared him a startled glance, afraid that he was delirious and went back to rolling him onto his side.

"I know you were counting on this one," he went on, not resisting me at all. "It was bound to happen sooner or later with all these roofs. Only I went after it. What'll you tell your friends?"

His asbestos coat was torn down the back in a long gash. Under it his back was charred and smoking. He had fallen on the incendiary. "Oh, my God," I said, trying frantically to see how badly he was burned without touching him. I had no way of knowing how deep the burns went, but they seemed to extend only in the narrow space where the coat had torn. I tried to pull the bomb out from under him, but the casing was as hot as a stove. It was not melting, though. My sand and Langby's body had smothered it. I had no idea if it would start up again when it was exposed to the air. I looked around, a little wildly, for the bucket and stirrup pump Langby must have dropped when he fell.

"Looking for a weapon?" Langby said, so clearly it was hard to believe he was hurt at all. "Why not just leave me here? A bit of overexposure and I'd be done for by morning. Or would you rather do your dirty work in private?"

I stood up and yelled to the men on the roof above us. One of them shone a pocket torch down at us, but its light didn't reach.

"Is he dead?" somebody shouted down to me.

"Send for an ambulance," I said. "He's been burned."

I helped Langby up, trying to support his back without touching the burn. He staggered a little and then leaned against the wall, watching me as I tried to bury the incendiary, using a piece of the planking as a scoop. The rope came down and I tied Langby to it. He had not spoken since I helped him up. He let me tie the rope around his waist, still looking steadily at me. "I should have let you smother in the crypt," he said.

He stood leaning easily, almost relaxed against the wooden supports, his hands holding him up. I put his hands on the slack rope and wrapped it once around them for the grip I knew he didn't have. "I've been on to you since that day in the Gallery. I knew you weren't afraid of heights. You came down here without any fear of heights when you thought I'd ruined your precious plans. What was it? An attack of conscience? Kneeling there like a baby, whining. 'What have we done? What have we done?' You made me sick. But you know what gave you away first? The cat. Everybody knows cats hate water. Everybody but a dirty Nazi spy."

There was a tug on the rope. "Come ahead," I said, and the rope tautened.

"That WVS tart? Was she a spy, too? Supposed to meet you in Marble Arch? Telling me it was going to be bombed. You're a rotten spy, Bartholomew. Your friends already blew it up in September. It's open again."

The rope jerked suddenly and began to lift Langby. He twisted his hands to get a better grip. His right shoulder scraped the wall. I put up my hands and pushed him gently so that his left side was to the wall. "You're making a big mistake, you know," he said. "You should have killed me. I'll tell."

I stood in the darkness, waiting for the rope. Langby was unconscious when he reached the roof. I walked past the fire watch to the dome and down to the crypt.

This morning the letter from my uncle came and with it a five-pound note.

December 31—Two of Dunworthy's flunkies met me in St. John's Wood to tell me I was late for my exams. I did not even protest. I shuffled obediently after them without even considering how unfair it was to give an exam to one of the walking dead. I had not slept in—how long? Since yesterday when I went to find Enola. I had not slept in a hundred years.

Dunworthy was in the Examination Buildings, blinking at me. One of the flunkies handed me a test paper and the other one called time. I turned the paper over and left an oily smudge from the ointment on my burns. I stared uncomprehendingly at them. I had grabbed at the incendiary when I turned Langby over, but these burns were on the backs of my hands. The answer came to me suddenly in Langby's unyielding voice. "They're rope burns, you fool. Don't they teach you Nazi spies the proper way to come up a rope?"

I looked down at the test. I read, "Number of incendiaries that fell on St. Paul's——— Number of land mines——— Number of high explosive bombs——— Method most commonly used for extinguishing incendiaries——— land mines——— high explosive bombs——— Number of volunteers on first watch——— second watch——— Casualties——— Fatalities———" The questions made no sense. There was only a short space, long enough for the writing of a number, after any of the questions. Method most commonly used for extinguishing incendiaries. How would I ever fit what I knew into that narrow space? Where were the questions about Enola and Langby and the cat?

I went up to Dunworthy's desk. "St. Paul's almost burned down last night," I said. "What kind of questions are these?"

"You should be answering questions, Mr. Bartholomew, not asking them."

"There aren't any questions about the people," I said. The outer casing of my anger began to melt.

"Of course there are," Dunworthy said, flipping to the second page of the test. "Number of casualties, 1940. Blast, shrapnel, other."

"Other?" I said. At any moment the roof would collapse on me in a shower of plaster dust and fury. "Other? Langby put out a fire with his own body. Enola has a cold that keeps getting worse. The cat . . ." I snatched the paper back from him and scrawled "one cat" in the narrow space next to "blast." "Don't you care about them at all?"

"They're important from a statistical point of view," he said, "but as individuals they are hardly relevant to the course of history."

My reflexes were shot. It was amazing to me that Dunworthy's were almost as slow. I grazed the side of his jaw and knocked his glasses off. "Of course they're relevant!" I shouted. "They *are* the history, not all these bloody numbers!"

The reflexes of the flunkies were very fast. They did not let me start another swing at him before they had me by both arms and were hauling me out of the room.

"They're back there in the past with nobody to save them. They can't see their hands in front of their faces and there are bombs falling down on them and you tell me they aren't important? You call that being an historian?"

The flunkies dragged me out the door and down the hall. "Langby saved St. Paul's. How much more important can a person get? You're no historian! You're nothing but a—" I wanted to call him a terrible name, but the only curses I could summon up were Langby's. "You're nothing but a dirty Nazi spy!" I bellowed. "You're nothing but a lazy bourgeois tart!"

They dumped me on my hands and knees outside the door and slammed it in my face. "I wouldn't be an historian if you paid me!" I shouted, and went to see the fire watch stone.

I am having to write this in bits and pieces. My hands are in pretty bad shape, and Dunworthy's boys didn't help matters much. Kivrin comes in periodically, wearing her St. Joan look, and smears so much salve on my hands that I can't hold a pencil.

St. Paul's Station is not there, of course, so I got out at Holborn and walked, thinking about my last meeting with Dean Matthews on the morning after the burning of the city. This morning.

"I understand you saved Langby's life," he said. "I also understand that between you, you saved St. Paul's last night."

I showed him the letter from my uncle and he stared at it as if he could not think what it was. "Nothing stays saved forever," he said, and for a terrible moment I thought he was going to tell me Langby had died. "We shall have to keep on saving St. Paul's until Hitler decides to bomb something else."

The raids on London are almost over, I wanted to tell him. He'll start bombing the countryside in a matter of weeks. Canterbury, Bath, aiming always at the cathedrals. You and St. Paul's will both outlast the war and live to dedicate the fire watch stone.

"I am hopeful, though," he said. "I think the worst is over."

"Yes, sir," I thought of the stone, its letters still readable after all this time. No, sir, the worst is not over.

I managed to keep my bearings almost to the top of Ludgate Hill. Then I lost my way completely, wandering about like a man in a graveyard. I had not remembered that the rubble looked so much like the white plaster dust Langby had tried to dig me out of. I could not find the stone anywhere. In the end I nearly fell over it, jumping back as if I had stepped on a body.

It is all that's left. Hiroshima is supposed to have had a handful of untouched trees at ground zero. Denver the capitol steps. Neither of them says, "Remember men and women of St. Paul's Watch who by the grace of God saved this cathedral." The grace of God.

Part of the stone is sheared off. Historians argue there was another line that said, "for all time," but I do not believe that, not if Dean Matthews had anything to do with it. And none of the watch it was dedicated to would have believed it for a minute. We saved St. Paul's every time we put out an incendiary, and only until the next one fell. Keeping watch on the danger spots, putting out the little fires with sand and stirrup pumps, the big ones with our bodies, in order to keep the whole vast complex structure from burning down. Which sounds to me like a course description for History Practicum 401. What a fine time to discover what historians are for when I have tossed my chance for being one out the windows as easily as they tossed the pinpoint bomb in! No, sir, the worst is not over.

There are flash burns on the stone, where legend says the Dean of St. Paul's was kneeling when the bomb went off. Totally apocryphal, of course, since the front door is hardly an appropriate place for prayers. It is more likely the shadow of a tourist who wandered in to ask the whereabouts of the Windmill Theatre, or the imprint of a girl bringing a volunteer his muffler. Or a cat.

Nothing is saved forever, Dean Matthews, and I knew that when I walked in the west doors that first day, blinking into the gloom, but it is pretty bad nevertheless. Standing here knee-deep in rubble out of which I will not be able to dig any folding chairs or friends, knowing that Langby died thinking I was a Nazi spy, knowing that Enola came one day and I wasn't there. It's pretty bad.

But it is not as bad as it could be. They are both dead, and Dean Matthews too, but they died without knowing what I knew all along, what sent me to my knees in the Whispering Gallery, sick with grief

and guilt: that in the end none of us saved St. Paul's. And Langby
cannot turn to me, stunned and sick at heart, and say, "Who did
this? Your friends the Nazis?" And I would have to say, "No, the
communists." That would be the worst.

I have come back to the room and let Kivrin smear more salve on
my hands. She wants me to get some sleep. I know I should pack
and get gone. It will be humiliating to have them come and throw
me out, but I do not have the strength to fight her. She looks so much
like Enola.

January 1—I have apparently slept not only through the night, but
through the morning mail drop as well. When I woke up just now,
I found Kivrin sitting on the end of the bed holding an envelope.
"Your grades came," she said.

I put my arm over my eyes. "They can be marvelously efficient
when they want to, can't they?"

"Yes," Kivrin said.

"Well, let's see it," I said, sitting up. "How long do I have before
they come and throw me out?"

She handed the flimsy computer envelope to me. I tore it along the
perforation. "Wait," she said. "Before you open it, I want to say
something." She put her hand gently on my burns. "You're wrong
about the history department. They're very good."

It was not exactly what I expected her to say. "Good is not the
word I'd use to describe Dunworthy," I said and yanked the inside
slip free.

Kivrin's look did not change, not even when I sat there with the
printout on my knees where she could surely see it.

"Well," I said.

The slip was hand-signed by the esteemed Dunworthy. I have
taken a first. With honors.

January 2—Two things came in the mail today. One was Kivrin's
assignment. The history department thinks of everything—even to
keeping her here long enough to nursemaid me, even to coming up
with a prefabricated trial by fire to send their history majors through.

I think I wanted to believe that was what they had done. Enola and
Langby only hired actors, the cat a clever android with its clockwork
innards taken out for the final effect, not so much because I wanted

to believe Dunworthy was not good at all, but because then I would not have this nagging pain at not knowing what had happened to them.

"You said your practicum was England in 1400?" I said, watching her as suspiciously as I had watched Langby.

"Thirteen forty-nine," she said, and her face went slack with memory. "The plague year."

"My God," I said. "How could they do that? The plague's a ten."

"I have a natural immunity," she said, and looked at her hands.

Because I could not think of anything to say, I opened the other piece of mail. It was a report on Enola. Computer-printed, facts and dates and statistics, all the numbers the history department so dearly loves, but it told me what I thought I would have to go without knowing: that she had gotten over her cold and survived the Blitz. Young Tom had been killed in the Baedaker raids on Bath, but Enola had lived until 2006, the year before they blew up St. Paul's.

I don't know whether I believe the report or not, but it does not matter. It is, like Langby's reading aloud to the old man, a simple act of human kindness. They think of everything.

Not quite. They did not tell me what happened to Langby. But I find as I write this that I already know: I saved his life. It does not seem to matter that he might have died in the hospital the next day, and I find, in spite of all the hard lessons the history department has tried to teach me, I do not quite believe this one: that nothing is saved forever. It seems to me that perhaps Langby is.

January 3—I went to see Dunworthy today. I don't know what I intended to say—some pompous drivel about my willingness to serve in the fire watch of history, standing guard against the falling incendiaries of the human heart, silent and saintly.

But he blinked at me nearsightedly across his desk, and it seemed to me that he was blinking at that last bright image of St. Paul's in sunlight before it was gone forever and that he knew better than anyone that the past cannot be saved, and I said instead, "I'm sorry that I broke your glasses, sir."

"How did you like St. Paul's?" he said, and like my first meeting with Enola, I felt I must be somehow reading the signals all wrong, that he was not feeling loss, but something quite different.

"I loved it, sir," I said.

"Yes," he said. "So do I."

Dean Matthews is wrong. I have fought with memory my whole practicum only to find that it is not the enemy at all, and being an historian is not some saintly burden after all. Because Dunworthy is not blinking against the fatal sunlight of the last morning, but into the gloom of that first afternoon, looking in the great west doors of St. Paul's at what is, like Langby, like all of it, every moment, in us, saved forever.

In Hugo Winners, Volume Four *Spider Robinson appeared twice, once on his own and once in collaboration with his wife, Jeanne Robinson. This, then, is his third appearance.*

"Melancholy Elephants" is what I consider an example of a "dense" story. By that I don't mean it is stupid; it isn't. I don't mean that it is hard to understand; it isn't. What I mean is that in the course of telling it, Spider reveals a great deal about the society in which the story is set. The social information is densely packed.

This is important. I have always maintained that what makes good science fiction so difficult to write is that it must construct an imaginary society within which the plot takes place. This imaginary society must be interesting and self-consistent, and must delight the reader without getting in the way of the plot. And the plot must be recounted without having it obscure the background. This double task is very difficult. Try it, if you don't believe me.

I wrote one science fiction novel in which I carried my hero through every moment of the several days in which the events took place. Since I didn't want to skip anything significant, I had to accompany him to the bathroom on a number of occasions. It seemed to me important to describe the bathroom each time; how each differed from the others; how all differed from ours. This is not the usual thing to do since the excretory process is skimped even in those stories that go into the sexual process in full clinical detail. Sure enough, there were reviewers who complained of this, though no reader did. (I have often wondered as to how the qualifications for reviewers are worked out; do they have to present an official certificate of failure on an intelligence test?)

Anyway, I like "density" in science fiction. I wish I were better at it than I am. Spider, in this story, is very good indeed. Watch for it as you read.

—Isaac Asimov

Melancholy Elephants

by Spider Robinson

She sat zazen, concentrating on not concentrating, until it was time to prepare for the appointment. Sitting *seemed* to produce the usual serenity, put everything into perspective. Her hand did not tremble as she applied her makeup; tranquil features looked back at her from the mirror. She was mildly surprised, in fact, at just how calm she was, until she got out of the hotel elevator at the garage level and the mugger made his play. She killed him instead of disabling him. Which was obviously not a measured, balanced action—the official fuss and paperwork could make her late. Annoyed at herself, she stuffed the corpse under a shiny new Westinghouse roadable whose owner she knew to be in Luna, and continued on to her own car. This would have to be squared later, and it would cost. No help for it—she fought to regain at least the semblance of tranquility as her car emerged from the garage and turned north.

Nothing must interfere with this meeting, or with her role in it.

Dozens of man-years and God knows how many dollars, she thought, *funneling down to perhaps a half hour of conversation. All the effort, all the hope. Insignificant on the scale of the Great Wheel, of course . . . but when you balance it all on a half hour of talk, it's like balancing a stereo cartridge on a needlepoint: it only takes a gram or so of weight to wear out a piece of diamond. I must be harder than diamond.*

Rather than clear a window and watch Washington, D.C., roll by beneath her car, she turned on the television. She absorbed and integrated the news, on the chance that there might be some late-breaking item she could turn to her advantage in the conversation to come; none developed. Shortly the car addressed her: "Grounding, ma'am. ID eyeball request." When the car landed, she cleared and then opened her window, presented her pass and ID to a marine in dress blues, and was cleared at once. At the marine's direction she re-opaqued the window and surrendered control of her car to the house computer, and when the car parked itself and powered down she got out without haste. A man she knew was waiting to meet her, smiling.

"Dorothy, it's good to see you again."

"Hello, Phillip. Good of you to meet me."

"You look lovely this evening."

"You're too kind."

She did not chafe at the meaningless pleasantries. She needed Phil's support, or she might. But she did reflect on how many, many sentences have been worn smooth with use, rendered meaningless by centuries of repetition. It was by no means a new thought.

"If you'll come with me, he'll see you at once."

"Thank you, Phillip." She wanted to ask what the old man's mood was, but knew it would put Phil in an impossible position.

"I rather think your luck is good; the old man seems to be in excellent spirits tonight."

She smiled her thanks, and decided that if and when Phil got around to making his pass she would accept him.

The corridors through which he led her then were broad and high and long; the building dated back to a time of cheap power. Even in Washington, few others would have dared to live in such an energy-wasteful environment. The extremely spare decor reinforced the impression created by the place's very dimensions: bare space from carpet to ceiling, broken approximately every forty meters by some exquisitely simple objet d'art of at least a megabuck's value, appropriately displayed. An unadorned, perfect, white porcelian bowl, over a thousand years old, on a rough cherrywood pedestal. An arresting color photograph of a snow-covered country road, silk-screened onto stretched silver foil; the time of day changed as one walked past it. A crystal globe, a meter in diameter, within which danced a hologram of the immortal Shara Drummond; since she had ceased performing before the advent of holo technology, this had to be an expensive computer reconstruction. A small sealed glassite chamber containing the first vacuum-sculpture ever made, Nakagawa's legendary Starstone. A visitor in no hurry could study an object at leisure, then walk quite a distance in undistracted contemplation before encountering another. A visitor in a hurry, like Dorothy, would not *quite* encounter peripherally astonishing stimuli often enough to get the trick of filtering them out. Each tugged at her attention, intruded on her thoughts; they were distracting both intrinsically and as a reminder of the measure of their owner's wealth. To approach this man in his own home, whether at leisure or in haste, was to be humbled. She knew the effect was intentional, and could not transcend it; this irritated her, which irritated her. She struggled for detachment.

At the end of the seemingly endless corridors was an elevator. Phillip handed her into it, punched a floor button without giving her a chance to see which one, and stepped back into the doorway. "Good luck, Dorothy."

"Thank you, Phillip. Any topics to be sure and avoid?"

"Well . . . don't bring up hemorrhoids."

"I didn't know one could."

He smiled. "Are we still on for lunch Thursday?"

"Unless you'd rather make it dinner."

One eyebrow lifted. "And breakfast?"

She appeared to consider it. "Brunch," she decided. He half bowed and stepped back.

The elevator door closed and she forgot Phillip's existence.

Sentient beings are innumerable; I vow to save them all. The deluding passions are limitless; I vow to extinguish them all. The truth is limitless; I—

The elevator door opened again, truncating the Vow of the Boddhisattva. She had not felt the elevator stop—yet she knew that she must have descended at least a hundred meters. She left the elevator.

The room was larger than she had expected; nonetheless the big powered chair dominated it easily. The chair also seemed to dominate—at least visually—its occupant. A misleading impression, as he dominated all this massive home, everything in it and, to a great degree, the country in which it stood. But he did not look like much.

A scent symphony was in progress, the cinnamon passage of Bulachevski's *Childhood*. It happened to be one of her personal favorites, and this encouraged her.

"Hello, Senator."

"Hello, Mrs. Martin. Welcome to my home. Forgive me for not rising."

"Of course. It was most gracious of you to receive me."

"It is my pleasure and privilege. A man my age appreciates a chance to spend time with a woman as beautiful and intelligent as yourself."

"Senator, how soon do we start talking to each other?"

He raised that part of his face which had once held an eyebrow. "We haven't *said* anything yet that is true. You do not stand because you cannot. Your gracious reception cost me three carefully hoarded favors and a good deal of folding cash. More than the going rate; you are seeing me reluctantly. You have at least eight mistresses that I know of, each of whom makes me look like a dull matron. I concealed a warm corpse on the way here because I dared not be late; my time is short and my business urgent. Can we begin?"

She held her breath and prayed silently. Everything she had been able to learn about the Senator told her that this was the correct way to approach him. But was it?

The mummy-like face fissured in a broad grin. "Right away. Mrs. Martin, I like you and that's the truth. My time is short, too. What do you want of me?"

"Don't you know?"

"I can make an excellent guess. I hate guessing."

"I am heavily and publicly committed to the defeat of S. 4217896."

"Yes, but for all I know you might have come here to sell out."

"Oh." She tried not to show her surprise. "What makes you think that possible?"

"Your organization is large and well financed and fairly efficient, Mrs. Martin, and there's something about it I don't understand."

"What is that?"

"Your objective. Your arguments are weak and implausible, and whenever this is pointed out to one of you, you simply keep on pushing. Many times I have seen people take a position without apparent logic to it—but I've always been able to see the logic if I kept on looking hard enough. But as I see it, S. '896 would work to the clear and lasting advantage of the group you claim to represent, the artists. There's too much intelligence in your organization to square with your goals. So I have to wonder what you *are* working for, and why. One possibility is that you're willing to roll over on this copyright thing in exchange for whatever it is that you *really* want. Follow me?"

"Senator, I *am* working on behalf of all artists—and in a broader sense—"

He looked pained, or rather, more pained. ". . . 'for all mankind,' oh my *God*, Mrs. Martin, really now."

"I *know* you have heard that countless times, and probably said it as often." He grinned evilly. "This is one of those rare times when it happens to be true. I believe that if S. '896 does pass, our species will suffer significant trauma."

He raised a skeletal hand, tugged at his lower lip. "Now that I have ascertained where you stand, I believe I can save you a good deal of money. By concluding this audience, and seeing that the squeeze you paid for half an hour of my time is refunded pro rata."

Her heart sank, but she kept her voice even. "Without even hearing the hidden logic behind our arguments?"

"It would be pointless and cruel to make you go into your spiel, ma'am. You see, I cannot help you."

She wanted to cry out, and savagely refused herself permission. *Control*, whispered a part of her mind, while another part shouted that a man such as this did not lightly use the words, "I cannot." But he *had* to be wrong. Perhaps the sentence was only a bargaining gambit . . .

No sign of the internal conflict showed; her voice was calm and measured. "Sir, I have not come here to lobby. I simply wanted to inform you personally that our organization intends to make a no-strings campaign donation in the amount of—"

"Mrs. Martin, please! Before you commit yourself, I repeat, I cannot help you. Regardless of the sum offered."

"Sir, it is substantial."

"I'm sure. Nonetheless it is insufficient."

She knew she should not ask. "Senator, *why?*"

He frowned, a frightening sight.

"Look," she said, the desperation almost showing through now, "keep the pro rata if it buys me an answer! Until I'm convinced that my mission is utterly hopeless, I must not abandon it: answering me is the quickest way to get me out of your office. Your scanners have searched me quite thoroughly; you know that I'm not abscamming you."

Still frowning, he nodded. "Very well. I cannot accept your campaign donation because I have already accepted one from another source."

Her very worst secret fear was realized. He had already taken money from the other side. The one thing any politician must do, no matter how powerful, is stay bought. It was all over.

All her panic and tension vanished, to be replaced by a sadness so great and so pervasive that for a moment she thought it might literally stop her heart.

Too late! Oh my darling, I was too late!

She realized bleakly that there were too many people in her life, too many responsibilities and entanglements. It would be at least a month before she could honorably suicide.

"—you all right, Mrs. Martin?" the old man was saying, sharp concern in his voice.

She gathered discipline around her like a familiar cloak. "Yes, sir, thank you. Thank you for speaking plainly." She stood up and smoothed her skirt. "And for your—"

"Mrs. Martin."

"—gracious hos—Yes?"

"Will you tell me your arguments? Why shouldn't I support '896?"

She blinked sharply. "You just said it would be pointless and cruel."

"If I held out the slightest hope, yes, it would be. If you'd rather not waste your time, I will not compel you. But I am curious."

"Intellectual curiosity?"

He seemed to sit up a little straighter—surely an illusion, for a prosthetic spine is not motile. "Mrs. Martin, I happen to be committed to a course of action. That does not mean I don't care whether the action is good or bad."

"Oh." She thought for a moment. "If I convince you, you will not thank me."

"I know. I saw the look on your face a moment ago, and . . . it reminded me of a night many years ago. Night my mother died. If you've got a sadness that big, and I can take on a part of it, I should try. Sit down."

She sat.

"Now tell me: What's so damned awful about extending copyright to meet the realities of modern life? Customarily I try to listen to both sides before accepting a campaign donation—but this seemed so open and shut, so straightforward . . ."

"Senator, that bill is a short-term boon, to some artists—and a long-term disaster for all artists, on Earth and off."

" 'In the long run, Mr. President—' " he began, quoting Keynes.

" '—we are some of us still alive,' " she finished softly and pointedly. "Aren't we? You've put your finger on part of the problem."

"What is this disaster you speak of?" he asked.

"The worst psychic trauma the race has yet suffered."

He studied her carefully and frowned again. "Such a possibility is not even hinted at in your literature or materials."

"To do so would precipitate the trauma. At present only a handful of people know, even in my organization. I'm telling you because you asked, and because I am certain that you are the only person recording this conversation. I'm betting that you will wipe the tape."

He blinked, and sucked at the memory of his teeth. "My, my," he said mildly. "Let me get comfortable." He had the chair recline sharply and massage his lower limbs; she saw that he could still watch her by overhead mirror if he chose. His eyes were closed. "All right, go ahead."

She needed no time to choose her words. "Do you know how old art is, Senator?"

"As old as man, I suppose. In fact, it may be part of the definition."

"Good answer," she said. "Remember that. But for all present-day intents and purposes, you might as well say that art is a little over 15,600 years old. That's the age of the oldest surviving artwork, the cave paintings at Lascaux. Doubtless the cave-painters sang, and danced, and even told stories—but these arts left no record more durable than the memory of a man. Perhaps it was the storytellers who next learned how to preserve their art. Countless more generations would pass before a workable method of musical notation was devised and standardized. Dancers only learned in the last few centuries how to leave even the most rudimentary record of their art.

"The racial memory of our species has been getting longer since Lascaux. The biggest single improvement came with the invention of writing: our memory span went from a few generations to as many as the Bible has been around. But it took a massive effort to sustain a memory that long; it was difficult to hand-copy manuscripts faster than barbarians, plagues, or other natural disasters could destroy them. The obvious solution was the printing press: to make and disseminate so many copies of a manuscript or art work that *some* would survive any catastrophe.

"But with the printing press a new idea was born. Art was suddenly mass-marketable, and there was money in it. Writers decided that they should own the right to copy their work. The notion of copyright was waiting to be born.

"Then in the last hundred and fifty years came the largest quantum jumps in human racial memory. Recording technologies. Visual: photography, film, video, Xerox, holo. Audio: low-fi, hi-fi, stereo, and digital. Then computers, the ultimate in information storage. Each of these technologies generated new art forms, and new ways of preserving the ancient art forms. And each required a reassessment of the idea of copyright.

"You know the system we have now, unchanged since the mid twentieth century. Copyright ceases to exist fifty years after the death of the copyright holder. But the size of the human race has increased drastically since the 1900s—and so has the average human lifespan. Most people in developed nations now expect to live to be a hundred and twenty; you yourself are considerably older. And so, naturally, S. '896 now seeks to extend copyright into perpetuity."

"Well," the senator interrupted, "what is *wrong* with that? Should a man's work cease to be his simply because he has neglected to keep on breathing? Mrs. Martin, you yourself will be wealthy all your life if that bill passes. Do you truly wish to give away your late husband's genius?"

She winced in spite of herself.

"Forgive my bluntness, but that is what I understand *least* about your position."

"Senator, if I try to hoard the fruits of my husband's genius, I may cripple my race. Don't you see what perpetual copyright implies? It is perpetual racial memory! That bill will give the human race an elephant's memory. *Have you ever seen a cheerful elephant?*"

He was silent for a time. Then: "I'm still not sure I understand the problem."

"Don't feel bad, sir. The problem has been directly under the nose of all of us, for at *least* eighty years, and hardly anyone has noticed."

"Why is that?"

"I think it comes down to a kind of innate failure of mathematical intuition, common to most humans. We tend to confuse any sufficiently high number with infinity."

"Well, anything above ten to the eighty-fifth might as well be infinity."

"Beg pardon?"

"Sorry—I should not have interrupted. That is the current best guess for the number of atoms in the Universe. Go on."

She struggled to get back on the rails. "Well, it takes a lot less than that to equal 'infinity' in most minds. For millions of years we looked at the ocean and said. 'That is infinite. It will accept our garbage and waste forever.' We looked at the sky and said, 'That is infinite; it will hold an infinite amount of smoke.' We *like* the idea of infinity. A problem with infinity in it is easily solved. How long can you pollute a planet infinitely large? Easy: forever. Stop thinking.

"Then one day there are so many of us that the planet no longer seems infinitely large.

"So we go elsewhere. There are infinite resources in the *rest* of the solar system, aren't there? I think you are one of the few people alive wise enough to realize that there are *not* infinite resources in the solar system, and sophisticated enough to have included that awareness in your plans."

The senator now looked troubled. He sipped something from a straw. "Relate all this to your problem."

"Do you remember a case from about eighty years ago, involving the song 'My Sweet Lord' by George Harrison?"

"Remember it? I did research on it. My firm won."

"Your firm convinced the court that Harrison had gotten the tune for that song from a song called 'He's So Fine,' written over ten years earlier. Shortly thereafter Yoko Ono was accused of stealing 'You're My Angel' from the classic 'Makin' Whoopee,' written more than thirty years earlier. Chuck Berry's estate eventually took John Lennon's estate to court over 'Come Together.' Then in the late eighties the great Plagiarism Plague *really* got started in the courts. From then on it was open season on popular composers, and still is. But it really hit the fan at the turn of the century, when Brindle's *Ringsong* was shown to be 'substantially similar' to one of Corelli's concertos.

"There are eighty-eight notes. One hundred and seventy-six, if your ear is good enough to pick out quarter tones. Add in rests and so forth, different time signatures. Pick a figure for maximum number of notes a melody can contain. I do not know the figure for the maximum possible number of melodies—too many variables—but I am sure it is quite high.

"I am certain that it is not infinity.

"For one thing, a great many of those possible arrays of eighty-eight notes will not be perceived as music, as melody, by the human ear. Perhaps more than half. They will not be hummable, whistle-able, listenable—some will be actively unpleasant to hear. Another large fraction will be so similar to one another as to be effectively identical: if you change three notes of the Moonlight Sonata, you have not created something new.

"I do not know the figure for the maximum number of discretely appreciable melodies, and again I'm certain it is quite high, and again I am certain that it is not infinity. There are sixteen billion of us alive, Senator, more than all the people that have ever lived. Thanks to our technology, better than half of us have no meaningful work to do; fifty-four percent of our population is entered on the tax rolls as artists. Because the synthesizer is so cheap and versatile, a majority of those artists are musicians, and a great many are composers. Do you know what it is like to be a composer these days, Senator?"

"I know a few composers."

"Who are still working?"

"Well . . . three of 'em."

"How often do they bring out a new piece?"

Pause. "I would say once every five years on the average. Hmmm. Never thought of it before, but—"

"Did you know that at present two out of every five copyright submissions to the Music Division are rejected on the first computer search?"

The old man's face had stopped registering surprise, other than for histrionic purposes, more than a century before; nonetheless, she knew she had rocked him. "No, I did not."

"Why would you know? Who would talk about it? But it is a fact nonetheless. Another fact is that, when the increase in number of working composers is taken into account, the *rate* of submissions to the Copyright Office is decreasing significantly. There are more composers than ever, but their individual productivity is declining. Who is the most popular composer alive?"

"Uh . . . I suppose that Vachandra fellow."

"Correct. He has been working for a little over fifty years. If you began now to play every note he ever wrote, in succession, you would be done in twelve hours. Wagner wrote well over sixty hours of music—the Ring alone runs twenty-one hours. The Beatles—essentially two composers—produced over twelve hours of original music in *less than ten years*. Why were the greats of yesteryear so much more prolific?

"There were more enjoyable permutations of eighty-eight notes for them to find."

"Oh my," the senator whispered.

"Now go back to the seventies again. Remember the *Roots* plagiarism case? And the dozens like it that followed? Around the same time a writer named van Vogt sued the makers of a successful film called *Alien*, for plagiarism of a story written forty years earlier. Two other writers named Bova and Ellison sued a television studio for stealing a series idea. All three collected.

"That ended the legal principle that one does not copyright *ideas* but *arrangements of words*. The number of word arrangements is finite, but the number of *ideas* is *much* smaller. Certainly, they can be retold in endless ways—*West Side Story* is a brilliant reworking of *Romeo and Juliet*. But it was only possible because *Romeo and Juliet* was in the public domain. Remember too that of the infinite number of stories that can be told, a certain number will be *bad stories*.

"As for visual artists—well, once a man demonstrated in the laboratory an ability to distinguish between eighty-one distinct shades of color accurately. I think that's an upper limit. There is a maximum amount of information that the eye is capable of absorbing, and much of that will be the equivalent of noise—"

"But . . . but . . ." This man was reputed never to have hesitated in any way under any circumstances. "But there'll always be change . . . there'll always be new discoveries, new horizons, new social attitudes, to infuse art with new—"

"Not as fast as artists breed. Do you know about the great split in literature at the beginning of the twentieth century? The mainstream essentially abandoned the Novel of Ideas after Henry James, and turned its collective attention to the Novel of Character. They had sucked that dry by mid-century, and they're still chewing on the pulp today. But meanwhile a small group of writers, desperate for something new to write about, for a new story to tell, invented a new genre called science fiction. They mined the future for ideas. The infinite future—like the infinite coal and oil and copper they had then too. In less than a century they had mined it out; there hasn't been a genuinely original idea in science fiction in over fifty years. Fantasy has always been touted as the 'literature of infinite possibility'—but there is even a theoretical upper limit to the 'meaningfully impossible,' and we are fast reaching it."

"We can create new art forms," he said.

"People have been trying to create new art forms for a long time, sir. Almost all fell by the wayside. People just didn't like them."

"We'll *learn* to like them. Damn it, we'll have to."

"And they'll help, for a while. More new art forms have been born in the last two centuries than in the previous million years—though none in the last fifteen years. Scent symphonies, tactile sculpture, kinetic sculpture, zero-gravity dance—they're all rich new fields, and they are generating mountains of new copyrights. Mountains of finite size. The ultimate bottleneck is this: that *we have only five senses with which to apprehend art, and that is a finite number.* Can I have some water, please?"

"Of course." The old man appeared to have regained his usual control, but the glass which emerged from the arm of her chair contained apple juice. She ignored this and continued.

"But that's not what I'm afraid of Senator. The theoretical heat-death of artistic expression is something we may never really approach in fact. Long before that point, the game will collapse."

She paused to gather her thoughts, sipped her juice. A part of her mind noted that it harmonized with the recurrent cinnamon motif of Bulachevski's scent symphony, which was still in progress.

"Artists have been deluding themselves, for centuries, with the notion that they create. In fact they do nothing of the sort. They discover. Inherent in the nature of reality are a number of combinations of musical tones that will be perceived as pleasing by a human central nervous system. For millennia we have been discovering them, implicit in the universe—and telling ourselves that we 'created' them. To create implies infinite possibility, to discover implies finite possibility. As a species I think we will react poorly to having our noses rubbed in the fact that we are discoverers and not creators."

She stopped speaking and sat very straight. Unaccountably her feet hurt. She closed her eyes, and continued speaking.

"My husband wrote a song for me, on the occasion of our fortieth wedding anniversary. It was our love in music, unique and special and intimate, the most beautiful melody I ever heard in my life. It made him so happy to have written it. Of his last ten compositions he had burned five for being derivative, and the others had all failed of copyright clearance. But this was fresh, special—he joked that my love for him had inspired him. The next day he submitted it for clearance, and learned that it had been a popular air during his early childhood, and had already been unsuccessfully submitted fourteen times since its original registration. A week later he burned all his manuscripts and working tapes and killed himself."

She was silent for a long time, and the senator did not speak.

" 'Ars longa, vita brevis,' " she said at last. "There's been comfort of a kind in that for thousands of years. But art is long, not infinite. 'The Magic goes away.' One day we will *use it up*—unless we can learn to recycle it like any other finite resource." Her voice gained strength. "Senator, that bill has to fail, if I have to take you on to do it. Perhaps I can't win—but I'm going to fight you! A copyright must not be allowed to last more than fifty years—after which it should be flushed from the memory banks of the Copyright Office. We need selective voluntary amnesia, if Discoverers of Art are to continue to work without psychic damage. Facts should be remembered—but dreams?" She shivered. ". . . dreams should be forgotten when we awake. Or one day we will find ourselves unable to sleep. Given eight billion artists with effective working lifetimes in excess of a century, we can no longer allow individuals to own their discoveries in perpetuity. We must do it the way the human race did it for a million years—by forgetting, and rediscovering. Because one day, the infinite number of monkeys will have nothing else to write *except* the complete works of Shakespeare. And they would probably rather not *know* that when it happens."

Now she was finished, nothing more to say. So was the scent symphony, whose last motif was fading slowly from the air. No clock ticked, no artifact hummed. The stillness was complete, for perhaps half a minute.

"If you live long enough," the senator said slowly at last, "there is nothing new under the sun." He shifted in his great chair. "If you're lucky, you die sooner than that. I haven't heard a new dirty joke in fifty years." He seemed to sit up straight in his chair. "I will kill S. 4217896."

She stiffened in shock. After a time, she slumped slightly and resumed breathing. So many emotions fought for ascendancy that she barely had time to recognize them as they went by. She could not speak.

"Furthermore," he went on, "I will not tell anyone why I'm doing it. It will begin the end of my career in public life, which I did not ever plan to leave, but you have convinced me that I must. I am both . . . glad, and—" his face tightened with pain—"and *bitterly* sorry that you told me why I must."

"So am I, sir," she said softly, almost inaudibly.

He looked at her sharply. "Some kinds of fight, you can't feel good even if you win them. Only two kinds of people take on fights like that: fools, and remarkable people. I think you are a remarkable person, Mrs. Martin."

She stood, knocking over her juice. "I wish to God I were a fool," she cried, feeling her control begin to crack at last.

"Dorothy!" he thundered.

She flinched as if he had struck her. "Sir?" she said automatically.

"Do *not* go to pieces! That is an order. You're wound up too tight; the pieces might not go back together again."

"So what?" she asked bitterly.

He was using the full power of his voice now, the voice which had stopped at least one war. "So how many friends do you think a man my age has *got*, damn it? Do you think minds like yours are common? We *share* this business now, and that makes us friends. You are the first person to come out of that elevator and really surprise me in a quarter of a century. And soon, when the word gets around that I've broken faith, people will stop coming out of the elevator. You think like me, and I can't afford to lose you." He smiled, and the smile seemed to melt decades from his face. "Hang on, Dorothy," he said, "and we will comfort each other in our terrible knowledge. All right?"

For almost a full minute she concentrated exclusively on her breathing, slowing and regularizing it. Then, tentatively, she probed at her emotions.

"Why," she said wonderingly, "it *is* better . . . shared."

"Anything is."

She looked at him then, and tried to smile and finally succeeded. "Thank you, Senator."

He returned her smile as he wiped all recordings of their conversation. "Call me Bob."

"Yes, Robert."

1984
Forty-second Convention
Anaheim

Cascade Point, by Timothy Zahn
Blood Music, by Greg Bear
Speech Sounds, by Octavia E. Butler

I don't think I ever met Timothy Zahn. That's not surprising. Considering how many science fiction writers there are, my own aversion to travel so that I don't get to places where the writers are congregating very often, and my failure as a visual person so that I'm apt not to see even those standing directly in front of me and waving to attract my attention, the surprise is that I know as many science fiction writers as I do.

Timothy has written, here, a piece of hard science fiction, and that's my baby. The question arises at once: What do you mean by hard science fiction, Isaac?

Like science fiction itself, I imagine that hard science fiction has as many definitions as there are people who are interested in it. I define hard science fiction as those science fiction stories in which the main thrust of a plot rests on a technological or scientific puzzle that must be solved in terms that do not offend the laws of nature as we know them.

There aren't many science fiction stories that are both hard and good. That requires a writer who is not only good at his trade but also has a knowledge of science and technology and a feel for it.

I recently read an essay by a respected science fiction writer (of whom I am very fond) who maintained that hard science fiction is approved of by people who want to have it around but who don't read it, or if they do, they skip the science parts (presumably, I suppose, because they think the science is too difficult).

I suspect the essayist wouldn't dream of dismissing stories with experimental styles because they are too wearisome to read; or objecting to stories that are very symbolic and involuted because they are too hard to grasp. After all, it would be the act of a despicable dimwit to find experimental style and involuted symbolism hard to understand. You have to labor at it if you have any self-respect at all. But, it's perfectly all right not to understand science and technology, and you need make no effort to do so. At least, that seems to be the attitude of the essayist.

And how intensely I disagree with that attitude!

Of course, the science in "Cascade Point" is very imaginative. There's nothing in the laws of nature, as we know them, that would really produce the effects described in the story. But the mode of treatment is scientific and it just warms my heart, in consequence, to have it chosen as a Hugo winner.

—Isaac Asimov

Cascade Point

by Timothy Zahn

In retrospect, I suppose I should have realized my number had come up on the universe's list right from the very start, right from the moment it became clear that I was going to be stuck with the job of welcoming the *Aura Dancer*'s latest batch of passengers aboard. Still, I suppose it's just as well it was me and not Tobbar who let Rik Bradley and his psychiatrist onto my ship. There are some things that a captain should have no one to blame for but himself, and this was definitely in that category.

Right away I suppose that generates a lot of false impressions. A star liner captain, resplendent in white and gold, smiling toothily at elegantly dressed men and women as the ramp carries them through the polished entry portal—forget all of that. A tramp starmer isn't polished anywhere it doesn't absolutely have to be, the captain is lucky if he's got a clean jumpsuit—let alone some pseudo-military Christmas tree frippery—and the passengers we get are the steerage of the star-traveling community. And look it.

Don't get me wrong; I have nothing against passengers aboard my ship. As a matter of fact, putting extra cabins in the *Dancer* had been my idea to start with, and they'd all too often made the difference between profit and loss in our always marginal business. But one of the reasons I had gone into space in the first place was to avoid having to make small talk with strangers, and I would rather solo through four cascade points in a row than spend those agonizing minutes at the entry portal. In this case, though, I had no choice. Tobbar, our master of drivel—and thus the man unofficially in charge of civilian small talk—was up to his elbows in grease and balky hydraulics; and my second choice, Alana Keal, had finally gotten through to an equally balky tower controller who wanted to bump us ten ships back in the lift pattern. Which left exactly one person—me—because there was no one else I'd trust with giving a good first impression of my ship to paying customers. And so I was the one standing on the ramp when Bradley and his eleven fellow passengers hoved into sight.

They ranged from semiscruffy to respectable-but-not-rich—about par for the *Dancer*—but even in such a diverse group Bradley stood out like a red light on the status board. He was reasonably good-looking, reasonably average in height and build; but there was something in the way he walked that immediately caught my attention. Sort of a cross between nervous fear and something I couldn't help but identify as swagger. The mix was so good that it was several seconds before it occurred to me how mutually contradictory the two impressions were, and the realization left me feeling more uncomfortable than I already did.

Bradley was eighth in line, with the result that my first seven greetings were carried out without a lot of attention from my conscious mind—which I'm sure only helped. Even standing still, I quickly discovered, Bradley's strangeness made itself apparent, both in his posture and also in his face and eyes. Especially his eyes.

Finally it was his turn at the head of the line. "Good morning, sir," I said, shaking his hand. "I'm Captain Pall Durriken. Welcome aboard."

"Thank you." His voice was bravely uncertain, the sort my mother used to describe as mousy. His eyes flicked the length of the *Dancer*, darted once into the portal, and returned to my face. "How often do ships like this crash?" he asked.

I hadn't expected any questions quite so blunt, but the fact that it was outside the realm of small talk made it easy to handle. "Hardly ever," I told him. "The last published figures showed a death rate of less than one per million passengers. You're more likely to be hit by a chunk of roof tile off the tower over there."

He actually cringed, turning halfway around to look at the tower. I hadn't dreamed he would take my comment so seriously, but before I could get my mouth working the man behind Bradley clapped a reassuring hand on his shoulder. "It's all right, Rik— nothing's going to hurt you. Really. This is a good ship, and we're going to be perfectly safe aboard her."

Bradley slowly straightened, and the other man shifted his attention to me. "I'm Dr. Hammerfeld Lanton, Captain," he said, extending his hand. "This is Rik Bradley. We're traveling in adjoining cabins."

"Of course," I said, nodding as if I'd already known that. In reality I hadn't had time to check out the passenger lists and assignments, but I could trust Leeds to have set things up properly. "Are you a doctor of medicine, sir?"

"In a way," Lanton said. "I'm a psychiatrist."

"Ah," I said, and managed two or three equally brilliant conversational gems before the two of them moved on. The last three passengers I dispatched with similar polish, and when everyone was inside I sealed the portal and headed for the bridge.

Alana had finished dickering with the tower and was running the prelift computer check when I arrived. "What's the verdict?" I asked as I slid into my chair and keyed for helm check.

"We've still got our lift slot," she said. "That's conditional on Matope getting the elevon system working within the next half hour, of course."

"Idiots," I muttered. The elevons wouldn't be needed until we arrived at Taimyr some six weeks from now, and Matope could practically rebuild them from scratch in that amount of time. To insist they be in prime condition before we could lift was unreasonable even for bureaucrats.

"Oh, there's no problem—Tobbar reported they were closing things up a few minutes ago. They'll put it through its paces, it'll work perfectly, they'll transmit the readout, and that'll be that." She cleared her throat. "Incidentally . . . are you aware we've got a skull-diver and his patient aboard?"

"Yes; I met—*patient?*" I interrupted myself as the last part of her sentence registered. "Who?"

"Name's Bradley," she said. "No further data on him, but apparently he and this Lanton character had a fair amount of electronic and medical stuff delivered to their cabins."

A small shiver ran up my back as I remembered Bradley's face. No wonder he'd struck me as strange. "No mention at all of what's wrong—of why Bradley needs a psychiatrist?"

"Nothing. But it can't be anything serious." The test board bleeped, and Alana paused to peer at the results. Apparently satisfied, she keyed in the next test on the check list. "The Swedish Psychiatric Institute seems to be funding the trip, and they presumably know the regulations about notifying us of potential health risks."

"Um." On the other hand, a small voice whispered in my ear, if there was some problem with Bradley that made him marginal for space certification, they were more likely to get away with slipping him aboard a tramp than on a liner. "Maybe I should give them a call, anyway. Unless you'd like to?"

I glanced over in time to see her face go stony. "No, thank you," she said firmly.

"Right." I felt ashamed of the comment, not really having meant it the way it had come out. All of us had our own reasons for being where we were; Alana's was an overdose of third-degree emotional burns. She was the type who'd seemingly been born to nurse broken wings and bruised souls, the type who by necessity kept her own heart in full view of both friends and passersby. Eventually, I gathered, one too many of her mended souls had torn out the emotional IVs she'd set up and flown off without so much as a backward glance, and she had renounced the whole business and run off to space. Ice to Europa, I'd thought once; there were enough broken wings out here for a whole shipload of Florence Nightingales. But what I'd expected to be a short vacation for her had become four years worth of armor plate over her emotions, until I wasn't sure she even knew anymore how to care for people. The last thing in the universe she would be interested in doing would be getting involved in any way with Bradley's problems. "Is all the cargo aboard now?" I asked, to change the subject.

"Yes, and Wilkinson certifies it's properly stowed."

"Good." I got to my feet. "I guess I'll make a quick spot survey of the ship, if you can handle things here."

"Go ahead," she said, not bothering to look up. Nodding anyway, I left.

I stopped first at the service shafts where Matope and Tobbar were just starting their elevon tests, staying long enough to satisfy myself the resulting data were adequate to please even the tower's bit-pickers. Then it was to each of the cargo holds to double-check Wilkinson's stowing arrangement, to the passenger area to make sure all their luggage had been properly brought on board, to the computer room to look into a reported malfunction—a false alarm, fortunately—and finally back to the bridge for the lift itself. Somehow, in all the running around, I never got around to calling Sweden. Not, as I found out later, that it would have done me any good.

We lifted right on schedule, shifting from the launch field's grav booster to ramjet at ten kilometers and kicking in the fusion drive as soon as it was legal to do so. Six hours later we were past Luna's orbit and ready for the first cascade maneuver.

Leeds checked in first, reporting officially that the proper number of dosages had been drawn from the sleeper cabinet and were being distributed to the passengers. Pascal gave the okay from the computer room, Matope from the engine room, and Sarojis from the small chamber housing the field generator itself. I had just pulled a hard copy of the computer's course instructions when Leeds called back. "Captain, I'm in Dr. Lanton's cabin," he said without preamble. "Both he and Mr. Bradley refuse to take their sleepers."

Alana turned at that, and I could read my own thought in her face: Lanton and Bradley had to be nuts. "Has Dr. Epstein explained the reasons behind the procedure?" I asked carefully, mindful of both my responsibilities and my limits here.

"Yes, I have," Kate Epstein's clear soprano came. "Dr. Lanton says that his work requires both of them to stay awake through the cascade point."

"Work? What sort of work?"

A pause, and Lanton's voice replaced Kate's. "Captain, this is Dr. Lanton. Rik and I are involved in an experimental type of therapy here. The personal details are confidential, but I assure you that it presents no danger either to us or to you."

Therapy. Great. I could feel anger starting to churn in my gut at Lanton's casual arrogance in neglecting to inform me ahead of time that he had more than transport in mind for my ship. By all rights I should freeze the countdown and sit Lanton down in a corner somewhere until I was convinced everything was as safe as he said. But time was money in this business; and if Lanton was glossing things over he could probably do so in finer detail than I could catch him on, anyway. "Mr. Bradley?" I called. "You agree to pass up your sleeper, as well?"

"Yes, sir," came the mousy voice.

"All right. Dr. Epstein, you and Mr. Leeds can go ahead and finish your rounds."

"Well," Alana said as I flipped off the intercom, "at least if something goes wrong the record will clear us of any fault at the inquest."

"You're a genuine ray of sunshine," I told her sourly. "What else could I have done?"

"Raked Lanton over the coals for some information. We're at least entitled to know what's going on."

"Oh, we'll find out, all right. As soon as we're through the point I'm going to haul Lanton up here for a long, cozy chat." I checked the readouts. Cascade point in seventeen minutes. "Look, you might as well go to your cabin and hit the sack. I know it's your turn, but you were up late with that spare parts delivery and you're due some downtime."

She hesitated; wanting to accept, no doubt, but slowed by considerations of duty. "Well . . . all right. I'm taking the next one, then. I don't know, though; maybe you shouldn't be up here alone. In case Lanton's miscalculated."

"You mean if Bradley goes berserk or something?" That thought had been lurking in my mind, too, though it sounded rather ridiculous when spoken out loud. Still . . . "I can lower the pressure in the passenger deck corridor to half an atmosphere. That'll be enough to lock the doors without triggering any vacuum alarms."

"Leaves Lanton on his own in case of trouble . . . but I suppose that's okay."

"He's the one who's so sure it's safe. Go on, now—get out of here."

She nodded and headed for the door. She paused there, though, her hand resting on the release. "Don't just haul Lanton away from Bradley when you want to talk to him," she called back over her shoulder. "Try to run into him in the lounge or somewhere instead when he's already alone. It might be hard on Bradley to know when you two were off somewhere together talking about him." She slapped the release, almost viciously, and was gone.

I stared after her for a long minute, wondering if I'd actually seen a crack in that heavy armor plate. The bleep of the intercom brought me back to the task at hand, Kate telling me the passengers were all down and that she, Leeds, and Wilkinson had taken their own sleepers. One by one the other six crewers also checked in. Within ten minutes they would be asleep, and I would be in sole charge of my ship.

Twelve minutes to go. Even with the *Dancer*'s old manual setup there was little that needed to be done. I laid the hard copy of the computer's instructions where it would be legible but not in the way, shut down all the external sensors and control surfaces, and put the computer and other electronic equipment into neutral/standby mode. The artificial gravity I left on; I'd tried a cascade point without it once and would never do so again. Then I waited, trying not to think of what was coming . . . and at the appropriate time I lifted the safety cover and twisted the field generator control knob.

And suddenly there were five of us in the room.

I will never understand how the first person to test the Colloton Drive ever made it past this point. The images silently surrounding me a bare arm's length away were life-size, lifelike, and—at first glance, anyway—as solid as the panels and chairs they seemed to have displaced. It took a careful look to realize they were actually slightly transparent, like some kind of colored glass, and a little experimentation at that point would show they had less substance than air. They were nothing but ghosts, specters straight out of childhood's scariest stories. Which merely added to the discomfort . . . because all of them were me.

Five seconds later the second set of images appeared, perfectly aligned with the first. After that they came more and more quickly, as the spacing between them similarly decreased, forming an ever-expanding horizontal cross with me at the center. I watched—forced myself to watch—knew I *had* to watch—as the lines continued to lengthen, watched until they were so long that I could no longer discern whether any more were being added.

I took a long, shuddering breath—peripherally aware that the images nearest me were doing the same—and wiped a shaking hand across my forehead. *You don't have to look,* I told myself, eyes rigidly fixed on the back of the image in front of me. *You've seen it all before. What's the point?* But I'd fought this fight before, and I knew in advance I would lose. There was indeed no more point to it than there was to pressing a bruise, but it held an equal degree of compulsion. Bracing myself, I turned my head and gazed down the line of images strung out to my left.

The armchair philosophers may still quibble over what the cascade point images "really" are, but those of us who fly the small ships figured it out long ago. The Colloton field puts us into a different type of space, possibly an entire universe worth of it—that much is established fact. Somehow this space links us into a set of alternate realities, universes that might have been if things had gone differently . . . and what I was therefore seeing around me were images of what I would be doing in each of those universes.

Sure, the theory has problems. Obviously, I should generate a separate pseudo-reality every time I choose ham instead of turkey for lunch, and just as obviously such trivial changes don't make it into the pattern. Only the four images closest to me are ever exactly my doubles; even the next ones in line are noticeably if subtly different. But it's not a matter of subconscious suggestion, either. Too many of the images are . . . unexpected . . . for that.

It was no great feat to locate the images I particularly needed to see: the white-and-gold liner captain's uniforms stood out brilliantly among the more dingy jumpsuits and coveralls on either side. Liner captain. In charge of a fully equipped, fully modernized ship; treated with the respect and admiration such a position brought. It could have been—*should* have been. And to make things worse, I knew the precise decision that had lost it to me.

It had been eight years now since the uniforms had appeared among my cascade images; ten since the day I'd thrown Lord Hendrik's son off the bridge of the training ship and simultaneously guaranteed myself a blackballing with every major company in the business. Could I have handled the situation differently? Probably. Should I have? Given the state of the art then, no. A man who, after three training missions, still went borderline claustrophobic every time he had to stay awake through a cascade point had no business aboard a ship, let alone on its bridge. Hendrik might have forgiven me once he thought things through. The kid, who was forced into a ground position with the firm, never did. Eventually, of course, he took over the business.

I had no way of knowing that four years later the Aker-Ming Autotorque would eliminate the need for *anyone* to stay awake through cascade maneuvers. I doubt seriously the kid appreciated the irony of it all.

In the eight years since the liner captain uniforms had appeared they had been gradually moving away from me along all four arms of the cross. Five more years, I estimated, and they would be far enough down the line to disappear into the mass of images crowded together out there. Whether my reaction to that event would be relief or sadness I didn't yet know, but there was no doubt in my mind that it would in some way be the end of a chapter in my life. I gazed at

the figures for another minute . . . and then, with my ritual squeezing of the bruise accomplished, I let my eyes drift up and down the
rest of the line.

They were unremarkable, for the most part: minor variations in my
appearance or clothing. The handful that had once showed me in
some nonspacing job had long since vanished toward infinity; I'd
been out here a long time. Perhaps too long . . . a thought the half
dozen or so gaps in each arm of the pattern underlined with unnecessary force. I'd told Bradley that ships like the *Dancer* rarely crashed,
a perfectly true statement; but what I hadn't mentioned was that the
chances of simply disappearing en route were something rather
higher. None of us liked to think about that, especially during critical
operations like cascade point maneuvers. But the gaps in the image
pattern were a continual reminder that people still died in space. In
six possible realities, apparently, I'd made a decision that killed me.

Taking another deep breath, I forced all of that as far from my
mind as I could and activated the *Dancer*'s flywheel.

Even on the bridge the hum was audible as the massive chunk of
metal began to spin. A minute later it had reached its top speed . . .
and the entire ship's counterrotation began to register on the gyroscope set behind glass in the ceiling above my head. The device
looked out of place, a decided anachronism among the modern
instruments, control circuits, and readouts filling the bridge. But
using it was the only way a ship our size could find its way safely
through a cascade point. The enhanced electron tunneling effect that
fouled up electronic instrument performance was well understood;
what was still needed was a way to predict the precise effect a given
cascade point rotation would generate. Without such predictability,
readings couldn't even be given adjustment factors. Cascade nav-
igation thus had to fall back on gross electrical and purely mechan-
ical systems: flywheel, physical gyroscope, simple on-off controls,
and a nonelectronic decision-maker. Me.

Slowly, the long needle above me crept around its dial. I watched
its reflection carefully in the magnifying mirror, a system that allowed me to see the indicator without having to break my neck
looking up over my shoulder. Around me, the cascade images did
their own slow dance, a strange kaleidoscopic thing that moved the
images and gaps around within each branch of the cross, while the
branches themselves remained stationary relative to me. The effect

was unexplained; but then, Colloton field theory left a lot of things unexplained. Mathematically, the basic idea was relatively straightforward: the space we were in right now could be described by a type of bilinear conformal mapping—specifically, a conjugate inversion that maps lines into circles. From that point it was all downhill, the details tangling into a soup of singularities, branch points, and confluent Riemann surfaces; but what it all eventually boiled down to was that a yaw rotation of the ship here would become a linear translation when I shut down the field generator and we reentered normal space. The *Dancer's* rotation was coming up on two degrees now, which for the particular configuration we were in meant we were already about half a light-year closer to our destination. Another—I checked the printout—one point three six and I would shut down the flywheel, letting the *Dancer's* momentum carry her an extra point two degree for a grand total of eight light-years.

The needle crept to the mark, and I threw the flywheel switch, simultaneously giving my full attention over to the gyro. Theoretically, over- or undershooting the mark could be corrected during the next cascade point—or by fiddling the flywheel back and forth now—but it was simpler not to have to correct at all. The need to make sure we were stationary was another matter entirely; if the *Dancer* were still rotating when I threw the field switch we would wind up strung out along a million kilometers or more of space. I thought of the gaps in my cascade image pattern and shivered.

But that was as close as death was going to get to me, at least this time. The delicately balanced spin lock worked exactly as it was supposed to, freezing the field switch in place until the ship's rotation was as close to zero as made no difference. I shut off the field and watched my duplicates disappear in reverse order, waiting until the last four vanished before confirming the stars were once again visible through the bridge's tiny viewport. I sighed; and fighting the black depression that always seized me at this point, I turned the *Dancer's* systems back on and set the computer to figuring our exact position. Someday, I thought, I'd be able to afford to buy Aker-Ming Autotorques and never, *never* have to go through this again.

And someday I'd swim the Pacific Ocean, too.

Slumping back in my chair, I waited for the computer to finish its job and allowed the tears to flow.

*   *   *

Crying, for me, has always been the simplest and fastest way of draining off tension, and I've always felt a little sorry for men who weren't able to appreciate its advantages. This time was no exception, and I was feeling almost back to normal by the time the computer produced its location figures. I was still poring over them twenty minutes later when Alana returned to the bridge. "Another cascade point successfully hurdled, I see," she commented tiredly. "Hurray for our side."

"I thought you were supposed to be taking a real nap, not just a sleeper's worth," I growled at her over my shoulder.

"I woke up and decided to take a walk," she answered, her voice suddenly businesslike. "What's wrong?"

I handed her a printout, pointed to the underlined numbers. "The gyroscope reading says we're theoretically dead on position. The stars say we're short."

"Wumph!" Frowning intently at the paper, she kicked around the other chair and sat down. "Twenty light-days. That's what, twice the expected error for this point? Great. You double-checked everything, of course?"

"Triple-checked. The computer confirmed the gyro reading, and the astrogate program's got positive ident on twenty stars. Margin of error's no greater than ten light-minutes on either of those."

"Yeah." She eyed me over the pages. "Anything funny in the cargo?"

I gestured to the manifest in front of me. "We've got three boxes of technical equipment that include Ming metal," I said. "All three are in the shield. I checked that before we lifted."

"Maybe the shield's sprung a leak," she suggested doubtfully.

"It's supposed to take a hell of a break before the stuff inside can affect cascade point configuration."

"I can go check if you'd like."

"No, don't bother. There's no rush now, and Wilkinson's had more experience with shield boxes. He can take a look when he wakes up. I'd rather you stay here and help me do a complete programming check. Unless you'd like to obey orders and go back to bed."

She smiled faintly. "No, thanks; I'll stay. Um . . . I could even start things along if you'd like to go to the lounge for a while."

"I'm fine," I growled, irritated by the suggestion.

"I know," she said. "But Lanton was down there alone when I passed by on my way here."

I'd completely forgotten about Lanton and Bradley, and it took a couple of beats for me to catch on. Cross-examining a man in the middle of cascade depression wasn't a terrifically nice thing to do, but I wasn't feeling terrifically nice at the moment. "Start with the astrogate program," I told Alana, getting to my feet. "Give me a shout if you find anything."

Lanton was still alone in the lounge when I arrived. "Doctor," I nodded to him as I sat down in the chair across from his. "How are you feeling?" The question was more for politeness than information; the four empty glasses on the end table beside him and the half-full one in his hand showed how he'd chosen to deal with his depression. I'd learned long ago that crying was easier on the liver.

He managed a weak smile. "Better, Captain; much better. I was starting to think I was the only one left on the ship."

"You're not even the only one awake," I said. "The other passengers will be wandering in shortly—you people get a higher-dose sleeper than the crew takes."

He shook his head. "Lord, but that was weird. No wonder you want everyone to sleep through it. I can't remember the last time I felt this rotten."

"It'll pass," I assured him. "How did Mr. Bradley take it?"

"Oh, fine. Much better than I did, though he fell apart just as badly when it was over. I gave him a sedative—the coward's way out, but I wasn't up to more demanding therapy at the moment."

So Bradley wasn't going to be walking in on us anytime soon. Good. "Speaking of therapy, Doctor, I think you owe me a little more information about what you're doing."

He nodded and took a swallow from his glass. "Beginning, I suppose, with what exactly Rik is suffering from?"

"That would be nice," I said, vaguely surprised at how civil I was being. Somehow, the sight of Lanton huddled miserably with his liquor had taken all the starch out of my fire-and-brimstone mood. Alana was clearly having a bad effect on me.

"Okay. Well, first and foremost, he is *not* in any way dangerous, either to himself or other people. He has no tendencies even remotely suicidal or homicidal. He's simply . . . permanently disoriented, I suppose, is one way to think of it. His personality seems to

slide around in strange ways, generating odd fluctuations in behavior and perception."

Explaining psychiatric concepts in layman's terms obviously
wasn't Lanton's forte. "You mean he's schizophrenic? Or para-
noid?" I added, remembering our launch-field conversation.

"Yes and no. He shows some of the symptoms of both—along
with those of five or six other maladies—but he doesn't demonstrate
the proper biochemical syndrome for any known mental disease.
He's a fascinating, scientifically annoying anomaly. I've got whole
bubble-packs of data on him, taken over the past five years, and I'm
convinced I'm teetering on the edge of a breakthrough. But I've
already exhausted all the standard ways of probing a patient's
subconscious, and I had to come up with something new." He
gestured around him. "This is it."

"This is what? A new form of shock therapy?"

"No, no—you're missing the point. I'm studying Rik's cascade
images."

I stared at him for a long moment. Then, getting to my feet, I went
to the autobar and drew myself a lager. "With all due respect," I said
as I sat down again, "I think you're out of your mind. First of all, the
images aren't a product of the deep subconscious or whatever;
they're reflections of universes that might have been."

"Perhaps. There is some argument about that." He held up a hand
as I started to object. "But either way, you have to admit that your
conscious or unconscious mind must have an influence on them.
Invariably, the images that appear show the results of major decisions or events in one's life; never the plethora of insignificant
choices we all make. Whether the subconscious is choosing among
actual images or generating them by itself, it is involved with them
and therefore can be studied through them."

He seemed to settle slightly in his chair, and I got the feeling this
wasn't the first time he'd made that speech.

"Even if I grant you all that," I said, "which I'm not sure I do, I
think you're running an incredibly stupid risk that the cascade point
effects will give Bradley a shove right over the edge. They're hard
enough on those of us who haven't got psychological problems—
what am I telling you this for? You saw what it was like, damn it. The
last thing I want on my ship is someone who's going to need either
complete sedation or a restraint couch all the way to Taimyr!"

I stopped short, suddenly aware that my volume had been steadily increasing. "Sorry," I muttered, draining half of my lager. "Like I said, cascade points are hard on all of us."

He frowned. "What do you mean? You were asleep with everyone else, weren't you?"

"Somebody's got to be awake to handle the maneuver," I said.

"But . . . I thought there were autopilots for cascade points now."

"Sure—the Aker-Ming Autotorque. But they cost nearly twenty-two thousand apiece and have to be replaced every hundred cascade points or so. The big liners and freighters can afford luxuries like that; tramp starmers can't."

"I'm sorry—I didn't know." His expression suggested he was also sorry he hadn't investigated the matter more thoroughly before booking aboard the *Dancer*.

I'd seen that look on people before, and I always hated it. "Don't worry; you're perfectly safe. The manual method's been used for nearly two centuries, and my crew and I know what we're doing."

His mind was obviously still a half kilometer back. "But how can it be that expensive? I mean, Ming metal's an exotic alloy, sure, but it's only selenium with a little bit of rhenium, after all. You can buy psy-test equipment with Ming-metal parts for a fraction of the cost you quoted."

"And we've got an entire box made of the stuff in our number one cargo hold," I countered. "But making a consistent-property rotation gauge is a good deal harder than rolling sheets or whatever. Anyway, you're evading my question. What are you going to do if Bradley can't take the strain?"

He shrugged, but I could see he didn't take the possibility seriously. "If worst comes to worst, I suppose I could let him sleep while I stayed awake to observe his images. They *do* show up even in your sleep, don't they?"

"So I've heard." I didn't add that I'd feel like a voyeur doing something like that. Psychiatrists, accustomed to poking into other people's minds, clearly had different standards than I did.

"Good. Though that would add another variable," he added thoughtfully. "Well . . . I think Rik can handle it. We'll do it conscious as long as we can."

"And what's going to be your clue that he's *not* handling it? The

first time he tries to strangle one of his images? Or maybe when he
goes catatonic?"

He gave me an irritated look. "Captain, I *am* a psychiatrist. I'm
perfectly capable of reading my patient and picking up any signs of
trouble before they become serious. Rik is going to be all right; let's
just leave it at that."

I had no intention of leaving it at that; but just then two more of
the passengers wandered into the lounge, so I nodded to Lanton and
left. We had five days before the next cascade point, and there would
be other opportunities in that time to discuss the issue. If necessary,
I would manufacture them.

Alana had only negatives for me when I got back to the bridge. "The
astrogate's clean," she told me. "I've pulled a hard copy of the
program to check, but the odds that a glitch developed that just
happened to look reasonable enough to fool the diagnostic are
essentially nil." She waved at the long gyroscope needle above us.
"Computer further says the vacuum in the gyro chamber stayed
hard throughout the maneuver and that there was no malfunction
of the mag-bearing fields."

So the gyroscope hadn't been jinxed by friction into giving a false
reading. Combined with the results on the astrogate program, that
left damn few places to look. "Has Wilkinson checked in?"

"Yes, and I've got him testing the shield for breaks."

"Good. I'll go down and give him a hand. Have you had time to
check out our current course?"

"Not in detail, but the settings look all right to me."

"They did to me, too, but if there's any chance the computer's
developed problems we can't take anything for granted. I don't want
to be in the wrong position when it's time for the next point."

"Yeah. Well, Pascal's due up here in ten minutes. I guess the
astrogate deep-check can wait until then. What did you find out
from Lanton?"

With an effort I switched gears. "According to him, Bradley's not
going to be any trouble. He sounds more neurotic than psychotic,
from Lanton's description, at least at the moment. Unfortunately,
Lanton's got this great plan to use cascade images as a research tool,
and intends to keep Bradley awake through every point between
here and Taimyr."

"He *what*? I don't suppose he's bothered to consider what that might do to Bradley's problems?"

"That's what *I* wanted to know. I never did get an acceptable answer." I moved to the bridge door, poked the release. "Don't worry, we'll pound some sense into him before the next point. See you later."

Wilkinson and Sarojis were both in the number one hold when I arrived, Sarojis offering minor assistance and lots of suggestions as Wilkinson crawled over the shimmery metal box that took up the forward third of the narrow space. Looking down at me as I threaded my way between the other boxes cramming the hold, he shook his head. "Nothing wrong here, Cap'n," he said. "The shield's structurally sound; there's no way the Ming metal inside could affect our configuration."

"No chance of hairline cracks?" I asked.

He held up the detector he'd been using. "I'm checking, but nothing that small would do anything."

I nodded acknowledgment and spent a moment frowning at the box. Ming metal had a number of unique properties inside cascade points, properties that made it both a blessing and a curse to those of us who had to fly with it. Its unique blessing, of course, was that its electrical, magnetic, and thermodynamic properties were affected only by the absolute angle the ship rotated through, and not by any of the hundred or so other variables in a given cascade maneuver. It was this predictability that finally had made it possible for a cascade point autodrive mechanism to be developed. Of more concern to smaller ships like mine, though, was that Ming metal drastically changed a ship's "configuration"—the size, shape, velocity profile, and so on from which the relation between rotation angle and distance traveled on a given maneuver could be computed. Fortunately, the effect was somewhat analogous to air resistance, in that if one piece of Ming metal were completely enclosed in another, only the outer container's shape, size, and mass would affect the configuration. Hence, the shield. But if it hadn't been breached, then the cargo inside it couldn't have fouled us up. . . . "What are the chances," I asked Wilkinson, "that one of these other boxes contains Ming metal?"

"Without listing it on the manifest?" Sarojis piped up indignantly. He was a dark, intense little man who always seemed loudly as-

tonished whenever anyone did anything either unjust or stupid.
Most everyone on the *Dancer* OD'd periodically on his chatter and
spent every third day or so avoiding him. Alana and Wilkinson were
the only exceptions I knew of, and even Alana got tired of him every
so often. "They couldn't do that," Sarojis continued before I could
respond. "We could sue them into bankruptcy."

"Only if we make it to Taimyr," I said briefly, my eyes on Wilkinson.

"One way to find out," he returned. Dropping lightly off the
shield, he replaced his detector in the open tool box lying on the deck
and withdrew a wand-like gadget.

It took two hours to run the wand over every crate in the *Dancer*'s
three holds, and we came up with precisely nothing. "Maybe one of
the passengers brought some aboard," Sarojis suggested.

"You've got to be richer than any of *our* customers to buy cases
with Ming-metal buckles." Wilkinson shook his head. "Cap'n, it's
got to be a computer fault, or else something in the gyro."

"Um," I said noncommittally. I hadn't yet told them that I'd
checked with Alana midway through all the cargo testing and that
she and Pascal had found nothing wrong in their deep-checks of both
systems. There was no point in worrying them more than necessary.

I returned to the bridge to find Pascal there alone, slouching in the
helm chair and gazing at the displays with a dreamy sort of expression on his face. "Where's Alana?" I asked him, dropping into the
other chair and eyeing the pile of diagnostic printouts they'd
thoughtfully left for me. "Finally gone to bed?"

"She said she was going to stop by the dining room first and have
some dinner," Pascal said, the dreamy expression fading somewhat. "Something about meeting the passengers."

I glanced at my watch, realizing with a start that it was indeed
dinnertime. "Maybe I'll go on down, too. Any problems here, first?"

He shook his head. "I have a theory about the cascade point
error," he said, lowering his voice conspiratorially. "I'd rather not
say what it is, though, until I've had more time to think about it."

"Sure," I said, and left. Pascal fancied himself a great scientific
detective and was always coming up with complex and wholly
unrealistic theories in areas far outside his field, with predictable
results. Still, nothing he'd ever come up with had been actually

dangerous, and there was always the chance he would someday hit on something useful. I hoped this would be the day.

The *Dancer*'s compact dining room was surprisingly crowded for so soon after the first cascade point, but a quick scan of the faces showed me why. Only nine of our twelve passengers had made it out of bed after their first experience with sleepers, but their absence was more than made up for by the six crewers who had opted to eat here tonight instead of in the duty mess. The entire off-duty contingent . . . and it wasn't hard to figure out why.

Bradley, seated between Lanton and Tobbar at one of the two tables, was speaking earnestly as I slipped through the door. ". . . less symbolic than it was an attempt to portray the world from a truly alien viewpoint, a viewpoint he would change every few years. Thus *A Midsummer Wedding* has both the slight fish-eye distortion *and* the color shifts you might get from a water-dwelling creature; also the subtleties of posture and expression that such an alien would understand and might therefore not get right."

"But isn't strange sensory expression one of the basic foundations of art?" That was Tobbar—so glib on any topic that you were never quite sure whether he actually knew anything about it or not. "Drawing both eyes on one side of the head, putting nudes at otherwise normal picnics—that sort of thing."

"True, but you mustn't confuse weirdness for its own sake, with the consistent, scientifically accurate variations Meyerhäus used."

There was more, but just then Alana caught my eye from her place at the other table and indicated the empty seat next to her. I went over and sat down, losing the train of Bradley's monologue in the process. "Anything?" she whispered to me.

"A very flat zero," I told her.

She nodded once but didn't say anything, and I noticed her gaze drift back to Bradley. "Knows a lot about art, I see," I commented, oddly irritated by her shift in attention.

"You missed his talk on history," she said. "He got quite a discussion going over there—that mathematician, Dr. Chileogu, also seems to be a history buff. First time I've ever seen Tobbar completely frozen out of a discussion. He certainly seems normal enough."

"Tobbar?"

"Bradley."

"Oh." I looked over at Bradley, who was now listening intently to someone holding forth from the other end of his table. *Permanently disoriented*, Lanton had described him. Was he envisioning himself a professor of art or something right now? Or were his delusions that complete? I didn't know; and at the moment I didn't care. "Well, good for him. Now if you'd care to bring your mind back to ship's business, we still have a problem on our hands."

Alana turned back to me, a slight furrow across her forehead. "I'm open to suggestions," she said. "I was under the impression that we were stuck for the moment."

I clenched my jaw tightly over the retort that wanted to come out. We *were* stuck; and until someone else came up with an idea there really wasn't any reason why Alana shouldn't be down here relaxing. "Yeah," I growled, getting to my feet. "Well, keep thinking about it."

"Aren't you going to eat?"

"I'll get something later in the duty mess," I said.

I paused at the door and glanced back. Already her attention was back on Bradley. Heading back upstairs to the duty mess, I programmed myself an unimaginative meal that went down like so much wet cardboard. Afterwards, I went back to my cabin and pulled a tape on cascade point theory.

I was still paging through it two hours later when I fell asleep.

I tried several times in the next five days to run into Lanton on his own, but it seemed that every time I saw him Bradley was tagging along like a well-behaved cocker spaniel. Eventually, I was forced to accept Alana's suggestion that she and Tobbar offer Bradley a tour of the ship, giving me a chance to waylay Lanton in the corridor outside his cabin. The psychiatrist seemed preoccupied and a little annoyed at being so accosted, but I didn't let it bother me.

"No, of course there's no progress yet," he said in response to my question. "I also didn't expect any. The first cascade point observations were my baseline. I'll be asking questions during the next one, and after that I'll start introducing various treatment techniques and observing Rik's reactions to them."

He started to slide past me, but I moved to block him. "Treatment? You never said anything about treatment."

"I didn't think I had to. I *am* legally authorized to administer drugs and such, after all."

"Maybe on the ground," I told him stiffly. "But out here the ship's doctor is the final medical authority. You will *not* give Bradley any drugs or electronic treatment without first clearing it with Dr. Epstein." Something tugged at my mind, but I couldn't be bothered with tracking it down. "As a matter of fact, I want you to give her a complete list of all the drugs you've brought aboard before the next cascade point. Anything addictive or potentially dangerous is to be turned over to her for storage in the sleeper cabinet. Understand?"

Lanton's expression stuck somewhere between irritated and stunned. "Oh, come on, Captain, be reasonable—practically every medicine in the book can be dangerous if taken in excessive doses." His face seemed to recover, settling into a bland sort of neutral as his voice similarly adjusted to match it. "Why do you object so strongly to what I'm trying to do for Rik?"

"I'd hurry with that list, Doctor—the next point's scheduled for tomorrow. Good day." Spinning on my heel, I turned and stalked away.

I called back Kate Epstein as soon as I reached my cabin and told her about the list Lanton would be delivering to her. I got the impression that she, too, thought I was overreacting, but she nevertheless agreed to cooperate. I extracted a promise to keep me informed on what Lanton's work involved, then signed off and returned once more to the Colloton theory tapes that had occupied the bulk of my time the past four days.

But despite the urgency I was feeling—we had less than twenty hours to the next cascade point—the words on my reader screen refused to coalesce into anything that made sense. I gritted my teeth and kept at it until I discovered myself reading the same paragraph for the fourth time and still not getting a word of it. Snapping off my reader in disgust, I stretched out on my bed and tried to track down the source of my distraction.

Obviously, my irritation at Lanton was a good fraction of it. Along with the high-handed way he treated the whole business of Bradley, he'd now added the insult of talking to me in a tone of voice that implied I needed his professional services—and for nothing worse than insisting on my rights as captain of the *Dancer*. I wished to hell

I'd paid more attention to the passenger manifest before I'd let the two of them aboard. Next time I'd know better.

Still . . . I had to admit that maybe I *had* overreacted a bit. But it wasn't as if I was being short-tempered without reason. I had plenty of reasons to be worried: Lanton's game of cascade image tag and its possible effects on Bradley; the still-unexplained discrepancy in the last point's maneuvers; the changes I was seeing in Alana—

Alana. Up until that moment I hadn't consciously admitted to myself that she was behaving any differently than usual. But I hadn't flown with her for four years without knowing all of her moods and tendencies, and it was abundantly clear to me that she was slowly getting involved with Bradley.

My anger over such an unexpected turn of events was not in any way motivated by jealousy. Alana was her own woman, and any part of her life not directly related to her duties was none of my business. But I knew that, in this case, her involvement was more than likely her old affinity for broken wings, rising like the phoenix—except that the burning would come afterwards instead of beforehand. I didn't want to see Alana go through that again, especially with someone whose presence I felt responsible for. There was, of course, little I could do directly without risking Alana's notice and probable anger; but I could let Lanton know how I felt by continuing to make things as difficult as possible. And I would.

And with that settled, I managed to push it aside and return to my studies. It is, I suppose, revealing that it never occurred to me at the time how inconsistent my conclusion and proposed course of action really were. After all, the faster Lanton cured Bradley, the faster the broken-wing attraction would disappear and—presumably—the easier Alana would be able to extricate herself. Perhaps, even then, I was secretly starting to wonder if her attraction to him was something more than altruistic.

"Two minutes," Alana said crisply from my right, her tone almost but not quite covering the tension I knew she must be feeling. "Gyro checks out perfectly."

I made a minor adjustment in my mirror, confirmed that the long needle was set dead on zero. Behind the mirror, the displays stared blankly at me from the control board, their systems having long since been shut down. I looked at the computer's printout, the field generator control cover, my own hands—anything to keep from looking at Alana. Like me, she was unaccustomed to company during a cascade point, and I was determined to give her what little privacy I could.

"One minute," she said. "You sure we made up enough distance for this to be safe?"

"Positive. The only possible trouble could have come from Epsilon Eridani, and we've made up enough lateral distance to put it the requisite six degrees off our path."

"Do you suppose that could have been the trouble last time? Could we have come too close to something—a black dwarf, maybe, that drifted into our corridor?"

I shrugged, eyes on the clock. "Not according to the charts. Ships have been going to Taimyr a long time, you know, and the whole route's been pretty thoroughly checked out. Even black dwarfs have to come *from* somewhere." Gritting my teeth, I flipped the cover off the knob. "Brace yourself; here we go."

Doing a cascade point alone invites introspection, memories of times long past, and melancholy. Doing it with someone else adds instant vertigo and claustrophobia to the list. Alana's images and mine still appeared in the usual horizontal cross shape, but since we weren't seated facing exactly the same direction, they didn't overlap. The result was a suffocatingly crowded bridge—crowded, to make things worse, with images that were no longer tied to your own motions, but would twitch and jerk apparently on their own.

For me, the disadvantages far outweighed the single benefit of having someone there to talk to, but in this case I had had little choice. Alana had steadfastly refused to let me take over from her on two points in a row, and I'd been equally insistent on being awake to watch the proceedings. It was a lousy compromise, but I'd known better than to order Alana off the bridge. She had her pride too.

"Activating flywheel."

Alana's voice brought my mind back to business. I checked the printout one last time, then turned my full attention to the gyro needle. A moment later it began its slow creep, and the dual set of cascade images started into their own convoluted dances. Swallowing hard, I gave my stomach stern orders and held on.

It seemed at times to be lasting forever, but finally it was over. The *Dancer* had been rotated, had been brought to a stop, and had successfully made the transition to real space. I slumped in my seat, feeling a mixture of cascade depression and only marginally decreased tension. The astrogate program's verdict, after all, was still to come.

But I was spared the ordeal of waiting with twiddled thumbs for the computer. Alana had barely gotten the ship's systems going again when the intercom bleeped at me. "Bridge," I answered.

"This is Dr. Lanton," the tight response came. "There's something very wrong with the power supply to my cabin—one of my instruments just burned out on me."

"Is it on fire?" I asked sharply, eyes flicking to the status display. Nothing there indicated any problem.

"Oh, no—there was just a little smoke and that's gone now. But the thing's ruined."

"Well, I'm sorry, Doctor," I said, trying to sound like I meant it. "But I can't be responsible for damage to electronics that are left running through a cascade point. Even something as simple as an AC power line can show small voltage fluc—*oh, damn it!*"

Alana jerked at my exclamation. "What—"

"Lanton!" I snapped, already halfway out of my seat. "Stay put and *don't touch anything.* I'm coming down."

His reply was more question than acknowledgment, but I ignored it. "Alana," I called to her, "call Wilkinson and have him meet me at Lanton's cabin—and tell him to bring a Ming-metal detector."

I caught just a glimpse of her suddenly horrified expression before the door slid shut and I went running down the corridor. There was no reason to run, but I did so anyway.

It was there, of course: a nice, neat Ming-metal dual crossover coil, smack in the center of the ruined neural tracer. At least it *had* been neat; now it was stained with a sticky goo that had dripped onto it from the blackened circuit board above. "Make sure none of it melted off onto something else," I told Wilkinson as he carefully removed the coil. "If it has we'll either have to gut the machine or find a way to squeeze it inside the shield." He nodded and I stepped over to where Lanton was sitting, the white-hot anger inside me completely overriding my usual depression. "What the *hell* did you think you were doing, bringing that damn thing aboard?" I thundered, dimly aware that the freshly sedated Bradley might hear me from the next cabin but not giving a damn.

His voice, when he answered, was low and artificially calm—whether in stunned reaction to my rage or simply a reflexive habit I didn't know. "I'm very sorry, Captain, but I swear I didn't know the tracer had any Ming metal in it."

"Why not? You told me yourself you could buy things with Ming-metal parts." And I'd let that fact sail blithely by me, a blunder on my part that was probably fueling ninety percent of my anger.

"But I never see the manufacturing specs on anything I use," he said. "It all comes through the Institute's receiving department, and all I get are the operating manuals and such." His eyes flicked to his machine as if he were going to object to Wilkinson's manhandling of it. "I guess they must have removed any identification tags, as well."

"I guess they must have," I ground out. Wilkinson had the coil out now, and I watched as he laid it aside and picked up the detector wand again. A minute later he shook his head.

"Clean, Cap'n," he told me, picking up the coil again. "I'll take this one to One Hold and put it away."

I nodded and he left. Gesturing to the other gadgets spread around the room, I asked, "Is this all you've got, or is there more in Bradley's cabin?"

"No, this is it," Lanton assured me.

"What about your stereovision camera? I know some of those have Ming metal in them."

He frowned. "I don't have any cameras. Who told you I did?"

"I—" I frowned in turn. "You said you were studying Bradley's cascade images."

"Yes, but you can't take pictures of them. They don't register on any kind of film."

I opened my mouth, closed it again. I was sure I'd known that once, but after years of watching the images I'd apparently clean forgotten it. They were so lifelike . . . and I was perhaps getting old. "I assumed someone had come up with a technique that worked," I said stiffly, acutely aware that my attempt to save face wasn't fooling either of us. "How *do* you do it, then?"

"I memorize all of it, of course. Psychiatrists have to have good memories, you know, and there are several drugs that can enhance one's basic abilities."

I'd heard of mnemonic drugs. They were safe, extremely effective, and cost a small fortune. "Do you have any of them with you? If so, I'm going to insist they be locked away."

He shook his head. "I was given a six-month treatment at the Institute before we left. That's the main reason we're on your ship, by the way, instead of something specially chartered. Mnemonic drugs play havoc with otherwise reasonable budgets."

He was making a joke, of course, but it was an exceedingly tasteless one, and the anger that had been draining out of me reversed its flow. No one needed to remind me that the *Dancer* wasn't up to the Cunard line's standards. "My sympathies to your budget," I said briefly. Turning away, I strode to the door.

"Wait a minute," he called after me. "What are my chances of getting that neural tracer fixed?"

I glanced back over my shoulder. "That probably depends on how good you are with a screwdriver and solder gun," I said, and left.

Alana was over her own cascade depression by the time I returned to the bridge. "I was right," I said as I dropped into my seat. "One of the damned black boxes had a Ming-metal coil."

"I know; Wilkinson called from One Hold." She glanced sideways at me. "I hope you didn't chew Lanton out in front of Bradley."

"Why not?"

"Did you?"

"As it happens, no. Lanton sedated him right after the point again. Why does it matter?"

"Well . . ." She seemed embarrassed. "It might . . . upset him to see you angry. You see, he sort of looks up to you—captain of a star ship and all—"

"Captain of a struggling tramp," I corrected her more harshly than was necessary. "Or didn't you bother to tell him that we're the absolute bottom of the line?"

"I told him," she said steadily. "But he doesn't see things that way. Even in five days aboard he's had a glimpse of how demanding this kind of life is. He's never been able to hold down a good job himself for very long, and that adds to the awe he feels for all of us."

"I can tell he's got a lot to learn about the universe," I snorted. For some reason the conversation was making me nervous, and I hurried to bring it back to safer regions. "Did your concern for Bradley's idealism leave you enough time to run the astrogate?"

She actually blushed, the first time in years I'd seen her do that.

"Yes," she said stiffly. "We're about thirty-two light-days short this time."

"Damn." I hammered the edge of the control board once with my clenched fist, and then began punching computer keys.

"I've already checked that," Alana spoke up. "We'll dig pretty deep into our fuel reserve if we try to make it up through normal space."

I nodded, my fingers coming to a halt. My insistence on maintaining a high fuel reserve was one of the last remnants of Lord Hendrik's training that I still held on to, and despite occasional ribbing from other freighter captains I felt it was a safety precaution worth taking. The alternative to using it, though, wasn't especially pleasant. "All right," I sighed. "Let's clear out enough room for the computer to refigure our course profile. If possible, I'd like to tack the extra fifty light-days onto one of the existing points instead of adding a new one."

She nodded and started typing away at her console as I called down to the engine room to alert Matope. It was a semi-major pain, but the *Dancer*'s computer didn't have enough memory space to handle the horribly complex Colloton calculations we needed while all the standard operations programming was in place. We would need to shift all but the most critical functions to Matope's manual control, replacing the erased programs later from Pascal's set of master tapes.

It took nearly an hour to get the results, but they turned out to be worth the wait. Not only could we make up our shortfall without an extra point, but with the slightly different stellar configuration we faced now it was going to be possible to actually shorten the duration of one of the points further down the line. That was good news from both practical and psychological considerations. Though I've never been able to prove it, I've long believed that the deepest depressions follow the longest points.

I didn't see any more of Lanton that day, though I heard later that he and Bradley had mingled with the passengers as they always did, Lanton behaving as if nothing at all had happened. Though I knew my crew wasn't likely to go around blabbing about Lanton's Ming-metal blunder, I issued an order anyway to keep the whole matter quiet. It wasn't to save Lanton any embarrassment—that much I was certain of—but beyond that my motives became uncomfortably fuzzy. I finally decided I was doing it for Alana, to keep her from having to explain to Bradley what an idiot his therapist was.

The next point, six days later, went flawlessly, and life aboard ship finally settled into the usual deep-space routine. Alana, Pascal, and I each took eight-hour shifts on the bridge; Matope, Tobbar, and Sarojis did the same back in the engine room; and Kate Epstein, Leeds, and Wilkinson took turns catering to the occasional whims of our passengers. Off duty, most of the crewers also made an effort to spend at least a little time in the passenger lounge, recognizing the need to be friendly in the part of our business that was mainly word of mouth. Since that first night, though, the exaggerated interest in Bradley the Mental Patient had pretty well evaporated, leaving him as just another passenger in nearly everyone's eyes.

The exception, of course, was Alana.

In some ways, watching her during those weeks was roughly akin to watching a baby bird hacking its way out of its shell. Alana's bridge shift followed mine, and I was often more or less forced to hang around for an hour or so listening to her talk about her day. *Forced* is perhaps the wrong word; obviously, no one was nailing me to my chair. And yet, in another sense, I really *did* have no choice. To the best of my knowledge, I was Alana's only real confidant aboard the *Dancer*, and to have refused to listen would have deprived her of her only verbal sounding board. And the more I listened, the more I realized how vital my participation really was . . . because along with the usual rolls, pitches, and yaws of every embryo relationship, this one had an extra complication: Bradley's personality was beginning to change.

Lanton had said he was on the verge of a breakthrough, but it had never occurred to me that he might be able to begin genuine treatment aboard ship, let alone that any of its effects would show up en route. But even to me, who saw Bradley for maybe ten minutes at a time three times a week, the changes were obvious. All the conflicting signals in posture and expression that had bothered me so much at our first meeting diminished steadily until they were virtually gone, showing up only on brief occasions. At the same time, his self-confidence began to increase, and a heretofore unnoticed—by me, at least—sense of humor began to manifest itself. The latter effect bothered me, until Alana explained that a proper sense of humor required both a sense of dignity and an ability to take oneself less than seriously, neither of which Bradley had ever had before. I was duly pleased for her at the progress this showed; privately, I sought out Lanton to find out exactly what he was doing to his patient and the possible hazards thereof. The interview was easy to obtain—Bradley was soloing quite a bit these days—but relatively uninformative. Lanton tossed around a lot of stuff about synaptic fixing and duplicate messenger chemistry, but with visions of a Nobel Prize almost visibly orbiting his head he was in no mood to worry about dangerous side effects. He assured me that nothing he was using was in the slightest way experimental, and that I should go back to flying the *Dancer* and let him worry about Bradley. Or words to that effect.

I really *was* happy for Bradley, of course, but the fact remained that his rapid improvement was playing havoc with Alana's feelings. After years away from the wing-mending business she felt herself painfully rusty at it; and as Bradley continued to get better despite that, she began to wonder out loud whether she was doing any good, and if not, what right she had to continue hanging around him. At first I thought this was just an effort to hide the growth of other feelings from me, but gradually I began to realize that she was as confused as she sounded about what was happening. Never before in her life, I gathered, had romantic feelings come to her without the framework of a broken-wing operation to both build on and help disguise, and with that scaffolding falling apart around her she was either unable or unwilling to admit to herself what was really going on.

I felt pretty rotten having to sit around watching her flounder, but until she was able to recognize for herself what was happening there wasn't much I could do except listen. I wasn't about to offer any suggestions, especially since I didn't believe in love at first sight in the first place. My only consolation was that Bradley and Lanton were riding round trip with us, which meant that Alana wouldn't have to deal with any sort of separation crisis until we were back on Earth. I'd never had much sympathy for people who expected time to solve all their problems for them, but in this case I couldn't think of anything better to do.

And so matters stood as we went through our eighth and final point and emerged barely eight hundred thousand kilometers from the thriving colony world Taimyr . . . and found it deserted.

"Still nothing," Alana said tightly, her voice reflecting both the remnants of cascade depression and the shock of our impossible discovery. "No response to our call; nothing on any frequency I can pick up. I can't even find the comm satellites' lock signal."

I nodded, my eyes on the scope screen as the *Dancer's* telescope slowly scanned Taimyr's dark side. No lights showed anywhere. Shifting the aim, I began searching for the nine comm and nav satellites that should be circling the planet. "Alana, call up the astrogate again and find out what it's giving as position uncertainty."

"If you're thinking we're in the wrong system, forget it," she said as she tapped keys.

"Just checking all possibilities," I muttered. The satellites, too, were gone. I leaned back in my seat and bit at my lip.

"Yeah. Well, from eighteen positively identified stars we've got an error of no more than half a light-hour." She swiveled to face me and I saw the fear starting to grow behind her eyes. "Pall, what is going *on* here? Two hundred million people can't just disappear without a trace."

I shrugged helplessly. "A nuclear war could do it, I suppose, and might account for the satellites being gone as well. But there's no reason why anyone on Taimyr should *have* any nuclear weapons." Leaning forward again, I activated the helm. "A better view might help. If there's been some kind of war the major cities should now be big craters surrounded by rubble. I'm going to take us in and see what the day side looks like from high orbit."

"Do you think that's safe? I mean—" She hesitated. "Suppose the attack came from outside Taimyr?"

"What, you mean like an invasion?" I shook my head. "Even if there are alien intelligences somewhere who would want to invade us, we stand just as good a chance of getting away from orbit as we do from here."

"All right," she sighed. "But I'm setting up a cascade point maneuver, just in case. Do you think we should alert everybody yet?"

"Crewers, yes; passengers, no. I don't want any silly questions until I'm ready to answer them."

We took our time approaching Taimyr, but caution turned out to be unnecessary. No ships, human or otherwise, waited in orbit for us; no one hailed or shot at us; and as I turned the telescope planetward I saw no signs of warfare.

Nor did I see any cities, farmland, factories, or vehicles. It was as if Taimyr the colony had never existed.

"It doesn't make any sense," Matope said after I'd explained things over the crew intercom hookup. "How could a whole colony disappear?"

"I've looked up the records we've got on Taimyr," Pascal spoke up. "Some of the tropical vegetation is pretty fierce in the growth department. If everyone down there was killed by a plague or something, it's possible the plants have overgrown everything."

"Except that most of the cities are in temperate regions," I said shortly, "and two are smack in the middle of deserts. I can't find any of those, either."

"Hmm," Pascal said and fell silent, probably already hard at work on a new theory.

"Captain, you don't intend to land, do you?" Sarojis asked. "If launch facilities are gone and not merely covered over we'd be unable to lift again to orbit."

"I'm aware of that, and I have no intention of landing," I assured him. "But something's happened down there, and I'd like to get back to Earth with at least *some* idea of what."

"Maybe nothing's happened to the colony," Wilkinson said slowly. "Maybe something's happened to *us*."

"Such as?"

"Well . . . this may sound strange, but suppose we've somehow gone back in time, back to before the colony was started."

"That's crazy," Sarojis scoffed before I could say anything. "How could we possibly do something like that?"

"Malfunction of the field generator, maybe?" Wilkinson suggested. "There's a lot we don't know about Colloton space."

"It *doesn't* send ships back in—"

"All right, ease up," I told Sarojis. Beside me Alana snorted suddenly and reached for her keyboard. "I agree the idea sounds crazy, but whole cities don't just walk off, either," I continued. "It's not like there's a calendar we can look at out here, either. If we *were* a hundred years in the past, how would we know it?"

"Check the star positions," Matope offered.

"No good; the astrogate program would have noticed if anything was too far out of place. But I expect that still leaves us a possible century or more to rattle around in."

"No, it doesn't." Alana turned back to me with a grimly satisfied look on her face. "I've just taken signals from three pulsars. Compensating for our distance from Earth gives the proper rates for all three."

"Any comments on that?" I asked, not expecting any. Pulsar signals occasionally break their normal pattern and suddenly increase their pulse frequency, but it was unlikely to have happened in three of the beasts simultaneously; and in the absence of such a glitch the steady decrease in frequency was as good a calendar as we could expect to find.

There was a short pause; then Tobbar spoke up. "Captain, I think maybe it's time to bring the passengers in on this. We can't hide the fact that we're in Taimyr system, so they're bound to figure out sooner or later that something's wrong. And I think they'll be more cooperative if we volunteer the information rather than making them demand it."

"What do we need *their* cooperation for?" Sarojis snorted.

"If you bothered to listen as much as you talked," Tobbar returned, a bit tartly, "you'd know that Chuck Raines is an advanced student in astrophysics and Dr. Chileogu has done a fair amount of work on Colloton field mathematics. I'd say chances are good that we're going to need help from one or both of them before this is all over."

I looked at Alana, raised my eyebrows questioningly. She hesitated, then nodded. "All right," I said. "Matope, you'll stay on duty down there; Alana will be in command here. Everyone else will assemble in the dining room. The meeting will begin in ten minutes."

I waited for their acknowledgments and then flipped off the intercom. "I'd like to be there," Alana said.

"I know," I said, raising my palms helplessly. "But I *have* to be there, and someone's got to keep an eye on things outside."

"Pascal or Sarojis could do it."

"True—and under normal circumstances I'd let them. But we're facing an unknown and potentially dangerous situation, and I need someone here whose judgment I trust."

She took a deep breath, exhaled loudly. "Yeah. Well . . . at least let me listen in by intercom, okay?"

"I'd planned to," I nodded. Reaching over, I touched her shoulder. "Don't worry; Bradley can handle the news."

"I know," she said, with a vehemence that told me she wasn't anywhere near that certain.

Sighing, I flipped the PA switch and made the announcement.

They took the news considerably better than I'd expected them to—possibly, I suspected, because the emotional kick hadn't hit them yet.

"But this is absolutely unbelievable, Captain Durriken," Lissa Steadman said when I'd finished. She was a rising young business administration type who I half expected to call for a committee to study the problem. "How could a whole colony simply vanish?"

"My question exactly," I told her. "We don't know yet, but we're going to try and find out before we head back to Earth."

"We're just going to leave?" Mr. Eklund asked timidly from the far end of the table. His hand, on top of the table, gripped his wife's tightly, and I belatedly remembered they'd been going to Taimyr to see a daughter who'd emigrated some thirty years earlier. Of all aboard, they had lost the most when the colony vanished.

"I'm sorry," I told him, "but there's no way we could land and take off again, not if we want to make Earth again on the fuel we have left."

Eklund nodded silently. Beside them, Chuck Raines cleared his throat. "Has anybody considered the possibility that *we're* the ones something has happened to? After all, it's the *Aura Dancer*, not Taimyr, that's been dipping in and out of normal space for the last six weeks. Maybe during all that activity something went wrong."

"The floor is open for suggestions," I said.

"Well . . . I presume you've confirmed we *are* in the Taimyr system. Could we be—oh—out of phase or something with the real universe?"

"Highly poetic," Tobbar spoke up from his corner. "But what does *out of phase* physically mean in this case?"

"Something like a parallel universe, or maybe an alternate time line," Raines suggested. "Some replica of our universe where humans never colonized Taimyr. After all, cascade images are supposed to be views of alternate universes, aren't they? Maybe cascade points are somehow where all the possible paths intersect."

"You've been reading too much science fiction," I told him. "Cascade images are at least partly psychological, and they certainly have no visible substance. Besides, if you had to trace the proper path through a hundred universes every time you went through a cascade point, you'd lose ninety-nine ships out of every hundred that tried it."

"Actually, Mr. Raines is not being all *that* far out," Dr. Chileogu put in quietly. "It's occasionally been speculated that the branch cuts and Riemann surfaces that show up in Colloton theory represent distinct universes. If so, it would be theoretically possible to cross between them." He smiled slightly. "But it's extremely unlikely that a responsible captain would put his ship through the sort of maneuver that would be necessary to do such a thing."

"What sort of maneuver would it take?" I asked.

"Basically, a large-angle rotation within the cascade point. Say, eight degrees or more."

I shook my head, feeling relieved and at the same time vaguely disappointed that a possible lead had evaporated. "Our largest angle was just under four point five degrees."

He shrugged. "As I said."

I glanced around the table, wondering what avenue to try next. But Wilkinson wasn't ready to abandon this one yet. "I don't understand what the ship's rotation has to do with it, Dr. Chileogu," he said. "I thought the further you rotated, the further you went in real space, and that was all."

"Well . . . it would be easier if I could show you the curves involved. Basically, you're right about the distance-angle relation as long as you stay below that eight degrees I mentioned. But above that point there's a discontinuity, similar to what you get in the curve of the ordinary tangent function at ninety degrees; though unlike the tangent the next arm doesn't start at minus infinity." Chileogu glanced around the room, and I could see him revising the level of his explanation downward. "Anyway, the point is that the first arm of the curve—real rotations of zero to eight point six degrees—gives the complete range of translation distance from zero to infinity, and so that's all a star ship ever uses. If the ship rotates *past* that discontinuity, mathematical theory would say it had gone off the edge of the universe and started over again on a different Riemann surface. What that means physically I don't think anyone knows; but as Captain Durriken pointed out, all our real rotations have been well below the discontinuity."

Wilkinson nodded, apparently satisfied; but the term "real rotation" had now set off a warning bell deep in my own mind. It was an expression I hadn't heard—much less thought about—in years, but I vaguely remembered now that it had concealed a seven-liter can of worms. "Doctor, when you speak of a 'real' rotation, you're referring to a mathematical entity, as opposed to an actual, physical one," I said slowly. "Correct?"

He shrugged. "Correct, but with a ship such as this one the two are for all practical purposes identical. The *Aura Dancer* is a long, perfectly symmetrical craft, with both the Colloton-field generator and Ming-metal cargo shield along the center line. It's only when you start working with the fancier lines, with their towers and blister lounges and all, that you get a serious divergence."

I nodded carefully and looked around the room. Pascal had already gotten it, from the expression on his face; Wilkinson and Tobbar were starting to. "Could an extra piece of Ming metal, placed several meters off the ship's center line, cause such a divergence?" I asked Chileogu.

"Possibly." He frowned. "Very possibly."

I shifted my gaze to Lanton. His face had gone white. "I think," I said, "I've located the problem."

Seated at the main terminal in Pascal's cramped computer room, Chileogu turned the Ming-metal coil over in his hands and shook his head. "I'm sorry, Captain, but it simply can't be done. A dual crossover winding is one of the most complex shapes in existence, and there's no way I can calculate its effect with a computer this small."

I glanced over his head at Pascal and Lanton, the latter having tagged along after I cut short the meeting and hustled the mathematician down here. "Can't you even get us an estimate?" I asked.

"Certainly. But the estimate could be anywhere up to a factor of three off, which would be worse than useless to you."

I nodded, pursing my lips tightly. "Well, then, how about going on from here? With that coil back in the shield, the real and physical rotations coincide again. Is there some way we can get back to our universe; say, by taking a long step out from Taimyr and two short ones back?"

Chileogu pondered that one for a long minute. "I would say that it depends on how many universes we're actually dealing with," he said at last. "If there are just two—ours and this one—then rotating past any one discontinuity should do it. But if there are more than two, you'd wind up just going one deeper into the stack if you crossed the wrong line."

"Ouch," Pascal murmured. "And if there are an infinite number, I presume, we'd never get back out?"

The mathematician shrugged uncomfortably. "Very likely."

"But don't the mathematics show how many universes there are?" Lanton spoke up.

"They show how many Riemann surfaces there are," Chileogu corrected. "But physical reality is never obliged to correspond with our theories and constructs. Experimental checks are always required, and to the best of my knowledge no one has ever tried this one."

I thought of all the ships that had simply disappeared, and shivered slightly. "In other words, trying to find the Taimyr colony is out. All right, then. What about the principle of reversibility? Will that let us go back the way we came?"

"Back to Earth?" Chileogu hesitated. "Ye-e-s, I think that would apply here. But to go back don't you need to know—?"

"The real rotations we used to get here," I nodded heavily. "Yeah." We looked at each other, and I saw that he, too, recognized the implications of that requirement.

Lanton, though, was still light-years behind us. "You act like there's still a problem," he said, looking back and forth between us. "Don't you have the records of the rotations we made at each point?"

I was suddenly tired of the psychiatrist. "Pascal, would you explain things to Dr. Lanton—on your way back to the passenger area?"

"Sure." Pascal stepped to Lanton's side and took his arm. "This way, Doctor."

"But—" Lanton's protests were cut off by the closing door.

I sat down carefully on a corner of the console, staring back at the

Korusyn 630 that took up most of the room's space. "I take it," Chileogu said quietly, "that you can't get the return-trip parameters?"

"We can get all but the last two points we'd need," I told him. "The ship's basic configuration was normal for all of those, and the Korusyn there can handle them." I shook my head. "But even for those the parameters will be totally different—a two-degree rotation one way might become a one or three on the return trip. It depends on our relation to the galactic magnetic field and angular momentum vectors, closest-approach distance to large masses, and a half dozen other parameters. Even if we *had* a mathematical expression for the influence Lanton's damn coil had on our first two points, I wouldn't know how to reprogram the machine to take that into account."

Chileogu was silent for a moment. Then, straightening up in his seat, he flexed his fingers. "Well, I suppose we have to start somewhere. Can you clear me a section of memory?"

"Easily. What are you going to do?"

He picked up the coil again. "I can't do a complete calculation, but there are several approximation methods that occasionally work pretty well; they're scattered throughout my technical tapes if your library doesn't have a list. If they give widely varying results—as they probably will, I'm afraid—then we're back where we started. But if they happen to show a close agreement, we can probably use the result with reasonable confidence." He smiled slightly. "*Then* we get to worry about programming it in."

"Yeah. Well, first things first. Alana, have you been listening in?"

"Yes," her voice came promptly through the intercom. "I'm clearing the computer now."

Chileogu left a moment later to fetch his tapes. Pascal returned while he was gone, and I filled him in on what we were going to try. Together, he and Alana had the computer ready by the time Chileogu returned. I considered staying to watch, but common sense told me I would just be in the way, so instead I went up to the bridge and relieved Alana. It wasn't really my shift, but I didn't feel like mixing with the passengers, and I could think and brood as well on the bridge as I could in my cabin. Besides, I had a feeling Alana would like to check up on Bradley.

I'd been sitting there staring at Taimyr for about an hour when the intercom bleeped. "Captain," Alana's voice said, "can you come down to the dining room right away? Dr. Lanton's come up with an idea I think you'll want to hear."

I resisted my reflexive urge to tell her what Lanton could do with his ideas; her use of my title meant she wasn't alone. "All right," I sighed. "I'll get Sarojis to take over here and be down in a few minutes."

"I think Dr. Chileogu and Pascal should be here, too."

Something frosty went skittering down my back. Alana knew the importance of what those two were doing. Whatever Lanton's brain-storm was, she must genuinely think it worth listening to. "All right. We'll be there shortly."

They were all waiting quietly around one of the tables when I arrived. Bradley, not surprisingly, was there too, seated next to Alana and across from Lanton. Only the six of us were present; the other passengers, I guessed, were keeping the autobar in the lounge busy. "Okay, let's have it," I said without preamble as I sat down.

"Yes, sir," Lanton said, throwing a quick glance in Pascal's di-rection. "If I understood Mr. Pascal's earlier explanation correctly, we're basically stuck because there's no way to calibrate the *Aura Dancer*'s instruments to take the, uh, extra Ming metal into account."

"Close enough," I grunted. "So?"

"So, it occurred to me that this 'real' rotation you were talking about ought to have some external manifestations, the same way a gyro needle shows the ship's physical rotation."

"You mean like something outside the viewports?" I frowned.

"No; something inside. I'm referring to the cascade images."

I opened my mouth, closed it again. My first thought was that it was the world's dumbest idea, but my second was *why not?* "You're saying, what, that the image-shuffling that occurs while we rotate is tied to the real rotation, each shift being a hundredth of a radian or something?"

"Right"—he nodded—"although I don't know whether that kind of calibration would be possible."

I looked at Chileogu. "Doctor?"

The mathematician brought his gaze back from infinity. "I'm not sure what to say. The basic idea is actually not new—Colloton himself showed such a manifestation ought to be present, and several others have suggested the cascade images were it. But I've never heard of any actual test being made of the hypothesis; and from what I've heard of the images, I suspect there are grave practical problems besides. The pattern doesn't change in any mathematically predictable way, so I don't know how you would keep track of the shifts."

"I wouldn't have to," Lanton said. "I've been observing Rik's cascade images throughout the trip. I remember what the pattern looked like at both the beginning and ending of each rotation."

I looked at Bradley, suddenly understanding. His eyes met mine and he nodded fractionally.

"The only problem," Lanton continued, "is that I'm not sure we could set up at either end to do the reverse rotation."

"Chances are good we can," I said absently, my eyes still on Bradley. His expression was strangely hard for someone who was supposedly seeing the way out of permanent exile. Alana, if possible, looked even less happy. "All rotations are supposed to begin at zero, and since we always go 'forward' we always rotate in the same direction."

I glanced back at Lanton to see his eyes go flat, as if he were watching a private movie. "You're right; it *is* the same starting pattern each time. I hadn't really noticed that before, with the changes and all."

"It should be easy enough to check, Captain," Pascal spoke up. "We can compute the physical rotations for the first six points we'll be going through. The real rotations should be the same as on the outbound leg, though, so if Dr. Lanton's right the images will wind up in the same pattern they did before."

"But how—?" Chileogu broke off suddenly. "Ah. You've had a mnemonic treatment?"

Lanton nodded and then looked at me. "I think Mr. Pascal's idea is a good one, Captain, and I don't see any purpose in hanging around here any longer than necessary. Whenever you want to start back—"

"I have a few questions to ask first," I interrupted mildly. I glanced at Bradley, decided to tackle the easier ones first. "Dr. Chileogu, what's the status of your project?"

"The approximations? We've just finished programming the first one, it'll take another hour or so to collect enough data for a plot. I agree with Dr. Lanton, though—we can do the calculations between cascade points as easily as we can do them in orbit here."

"Thank you. Dr. Lanton, you mentioned something about *changes* a minute ago. What exactly did you mean?"

Lanton's eyes flicked to Bradley for an instant. "Well . . . as I told you several weeks ago, a person's mind has a certain effect on the cascade image pattern. Some of the medicines Rik's been taking have slightly altered the—oh, I guess you could call it the *texture* of the pattern."

"Altered it how much?"

"In some cases, fairly extensively." He hesitated, just a bit too long. "But nothing I've done is absolutely irreversible. I should be able to re-create the original conditions before each cascade point."

Deliberately, I leaned back in my chair. "All right. Now let's hear what the problem is."

"I beg your pardon?"

"You heard me." I waved at Bradley and Alana. "Your patient and my first officer look like they're about to leave for a funeral. I want to know why."

Lanton's cheek twitched. "I don't think this is the time or the place to discuss—"

"The problem, Captain," Bradley interrupted quietly, "is that the reversing of the treatments may turn out to be permanent."

It took a moment for that to sink in. When it did I turned my eyes back on Lanton. "Explain."

The psychiatrist took a deep breath. "The day after the second point I used ultrasound to perform a type of minor neurosurgery called synapse fixing. It applies heat to selected regions of the brain to correct a tendency of the nerves to misfire. The effects *can* be reversed . . . but the procedure's been done only rarely, and usually involves unavoidable peripheral damage."

I felt my gaze hardening into an icy stare. "In other words," I bit out, "not only will the progress he's made lately be reversed, but he'll likely wind up worse off than he started. Is that it?"

Lanton squirmed uncomfortably, avoiding my eyes. "I don't *know* that he will. Now that I've found a treatment—"

"You're about to give him a brand-new disorder," I snapped. "*Damn* it all, Lanton, you are the most cold-blooded—"

"Captain."

Bradley's single word cut off my flow of invective faster than anything but hard vacuum could have. "What?" I said.

"Captain, I understand how you feel." His voice was quiet but firm; and though the tightness remained in his expression, it had been joined by an odd sort of determination. "But Dr. Lanton wasn't really trying to maneuver you into supporting something unethical. For the record, I've already agreed to work with him on this; I'll put that on tape if you'd like." He smiled slightly. "And before you bring it up, I *am* recognized as legally responsible for my actions, so as long as Dr. Lanton and I agree on a course of treatment your agreement is not required."

"That's not entirely true," I ground out. "As a ship's captain in deep space, I have full legal power here. If I say he can't do something to you, he can't. Period."

Bradley's face never changed. "Perhaps. But unless you can find another way to get us back to Earth, I don't see that you have any other choice."

I stared into those eyes for a couple of heartbeats. Then, slowly, my gaze swept the table, touching in turn all the others as they sat watching me, awaiting my decision. The thought of deliberately sending Bradley back to his permanent disorientation—*really* permanent, this time—left a taste in my mouth that was practically gagging in its intensity. But Bradley was right . . . and at the moment I didn't have any better ideas.

"Pascal," I said, "you and Dr. Chileogu will first of all get some output on that program of yours. Alana, as soon as they're finished you'll take the computer back and calculate the parameters for our first point. *You* two"—I glared in turn at Bradley and Lanton—"will be ready to test this image theory of yours. You'll do the observations in your cabin as usual, and tell me afterwards whether we duplicated the rotation exactly or came out short or long. Questions? All right; dismissed."

After all, I thought amid the general scraping of chairs, *for the first six points all Bradley will need to do is cut back on medicines. That means twenty-eight days or so before any irreversible surgery is done.*

I had just that long to come up with another answer.

We left orbit three hours later, pushing outward on low drive to conserve fuel. That plus the course I'd chosen meant another ten hours until we were in position for the first point, but none of that time was wasted. Pascal and Chileogu were able to program and run two more approximation schemes; the results, unfortunately, were not encouraging. Any two of the three plots had a fair chance of agreeing over ranges of half a degree or so, but there was no consistency at all over the larger angles we would need to use. Chileogu refused to throw in the towel, pointing out that he had another six methods to try and making vague noises about statistical curve-fitting schemes. I promised him all the computer time he needed between point maneuvers, but privately I conceded defeat. Lanton's method now seemed our only chance . . . if it worked.

I handled the first point myself, double-checking all parameters beforehand and taking special pains to run the gyro needle as close to the proper angle as I could. As with any such hand operation, of course, perfection was not quite possible, and I ran the *Dancer* something under a hundredth of a degree long. I'm not sure what I was expecting from this first test, but I *was* more than a little surprised when Lanton accurately reported that we'd slightly overshot the mark.

"It looks like it'll work," Alana commented from her cabin when I relayed the news. She didn't sound too enthusiastic.

"Maybe," I said, feeling somehow the need to be as skeptical as possible. "We'll see what happens when he starts taking Bradley off the drugs. I find it hard to believe that the man's mental state can be played like a yo-yo, and if it can't be we'll have to go with whatever statistical magic Chileogu can put together."

Alana gave a little snort that she'd probably meant to be a laugh. "Hard to know which way to hope, isn't it?"

"Yeah." I hesitated for a second, running the duty arrangements over in my mind. "Look, why don't you take the next few days off, at least until the next point. Sarojis can take your shift up here."

"That's all right," she sighed. "I—if it's all the same with you, I'd rather save any offtime until later. Rik will . . . need my help more then."

"Okay," I told her. "Just let me know when you want it and the time's yours."

We continued on our slow way, and with each cascade point I became more and more convinced that Lanton really would be able to guide us through those last two critical points. His accuracy for the first four maneuvers was a solid hundred percent, and on the fifth maneuver we got to within point zero two percent of the computer's previous reading by deliberately jockeying the *Dancer* back and forth until Bradley's image pattern was exactly as Lanton remembered it. After that even Matope was willing to be cautiously optimistic; and if it hadn't been for one small cloud hanging over my head I probably would have been as happy as the rest of the passengers had become.

The cloud, of course, being Bradley.

I'd been wrong about how much his improvement had been due to the drugs Lanton had been giving him, and every time I saw him that ill-considered line about playing his mind like a yo-yo came back to haunt me. Slowly, but very steadily, Bradley was regressing toward his original mental state. His face went first, his expressions beginning to crowd each other again as if he were unable to decide which of several moods should be expressed at any given moment. His eyes took on that shining, nervous look I hated so much: just occasionally at first, but gradually becoming more and more frequent, until it seemed to be almost his norm. And yet, even though he certainly saw what was happening to him, not once did I hear him say anything that could be taken as resentment or complaint. It was as if the chance to save twenty other lives was so important to him that it was worth any sacrifice. I thought occasionally about Alana's comment that he'd never before had a sense of dignity, and wondered if he would lose it again to his illness. But I didn't wonder about it all that much; I was too busy worrying about Alana.

I hadn't expected her to take Bradley's regression well, of course—to someone with Alana's wing-mending instincts a backsliding patient would be both insult *and* injury. What I wasn't prepared for was her abrupt withdrawal into a shell of silence on the issue, which no amount of gentle probing could crack open. I tried to be patient with her, figuring that eventually the need to talk would overcome her reticence; but as the day for what Lanton described as "minor surgery" approached, I finally decided I couldn't wait any longer. On the day after our sixth cascade point, I quit being subtle and forced the issue.

"Whatever I'm feeling, it isn't any concern of yours," she said, her fingers playing across the bridge controls as she prepared to take over from me. Her hands belied the calmness in her voice: I knew her usual checkout routine as well as my own, and she lost the sequence no fewer than three times while I watched.

"I think it is," I told her. "Aside from questions of friendship, you're a member of my crew, and anything that might interfere with your efficiency is my concern."

She snorted. "I've been under worse strains than this without falling apart."

"I know. But you've never buried yourself this deeply before, and it worries me."

"I know. I'm . . . sorry. If I could put it into words—" She shrugged helplessly.

"Are you worried about Bradley?" I prompted. "Don't forget that, whatever Lanton has to do here, he'll have all the resources of the Swedish Psychiatric Institute available to undo it."

"I know. But . . . he's going to come out of it a different person. Even Lanton has to admit that."

"Well . . . maybe it'll wind up being a change for the better."

It was a stupid remark, and her scornful look didn't make me feel any better about having made it. "Oh, come *on*. Have you *ever* heard of an injury that did any real good? Because that's what it's going to be—an injury."

And suddenly I understood. "You're afraid you won't like him afterwards, aren't you? At least not the way you do now?"

"Why should that be so unreasonable?" she snapped. "I'm a damn fussy person, you know—I don't like an awful lot of people. I can't afford to . . . to lose any of them." She turned her back on me abruptly, and I saw her shoulders shake once.

I waited a decent interval before speaking. "Look, Alana, you're not in any shape to stay up here alone. Why don't you go down to your cabin and pull yourself together, and then go and spend some time with Bradley."

"I'm all right," she mumbled. "I can take my shift."

"I know. But . . . at the moment I imagine Rik needs you more than I do. Go on, get below."

She resisted for a few more minutes, but eventually I bent her sense of duty far enough and she left. For a long time afterwards I just sat and stared at the stars, my thoughts whistling around my head in tight orbit. What *would* the effect of the new Bradley be on Alana? She'd been right—whatever happened, it wasn't likely to be an improvement. If her interest was really only in wing-mending, Lanton's work would provide her with a brand-new challenge. But

I didn't think even Alana was able to fool herself like that anymore. She cared about him, for sure, and if he changed too much that feeling might well die.

And I wouldn't lose her when we landed.

I thought about it long and hard, examining it and the rest of our situation from several angles. Finally, I leaned forward and keyed the intercom. Wilkinson was off duty in his cabin; from the time it took him to answer he must have been asleep as well. "Wilkinson, you got a good look at the damage in Lanton's neural whatsis machine. How hard would it be to fix?"

"Uh . . . well, that's hard to say. The thing that spit goop all over the Ming-metal coil was a standard voltage regulator board—we're bound to have spares aboard. But there may be other damage, too. I'd have to run an analyzer over it to find out if anything else is dead. Whether we would have replacements is another question."

"Okay. Starting right now, you're relieved of all other duty until you've got that thing running again. Use anything you need from ship's spares—" I hesitated—"and you can even pirate from our cargo if necessary."

"Yes, sir." He was wide awake now. "I gather there's a deadline?"

"Lanton's going to be doing some ultrasound work on Bradley in fifty-eight hours. You need to be done before that. Oh, and you'll need to work in Lanton's cabin—I don't want the machine moved at all."

"Got it. If you'll clear it with Lanton, I can be up there in twenty minutes."

Lanton wasn't all that enthusiastic about letting Wilkinson set up shop in his cabin, especially when I wouldn't explain my reasons to him, but eventually he gave in. I alerted Kate Epstein that she would have to do without Wilkinson for a while, and then called Matope to confirm the project's access to tools and spares.

And then, for the time being, it was all over but the waiting. I resumed my examination of the viewport, wondering if I were being smart or just pipe-dreaming.

Two days later—barely eight hours before Bradley's operation was due to begin—Wilkinson finally reported that the neural tracer was once again operational.

*   *   *

"This better be important," Lanton fumed as he took his place at the dining-room table. "I'm already behind schedule in my equipment setup as it is."

I glanced around at the others before replying. Pascal and Chileogu, fresh from their latest attempt at making sense from their assortment of plots, seemed tired and irritated by this interruption. Bradley and Alana, holding hands tightly under the table, looked more resigned than anything else. Everyone seemed a little gaunt, but that was probably my imagination—certainly we weren't on anything approaching starvation rations yet. "Actually, Doctor," I said, looking back at Lanton, "you're not in nearly the hurry you think. There's not going to be any operation."

That got everyone's full attention. "You've found another way?" Alana breathed, a hint of life touching her eyes for the first time in days.

"I think so. Dr. Chileogu, I need to know first whether a current running through Ming metal would change its effect on the ship's real rotation."

He frowned, then shrugged. "Probaby. I have no idea how, though."

A good thing I'd had the gadget fixed, then. "Doesn't matter. Dr. Lanton, can you tell me approximately when in the cascade point your neural tracer burned out?"

"I can tell you exactly. It was just as the images started disappearing, right at the end."

I nodded; I'd hoped it was either the turning on or off of the field generator that had done it. That would make the logistics a whole lot easier. "Good. Then we're all set. What we're going to do, you see, is reenact that particular maneuver."

"What good will *that* do?" Lanton asked, his tone more puzzled than belligerent.

"It should get us home." I waved toward the outer hull. "For the past two days we've been moving toward a position where the galactic field and other parameters are almost exactly the same as we had when we went through that point—providing your neural tracer is on and we're heading back toward Taimyr. In another two days we'll turn around and get our velocity vector lined up correctly. Then, with your tracer running, we're going to fire up the generator and rotate the same amount—by gyro reading—as we did then.

You"—I leveled a finger at Lanton—"will be on the bridge during that operation, and you will note the exact configuration of your cascade images at that moment. Then, *without shutting off the generator*, we'll rotate *back* to zero; zero as defined by your cascade pattern, since it may be different from gyro zero. At that time, I'll take the Ming metal from your tracer, walk it to the number one hold, and stuff it into the cargo shield; and we'll rotate the ship again until we reach your memorized cascade pattern. Since the physical and real rotations are identical in that configuration, that'll give us the real angle we rotated through the last time—"

"And from *that* we can figure the angle we'll need to make going the other direction!" Alana all but shouted.

I nodded. "Once we've rotated back to zero to regain our starting point, of course." I looked around at them again. Lanton and Bradley still seemed confused, though the latter was starting to catch Alana's enthusiasm. Chileogu was scribbling on a notepad, and Pascal just sat there with his mouth slightly open. Probably astonished that he hadn't come up with such a crazy idea himself. "That's all I have to say," I told them. "If you have any comments later—"

"I have one now, Captain."

I looked at Bradley in some surprise. "Yes?"

He swallowed visibly. "It seems to me, sir, that what you're going to need is a set of cascade images that vary a lot, so that the pattern you're looking for is a distinctive one. I don't think Dr. Lanton's are suitable for that."

"I see." Of course; while Lanton had been studying Bradley's images, Bradley couldn't help but see his, as well. "Lanton? How about it?"

The psychiatrist shrugged. "I admit they're a little bland—I haven't had a very exciting life. But they'll do."

"I doubt it." Bradley looked back at me. "Captain, I'd like to volunteer."

"You don't know what you're saying," I told him. "Each rotation will take twice as long as the ones you've already been through. *And* there'll be two of them back to back; *and* the field won't be shut down between them, because I want to know if the images drift while I'm moving the coil around the ship. Multiply by about five what you've felt afterwards and you'll get some idea what it'll be like." I shook my head. "I'm grateful for your offer, but I can't let more people than necessary go through that."

"I appreciate that. But I'm still going to do it."

We locked eyes for a long moment . . . and the word *dignity* flashed through my mind. "In that case, I accept," I said. "Other questions? Thank you for stopping by."

They got the message and began standing up . . . all except Alana. Bradley whispered something to her, but she shook her head and whispered back. Reluctantly, he let go of her hand and followed the others out of the room.

"Question?" I asked Alana when we were alone, bracing for an argument over the role I was letting Bradley take.

"You're right about the extra stress staying in Colloton space that long will create," she said. "That probably goes double for anyone running around in it. I'd expect a lot more vertigo, for starters, and that could make movement dangerous."

"Would you rather Bradley had his brain scorched?"

She flinched, but stood her ground. "My objection isn't with the method—it's with who's going to be bouncing off the *Dancer*'s walls."

"Oh. Well, before you get the idea you're being left out of things, let me point out that *you're* going to be handling bridge duties for the maneuver."

"Fine; but since I'm going to be up anyway I want the job of running the Ming metal back and forth instead."

I shook my head. "No. You're right about the unknowns involved with this, which is why *I'm* going to do it."

"I'm five years younger than you are," she said, ticking off fingers. "I also have a higher stress index, better balance, and I'm in better physical condition." She hesitated. "And I'm not haunted by white uniforms in my cascade images," she added gently.

Coming from anyone else, that last would have been like a knife in the gut. But from Alana, it somehow didn't even sting. "The assignments are nonnegotiable," I said, getting to my feet. "Now if you'll excuse me, I have to catch a little sleep before my next shift."

She didn't respond. When I left she was still sitting there, staring through the shiny surface of the table.

*   *   *

"Here we go. Good Luck," were the last words I heard Alana say before the intercom was shut down and I was alone in Lanton's cabin. Alone, but not for long: a moment later my first doubles appeared. Raising my wrist, I keyed my chrono to stopwatch mode and waited, ears tingling with the faint ululation of the Colloton field generator. The sound, inaudible from the bridge, reminded me of my trainee days, before the *Dancer* . . . before Lord Hendrik and his fool-headed kid. . . . Shaking my head sharply, I focused on the images, waiting for them to begin their one-dimensional allemande.

They did, and I started my timer. With the lines to the bridge dead I was going to have to rely on the image movements to let me know when the first part of the maneuver was over; moving the Ming metal around the ship while we were at the wrong end of our rotation or—worse—while we were still moving would probably end our chances of getting back for good. Mindful of the pranks cascade points could play on a person's time sense, I'd had Pascal calculate the approximate times each rotation would take. Depending on how accurate they turned out to be, they might simply let me limit how soon I started worrying.

It wasn't a pleasant wait. On the bridge, I had various duties to perform; here, I didn't have even that much distraction from the ghosts surrounding me. Sitting next to the humming neural tracer, I watched the images flicker in and out, white uniforms do-si-doing with the coveralls and the gaps.

Ghosts. *Haunted.* I'd never seriously thought of them like that before, but now I found I couldn't see them in any other way. I imagined I could see knowing smiles on the liner captains' faces, or feel a coldness from the gaps where I'd died. Pure autosuggestion, of course . . . and yet, it forced me for probably the first time to consider what exactly the images were doing to me.

They were making me chronically discontented with my life.

My first reaction to such an idea was to immediately justify my resentment. I'd been cheated out of the chance to be a success in my field; trapped at the bottom of the heap by idiots who ranked political weaselcraft higher than flying skill. I had a *right* to feel dumped on.

And yet . . .

My watch clicked at me: the first rotation should be about over. I reset it and waited, watching the images. With agonizing slowness they came to a stop . . . and then started moving again in what I could persuade myself was the opposite direction. I started my watch again and let my eyes defocus a bit. The next time the dance stopped, it would be time to move Lanton's damn coil to the hold and bring my ship back to normal.

My ship. I listened to the way the words echoed around my brain. *My ship.* No liner captain owned his own ship. He was an employee, like any other in the company; forever under the basilisk eye of those selfsame idiots who'd fired me once for doing my job. The space junk being sparser and all that aside, would I *really* have been happier in a job like that? Would I have enjoyed being caught between management on one hand and upper-crusty passengers on the other? Enjoyed, hell—would I have *survived* it? For the first time in ten years I began to wonder if perhaps Lord Hendrik had known what he was doing when he booted me out of his company.

Deliberately, I searched out the white uniforms far off to my left and watched as they popped in and out of different slots in the long line. Perhaps that was why there were so few of them, I thought suddenly; perhaps, even while I was pretending otherwise, I'd been smart enough to make decisions that had kept me out of the running for that particular treadmill. The picture that created made me smile; my subconscious chasing around with secret memos, hiding basic policy matters from my righteously indignant conscious mind.

The click of my watch made me jump. Taking a deep breath, I picked up a screwdriver from the tool pouch laid out beside the neural tracer and gave my full attention to the images. Slow . . . slower . . . stopped. I waited a full two minutes to make sure, then flipped off the tracer and got to work.

I'd had plenty of practice in the past two days, but it still took me nearly five minutes to extricate the coil from the maze of equipment surrounding it. That was no particular problem—we'd allowed seven minutes for the disassembly—but I was still starting to sweat as I got to my feet and headed for the door.

And promptly fell on my face.

Alana's reference to enhanced vertigo apart, I hadn't expected anything that strong quite so soon. Swallowing hard, I tried to ignore the feeling of lying on a steep hill and crawled toward the nearest wall. Using it as a support, I got to my feet, waited for the cabin to stop spinning, and shuffled over to the door. Fortunately, all the doors between me and One Hold had been locked open, so I didn't have to worry about getting to the release. Still shuffling, I maneuvered through the opening and started down the corridor, moving as quickly as I could. The trip—fifteen meters of corridor, a circular stairway down, five more meters of corridor, and squeezing through One Hold's cargo to get to the shield—normally took less than three minutes. We'd allowed ten; but already I could see that was going to be tight. I kept my eyes on the wall beside me and concentrated on moving my feet . . . which was probably why I was nearly to the stairway before I noticed the kaleidoscope dance my cascade images were doing.

While the ship was at rest.

I stopped short, the pattern shifts ceasing as I did so. The thing I had feared most about this whole trick was happening: moving the Ming metal was changing our real angle in Colloton space.

I don't know how long I leaned there with the sweat trickling down my forehead, but it was probably no more than a minute before I forced myself to get moving again. There were now exactly two responses Alana could make: go on to the endpoint Lanton had just memorized, or try and compensate somehow for the shift I was causing. The former course felt intuitively wrong, but the latter might well be impossible to do—and neither had any particular mathematical backing that Chileogu had been able to find. For me, the worst part of it was the fact that I was now completely out of the decision process. No matter how fast I got the coil locked away, there was no way I was going to make it back up two flights of stairs to the bridge. Like everyone else on board, I was just going to have to trust Alana's judgment.

I slammed into the edge of the stairway opening, nearly starting my downward trip headfirst before I got a grip on the railing. The coil, jarred from my sweaty hand, went on ahead of me, clanging like a muffled bell as it bounced to the deck below. I followed a good deal more slowly, the writhing images around me adding to my vertigo. By now, the rest of my body was also starting to react to the stress, and I had to stop every few steps as a wave of nausea or fatigue washed over me. It seemed forever before I finally reached the bottom of the stairs. The coil had rolled to the middle of the corridor; retrieving it on hands and knees, I got back to the wall and hauled myself to my feet. I didn't dare look at my watch.

The cargo hold was the worst part yet. The floor was swaying freely by then, like an ocean vessel in heavy seas, and through the reddish haze surrounding me, the stacks of boxes I staggered between seemed ready to hurl themselves down upon my head. I don't remember how many times I shied back from what appeared to be a breaking wave of crates, only to slam into the stack behind me. Finally, though, I made it to the open area in front of the shield door. I was halfway across the gap, moving again on hands and knees, when my watch sounded the one-minute warning. With a desperate lunge, I pushed myself up and forward, running full tilt into the Ming-metal wall. More from good luck than anything else, my free hand caught the handle; and as I fell backwards the door swung open. For a moment I hung there, trying to get my trembling muscles to respond. Then, slowly, I got my feet under me and stood up. Reaching through the opening, I let go of the coil and watched it drop into the gap between two boxes. The hold was swaying more and more violently now; timing my move carefully, I shoved on the handle and collapsed to the deck. The door slammed shut with a thunderclap that tried to take the top of my head with it. I hung on just long enough to see that the door was indeed closed, and then gave in to the darkness.

I'm told they found me sleeping with my back against the shield door, making sure it couldn't accidentally come open.

I was lying on my back when I came to, and the first thing I saw when I opened my eyes was Kate Epstein's face. "How do you feel?" she asked.

"Fine," I told her, frowning as I glanced around. This wasn't my cabin. . . . With a start I recognized the humming in my ear. "What the hell am I doing in Lanton's cabin?" I growled.

Kate shrugged and reached over my shoulder, shutting off the neural tracer. "We needed Dr. Lanton's neural equipment, and the tracer wasn't supposed to be moved. A variant of the mountain/ Mohammed problem, I guess you could say."

I grunted. "How'd the point maneuver go? Was Alana able to figure out a correction factor?"

"It went perfectly well," Alana's voice came from my right. I turned my head, to find her sitting next to the door. "I think we're out of the woods now, Pall—that four-point-four physical rotation turned out to be more like nine point one once the coil was out of the way. If Chileogu's right about reversibility applying here, we should be back in our own universe now. I guess we won't know for sure until we go through the next point and reach Earth."

"Is that nine point one with or without a correction factor?" I asked, my stomach tightening in anticipation. We might not be out of the woods quite yet.

"No correction needed," she said. "The images on the bridge stayed rock-steady the whole time."

"But . . . I saw them shifting."

"Yes, you told us that. Our best guess—excuse me; *Pascal*'s best guess—is that you were getting that because you were moving relative to the field generator, that if you'd made a complete loop around it you would've come back to the original cascade pattern again. Chileogu's trying to prove that mathematically, but I doubt he'll be able to until he gets to better facilities."

"Uh-huh." Something wasn't quite right here. "You say I *told* you about the images? When?"

Alana hesitated, looked at Kate. "Actually, Captain," the doctor said gently, "you've been conscious quite a bit during the past four days. The reason you don't remember any of it is that the connection between your short-term and long-term memories got a little scrambled—probably another effect of your jaunt across all those field lines. It looks like that part's healed itself, though, so you shouldn't have any more memory problems."

"Oh, great. What sort of problems *will* I have more of?"

"Nothing major. You might have balance difficulties for a while, and you'll likely have a mild migraine or two within the next couple of weeks. But indications are that all of it is very temporary."

I looked back at Alana. "Four days. We'll need to set up our last calibration run soon."

"All taken care of," she assured me. "We're turning around later today to get our velocity vector pointing back toward Taimyr again, and we'll be able to do the run tomorrow."

"Who's going to handle it?"

"Who do you think?" she snorted. "Rik, Lanton, and me, with maybe some help from Pascal."

I'd known that answer was coming, but it still made my mouth go dry. "No way," I told her, struggling to sit up. "You aren't going to go through this hell. I can manage—"

"Ease up, Pall," Alana interrupted me. "Weren't you paying attention? The real angle doesn't drift when the Ming metal is moved, and that means we can shut down the field generator while I'm taking the coil from here to One Hold again."

I sank back onto the bed, feeling foolish. "Oh. Right."

Getting to her feet, Alana came over to me and patted my shoulder. "Don't worry," she said in a kinder tone. "We've got things under control. You've done the hard part; just relax and let us do the rest."

"Okay," I agreed, trying to hide my misgivings.

It was just as well that I did. Thirty-eight hours later Alana used our last gram of fuel in a flawless bit of flying that put us into a deep Earth orbit. The patrol boats that had responded to her emergency signal were waiting there, loaded with the fuel we would need to land.

Six hours after that, we were home.

They checked me into a hospital, just to be on the safe side, and the next four days were filled with a flurry of tests, medical interviews, and bumpy wheelchair rides. Surprisingly—to me, anyway—I was also nailed by two media types who wanted the more traditional type of interview. Apparently, the *Dancer*'s trip to elsewhere and back was getting a fair amount of publicity. Just how widespread the coverage was, though, I didn't realize until my last day there, when an official-looking CompNote was delivered to my room.

It was from Lord Hendrik.

I snapped the sealer and unfolded the paper. The first couple of paragraphs—the greetings, congratulations on my safe return, and such—I skipped over quickly, my eyes zeroing in on the business portion of the letter:

> As you may or may not know, I have recently come out of semiretirement to serve on the Board of Directors of TranStar Enterprises, headquartered here in Nairobi. With excellent contacts both in Africa and in the so-called Black Colony chain, our passenger load is expanding rapidly, and we are constantly on the search for experienced and resourceful pilots we

can entrust them to. The news reports of your recent close call brought you to my mind again after all these years, and I thought you might be interested in discussing—

A knock on the door interrupted my reading. "Come in," I called, looking up.

It was Alana. "Hi, Pall, how are you doing?" she asked, walking over to the bed and giving me a brief once-over. In one hand she carried a slender plastic portfolio.

"Bored silly," I told her. "I think I'm about ready to check out—they've finished all the standard tests without finding anything, and I'm tired of lying around while they dream up new ones."

"What a shame," she said with mock sorrow. "And after I brought you all this reading material, too." She hefted the portfolio.

"What is it, your resignation?" I asked, trying to keep my voice light. There was no point making this any more painful for either of us than necessary.

But she just frowned. "Don't be silly. It's a whole batch of new contracts I've picked up for us in the past few days. Some really good ones, too, from name corporations. I think people are starting to see what a really good carrier we are."

I snorted. "Aside from the thirty-six or whatever penalty clauses we invoked on this trip?"

"Oh, that's all in here too. The Swedish Institute's not even going to put up a fight—they're paying off everything, including your hospital bills and the patrol's rescue fee. Probably figured Lanton's glitch was going to make them look bad enough without them trying to chisel us out of damages too." She hesitated, and an odd expression flickered across her face. "Were you really expecting me to jump ship?"

"I was about eighty percent sure," I said, fudging my estimate down about nineteen points. "After all, this is where Rik Bradley's going to be, and you . . . rather like him. Don't you?"

She shrugged. "I don't know what I feel for him, to be perfectly honest. I like him, sure—like him a lot. But my life's out there"—she gestured skyward—"and I don't think I can give that up for anyone. At least, not for him."

"You could take a leave of absence," I told her, feeling like a prize fool but determined to give her every possible option. "Maybe once you spend some real time on a planet, you'd find you like it."

"And maybe I wouldn't," she countered. "And when I decided I'd had enough, where would the *Dancer* be? Probably nowhere I'd ever be able to get to you." She looked me straight in the eye and all traces of levity vanished from her voice. "Like I told you once before, Pall, I can't afford to lose *any* of my friends."

I took a deep breath and carefully let it out. "Well. I guess that's all settled. Good. Now, if you'll be kind enough to tell the nurse out by the monitor station that I'm signing out, I'll get dressed and we'll get back to the ship."

"Great. It'll be good to have you back." Smiling, she disappeared out into the corridor.

Carefully, I got my clothes out of the closet and began putting them on, an odd mixture of victory and defeat settling into my stomach. Alana was staying with the *Dancer*, which was certainly what I'd wanted . . . and yet, I couldn't help but feel that in some ways her decision was more a default than a real, active choice. Was she coming back because she wanted to, or merely because we were a safer course than the set of unknowns that Bradley offered? If the latter, it was clear that her old burns weren't entirely healed; that she still had a ways—maybe a long ways—to go. But that was all right. I may not have the talent she did for healing bruised souls, but if time and distance were what she needed, the *Dancer* and I could supply her with both.

I was just sealing my boots when Alana returned. "Finished? Good. They're getting your release ready, so let's go. Don't forget your letter," she added, pointing at Lord Hendrik's CompNote.

"This? It's nothing," I told her, crumpling it up and tossing it toward the wastebasket. "Just some junk mail from an old admirer."

Six months later, on our third point out from Prima, a new image of myself in liner captain's white appeared in my cascade pattern. I looked at it long and hard . . . and then did something I'd never done before for such an image.

I wished it lots of luck.

The writer who has most frequently appeared in the *Hugo Winners* volumes so far has been Poul Anderson. He has appeared seven times, all told, in the first five volumes. He appeared once in the first, twice in the second, twice in the third, once in the fourth, and once in the fifth—the only writer to have appeared in each of the first five volumes. It distresses me, then, that he has finally missed and is not represented in the sixth.

Here, however, is Greg Bear. And who is Greg Bear—aside from the fact that he is an award-winning science fiction writer of great expertise, that he is currently the president of the Science Fiction Writers of America, and that he has an excellent sense of humor (since just a few nights ago he was laughing fiendishly at my bursts of spontaneous wit, and that's the best measure of a sense of humor that I can imagine)?

Well, I'll tell you. He's the husband of Astrid Bear, nee Anderson, who is the daughter of Poul and Karen Anderson. In other words, Greg is Poul's son-in-law, and perhaps that counts. If we can't have Poul, we have Greg.

"Blood Music," by the way, is in my judgment another example of hard science fiction, and on a biological theme, too, which makes it even rarer and more beautiful. Greg manages, in the end, to advance something brand-new in answer to Enrico Fermi's famous question "Well, then, where are they?" when the possibility of copious alien life arose. If they exist, in other words, why haven't they come to visit us?

Let Greg give you one answer I had not thought of myself. (And, just to show you my limitations, we'll have still another answer I haven't thought of myself before this volume is done.)

—Isaac Asimov

Blood Music

by Greg Bear

There is a principle in nature I don't think anyone has pointed out before. Each hour, a myriad of trillions of little live things—bacteria, microbes, "animalcules"—are born and die, not counting for much except in the bulk of their existence and the accumulation of their tiny effects. They do not perceive deeply. They don't suffer much. A hundred billion, dying, would not begin to have the same importance as a single human death.

Within the ranks of magnitude of all creatures, small as microbes or great as humans, there is an equality of "elan," just as the branches of a tall tree, gathered together, equal the bulk of the limbs below, and all the limbs equal the bulk of the trunk.

That, at least, is the principle. I believe Vergil Ulam was the first to violate it.

It had been two years since I'd last seen Vergil. My memory of him hardly matched the tan, smiling, well-dressed gentleman standing before me. We had made a lunch appointment over the phone the day before, and now faced each other in the wide double doors of the employee's cafeteria at the Mount Freedom Medical Center.

"Vergil?" I asked. "My God, Vergil!"

"Good to see you, Edward." He shook my hand firmly. He had lost ten or twelve kilos and what remained seemed tighter, better proportioned. At the university, Vergil had been the pudgy, shock-haired, snaggle-toothed whiz kid who hot-wired doorknobs, gave us punch that turned our piss blue, and never got a date except with Eileen Termagent, who shared many of his physical characteristics.

"You look fantastic," I said. "Spend a summer in Cabo San Lucas?"

We stood in line at the counter and chose our food. "The tan," he said, picking out a carton of chocolate milk, "is from spending three months under a sun lamp. My teeth were straightened just after I last saw you. I'll explain the rest, but we need a place to talk where no one will listen close."

I steered him to the smoker's corner, where three die-hard puffers were scattered among six tables.

"Listen, I mean it," I said as we unloaded our trays. "You've changed. You're looking good."

"I've changed more than you know." His tone was motion-picture ominous, and he delivered the line with a theatrical lift of his brows. "How's Gail?"

Gail was doing well, I told him, teaching nursery school. We'd married the year before. His gaze shifted down to his food—pineapple slice and cottage cheese, piece of banana cream pie—and he said, his voice almost cracking, "Notice something else?"

I squinted in concentration. "Uh."

"Look closer."

"I'm not sure. Well, yes, you're not wearing glasses. Contacts?"

"No. I don't need them anymore."

"And you're a snappy dresser. Who's dressing you now? I hope she's as sexy as she is tasteful."

"Candice isn't—wasn't—responsible for the improvements in my clothes," he said. "I just got a better job, more money to throw around. My taste in clothes is better than my taste in food, as it happens." He grinned the old Vergil self-deprecating grin, but ended it with a peculiar leer. "At any rate, she's left me, I've been fired from my job, I'm living on savings."

"Hold it," I said. "That's a bit crowded. Why not do a linear breakdown? You got a job. Where?"

"Genetron Corp.," he said. "Sixteen months ago."

"I haven't heard of them."

"You will. They're putting out common stock in the next month. It'll shoot off the board. They've broken through with MABs. Medical—"

"I know what MABs are," I interrupted. "At least in theory. Medically Applicable Biochips."

"They have some that work."

"What?" It was my turn to lift my brows.

"Microscopic logic circuits. You inject them into the human body, they set up shop where they're told and troubleshoot. With Dr. Michael Bernard's approval."

That was quite impressive. Bernard's reputation was spotless. Not only was he associated with the genetic engineering biggies, but

he had made news at least once a year in his practice as a neuro-
surgeon before retiring. Covers on *Time*, *Mega*, *Rolling Stone*.

"That's supposed to be secret—stock, breakthrough, Bernard,
everything." He looked around and lowered his voice. "But you do
whatever the hell you want. I'm through with the bastards."

I whistled. "Make me rich, huh?"

"If that's what you want. Or you can spend some time with me
before rushing off to your broker."

"Of course." He hadn't touched the cottage cheese or pie. He had,
however, eaten the pineapple slice and drunk the chocolate milk.
"So tell me more."

"Well, in med school I was training for lab work. Biochemical
research. I've always had a bent for computers, too. So I put myself
through my last two years—"

"By selling software packages to Westinghouse," I said.

"It's good my friends remember. That's how I got involved with
Genetron, just when they were starting out. They had big money
backers, all the lab facilities I thought anyone would ever need. They
hired me, and I advanced rapidly.

"Four months and I was doing my own work. I made some
breakthroughs," he tossed his hand nonchalantly, "then I went off
on tangents they thought were premature. I persisted and they took
away my lab, handed it over to a certifiable flatworm. I managed to
save part of the experiment before they fired me. But I haven't
exactly been cautious . . . or judicious. So now it's going on outside
the lab."

I'd always regarded Vergil as ambitious, a trifle cracked, and not
terribly sensitive. His relations with authority figures had never
been smooth. Science, for him, was like the woman you couldn't
possibly have, who suddenly opens her arms to you, long before
you're ready for mature love—leaving you afraid you'll forever blow
the chance, lose the prize, screw up royally. Apparently, he had.

"Outside the lab? I don't get you."

"Edward, I want you to examine me. Give me a thorough physical. Maybe a cancer diagnostic. Then I'll explain more."

"You want a five-thousand-dollar exam?"

"Whatever you can do. Ultrasound, NMR, thermogram, everything."

"I don't know if I can get access to all that equipment. NMR full-scan has only been here a month or two. Hell, you couldn't pick a more expensive way—"

"Then ultrasound. That's all you'll need."

"Vergil, I'm an obstetrician, not a glamour-boy lab-tech. OB-GYN, butt of all jokes. If you're turning into a woman, maybe I can help you."

He leaned forward, almost putting his elbow into the pie, but swinging wide at the last instant by scant millimeters. The old Vergil would have hit it square. "Examine me closely and you'll . . ." He narrowed his eyes and shook his head. "Just examine me."

"So I make an appointment for ultrasound. Who's going to pay?"

"I'm on Blue Shield." He smiled and held up a medical credit card. "I messed with the personnel files at Genetron. Anything up to a hundred thousand dollars medical, they'll never check, never suspect."

He wanted secrecy, so I made arrangements. I filled out his forms myself. As long as everything was billed properly, most of the examination could take place without official notice. I didn't charge for my services. After all, Vergil had turned my piss blue. We were friends.

He came in late at night. I wasn't normally on duty then, but I stayed late, waiting for him on the third floor of what the nurses called the Frankenstein wing. I sat on an orange plastic chair. He arrived, looking olive-colored under the fluorescent lights.

He stripped, and I arranged him on the table. I noticed, first off, that his ankles looked swollen. But they weren't puffy. I felt them several times. They seemed healthy, but looked odd. "Hm," I said.

I ran the paddles over him, picking up areas difficult for the big unit to hit, and programmed the data into the imaging system. Then I swung the table around and inserted it into the enameled orifice of the ultrasound diagnostic unit, the hum-hole, so called by the nurses.

I integrated the data from the hum-hole with that from the paddle sweeps and rolled Vergil out, then set up a video frame. The image took a second to integrate, then flowed into a pattern showing Vergil's skeleton.

Three seconds of that—my jaw gaping—and it switched to his

thoracic organs, then his musculature, and finally, vascular system and skin.

"How long since the accident?" I asked, trying to take the quiver out of my voice.

"I haven't been in an accident," he said. "It was deliberate."

"Jesus, they beat you, to keep secrets?"

"You don't understand me, Edward. Look at the images again. I'm not damaged."

"Look, there's thickening here," I indicated the ankles, "and your ribs—that crazy zigzag pattern of interlocks. Broken sometime, obviously. And—"

"Look at my spine," he said. I rotated the image in the video frame.

Buckminster Fuller, I thought. It was fantastic. A cage of triangular projections, all interlocking in ways I couldn't begin to follow, much less understand. I reached around and tried to feel his spine with my fingers. He lifted his arms and looked off at the ceiling.

"I can't find it," I said. "It's all smooth back there." I let go of him and looked at his chest, then prodded his ribs. They were sheathed in something rough and flexible. The harder I pressed, the tougher it became. Then I noticed another change.

"Hey," I said. "You don't have any nipples." There were tiny pigment patches, but no nipple formations at all.

"See?" Vergil asked, shrugging on the white robe. "I'm being rebuilt from the inside out."

In my reconstruction of those hours, I fancy myself saying, "So tell me about it." Perhaps mercifully, I don't remember what I actually said.

He explained with his characteristic circumlocutions. Listening was like trying to get to the meat of a newspaper article through a forest of sidebars and graphic embellishments.

I simplify and condense.

Genetron had assigned him to manufacturing prototype biochips, tiny circuits made out of protein molecules. Some were hooked up to silicon chips little more than a micrometer in size, then sent through rat arteries to chemically keyed locations, to make connections with the rat tissue and attempt to monitor and even control lab-induced pathologies.

"*That* was something," he said. "We recovered the most complex microchip by sacrificing the rat, then debriefed it—hooked the silicon portion up to an imaging system. The computer gave us bar graphs, then a diagram of the chemical characteristics of about eleven centimeters of blood vessel . . . then put it all together to make a picture. We zoomed down eleven centimeters of rat artery. You never saw so many scientists jumping up and down, hugging each other, drinking buckets of bug juice." Bug juice was lab ethanol mixed with Dr Pepper.

Eventually, the silicon elements were eliminated completely in favor of nucleoproteins. He seemed reluctant to explain in detail, but I gathered they found ways to make huge molecules—as large as DNA, and even more complex—into electrochemical computers, using ribosome-like structures as "encoders" and "readers," and RNA as "tape." Vergil was able to mimic reproductive separation and reassembly in his nucleoproteins, incorporating program changes at key points by switching nucleotide pairs. "Genetron wanted me to switch over to supergene engineering, since that was the coming thing everywhere else. Make all kinds of critters, some out of our imagination. But I had different ideas." He twiddled his finger around his ear and made theremin sounds. "Mad scientist time, right?" He laughed, then sobered. "I injected my best nucleoproteins into bacteria to make duplication and compounding easier. Then I started to leave them inside, so the circuits could interact with the cells. They were heuristically programmed; they taught themselves more than I programmed them. The cells fed chemically coded information to the computers, the computers processed it and made decisions, the cells became smart. I mean, smart as planaria, for starters. Imagine an *E. coli* as smart as a planarian worm!"

I nodded. "I'm imagining."

"Then I really went off on my own. We had the equipment, the techniques; and I knew the molecular language. I could make really dense, really complicated biochips by compounding the nucleoproteins, making them into little brains. I did some research into how far I could go, theoretically. Sticking with bacteria, I could make them a biochip with the computing capacity of a sparrow's brain. Imagine how jazzed I was! Then I saw a way to increase the complexity a thousandfold, by using something we regarded as a nuisance—quantum chitchat between the fixed elements of the circuits. Down that small, even the slightest change could bomb a biochip. But I developed a program that actually predicted and took advantage of electron tunneling. Emphasized the heuristic aspects of the computer, used the chitchat as a method of increasing complexity."

"You're losing me," I said.

"I took advantage of randomness. The circuits could repair themselves, compare memories, and correct faulty elements. The whole schmeer. I gave them basic instructions: Go forth and multiply. Improve. By God, you should have seen some of the cultures a week later! It was amazing. They were evolving all on their own, like little cities. I destroyed them all. I think one of the petri dishes would have grown legs and walked out of the incubator if I'd kept feeding it."

"You're kidding." I looked at him. "You're not kidding."

"Man, they *knew* what it was like to improve! They knew where they had to go, but they were just so limited, being in bacteria bodies, with so few resources."

"How smart were they?"

"I couldn't be sure. They were associating in clusters of a hundred to two hundred cells, each cluster behaving like an autonomous unit. Each cluster might have been as smart as a rhesus monkey. They exchanged information through their pili, passed on bits of memory, and compared notes. Their organization was obviously different from a group of monkeys. Their world was so much simpler, for one thing. With their abilities, they were masters of the petri dishes. I put phages in with them; the phages didn't have a chance. They used every option available to change and grow."

"How is that possible?"

"What?" He seemed surprised I wasn't accepting everything at face value.

"Cramming so much into so little. A rhesus monkey is not your simple little calculator, Vergil."

"I haven't made myself clear," he said, obviously irritated. "I was using nucleoprotein computers. They're like DNA, but all the information can interact. Do you know how many nucleotide pairs there are in the DNA of a single bacteria?"

It had been a long time since my last biochemistry lesson. I shook my head.

"About two million. Add in the modified ribosome structures—

fifteen thousand of them, each with a molecular weight of about three million—and consider the combinations and permutations. The RNA is arranged like a continuous loop paper tape, surrounded by ribosomes ticking off instructions and manufacturing protein chains . . ." His eyes were bright and slightly moist. "Besides, I'm not saying every cell was a distinct entity. They cooperated."

"How many bacteria in the dishes you destroyed?"

"Billions. I don't know." He smirked. "You got it, Edward. Whole planetsful of *E. coli*."

"But they didn't fire you then?"

"No. They didn't know what was going on, for one thing. I kept compounding the molecules, increasing their size and complexity. When bacteria were too limited, I took blood from myself, separated out white cells, and injected them with the new biochips. I watched them, put them through mazes and little chemical problems. They were whizzes. Time is a lot faster at that level—so little distance for the messages to cross, and the environment is much simpler. Then I forgot to store a file under my secret code in the lab computers. Some managers found it and guessed what I was up to. Everybody panicked. They thought we'd have every social watchdog in the country on our backs because of what I'd done. They started to destroy my work and wipe my programs. Ordered me to sterilize my white cells. Christ." He pulled the white robe off and started to get dressed. "I only had a day or two. I separated out the most complex cells—"

"How complex?"

"They were clustering in hundred-cell groups, like the bacteria. Each group as smart as a ten-year-old kid, maybe." He studied my face for a moment. "Still doubting? Want me to run through how many nucleotide pairs there are in a mammalian cell? I tailored my computers to take advantage of the white cells' capacity. Ten billion nucleotide pairs, Edward. Ten E-f——ing ten. And they don't have a huge body to worry about, taking up most of their thinking time."

"Okay," I said. "I'm convinced. What did you do?"

"I mixed the cells back into a cylinder of whole blood and injected myself with it." He buttoned the top of his shirt and smiled thinly at me. "I'd programmed them with every drive I could, talked as high a level as I could using just enzymes and such. After that, they were on their own."

"You programmed them to go forth and multiply, improve?" I repeated.

"I think they developed some characteristics picked up by the biochips in their *E. coli* phases. The white cells could talk to one another with extruded memories. They almost certainly found ways to ingest other types of cells and alter them without killing them."

"You're crazy."

"You can see the screen! Edward, I haven't been sick since. I used to get colds all the time. I've never felt better."

"They're inside you, finding things, changing them."

"And by now, each cluster is as smart as you or I."

"You're absolutely nuts."

He shrugged. "They fired me. They thought I was going to get revenge for what they did to my work. They ordered me out of the labs, and I haven't had a real chance to see what's been going on inside me until now. Three months."

"So . . ." My mind was racing. "You lost weight because they improved your fat metabolism. Your bones are stronger, your spine has been completely rebuilt—"

"No more backaches even if I sleep on my old mattress."

"Your heart looks different."

"I didn't know about the heart," he said, examining the frame image from a few inches. "About the fat—I was thinking about that. They could increase my brown cells, fix up the metabolism. I haven't been as hungry lately. I haven't changed my eating habits that much—I still want the same old junk—but somehow I get around to eating only what I need. I don't think they know what my brain is yet. Sure, they've got all the glandular stuff—but they don't have the *big* picture, if you see what I mean. They don't know *I'm* in there. But boy, they sure did figure out what my reproductive organs are."

I glanced at the image and shifted my eyes away.

"Oh, they look pretty normal," he said, hefting his scrotum obscenely. He snickered. "But how else do you think I'd land a real looker like Candice? She was just after a one-night stand with a techie. I looked okay then, no tan but trim, with good clothes. She'd never screwed a techie before. Joke time, right? But my little geniuses kept us up half the night. I think they made improvements each time. I felt like I had a goddamned fever."

His smile vanished. "But then one night my skin started to crawl.

It really scared me. I thought things were getting out of hand. I wondered what they'd do when they crossed the blood-brain barrier and found out about *me*—about the brain's real function. So I began a campaign to keep them under control. I figured, the reason they wanted to get into the skin was the simplicity of running circuits across a surface. Much easier than trying to maintain chains of communication in and around muscles, organs, vessels. The skin was much more direct. So I bought a quartz lamp." He caught my puzzled expression. "In the lab, we'd break down the protein in biochip cells by exposing them to ultraviolet light. I alternated sun lamp with quartz treatments. Keeps them out of my skin, so far as I can tell, and gives me a nice tan."

"Give you skin cancer, too," I commented.

"They'll probably take care of that. Like police."

"Okay, I've examined you, you've told me a story I still find hard to believe . . . what do you want me to do?"

"I'm not as nonchalant as I act, Edward. I'm worried. I'd like to find some way to control them before they find out about my brain. I mean, think of it, they're in the trillions by now, each one smart. They're cooperating to some extent. I'm probably the smartest thing on the planet, and they haven't even begun to get their act together yet. I don't really want them to take over." He laughed very unpleasantly. "Steal my soul, you know? So think of some treatment to block them. Maybe we can starve the little buggers. Just think on it." He buttoned his shirt. "Give me a call." He handed me a slip of paper with his address and phone number. Then he went to the keyboard and erased the image on the frame, dumping the memory of the examination. "Just you," he said. "Nobody else for now. And please . . . hurry."

It was three o'clock in the morning when Vergil walked out of the examination room. He'd allowed me to take blood samples, then shaken my hand—his palm damp, nervous —and cautioned me against ingesting anything from the specimens.

Before I went home, I put the blood through a series of tests. The results were ready the next day.

I picked them up during my lunch break in the afternoon, then destroyed all the samples. I did it like a robot. It took me five days and nearly sleepless nights to accept what I'd seen. His blood was normal enough, though the machines diagnosed the patient as

having an infection. High levels of leukocytes—white blood cells—
and histamines. On the fifth day, I believed.

Gail was home before I, but it was my turn to fix dinner. She
slipped one of the school's disks into the home system and showed
me video art her nursery kids had been creating. I watched quietly,
ate with her in silence.

I had two dreams, part of my final acceptance. The first that
evening—which had me up thrashing in my sheets—I witnessed the
destruction of the planet Krypton, Superman's home world. Billions
of superhuman geniuses went screaming off in walls of fire. I related
the destruction to my sterilizing the samples of Vergil's blood.

The second dream was worse. I dreamed that New York City was
raping a woman. By the end of the dream, she was giving birth to
little embryo cities, all wrapped up in translucent sacs, soaked with
blood from the difficult labor.

I called him on the morning of the sixth day. He answered on the
fourth ring. "I have some results," I said. "Nothing conclusive. But
I want to talk with you. In person."

"Sure," he said. "I'm staying inside for the time being." His voice
was strained; he sounded tired.

Vergil's apartment was in a fancy high-rise near the lake shore. I
took the elevator up, listening to little advertising jingles and watching dancing holograms display products, empty apartments for
rent, the building's hostess discussing social activities for the week.

Vergil opened the door and motioned me in. He wore a checked
robe with long sleeves and carpet slippers. He clutched an unlit pipe
in one hand, his fingers twisting it back and forth as he walked away
from me and sat down, saying nothing.

"You have an infection," I said.

"Oh?"

"That's all the blood analyses tell me. I don't have access to the
electron microscopes."

"I don't think it's really an infection," he said. "After all, they're
my own cells. Probably something else . . . sign of their presence,
of the change. We can't expect to understand everything that's
happening."

I removed my coat. "Listen," I said, "you have me worried now."
The expression on his face stopped me: a kind of frantic beatitude.
He squinted at the ceiling and pursed his lips.

"Are you stoned?" I asked.

He shook his head, then nodded once, very slowly. "Listening," he said.

"To what?"

"I don't know. Not sounds . . . exactly. Like music. The heart, all the blood vessels, friction of blood along the arteries, veins. Activity. Music in the blood." He looked at me plaintively. "Why aren't you at work?"

"My day off. Gail's working."

"Can you stay?"

I shrugged. "I suppose." I sounded suspicious. I was glancing around the apartment, looking for ashtrays, packs of papers.

"I'm not stoned, Edward," he said. "I may be wrong, but I think something big is happening. I think they're finding out who I am."

I sat down across from Vergil, staring at him intently. He didn't seem to notice. Some inner process was involving him. When I asked for a cup of coffee, he motioned to the kitchen. I boiled a pot of water and took a jar of instant from the cabinet. With cup in hand, I returned to my seat. He was twisting his head back and forth, eyes open. "You always knew what you wanted to be, didn't you?" he asked me.

"More or less."

"A gynecologist. Smart moves. Never false moves. I was different. I had goals, but no direction. Like a map without roads, just places to be. I didn't give a shit for anything, anyone but myself. Even science. Just a means. I'm surprised I got so far. I even hated my folks."

He gripped his chair arms.

"Something wrong?" I asked.

"They're talking to me," he said. He shut his eyes.

For an hour he seemed to be asleep. I checked his pulse, which was strong and steady, felt his forehead—slightly cool—and made myself more coffee. I was looking through a magazine, at a loss what to do, when he opened his eyes again. "Hard to figure exactly what time is like for them," he said. "It's taken them maybe three, four days to figure out language, key human concepts. Now they're on to it. On to me. Right now."

"How's that?"

He claimed there were thousands of researchers hooked up to his neurons. He couldn't give details. "They're damned efficient, you know," he said. "They haven't screwed me up yet."

"We should get you into the hospital now."

"What in hell could they do? Did you figure out any way to control them? I mean, they're my own cells."

"I've been thinking. We could starve them. Find out what metabolic differences—"

"I'm not sure I want to be rid of them," Vergil said. "They're not doing any harm."

"How do you know?"

He shook his head and held up one finger. "Wait. They're trying to figure out what space is. That's tough for them. They break distances down into concentrations of chemicals. For them, space is like intensity of taste."

"Vergil—"

"Listen! Think, Edward!" His tone was excited but even. "Observe! Something big is happening inside me. They talk to one another across the fluid, through membranes. They tailor something—viruses?—to carry data stored in nucleic acid chains. I think they're saying 'RNA.' That makes sense. That's one way I programmed them. But plasmid-like structures, too. Maybe that's what your machines think is a sign of infection—all their chattering in my blood, packets of data. Tastes of other individuals. Peers. Superiors. Subordinates."

"Vergil, I'm listening, but I still think you should be in a hospital."

"This is my show, Edward," he said. "I'm their universe. They're amazed by the new scale." He was quiet again for a time. I squatted by his chair and pulled up the sleeve to his robe. His arm was crisscrossed with white lines. I was about to go to the phone and call for an ambulance when he stood and stretched. "Do you realize," he said, "how many body cells we kill each time we move?"

"I'm going to call for an ambulance," I said.

"No, you aren't." His tone stopped me. "I told you, I'm not sick; this is my show. Do you know what they'd do to me in a hospital? They'd be like cavemen trying to fix a computer the same way they fix a stone ax. It would be a farce."

"Then what the hell am I doing here?" I asked, getting angry. "I can't do anything. I'm one of those cavemen."

"You're a friend," Vergil said, fixing his eyes on me. I had the impression I was being watched by more than just Vergil. "I want you here to keep me company." He laughed. "But I'm not exactly alone."

He walked around the apartment for two hours, fingering things, looking out windows, making himself lunch slowly and methodically. "You know, they can actually feel their own thoughts," he said about noon. "I mean, the cytoplasm seems to have a will of its own, a kind of subconscious life counter to the rationality they've only recently acquired. They hear the chemical 'noise' or whatever of the molecules fitting and unfitting inside."

At two o'clock, I called Gail to tell her I would be late. I was almost sick with tension but I tried to keep my voice level. "Remember Vergil Ulam? I'm talking with him right now."

"Everything okay?" she asked.

Was it? Decidedly not. "Fine," I said.

"Culture!" Vergil said, peering around the kitchen wall at me. I said good-bye and hung up the phone. "They're always swimming in that bath of information. Contributing to it. It's a kind of gestalt thing, whatever. The hierarchy is absolute. They send tailored phages after cells that don't interact properly. Viruses specified to individuals or groups. No escape. One gets pierced by the virus, the cell blebs outward, it explodes and dissolves. But it's not just a dictatorship, I think they effectively have more freedom than in a democracy. I mean, they vary so differently from individual to individual. Does that make sense? They vary in different ways than we do."

"Hold it," I said, gripping his shoulders. "Vergil, you're pushing me close to the edge. I can't take this much longer. I don't understand, I'm not sure I believe—"

"Not even now?"

"Okay, let's say you're giving me the, the right interpretation. Giving it to me straight. The whole thing's true. Have you bothered to figure out all the consequences yet? What all this means, where it might lead?"

He walked into the kitchen and drew a glass of water from the tap, then returned and stood next to me. His expression had changed from childish absorption to sober concern. "I've never been very good at that."

"Aren't you afraid?"

"I was. Now I'm not sure." He fingered the tie of his robe. "Look, I don't want you to think I went around you, over your head or something. But I met with Michael Bernard yesterday. He put me through his private clinic, took specimens. Told me to quit the lamp treatments. He called this morning, just before you did. He says it all checks out. And he asked me not to tell anybody." He paused and his expression became dreamy again. "Cities of cells," he continued. "Edward, they push pili-like tubes through the tissues, spread information—"

"Stop it!" I shouted. "Checks out? What checks out?"

"As Bernard puts it, I have 'severely enlarged macrophages' throughout my system. And he concurs on the anatomical changes. So it's not just our common delusion."

"What does he plan to do?"

"I don't know. I think he'll probably convince Genetron to reopen the lab."

"Is that what you want?"

"It's not just having the lab again. I want to show you. Since I stopped the lamp treatments. I'm still changing." He undid his robe and let it slide to the floor. All over his body, his skin was criss-crossed with white lines. Along his back, the lines were starting to form ridges.

"My God," I said.

"I'm not going to be much good anywhere else but the lab soon. I won't be able to go out in public. Hospitals wouldn't know what to do, as I said."

"You're . . . you can talk to them, tell them to slow down," I said, aware how ridiculous that sounded.

"Yes, indeed I can, but they don't necessarily listen."

"I thought you were their god or something."

"The ones hooked up to my neurons aren't the big wheels. They're researchers, or at least serve the same function. They know I'm here, what I am, but that doesn't mean they've convinced the upper levels of the hierarchy."

"They're disputing?"

"Something like that. It's not all that bad, anyway. If the lab is reopened, I have a home, a place to work." He glanced out the window, as if looking for someone. "I don't have anything left but them. They aren't afraid, Edward. I've never felt so close to anything before." The beatific smile again. "I'm responsible for them. Mother to them all."

"You have no way of knowing what they're going to do."

He shook his head.

"No, I mean it. You say they're like a civilization—"

"Like a thousand civilizations."

"Yes, and civilizations have been known to screw up. Warfare, the environment—"

I was grasping at straws, trying to restrain a growing panic. I wasn't competent to handle the enormity of what was happening. Neither was Vergil. He was the last person I would have called insightful and wise about large issues.

"But I'm the only one at risk."

"You don't know that. Jesus, Vergil, look what they're *doing* to you!"

"To me, all to me!" he said. "Nobody else."

I shook my head and held up my hands in a gesture of defeat. "Okay, so Bernard gets them to reopen the lab, you move in, become a guinea pig. What then?"

"They treat me right. I'm more than just good old Vergil Ulam now. I'm a goddamned galaxy, a super-mother."

"Super-host, you mean." He conceded the point with a shrug.

I couldn't take any more. I made my exit with a few flimsy excuses, then sat in the lobby of the apartment building, trying to calm down. Somebody had to talk some sense into him. Who would he listen to? He had gone to Bernard . . .

And it sounded as if Bernard was not only convinced, but very interested. People of Bernard's stature didn't coax the Vergil Ulams of the world along, not unless they felt it was to their advantage.

I had a hunch, and I decided to play it. I went to a pay phone, slipped in my credit card, and called Genetron.

"I'd like you to page Dr. Michael Bernard," I told the receptionist.

"Who's calling, please?"

"This is his answering service. We have an emergency call and his beeper doesn't seem to be working."

A few anxious minutes later, Bernard came on the line. "Who the hell is this?" he asked quietly. "I don't have an answering service."

"My name is Edward Milligan. I'm a friend of Vergil Ulam's. I think we have some problems to discuss."

We made an appointment to talk the next morning.

I went home and tried to think of excuses to keep me off the next day's hospital shift. I couldn't concentrate on medicine, couldn't give my patients anywhere near the attention they deserved.

Guilty, anxious, angry, afraid.

That was how Gail found me. I slipped on a mask of calm and we fixed dinner together. After eating, we watched the city lights come on in late twilight through the bayside window, holding on to each other. Odd winter starlings pecked at the yellow lawn in the last few minutes of light, then flew away with a rising wind which made the windows rattle.

"Something's wrong," Gail said softly. "Are you going to tell me, or just act like everything's normal?"

"It's just me," I said. "Nervous. Work at the hospital."

"Oh, lord," she said, sitting up. "You're going to divorce me for that Baker woman." Mrs. Baker weighed three hundred and sixty pounds and hadn't known she was pregnant until her fifth month.

"No," I said, listless.

"Rapturous relief," Gail said, touching my forehead lightly. "You know this kind of introspection drives me crazy."

"Well, it's nothing I can talk about yet, so . . ." I patted her hand.

"That's disgustingly patronizing," she said, getting up. "I'm going to make some tea. Want some?" Now she was miffed, and I was tense with not telling.

Why not just reveal all? I asked myself. An old friend of mine was turning himself into a galaxy.

I cleared away the table instead. That night, unable to sleep, I looked down on Gail in bed from my sitting position, pillow against the wall, and tried to determine what I knew was real, and what wasn't.

I'm a doctor, I told myself. A technical, scientific profession. I'm supposed to be immune to things like future shock.

Vergil Ulam was turning into a galaxy.

How would it feel to be topped off with a trillion Chinese? I grinned in the dark, and almost cried at the same time. What Vergil had inside him was unimaginably stranger than Chinese. Stranger than anything I—or Vergil—could easily understand. Perhaps ever understand.

But I knew what was real. The bedroom, the city lights faint through gauze curtains. Gail sleeping. Very important. Gail, in bed, sleeping.

The dream came again. This time the city came in through the window and attacked Gail. It was a great, spiky lighted-up prowler and it growled in a language I couldn't understand, made up of auto horns, crowded noises, construction bedlam. I tried to fight it off, but it got to her—and turned into a drift of stars, sprinkling all over the bed, all over everything. I jerked awake and stayed up until dawn, dressed with Gail, kissed her, savored the reality of her human, unviolated lips.

And went to meet with Bernard. He had been loaned a suite in a big downtown hospital; I rode the elevator to the sixth floor, and saw what fame and fortune could mean.

The suite was tastefully furnished, fine serigraphs on wood-paneled walls, chrome and glass furniture, cream-colored carpet, Chinese brass, and wormwood-grain cabinets and tables.

He offered me a cup of coffee, and I accepted. He took a seat in the breakfast nook, and I sat across from him, cradling my cup in moist palms. He was dapper, wearing a gray suit; had graying hair and a sharp profile. He was in his mid-sixties and he looked quite a bit like Leonard Bernstein.

"About our mutual acquaintance," he said. "Mr. Ulam. Brilliant. And, I won't hesitate to say, courageous."

"He's my friend. I'm worried about him."

Bernard held up one finger. "Courageous—and a bloody damned fool. What's happening to him should never have been allowed. He may have done it under duress, but that's no excuse. Still, what's done is done. He's talked to you, I take it."

I nodded. "He wants to return to Genetron."

"Of course. That's where all his equipment is. Where his home probably will be while we sort this out."

"Sort it out—how? What use is it?" I wasn't thinking too clearly. I had a slight headache.

"I can think of a large number of uses for small, super-dense computer elements with a biological base. Can't you? Genetron has already made breakthroughs, but this is something else again."

"What do you envision?"

Bernard smiled. "I'm not really at liberty to say. It'll be revolutionary. We'll have to get him in lab conditions. Animal experiments have to be conducted. We'll have to start from scratch, of course. Vergil's . . . um . . . colonies can't be transferred. They're based on his white blood cells. So we have to develop colonies that won't trigger immune reactions to other animals."

"Like an infection?" I asked.

"I suppose there are comparisons. But Vergil is not infected."

"My tests indicate he is."

"That's probably the bits of data floating around in his blood, don't you think?"

"I don't know."

"Listen, I'd like you to come down to the lab after Vergil is settled in. Your expertise might be useful to us."

Us. He was working with Genetron hand in glove. Could he be objective? "How will you benefit from all this?"

"Edward, I have always been at the forefront of my profession. I see no reason why I shouldn't be helping here. With my knowledge of brain and nerve functions, and the research I've been conducting in neurophysiology—"

"You could help Genetron hold off an investigation by the government," I said.

"That's being very blunt. Too blunt, and unfair."

"Perhaps. Anyway, yes. I'd like to visit the lab when Vergil's settled in. If I'm still welcome, bluntness and all." He looked at me sharply. I wouldn't be playing on *his* team; for a moment, his thoughts were almost nakedly apparent.

"Of course," Bernard said, rising with me. He reached out to shake my hand. His palm was damp. He was as nervous as I was, even if he didn't look it.

I returned to my apartment and stayed there until noon, reading, trying to sort things out. Reach a decision. What was real, what I needed to protect.

There is only so much change anyone can stand. Innovation, yes, but slow application. Don't force. Everyone has the right to stay the same until they decide otherwise.

The greatest thing in science since . . .

And Bernard would force it. Genetron would force it. I couldn't handle the thought. "Neo-Luddite," I said to myself. A filthy accusation.

When I pressed Vergil's number on the building security panel, Vergil answered almost immediately. "Yeah," he said. He sounded exhilarated now. "Come on up. I'll be in the bathroom. Door's unlocked."

I entered his apartment and walked through the hallway to the bathroom. Vergil was in the tub, up to his neck in pinkish water. He smiled vaguely at me and splashed his hands. "Looks like I slit my wrists, doesn't it?" he said softly. "Don't worry. Everything's fine now. Genetron's going to take me back. Bernard just called." He pointed to the bathroom phone and intercom.

I sat down on the toilet and noticed the sun lamp fixture standing unplugged next to the linen cabinets. The bulbs sat in a row on the edge of the sink counter. "You're sure that's what you want," I said, my shoulders slumping.

"Yeah, I think so," he said. "They can take better care of me. I'm getting cleaned up, go over there this evening. Bernard's picking me up in his limo. Style. From here on in, everything's style."

The pinkish color in the water didn't look like soap. "Is that bubble bath?" I asked. Some of it came to me in a rush then and I felt a little weaker: what had occurred to me was just one more obvious and necessary insanity.

"No," Vergil said. I knew that already.

"No," he repeated, "it's coming from my skin. They're not telling me everything, but I think they're sending out scouts. Astronauts." He looked at me with an expression that didn't quite equal concern; more like curiosity as to how I'd take it.

The confirmation made my stomach muscles tighten as if waiting for a punch. I had never even considered the possibility until now, perhaps because I had been concentrating on other aspects. "Is this the first time?" I asked.

"Yeah," he said. He laughed. "I've half a mind to let the little buggers down the drain. Let them find out what the world's really about."

"They'd go everywhere," I said.

"Sure enough."

"How . . . how are you feeling?"

"I'm feeling pretty good now. Must be billions of them." More splashing with his hands. "What do you think? Should I let the buggers out?"

Quickly, hardly thinking, I knelt down beside the tub. My fingers went for the cord on the sun lamp and I plugged it in. He had hot-wired doorknobs, turned my piss blue, played a thousand dumb practical jokes and never grown up, never grown mature enough to understand that he was just brilliant enough to really affect the world; he would never learn caution.

He reached for the drain knob. "You know, Edward, I—"

He never finished. I picked up the fixture and dropped it into the tub, jumping back at the flash of steam and sparks. Vergil screamed and thrashed and jerked and then everything was still, except for the low, steady sizzle and the smoke wafting from his hair.

I lifted the toilet and vomited. Then I clenched my nose and went into the living room. My legs went out from under me and I sat abruptly on the couch.

After an hour, I searched through Vergil's kitchen and found bleach, ammonia, and a bottle of Jack Daniel's. I returned to the bathroom, keeping the center of my gaze away from Vergil. I poured first the booze, then the bleach, then the ammonia into the water. Chlorine started bubbling up and I left, closing the door behind me.

The phone was ringing when I got home. I didn't answer. It could have been the hospital. It could have been Bernard. Or the police. I could envision having to explain everything to the police. Genetron would stonewall; Bernard would be unavailable.

I was exhausted, all my muscles knotted with tension and whatever name one can give to the feelings one has after—

Committing genocide?

That certainly didn't seem real. I could not believe I had just murdered a hundred trillion intelligent beings. Snuffed a galaxy. It was laughable. But I didn't laugh.

It was not at all hard to believe I had just killed one human being, a friend. The smoke, the melted lamp rods, the drooping electrical outlet and smoking cord.

Vergil.

I had dunked the lamp into the tub with Vergil.

I felt sick. Dreams, cities raping Gail (and what about his girl-friend, Candice?). Letting the water filled with them out. Galaxies sprinkling over us all. What horror. Then again, what potential beauty—a new kind of life, symbiosis and transformation.

Had I been thorough enough to kill them all? I had a moment of panic. Tomorrow, I thought, I will sterilize his apartment. Somehow. I didn't even think of Bernard.

When Gail came in the door, I was asleep on the couch. I came to, groggy, and she looked down at me.

"You feeling okay?" she asked, perching on the edge of the couch. I nodded.

"What are you planning for dinner?" My mouth wasn't working properly. The words were mushy. She felt my forehead.

"Edward, you have a fever," she said. "A very high fever."

I stumbled into the bathroom and looked in the mirror. Gail was close behind me. "What is it?" she asked.

There were lines under my collar, around my neck. White lines, like freeways. They had already been in me a long time, days.

"Damp palms," I said. So obvious.

I think we nearly died. I struggled at first, but within minutes I was too weak to move. Gail was just as sick within an hour.

I lay on the carpet in the living room, drenched in sweat. Gail lay on the couch, her face the color of talcum, eyes closed, like a corpse in an embalming parlor. For a time I thought she was dead. Sick as I was, I raged—hated, felt tremendous guilt at my weakness, my slowness to understand all the possibilities. Then I no longer cared. I was too weak to blink, so I closed my eyes and waited.

There was a rhythm in my arms, my legs. With each pulse of blood, a kind of sound welled up within me. A sound like an orchestra thousands strong, but not playing in unison; playing whole seasons of symphonies at once. Music in the blood. The sound or whatever became harsher, but more coordinated, wave-trains finally cancelling into silence, then separating into harmonic beats.

The beats seemed to melt into me, into the sound of my own heart.

First, they subdued our immune responses. The war—and it was a war, on a scale never before known on Earth, with trillions of combatants—lasted perhaps two days.

By the time I regained enough strength to get to the kitchen faucet, I could feel them working on my brain, trying to crack the code and

find the god within the protoplasm. I drank until I was sick, then
drank more moderately and took a glass to Gail. She sipped at it. Her
lips were cracked, her eyes bloodshot and ringed with yellowish
crumbs. There was some color in her skin. Minutes later, we were
eating feebly in the kitchen.

"What in hell was *that?*" was the first thing she asked. I didn't
have the strength to explain, so I shook my head. I peeled an orange
and shared it with her. "We should call a doctor," she said. But I
knew we wouldn't. I was already receiving messages; it was becoming apparent that any sensation of freedom we had was illusory.

The messages were simple at first. Memories of commands, rather
than the commands themselves, manifested themselves in my
thoughts. We were not to leave the apartment—a concept which
seemed quite abstract to those in control, even if undesirable—and
we were not to have contact with others. We would be allowed to
eat certain foods, and drink tap water, for the time being.

With the subsidence of the fevers, the transformations were quick
and drastic. Almost simultaneously, Gail and I were immobilized.
She was sitting at the table, I was kneeling on the floor. I was able
barely to see her in the corner of my eye.

Her arm was developing pronounced ridges.

They had learned inside Vergil; their tactics within the two of us
were very different. I itched all over for about two hours—two hours
in hell—before they made the breakthrough and found me. The
effort of ages on their time scale paid off and they communicated
smoothly and directly with this great, clumsy intelligence which had
once controlled their universe.

They were not cruel. When the concept of discomfort and its
undesirability was made clear, they worked to alleviate it. They
worked too effectively. For another hour, I was in a sea of bliss, out
of all contact with them.

With dawn the next day, we were allowed freedom to move again;
specifically, to go to the bathroom. There were certain waste products they could not deal with. I voided those—my urine was
purple—and Gail followed suit. We looked at each other vacantly in
the bathroom. Then she managed a slight smile. "Are they talking
to you?" she asked. I nodded. "Then I'm not crazy."

For the next twelve hours, control seemed to loosen on some
levels. During that time, I managed to pencil the majority of this

manuscript. I suspect there was another kind of war going on in me. Gail was capable of our previous limited motion, but no more.

When full control resumed, we were instructed to hold each other. We did not hesitate.

"Eddie . . ." she whispered. My name was the last sound I ever heard from outside.

Standing, we grew together. In hours, our legs expanded and spread out. Then extensions grew to the windows to take in sunlight, and to the kitchen to take water from the sink. Filaments soon reached to all corners of the room, stripping paint and plaster from the walls, fabric and stuffing from the furniture.

By the next dawn, the transformation was complete.

I no longer have any clear view of what we look like. I suspect we resemble cells—large, flat and filamented cells, draped purposefully across most of the apartment. The great shall mimic the small.

I have been asked to carry on recording, but soon that will not be possible. Our intelligence fluctuates daily as we are absorbed into the minds within. Each day, our individuality declines. We are, indeed, great clumsy dinosaurs. Our memories have been taken over by billions of them, and our personalities have been spread through the transformed blood.

Soon there will be no need for centralization.

I am informed that already the plumbing has been invaded. People throughout the building are undergoing transformation.

Within the old time frame of weeks, we will reach the lakes, rivers, and seas in force.

I can barely begin to guess the results. Every square inch of the planet will teem with thought. Years from now, perhaps much sooner, they will subdue their own individuality—what there is of it.

New creatures will come, then. The immensity of their capacity for thought will be inconceivable.

All my hatred and fear is gone now.

I leave them—us—with only one question.

How many times has this happened, elsewhere? Travelers never came through space to visit the Earth. They had no need.

They had found universes in grains of sand.

Here is Octavia Butler, the third of the women represented by stories in this volume. I have never met her, but I would certainly like to, for she is described to me as a large and impressive woman over six feet tall—and I like to admire statuesque women.

There's a queer double image of science fiction, by the way. To some people who don't read science fiction there is the feeling, I suspect, that the field is made up simply of a collection of stories in which writers predict the technological wonders of tomorrow. This insistence on "prediction" comes up whenever I am interviewed. I am constantly being asked to talk about the future, and a disquietingly large number of questions begin with "What do you predict for . . .?" It could be anything. The most recent question of the sort was, "What do you predict for the future of Philadelphia?"

On the other hand, there are also people who, through a surfeit of disaster movies, think of science fiction (which they call "sci-fi"—spit, spit) as a litany of terrible destructiveness. I guess that would be best epitomized by Harlan Ellison's favorite title for such things: "The Monster That Ate Cleveland."

Actually, science fiction is committed neither to marvels nor to disasters. It deals with possible situations. It tries to draw a rational and self-consistent society, different from ours, which may be better, even much better, than our society; or worse, even much worse; or better in some respects and worse in others. The point of the story, then, is how people live and react in such societies.

Naturally, trouble makes for greater drama than does happiness, and it asks more in the way of human response. Therefore, science fiction (like all forms of literature) is more likely to deal with discomfort than with comfort. Furthermore, it must be granted that given the direction in which our society is now moving, we seem much more likely to end in the soup than to be swimming in the cream.

But what counts, as always, is the way a story is written, and Octavia draws a picture of an all-but-destroyed society that is so vivid that you will find yourself living in it. And, oddly enough, she manages to end with a ray of hope that you will find yourself accepting gladly.

—Isaac Asimov

Speech Sounds
by Octavia E. Butler

There was trouble aboard the Washington Boulevard bus. Rye had expected trouble sooner or later in her journey. She had put off going until loneliness and hopelessness drove her out. She believed she might have one group of relatives left alive—a brother and his two children twenty miles away in Pasadena. That was a day's journey one-way, if she were lucky. The unexpected arrival of the bus as she left her Virginia Road home had seemed to be a piece of luck—until the trouble began.

Two young men were involved in a disagreement of some kind, or, more likely, a misunderstanding. They stood in the aisle, grunting and gesturing at each other, each in his own uncertain T stance as the bus lurched over the potholes. The driver seemed to be putting some effort into keeping them off balance. Still, their gestures stopped just short of contact—mock punches, hand games of intimidation to replace lost curses.

People watched the pair, then looked at one another and made small anxious sounds. Two children whimpered.

Rye sat a few feet behind the disputants and across from the back door. She watched the two carefully, knowing the fight would begin when someone's nerve broke or someone's hand slipped or someone came to the end of his limited ability to communicate. These things could happen anytime.

One of them happened as the bus hit an especially large pothole and one man, tall, thin, and sneering, was thrown into his shorter opponent.

Instantly, the shorter man drove his left fist into the disintegrating sneer. He hammered his larger opponent as though he neither had nor needed any weapon other than his left fist. He hit quickly enough, hard enough to batter his opponent down before the taller man could regain his balance or hit back even once.

People screamed or squawked in fear. Those nearby scrambled to get out of the way. Three more young men roared in excitement and gestured wildly. Then, somehow, a second dispute broke out be-

199

tween two of these three—probably because one inadvertently touched or hit the other.

As the second fight scattered frightened passengers, a woman shook the driver's shoulder and grunted as she gestured toward the fighting.

The driver grunted back through bared teeth. Frightened, the woman drew away.

Rye, knowing the methods of bus drivers, braced herself and held on to the crossbar of the seat in front of her. When the driver hit the brakes, she was ready and the combatants were not. They fell over seats and onto screaming passengers, creating even more confusion. At least one more fight started.

The instant the bus came to a full stop, Rye was on her feet, pushing the back door. At the second push, it opened and she jumped out, holding her pack in one arm. Several other passengers followed, but some stayed on the bus. Buses were so rare and irregular now, people rode when they could, no matter what. There might not be another bus today—or tomorrow. People started walking, and if they saw a bus they flagged it down. People making intercity trips like Rye's from Los Angeles to Pasadena made plans to camp out, or risked seeking shelter with locals who might rob or murder them.

The bus did not move, but Rye moved away from it. She intended to wait until the trouble was over and get on again, but if there was shooting, she wanted the protection of a tree. Thus, she was near the curb when a battered blue Ford on the other side of the street made a U-turn and pulled up in front of the bus. Cars were rare these days—as rare as a severe shortage of fuel and of relatively unimpaired mechanics could make them. Cars that still ran were as likely to be used as weapons as they were to serve as transportation. Thus, when the driver of the Ford beckoned to Rye, she moved away warily. The driver got out—a big man, young, neatly bearded with dark, thick hair. He wore a long overcoat and a look of wariness that matched Rye's. She stood several feet from him, waiting to see what he would do. He looked at the bus, now rocking with the combat inside, then at the small cluster of passengers who had gotten off. Finally he looked at Rye again.

She returned his gaze, very much aware of the old forty-five automatic her jacket concealed. She watched his hands.

He pointed with his left hand toward the bus. The dark-tinted windows prevented him from seeing what was happening inside.

His use of the left hand interested Rye more than his obvious question. Left-handed people tended to be less impaired, more reasonable and comprehending, less driven by frustration, confusion, and anger.

She imitated his gesture, pointing toward the bus with her own left hand, then punching the air with both fists.

The man took off his coat revealing a Los Angeles Police Department uniform complete with baton and service revolver.

Rye took another step back from him. There was no more LAPD, no more *any* large organization, governmental or private. There were neighborhood patrols and armed individuals. That was all.

The man took something from his coat pocket, then threw the coat into the car. Then he gestured Rye back, back toward the rear of the bus. He had something made of plastic in his hand. Rye did not understand what he wanted until he went to the rear door of the bus and beckoned her to stand there. She obeyed mainly out of curiosity. Cop or not, maybe he could do something to stop the stupid fighting.

He walked around the front of the bus, to the street side where the driver's window was open. There, she thought she saw him throw something into the bus. She was still trying to peer through the tinted glass when people began stumbling out the rear door, choking and weeping. Gas.

Rye caught an old woman who would have fallen, lifted two little children down when they were in danger of being knocked down and trampled. She could see the bearded man helping people at the front door. She caught a thin old man shoved out by one of the combatants. Staggered by the old man's weight, she was barely able to get out of the way as the last of the young men pushed his way out. This one, bleeding from nose and mouth, stumbled into another and they grappled blindly, still sobbing from the gas.

The bearded man helped the bus driver out through the front door, though the driver did not seem to appreciate his help. For a moment, Rye thought there would be another fight. The bearded man stepped back and watched the driver gesture threateningly, watched him shout in wordless anger.

The bearded man stood still, made no sound, refused to respond to clearly obscene gestures. The least impaired people tended to do

this—stand back unless they were physically threatened and let
those with less control scream and jump around. It was as though
they felt it beneath them to be as touchy as the less comprehending.
This was an attitude of superiority and that was the way people like
the bus driver perceived it. Such "superiority" was frequently punished by beatings, even by death. Rye had had close calls of her own.
As a result, she never went unarmed. And in this world where the
only likely common language was body language, being armed was
often enough. She had rarely had to draw her gun or even display it.

The bearded man's revolver was on constant display. Apparently
that was enough for the bus driver. The driver spat in disgust, glared
at the bearded man for a moment longer, then strode back to his
gas-filled bus. He stared at it for a moment, clearly wanting to get
in, but the gas was still too strong. Of the windows, only his tiny
driver's window actually opened. The front door was open, but the
rear door would not stay open unless someone held it. Of course,
the air conditioning had failed long ago. The bus would take some
time to clear. It was the driver's property, his livelihood. He had
pasted old magazine pictures of items he would accept as fare on its
sides. Then he would use what he collected to feed his family or to
trade. If his bus did not run, he did not eat. On the other hand, if
the inside of his bus was torn apart by senseless fighting, he would
not eat very well either. He was apparently unable to perceive this.
All he could see was that it would be some time before he could use
his bus again. He shook his fist at the bearded man and shouted.
There seemed to be words in his shout, but Rye could not understand them. She did not know whether this was his fault or hers. She
had heard so little coherent human speech for the past three years,
she was no longer certain how well she recognized it, no longer
certain of the degree of her own impairment.

The bearded man sighed. He glanced toward his car, then beckoned to Rye. He was ready to leave, but he wanted something from
her first. No. No, he wanted her to leave with him. Risk getting into
his car when, in spite of his uniform, law and order were nothing—
not even words any longer.

She shook her head in a universally understood negative, but the
man continued to beckon.

She waved him away. He was doing what the less-impaired rarely did—drawing potentially negative attention to another of his kind. People from the bus had begun to look at her.

One of the men who had been fighting tapped another on the arm, then pointed from the bearded man to Rye, and finally held up the first two fingers of his right hand as though giving two-thirds of a Boy Scout salute. The gesture was very quick, its meaning obvious even at a distance. She had been grouped with the bearded man. Now what?

The man who had made the gesture started toward her.

She had no idea what he intended, but she stood her ground. The man was half a foot taller than she was and perhaps ten years younger. She did not imagine she could outrun him. Nor did she expect anyone to help her if she needed help. The people around her were all strangers.

She gestured once—a clear indication to the man to stop. She did not intend to repeat the gesture. Fortunately, the man obeyed. He gestured obscenely and several other men laughed. Loss of verbal language had spawned a whole new set of obscene gestures. The man, with stark simplicity, had accused her of sex with the bearded man and had suggested she accommodate the other men present— beginning with him.

Rye watched him wearily. People might very well stand by and watch if he tried to rape her. They would also stand and watch her shoot him. Would he push things that far?

He did not. After a series of obscene gestures that brought him no closer to her, he turned contemptuously and walked away.

And the bearded man still waited. He had removed his service revolver, holster and all. He beckoned again, both hands empty. No doubt his gun was in the car and within easy reach, but his taking it off impressed her. Maybe he was all right. Maybe he was just alone. She had been alone herself for three years. The illness had stripped her, killing her children one by one, killing her husband, her sister, her parents . . .

The illness, if it was an illness, had cut even the living off from one another. As it swept over the country, people hardly had time to lay blame on the Soviets (though they were falling silent along with the rest of the world), on a new virus, a new pollutant, radiation, divine retribution. . . . The illness was stroke-swift in the way it cut people down and stroke-like in some of its effects. But it was highly specific.

Language was always lost or severely impaired. It was never regained. Often there was also paralysis, intellectual impairment, death.

Rye walked toward the bearded man, ignoring the whistling and applauding of two of the young men and their thumbs-up signs to the bearded man. If he had smiled at them or acknowledged them in any way, she would almost certainly have changed her mind. If she had let herself think of the possible deadly consequences of getting into a stranger's car, she would have changed her mind. Instead, she thought of the man who lived across the street from her. He rarely washed since his bout with the illness. And he had gotten into the habit of urinating wherever he happened to be. He had two women already—one tending each of his large gardens. They put up with him in exchange for his protection. He had made it clear that he wanted Rye to become his third woman.

She got into the car and the bearded man shut the door. She watched as he walked around to the driver's door—watched for his sake because his gun was on the seat beside her. And the bus driver and a pair of young men had come a few steps closer. They did nothing, though, until the bearded man was in the car. Then one of them threw a rock. Others followed his example, and as the car drove away, several rocks bounced off harmlessly.

When the bus was some distance behind them, Rye wiped sweat from her forehead and longed to relax. The bus would have taken her more than halfway to Pasadena. She would have had only ten miles to walk. She wondered how far she would have to walk now—and wondered if walking a long distance would be her only problem.

At Figuroa and Washington where the bus normally made a left turn, the bearded man stopped, looked at her, and indicated that she should choose a direction. When she directed him left and he actually turned left, she began to relax. If he was willing to go where she directed, perhaps he was safe.

As they passed blocks of burned, abandoned buildings, empty lots, and wrecked or stripped cars, he slipped a gold chain over his head and handed it to her. The pendant attached to it was a smooth, glassy, black rock. Obsidian. His name might be Rock or Peter or Black, but she decided to think of him as Obsidian. Even her sometimes useless memory would retain a name like Obsidian.

She handed him her own name symbol—a pin in the shape of a large golden stalk of wheat. She had bought it long before the illness and the silence began. Now she wore it, thinking it was as close as she was likely to come to Rye. People like Obsidian who had not known her before probably thought of her as Wheat. Not that it mattered. She would never hear her name spoken again.

Obsidian handed her pin back to her. He caught her hand as she reached for it and rubbed his thumb over her calluses.

He stopped at First Street and asked which way again. Then, after turning right as she had indicated, he parked near the Music Center. There, he took a folded paper from the dashboard and unfolded it. Rye recognized it as a street map, though the writing on it meant nothing to her. He flattened the map, took her hand again, and put her index finger on one spot. He touched her, touched himself, pointed toward the floor. In effect, "We are here." She knew he wanted to know where she was going. She wanted to tell him, but she shook her head sadly. She had lost reading and writing. That was her most serious impairment and her most painful. She had taught history at UCLA. She had done freelance writing. Now she could not even read her own manuscripts. She had a houseful of books that she could neither read nor bring herself to use as fuel. And she had a memory that would not bring back to her much of what she had read before.

She stared at the map, trying to calculate. She had been born in Pasadena, had lived for fifteen years in Los Angeles. Now she was near L.A. Civic Center. She knew the relative positions of the two cities, knew streets, directions, even knew to stay away from freeways which might be blocked by wrecked cars and destroyed overpasses. She ought to know how to point out Pasadena even though she could not recognize the word.

Hesitantly, she placed her hand over a pale orange patch in the upper right corner of the map. That should be right. Pasadena.

Obsidian lifted her hand and looked under it, then folded the map and put it back on the dashboard. He could read, she realized belatedly. He could probably write, too. Abruptly, she hated him— deep, bitter hatred. What did literacy mean to him—a grown man who played cops and robbers? But he was literate and she was not. She never would be. She felt sick to her stomach with hatred, frustration, and jealousy. And only a few inches from her hand was a loaded gun.

She held herself still, staring at him, almost seeing his blood. But her rage crested and ebbed and she did nothing.

Obsidian reached for her hand with hesitant familiarity. She looked at him. Her face had already revealed too much. No person still living in what was left of human society could fail to recognize that expression, that jealousy.

She closed her eyes wearily, drew a deep breath. She had experienced longing for the past, hatred of the present, growing hopelessness, purposelessness, but she had never experienced such a powerful urge to kill another person. She had left her home, finally, because she had come near to killing herself. She had found no reason to stay alive. Perhaps that was why she had gotten into Obsidian's car. She had never before done such a thing.

He touched her mouth and made chatter motions with thumb and fingers. Could she speak?

She nodded and watched his milder envy come and go. Now both had admitted what it was not safe to admit, and there had been no violence. He tapped his mouth and forehead and shook his head. He did not speak or comprehend spoken language. The illness had played with them, taking away, she suspected, what each valued most.

She plucked at his sleeve, wondering why he had decided on his own to keep the LAPD alive with what he had left. He was sane enough otherwise. Why wasn't he at home raising corn, rabbits, and children? But she did not know how to ask. Then he put his hand on her thigh and she had another question to deal with.

She shook her head. Disease, pregnancy, helpless, solitary agony . . . no.

He massaged her thigh gently and smiled in obvious disbelief.

No one had touched her for three years. She had not wanted anyone to touch her. What kind of world was this to chance bringing a child into even if the father were willing to stay and help raise it? It was too bad, though. Obsidian could not know how attractive he was to her—young, probably younger than she was, clean, asking for what he wanted rather than demanding it. But none of that mattered. What were a few moments of pleasure measured against a lifetime of consequences?

He pulled her closer to him and for a moment she let herself enjoy the closeness. He smelled good—male and good. She pulled away reluctantly.

He sighed, reached toward the glove compartment. She stiffened, not knowing what to expect, but all he took out was a small box. The writing on it meant nothing to her. She did not understand until he broke the seal, opened the box, and took out a condom. He looked at her and she first looked away in surprise. Then she giggled. She could not remember when she had last giggled.

He grinned, gestured toward the backseat, and she laughed aloud. Even in her teens, she had disliked backseats of cars. But she looked around at the empty streets and ruined buildings, then she got out and into the backseat. He let her put the condom on him, then seemed surprised at her eagerness.

Sometime later, they sat together, covered by his coat, unwilling to become clothed near-strangers again just yet. He made rock-the-baby gestures and looked questioningly at her.

She swallowed, shook her head. She did not know how to tell him her children were dead.

He took her hand and drew a cross in it with his index finger, then made his baby-rocking gesture again.

She nodded, held up three fingers, then turned away, trying to shut out a sudden flood of memories. She had told herself that the children growing up now were to be pitied. They would run through the downtown canyons with no real memory of what the buildings had been or even how they had come to be. Today's children gathered books as well as wood to be burned as fuel. They ran through the streets chasing one another and hooting like chimpanzees. They had no future. They were now all they would ever be.

He put his hand on her shoulder and she turned suddenly, fumbling for his small box, then urging him to make love to her again. He could give her forgetfulness and pleasure. Until now, nothing had been able to do that. Until now, every day had brought her closer to the time when she would do what she had left home to avoid doing: putting her gun in her mouth and pulling the trigger.

She asked Obsidian if he would come home with her, stay with her.

He looked surprised and pleased once he understood. But he did not answer at once. Finally he shook his head as she had feared he might. He was probably having too much fun playing cops and robbers and picking up women.

She dressed in silent disappointment, unable to feel any anger toward him. Perhaps he already had a wife and a home. That was likely. The illness had been harder on men than on women—had killed more men, had left male survivors more severely impaired. Men like Obsidian were rare. Women either settled for less or stayed alone. If they found an Obsidian, they did what they could to keep him. Rye suspected he had someone younger, prettier keeping him.

He touched her while she was strapping her gun on and asked with a complicated series of gestures whether it was loaded.

She nodded grimly.

He patted her arm.

She asked once more if he would come home with her, this time using a different series of gestures. He had seemed hesitant. Perhaps he could be courted.

He got out and into the front seat without responding.

She took her place in front again, watching him. Now he plucked at his uniform and looked at her. She thought she was being asked something, but did not know what it was.

He took off his badge, tapped it with one finger, then tapped his chest. Of course.

She took the badge from his hand and pinned her wheat stalk to it. If playing cops and robbers was his only insanity, let him play. She would take him, uniform and all. It occurred to her that she might eventually lose him to someone he would meet as he had met her. But she would have him for a while.

He took the street map down again, tapped it, pointed vaguely northeast toward Pasadena, then looked at her.

She shrugged, tapped his shoulder, then her own, and held up her index and second fingers tight together, just to be sure.

He grasped the two fingers and nodded. He was with her.

She took the map from him and threw it onto the dashboard. She pointed back southwest—back toward home. Now she did not have to go to Pasadena. Now she could go on having a brother there and two nephews—three right-handed males. Now she did not have to find out for certain whether she was as alone as she feared. Now she was not alone.

Obsidian took Hill Street south, then Washington west, and she leaned back, wondering what it would be like to have someone again. With what she had scavenged, what she had preserved, and what she grew, there was easily enough food for them. There was certainly room enough in a four-bedroom house. He could move his possessions in. Best of all, the animal across the street would pull back and possibly not force her to kill him.

Obsidian had drawn her closer to him and she had put her head on his shoulder when suddenly he braked hard, almost throwing her off the seat. Out of the corner of her eye, she saw that someone had run across the street in front of the car. One car on the street and someone had to run in front of it.

Straightening up, Rye saw that the runner was a woman, fleeing from an old frame house to a boarded-up storefront. She ran silently, but the man who followed her a moment later shouted what sounded like garbled words as he ran. He had something in his hand. Not a gun. A knife, perhaps.

The woman tried a door, found it locked, looked around desperately, finally snatched up a fragment of glass broken from the storefront window. With this she turned to face her pursuer. Rye thought she would be more likely to cut her own hand than to hurt anyone else with the glass.

Obsidian jumped from the car, shouting. It was the first time Rye had heard his voice—deep and hoarse from disuse. He made the same sound over and over the way some speechless people did, "Da, da, da!"

Rye got out of the car as Obsidian ran toward the couple. He had drawn his gun. Fearful, she drew her own and released the safety. She looked around to see who else might be attracted to the scene. She saw the man glance at Obsidian, then suddenly lunge at the woman. The woman jabbed his face with her glass, but he caught her arm and managed to stab her twice before Obsidian shot him. The man doubled, then toppled, clutching his abdomen. Obsidian shouted, then gestured Rye over to help the woman.

Rye moved to the woman's side, remembering that she had little more than bandages and antiseptic in her pack. But the woman was beyond help. She had been stabbed with a long, slender boning knife.

She touched Obsidian to let him know the woman was dead. He had bent to check the wounded man who lay still and also seemed dead. But as Obsidian looked around to see what Rye wanted, the man opened his eyes. Face contorted, he seized Obsidian's just-holstered revolver and fired. The bullet caught Obsidian in the temple and he collapsed.

It happened just that simply, just that fast. An instant later, Rye shot the wounded man as he was turning the gun on her.

And Rye was alone—with three corpses.

She knelt beside Obsidian, dry-eyed, frowning, trying to under-stand why everything had suddenly changed. Obsidian was gone. He had died and left her—like everyone else.

Two very small children came out of the house from which the man and woman had run—a boy and girl perhaps three years old. Holding hands, they crossed the street toward Rye. They stared at her, then edged past her and went to the dead woman. The girl shook the woman's arm as though trying to wake her.

This was too much. Rye got up, feeling sick to her stomach with grief and anger. If the children began to cry, she thought she would vomit.

They were on their own, those two kids. They were old enough to scavenge. She did not need any more grief. She did not need a stranger's children who would grow up to be hairless chimps.

She went back to the car. She could drive home, at least. She remembered how to drive.

The thought that Obsidian should be buried occurred to her before she reached the car, and she did vomit.

She had found and lost the man so quickly. It was as though she had been snatched from comfort and security and given a sudden, inexplicable beating. Her head would not clear. She could not think.

Somehow, she made herself go back to him, look at him. She found herself on her knees beside him with no memory of having knelt. She stroked his face, his beard. One of the children made a noise and she looked at them, at the woman who was probably their mother. The children looked back at her, obviously frightened. Perhaps it was their fear that reached her finally.

She had been about to drive away and leave them. She had almost done it, almost left two toddlers to die. Surely there had been enough dying. She would have to take the children home with her. She would not be able to live with any other decision. She looked around for a place to bury three bodies. Or two. She wondered if the murderer were the children's father. Before the silence, the police had always said some of the most dangerous calls they went out on were domestic disturbance calls. Obsidian should have known that—not that the knowledge would have kept him in the car. It would not have held her back either. She could not have watched the woman murdered and done nothing.

She dragged Obsidian toward the car. She had nothing to dig with her, and no one to guard for her while she dug. Better to take the bodies with her and bury them next to her husband and her children. Obsidian would come home with her after all.

When she had gotten him onto the floor in the back, she returned for the woman. The little girl, thin, dirty, solemn, stood up and unknowingly gave Rye a gift. As Rye began to drag the woman by her arms, the little girl screamed, "No!"

Rye dropped the woman and stared at the girl.

"No!" the girl repeated. She came to stand beside the woman. "Go away!" she told Rye.

"Don't talk," the little boy said to her. There was no blurring or confusing of sounds. Both children had spoken and Rye had understood. They boy looked at the dead murderer and moved further from him. He took the girl's hand. "Be quiet," he whispered.

Fluent speech! Had the woman died because she could talk and had taught her children to talk? Had she been killed by a husband's festering anger or by a stranger's jealous rage? And the children . . . they must have been born after the silence. Had the disease run its course, then? Or were these children simply immune? Certainly they had had time to fall sick and silent. Rye's mind leaped ahead. What if children of three or fewer years were safe and able to learn language? What if all they needed were teachers? Teachers and protectors.

Rye glanced at the dead murderer. To her shame, she thought she could understand some of the passions that must have driven him, whoever he was. Anger, frustration, hopelessness, insane jealousy . . . how many more of him were there—people willing to destroy what they could not have?

Obsidian had been the protector, had chosen that role for who knew what reason. Perhaps putting on an obsolete uniform and patrolling the empty streets had been what he did instead of putting a gun into his mouth. And now that there was something worth protecting, he was gone.

She had been a teacher. A good one. She had been a protector, too, though only of herself. She had kept herself alive when she had no reason to live. If the illness let these children alone, she could keep them alive.

Somehow she lifted the dead woman into her arms and placed her on the backseat of the car. The children began to cry, but she knelt on the broken pavement and whispered to them, fearful of frightening them with the harshness of her long unused voice.

"It's all right," she told them. "You're going with us, too. Come on." She lifted them both, one in each arm. They were so light. Had they been getting enough to eat?

The boy covered her mouth with his hand, but she moved her face away. "It's all right for me to talk," she told him. "As long as no one's around, it's all right." She put the boy down on the front seat of the car and he moved over without being told to, to make room for the girl. When they were both in the car Rye leaned against the window, looking at them, seeing that they were less afraid now, that they watched her with at least as much curiosity as fear.

"I'm Valerie Rye," she said, savoring the words. "It's all right for you to talk to me."

1985
Forty-third Convention
Melbourne

Press Enter ■, by John Varley
Blood Child, by Octavia E. Butler
The Crystal Spheres, by David Brin

John Varley didn't show up in this series until the fourth volume, but then he appeared in the fifth also, and here he is in the sixth. He's about six and a half feet tall and very handsome. At least, he was handsome the last time I saw him, but perhaps, unlike me, he ages quickly—which would be only fair, since one fellow shouldn't have everything. After all, he also writes like an angel.

"Press Enter ■" shows that we have come full circle. When I was a teenager, I was at the tail end of a cycle of stories that insisted on making robots evil. They were the symbol of human arrogance and hubris. They were the attempts of human beings to arrogate to themselves God's function of creating life—and all humanity was able to do was to create a soulless monster of destructive tendencies.

As the Bible says (Proverbs 16:18): "Pride goes before destruction, and a haughty spirit before a fall."

I got sick of it: robots, I decided, were not pseudo-life or soulless monsters. They were machines—very complicated levers. You can kill a man with a lever, but that's your choice, not its. So I built safeguards into my robots and made them useful—even noble. I liked it that way, and most science fiction writers tended to follow me in this respect.

But you can't win forever. My robots began before electronic computers were invented in 1944 (that's why I had to use "positronic brains"). Once we understood the apparent power of computers, they became a new variety of robots. So you can read John Varley reversing me and doing it very powerfully, too.

We can view robots and computers merely as symbols, of course—symbols of humanity's restless urge to increase knowledge, to understand the universe, to develop a technology. They are the modern version of the myth of our eviction from paradise as a result of our eating of the fruit of the tree of knowledge.

Isn't it through our increasing knowledge and understanding and technological know-how that we threaten the world with nuclear weapons, poison it with chemical and radiation pollution, destroy it from soil to ozone layer, and choke it with multiplying mouths? Isn't knowledge evil?

Well, I'm unregenerate. I will not give up.

We are meant to know, or we are amoebae.

Suppose that we are wise enough to learn and know—and yet not wise enough to control our learning and knowledge, so that we use it to destroy ourselves?

Even if that is so, knowledge remains better than ignorance. It is better to know—even if the knowledge endures only for the moment that comes before destruction—than to gain eternal life at the price of a dull and swinish lack of comprehension of a universe that swirls unseen before us in all its wonder. That was the choice of Achilles, and it is mine, too.

—Isaac Asimov

Press Enter ▪

by John Varley

"This is a recording. Please do not hang up until—"

I slammed the phone down so hard it fell onto the floor. Then I stood there, dripping wet and shaking with anger. Eventually, the phone started to make that buzzing noise they make when a receiver is off the hook. It's twenty times as loud as any sound a phone can normally make, and I always wondered why. As though it was such a terrible disaster: "Emergency! Your telephone is off the hook!!!"

Phone answering machines are one of the small annoyances of life. Confess, do you really *like* to talk to a machine? But what had just happened to me was more than a petty irritation. I had just been called by an automatic dialing machine.

They're fairly new. I'd been getting about two or three such calls a month. Most of them come from insurance companies. They give you a two-minute spiel and then a number to call if you are interested. (I called back, once, to give them a piece of my mind, and was put on hold, complete with Muzak.) They use lists. I don't know where they get them.

I went back to the bathroom, wiped water droplets from the plastic cover of the library book, and carefully lowered myself back into the water. It was too cool. I ran more hot water and was just getting my blood pressure back to normal when the phone rang again.

So I sat through fifteen rings, trying to ignore it.

Did you ever try to read with the phone ringing?

On the sixteenth ring I got up. I dried off, put on a robe, walked slowly and deliberately into the living room. I stared at the phone for a while.

On the fiftieth ring I picked it up.

"This is a recording. Please do not hang up until the message has been completed. This calls originates from the house of your next-door neighbor, Charles Kluge. It will repeat every ten minutes. Mr. Kluge knows he has not been the best of neighbors, and apologizes in advance for the inconvenience. He requests that you go immediately to his house. The key is under the mat. Go inside and do what needs to be done. There will be a reward for your services. Thank you."

Click. Dial tone.

I'm not a hasty man. Ten minutes later, when the phone rang again, I was still sitting there thinking it over. I picked up the receiver and listened carefully.

It was the same message. As before, it was not Kluge's voice. It was something synthesized, with all the human warmth of a Speak'n'Spell.

I heard it out again, and cradled the receiver when it was done.

I thought about calling the police. Charles Kluge had lived next door to me for ten years. In that time I may have had a dozen conversations with him, none lasting longer than a minute. I owed him nothing.

I thought about ignoring it. I was still thinking about that when the phone rang again. I glanced at my watch. Ten minutes. I lifted the receiver and put it right back down.

I could disconnect the phone. It wouldn't change my life radically.

But in the end I got dressed and went out the front door, turned left, and walked toward Kluge's property.

My neighbor across the street, Hal Lanier, was out mowing the lawn. He waved to me, and I waved back. It was about seven in the evening of a wonderful August day. The shadows were long. There was the smell of cut grass in the air. I've always liked that smell. About time to cut my own lawn, I thought.

It was a thought Kluge had never entertained. His lawn was brown and knee-high and choked with weeds.

I rang the bell. When nobody came I knocked. Then I sighed, looked under the mat, and used the key I found there to open the door.

"Kluge?" I called out as I stuck my head in.

I went along the short hallway, tentatively, as people do when unsure of their welcome. The drapes were drawn, as always, so it was dark in there, but in what had once been the living room ten television screens gave more than enough light for me to see Kluge. He sat in a chair in front of a table, with his face pressed into a computer keyboard and the side of his head blown away.

*   *   *

Hal Lanier operates a computer for the LAPD, so I told him what I had found and he called the police. We waited together for the first car to arrive. Hal kept asking if I'd touched anything, and I kept telling him no, except for the front door knob.

An ambulance arrived without the siren. Soon there were police all over, and neighbors standing out in their yards or talking in front of Kluge's house. Crews from some of the television stations arrived in time to get pictures of the body, wrapped in a plastic sheet, being carried out. Men and women came and went. I assumed they were doing all the standard police things, taking fingerprints, collecting evidence. I would have gone home, but had been told to stick around.

Finally I was brought in to see Detective Osborne, who was in charge of the case. I was led into Kluge's living room. All the television screens were still turned on. I shook hands with Osborne. He looked me over before he said anything. He was a short guy, balding. He seemed very tired until he looked at me. Then, though nothing really changed in his face, he didn't look tired at all.

"You're Victor Apfel?" he asked. I told him I was. He gestured at the room. "Mr. Apfel, can you tell if anything has been taken from this room?"

I took another look around, approaching it as a puzzle.

There was a fireplace and there were curtains over the windows. There was a rug on the floor. Other than those items, there was nothing else you would expect to find in a living room.

All the walls were lined with tables, leaving a narrow aisle down the middle. On the tables were monitor screens, keyboards, disc drives—all the glossy bric-a-brac of the new age. They were interconnected by thick cables and cords. Beneath the tables were still more computers, and boxes full of electronic items. Above the tables were shelves that reached the ceiling and were stuffed with boxes of tapes, discs, cartridges . . . there was a word for it which I couldn't recall just then. It was software.

"There's no furniture, is there? Other than that . . ."

He was looking confused.

"You mean there was furniture here before?"

"How would I know?" Then I realized what the misunderstanding was. "Oh. You thought I'd been here before. The first time I ever set foot in this room was about an hour ago."

He frowned, and I didn't like that much.

"The medical examiner says the guy had been dead about three hours. How come you came over when you did, Victor?"

I didn't like him using my first name, but didn't see what I could do about it. And I knew I had to tell him about the phone call.

He looked dubious. But there was one easy way to check it out, and we did that. Hal and Osborne and I and several others trooped over to my house. My phone was ringing as we entered.

Osborne picked it up and listened. He got a very sour expression on his face. As the night wore on, it just got worse and worse.

We waited ten minutes for the phone to ring again. Osborne spent the time examining everything in my living room. I was glad when the phone rang again. They made a recording of the message, and we went back to Kluge's house.

Osborne went into the backyard to see Kluge's forest of antennas. He looked impressed.

"Mrs. Madison down the street thinks he was trying to contact Martians," Hal said, with a laugh. "Me, I just thought he was stealing HBO." There were three parabolic dishes. There were six tall masts, and some of those things you see on telephone company buildings for transmitting microwaves.

Osborne took me to the living room again. He asked me to describe what I had seen. I didn't know what good that would do, but I tried.

"He was sitting in that chair, which was here in front of this table. I saw the gun on the floor. His hand was hanging down toward it."

"You think it was suicide?"

"Yes, I guess I did think that." I waited for him to comment, but he didn't. "Is that what you think?"

He sighed. "There wasn't any note."

"They don't always leave notes," Hal pointed out.

"No, but they do often enough that my nose starts to twitch when they don't." He shrugged. "It's probably nothing."

"That phone call," I said. "That might be a kind of suicide note."

Osborne nodded. "Was there anything else you noticed?"

I went to the table and looked at the keyboard. It was made by

Texas Instruments, model TI-99/4A. There was a large bloodstain on the right side of it, where his head had been resting.

"Just that he was sitting in front of this machine." I touched a key, and the monitor screen behind the keyboard immediately filled with words. I quickly drew my hand back, then stared at the message there.

```
PROGRAM NAME: GOODBYE REAL WORLD
DATE: 8/20
CONTENTS: LAST WILL AND TESTAMENT;
          MISC. FEATURES
PROGRAMMER: ''CHARLES KLUGE''
TO RUN
PRESS ENTER ▪
```

The black square at the end flashed on and off. Later I learned it was called a cursor.

Everyone gathered around. Hal, the computer expert, explained how many computers went blank after ten minutes of no activity, so the words wouldn't be burned into the television screen. This one had been green until I touched it, then displayed black letters on a blue background.

"Has this console been checked for prints?" Osborne asked. Nobody seemed to know, so Osborne took a pencil and used the eraser to press the ENTER key.

The screen cleared, stayed blue for a moment, then filled with little ovoid shapes that started at the top of the screen and descended like rain. There were hundreds of them in many colors.

"Those are pills," one of the cops said, in amazement. "Look, that's gotta be a Quaalude. There's a Nembutal." Other cops pointed out other pills. I recognized the distinctive red stripe around the center of a white capsule that had to be a Dilantin. I had been taking them every day for years.

Finally the pills stopped falling, and the damn thing started to play music at us. "Nearer My God to Thee," in three-part harmony.

A couple people laughed. I don't think any of us thought it was funny—it was creepy as hell listening to that eerie dirge—but it sounded like it had been scored for pennywhistle, calliope, and kazoo. What could you do but laugh?

As the music played a little figure composed entirely of squares entered from the left of the screen and jerked spastically toward the center. It was like one of those human figures from a video game, but not as detailed. You had to use your imagination to believe it was a man.

A shape appeared in the middle of the screen. The "man" stopped in front of it. He bent in the middle, and something that might have been a chair appeared under him.

"What's that supposed to be?"

"A computer. Isn't it?"

It must have been, because the little man extended his arms, which jerked up and down like Liberace at the piano. He was typing. The words appeared above him.

```
SOMEWHERE ALONG THE LINE I MISSED SOMETHING. I
SIT HERE, NIGHT AND DAY, A SPIDER IN THE CENTER
OF A COAXIAL WEB, MASTER OF ALL I SURVEY . . .
AND IT IS NOT ENOUGH. THERE MUST BE MORE.

ENTER YOUR NAME HERE ■
```

"Jesus Christ," Hal said. "I don't believe it. An interactive suicide note."

"Come on, we've got to see the rest of this."

I was nearest the keyboard, so I leaned over and typed my name. But when I looked up, what I had typed was VICT9R.

"How do you back this up?" I asked.

"Just enter it," Osborne said. He reached around me and pressed ENTER.

```
DO YOU EVER GET THAT FEELING, VICT9R? YOU HAVE
WORKED ALL YOUR LIFE TO BE THE BEST THERE IS AT
WHAT YOU DO, AND ONE DAY YOU WAKE UP TO WONDER
WHY YOU ARE DOING IT? THAT IS WHAT HAPPENED TO
ME.

DO YOU WANT TO HEAR MORE, VICT9R? Y/N ■
```

The message rambled from that point. Kluge seemed to be aware of it, apologetic about it, because at the end of each forty- or fifty-word paragraph the reader was given the Y/N option.

I kept glancing from the screen to the keyboard, remembering
Kluge slumped across it. I thought about him sitting here alone,
writing this.

He said he was despondent. He didn't feel like he could go on. He
was taking too many pills (more of them rained down the screen at
this point), and he had no further goal. He had done everything he
set out to do. We didn't understand what he meant by that. He said
he no longer existed. We thought that was a figure of speech.

```
ARE YOU A COP, VICT9R? IF YOU ARE NOT, A COP WILL
BE HERE SOON. SO TO YOU OR THE COP: I WAS NOT
SELLING NARCOTICS. THE DRUGS IN MY BEDROOM WERE
FOR MY OWN PERSONAL USE. I USED A LOT OF THEM AND
NOW I WILL NOT NEED THEM ANYMORE.


PRESS ENTER ▪
```

Osborne did, and a printer across the room began to chatter,
scaring the hell out of all of us. I could see the carriage zipping back
and forth, printing in both directions, when Hal pointed at the
screen and shouted.

"Look! Look at that!"

The compugraphic man was standing again. He faced us. He had
something that had to be a gun in his hand, which he now pointed
at his head.

"Don't do it!" Hal yelled.

The little man didn't listen. There was a denatured gunshot
sound, and the little man fell on his back. A line of red dripped down
the screen. Then the green background turned to blue, the printer
shut off, and there was nothing left but the little black corpse lying
on its back and the world **DONE** at the bottom of the screen.

I took a deep breath, and glanced at Osborne. It would be an
understatement to say he did not look happy.

"What's this about drugs in the bedroom?" he said.

We watched Osborne pulling out drawers in dressers and beside the
tables. He didn't find anything. He looked under the bed, and in the
closet. Like all the other rooms in the house, this one was full of
computers. Holes had been knocked in walls for the thick sheaves
of cables.

I had been standing near a big cardboard drum, one of several in the room. It was about thirty-gallon capacity, the kind you ship things in. The lid was loose, so I lifted it. I sort of wished I hadn't.

"Osborne," I said, "You'd better look at this."

The drum was lined with a heavy-duty garbage bag. And it was two-thirds full of Quaaludes.

They pried the lids off the rest of the drums. We found drums of amphetamines, of Nembutals, of Valium. All sorts of things.

With the discovery of the drugs a lot more police returned to the scene. With them came the television camera crews.

In all the activity no one seemed concerned about me, so I slipped back to my own house and locked the door. From time to time I peeked out the curtains. I saw reporters interviewing the neighbors. Hal was there, and seemed to be having a good time. Twice crews knocked on my door, but I didn't answer. Eventually they went away.

I ran a hot bath and soaked in it for about an hour. Then I turned the heat up as high as it would go and got in bed, under the blankets.

I shivered all night.

Osborne came over about nine the next morning. I let him in. Hal followed, looking very unhappy. I realized they had been up all night. I poured coffee for them.

"You'd better read this first," Osborne said, and handed me the sheet of computer printout. I unfolded it, got out my glasses, and started to read.

It was in that awful dot-matrix printing. My policy is to throw any such trash into the fireplace, unread, but I made an exception this time.

It was Kluge's will. Some probate court was going to have a lot of fun with it.

He stated again that he didn't exist, so he could have no relatives. He had decided to give all his worldly property to somebody who deserved it.

But who was deserving? Kluge wondered. Well, not Mr. and Mrs. Perkins, four houses down the street. They were child abusers. He cited court records in Buffalo and Miami, and a pending case locally.

Mrs. Radnor and Mrs. Polonski, who lived across the street from each other five houses down, were gossips.

The Andersons' oldest son was a car thief.

Marian Flores cheated on her high school algebra tests.

There was a guy nearby who was diddling the city on a freeway construction project. There was one wife in the neighborhood who made out with door-to-door salesmen, and two having affairs with men other than their husbands. There was a teenage boy who got his girlfriend pregnant, dropped her, and bragged about it to his friends.

There were no fewer than nineteen couples in the immediate area who had not reported income to the IRS, or who padded their deductions.

Kluge's neighbors in back had a dog that barked all night.

Well, I could vouch for the dog. He'd kept me awake often enough. But the rest of it was *crazy!* For one thing, where did a guy with two hundred gallons of illegal narcotics get the right to judge his neighbors so harshly? I mean, the child abusers were one thing, but was it right to tar a whole family because their son stole cars? And for another . . . how did he *know* some of this stuff?

But there was more. Specifically, four philandering husbands. One was Harold "Hal" Lanier, who for three years had been seeing a woman named Toni Jones, a co-worker at the LAPD Data Processing facility. She was pressuring him for a divorce; he was "waiting for the right time to tell his wife."

I glanced up at Hal. His red face was all the confirmation I needed.

Then it hit me. What had Kluge found out about *me?*

I hurried down the page, searching for my name. I found it in the last paragraph.

". . . for thirty years Mr. Apfel has been paying for a mistake he did not even make. I won't go so far as to nominate him for sainthood, but by default—if for no other reason—I hereby leave all deed and title to my real property and the structure thereon to Victor Apfel."

I looked at Osborne, and those tired eyes were weighing me.

"But I don't *want* it!"

"Do you think this is the reward Kluge mentioned in the phone call?"

"It must be," I said. "What else could it be?"

Osborne sighed, and sat back in his chair. "At least he didn't try to leave you the drugs. Are you still saying you didn't know the guy?"

"Are you accusing me of something?"

He spread his hands. "Mr. Apfel, I'm simply asking a question. You're never one-hundred-percent sure in a suicide. Maybe it was a murder. If it was, you can see that, so far, you're the only one we know of that's gained by it."

"He was almost a stranger to me."

He nodded, tapping his copy of the computer printout. I looked back at my own, wishing it would go away.

"What's this . . . mistake you didn't make?"

I was afraid that would be the next question.

"I was a prisoner of war in North Korea," I said.

Osborne chewed that over awhile.

"They brainwash you?"

"Yes." I hit the arm of my chair, and suddenly had to be up and moving. The room was getting cold. "No. I don't . . . there's been a lot of confusion about the word. Did they 'brainwash' me? Yes. Did they succeed? Did I offer a confession of my war crimes and denounce the U.S. Government? No."

Once more, I felt myself being inspected by those deceptively tired eyes.

"You still seem to have . . . strong feelings about it."

"It's not something you forget."

"Is there anything you want to say about it?"

"It's just that it was all so . . . no. No, I have nothing further to say. Not to you, not to anybody."

"I'm going to have to ask you more questions about Kluge's death."

"I think I'll have my lawyer present for those." Christ. Now I was going to have to get a lawyer. I didn't know where to begin.

Osborne just nodded again. He got up and went to the door.

"I was ready to write this one down as a suicide," he said. "The only thing that bothered me was there was no note. Now we've got a note." He gestured in the direction of Kluge's house, and started to look angry.

"This guy not only writes a note, he programs the fucking thing into his computer, complete with special effects straight out of Pac-Man.

"Now, I know people do crazy things. I've seen enough of them. But when I heard the computer playing a hymn, that's when I knew this was murder. Tell you the truth, Mr. Apfel, I don't think you did it. There must be two dozen motives for murder in that printout. Maybe he was blackmailing people around here. Maybe that's how he bought all those machines. And people with that amount of drugs usually die violently. I've got a lot of work to do on this one, and I'll find who did it." He mumbled something about not leaving town, and that he'd see me later, and left.

"Vic . . ." Hal said. I looked at him.

"About that printout," he finally said. "I'd appreciate it . . . well, they said they'd keep it confidential. If you know what I mean." He had eyes like a basset hound. I'd never noticed that before.

"Hal, if you'll just go home, you have nothing to worry about from me."

He nodded, and scuttled for the door.

"I don't think any of that will get out," he said.

It all did, of course.

It probably would have even without the letters that began arriving a few days after Kluge's death, all postmarked Trenton, New Jersey, all computer-generated from a machine no one was ever able to trace. The letters detailed the matters Kluge had mentioned in his will.

I didn't know about any of that at the time. I spent the rest of the day after Hal's departure lying in my bed, under the electric blanket. I couldn't get my feet warm. I got up only to soak in the tub or to make a sandwich.

Reporters knocked on the door but I didn't answer. On the second day I called a criminal lawyer—Martin Abrams, the first in the book—and retained him. He told me they'd probably call me down to the police station for questioning. I told him I wouldn't go, popped two Dilantin, and sprinted for the bed.

A couple of times I heard sirens in the neighborhood. Once I heard a shouted argument down the street. I resisted the temptation to look. I'll admit I was a little curious, but you know what happened to the cat.

I kept waiting for Osborne to return, but he didn't. The days turned into a week. Only two things of interest happened in that time.

The first was a knock on my door. This was two days after Kluge's death. I looked through the curtains and saw a silver Ferrari parked at the curb. I couldn't see who was on the porch, so I asked who it was.

"My name's Lisa Foo," she said. "You asked me to drop by."

"I certainly don't remember it."

"Isn't this Charles Kluge's house?"

"That's next door."

"Oh. Sorry."

I decided I ought to warn her Kluge was dead, so I opened the door. She turned around and smiled at me. It was blinding.

Where does one start in describing Lisa Foo? Remember when newspapers used to run editorial cartoons of Hirohito and Tojo, when the *Times* used the word "Jap" without embarrassment? Little guys with faces wide as footballs, ears like jug handles, thick glasses, two big rabbity buck teeth, and pencil-thin moustaches . . .

Leaving out only the moustache, she was a dead ringer for a cartoon Tojo. She had the glasses, and the ears, and the teeth. But her teeth had braces, like piano keys wrapped in barbed wire. And she was five eight or five nine and couldn't have weighed more than a hundred and ten. I'd have said a hundred, but added five pounds for each of her breasts, so improbably large on her scrawny frame that all I could read of the message on her T-shirt was POCK LIVE.

It was only when she turned sideways that I saw the S's before and after.

She thrust out a slender hand.

"Looks like I'm going to be your neighbor for a while," she said. "At least until we get that dragon's lair next door straightened out." If she had an accent, it was San Fernando Valley.

"That's nice."

"Did you know him? Kluge, I mean. Or at least that's what he called himself."

"You don't think that was his name?"

"I doubt it. 'Kluge' means clever in German. And it's hacker slang for being tricky. And he sure was a tricky bugger. Definitely some glitches in the wetware." She tapped the side of her head meaningfully. "Viruses and phantoms and demons jumping out every time they try to key in, software rot, bit buckets overflowing onto the floor . . ."

She babbled on in that vein for a time. It might as well have been Swahili.

"Did you say there were demons in his computers?"

"That's right."

"Sounds like they need an exorcist."

She jerked her thumb at her chest and showed me another half-acre of teeth.

"That's me. Listen, I gotta go. Drop in and see me anytime."

The second interesting event of the week happened the next day. My bank statement arrived. There were three deposits listed. The first was the regular check from the VA for $487.00. The second was for $392.54, interest on the money my parents had left me fifteen years ago.

The third deposit had come in on the twentieth, the day Charles Kluge died. It was for $700,083.04.

A few days later Hal Lanier dropped by.

"Boy, what a week," he said. Then he flopped down on the couch and told me all about it.

There had been a second death on the block. The letters had stirred up a lot of trouble, especially with the police going house to house questioning everyone. Some people had confessed to things when they were sure the cops were closing in on them. The woman who used to entertain salesmen while her husband was at work had admitted her infidelity, and the guy had shot her. He was in the County Jail. That was the worst incident, but there had been others, from fistfights to rocks thrown through windows. According to Hal, the IRS was thinking of setting up a branch office in the neighborhood, so many people were being audited.

I thought about the seven hundred thousand and eighty-three dollars.

And four cents.

I didn't say anything, but my feet were getting cold.

"I suppose you want to know about me and Betty," he said, at last. I didn't. I didn't want to hear *any* of this, but I tried for a sympathetic expression.

"That's all over," he said, with a satisfied sigh. "Between me and Toni, I mean. I told Betty all about it. It was real bad for a few days, but I think our marriage is stronger for it now." He was quiet for a moment, basking in the warmth of it all. I had kept a straight face under worse provocation, so I trust I did well enough then.

He wanted to tell me all they'd learned about Kluge, and he wanted to invite me over for dinner, but I begged off on both, telling him my war wounds were giving me hell. I just about had him to the door when Osborne knocked on it. There was nothing to do but let him in. Hal stuck around, too.

I offered Osborne coffee, which he gratefully accepted. He looked different. I wasn't sure what it was at first. Same old tired expression . . . no, it wasn't. Most of that weary look had been either an act of a cop's built-in cynicism. Today it was genuine. The tiredness had moved from his face to his shoulders, to his hands, to the way he walked and the way he slumped in the chair. There was a sour aura of defeat around him.

"Am I still a suspect?" I asked.

"You mean should you call your lawyer? I'd say don't bother. I checked you out pretty good. That will ain't gonna hold up, so your motive is pretty half-assed. Way I figure it, every coke dealer in the Marina had a better reason to snuff Kluge than you." He sighed. "I got a couple questions. You can answer them or not."

"Give it a try."

"You remember any unusual visitors he had? People coming and going at night?"

"The only visitors I *ever* recall were deliveries. Post Office, Federal Express, freight companies . . . that sort of thing. I suppose the drugs could have come in any of those shipments."

"That's what we figure, too. There's no way he was dealing nickel and dime bags. He must have been a middleman. Ship it in, ship it out." He brooded about that for a while, and sipped his coffee.

"So are you making any progress?" I asked.

"You want to know the truth? The case is going in the toilet. We've got too many motives, and not a one of them that works. As far as we can tell, nobody on the block had the slightest idea Kluge had all that information. We've checked bank accounts and we can't find evidence of blackmail. So the neighbors are pretty much out of the picture. Though if he were alive, most people around here would like to kill him *now*."

"Damn straight," Hal said.

Osborne slapped his thigh. "If the bastard was alive, I'd kill him," he said. "But I'm beginning to think he never *was* alive."

"I don't understand."

"If I hadn't seen the goddamn body . . ." He sat up a little straighter. "He said he didn't exist. Well, he practically didn't. PG&E never heard of him. He's hooked up to their lines and a meter reader came by every month, but they never billed him for a single kilowatt. Same with the phone company. He had a whole exchange in that house that was *made* by the phone company, and delivered by them, and installed by them, but they have no record of him. We talked to the guy who hooked it all up. He turned in his records, and the computer swallowed them. Kluge didn't have a bank account anywhere in California, and apparently he didn't need one. We've tracked down a hundred companies that sold things to him, shipped them out, and then either marked his account paid or forgot they ever sold him anything. Some of them have check numbers and account numbers in their books, for accounts or even *banks* that don't exist."

He leaned back in his chair, simmering at the perfidy of it all.

"The only guy we've found who ever heard of him was the guy who delivered his groceries once a month. Little store down on Sepulveda. They don't have a computer, just paper receipts. He paid by check. Wells Fargo accepted them and the checks never bounced. But Wells Fargo never heard of him."

I thought it over. He seemed to expect something of me at this point, so I made a stab at it.

"He was doing all this by computers?"

"That's right. Now, the grocery store scam I can understand, almost. But more often than not, Kluge got right into the basic programming of the computers and wiped himself out. The power company was never paid, by check or any other way, because as far as they were concerned, they weren't selling him anything.

"No government agency has ever heard of him. We've checked him with everybody from the Post Office to the CIA."

"Kluge was probably an alias, right?" I offered.

"Yeah. But the FBI doesn't have his fingerprints. We'll find out who he was, eventually. But it doesn't get us any closer to whether or not he was murdered."

He admitted there was pressure to simply close the felony part of the case, label it suicide, and forget it. But Osborne would not believe it. Naturally, the civil side would go on for some time, as they attempted to track down all Kluge's deceptions.

"It's all up to the dragon lady," Osborne said. Hal snorted.

"Fat chance," Hal said, and muttered something about boat people.

"That girl? She's still over there? Who is she?"

"She's some sort of giant brain from Cal Tech. We called out there and told them we were having problems, and she's what they sent." It was clear from Osborne's face what he thought of any help she might provide.

I finally managed to get rid of them. As they went down the walk I looked over at Kluge's house. Sure enough, Lisa Foo's silver Ferrari was sitting in his driveway.

I had no business going over there. I knew that better than anyone.

So I set about preparing my evening meal. I made a tuna casserole—which is not as bland as it sounds, the way I make it—put it in the oven and went out to the garden to pick the makings for a salad. I was slicing cherry tomatoes and thinking about chilling a bottle of white wine when it occurred to me that I had enough for two.

Since I never do anything hastily, I sat down and thought it over for a while. What finally decided me was my feet. For the first time in a week, they were warm. So I went to Kluge's house.

The front door was standing open. There was no screen. Funny how disturbing that can look, the dwelling wide open and un-guarded. I stood on the porch and leaned in, but all I could see was the hallway.

"Miss Foo?" I called. There was no answer.

The last time I'd been here I had found a dead man. I hurried in.

Lisa Foo was sitting on a piano bench before a computer console. She was in profile, her back very straight, her brown legs in lotus position, her fingers poised at the keys as words sprayed rapidly onto the screen in front of her. She looked up and flashed her teeth at me.

"Somebody told me your name was Victor Apfel," she said.

"Yes. Uh, the door was open . . ."

"It's hot," she said, reasonably, pinching the fabric of her shirt near her neck and lifting it up and down like you do when you're sweaty. "What can I do for you?"

"Nothing, really." I came into the dimness, and stumbled on something. It was a cardboard box, the large flat kind used for delivering a jumbo pizza.

"I was just fixing dinner, and it looks like there's plenty for two, so I was wondering if you . . ." I trailed off, as I had just noticed something else. I had thought she was wearing shorts. In fact, all she had on was the shirt and a pair of pink bikini underpants. This did not seem to make her uneasy.

". . . would you like to join me for dinner?"

Her smile grew even broader.

"I'd love to," she said. She effortlessly unwound her legs and bounced to her feet, then brushed past me, trailing the smells of perspiration and sweet soap. "Be with you in a minute."

I looked around the room again but my mind kept coming back to her. She liked Pepsi with her pizza; there were dozens of empty cans. There was a deep scar on her knee and upper thigh. The ashtrays were empty . . . and the long muscles of her calves bunched strongly as she walked. Kluge must have smoked, but Lisa didn't, and she had fine, downy hairs in the small of her back just visible in the green computer light. I heard water running in the bathroom sink, looked at a yellow notepad covered with the kind of penmanship I hadn't seen in decades, and smelled soap and remembered tawny brown skin and an easy stride.

She appeared in the hall, wearing cut-off jeans, sandals, and a new T-shirt. The old one had advertised BURROUGHS OFFICE SYSTEMS. This one featured Mickey Mouse and Snow White's Castle and smelled of fresh bleached cotton. Mickey's ears were laid back on the upper slopes of her incongruous breasts.

I followed her out the door. Tinkerbell twinkled in pixie dust from the back of her shirt.

"I like this kitchen," she said.

You don't really look at a place until someone says something like that.

The kitchen was a time capsule. It could have been lifted bodily from an issue of *Life* in the early fifties. There was the hump-shouldered Frigidaire, of a vintage when that word had been a generic term, like Xerox or Coke. The counter tops were yellow tile, the sort that's only found in bathrooms these days. There wasn't an ounce of Formica in the place. Instead of a dishwasher I had a wire rack and a double sink. There was no electric can opener, Cuisinart, trash compacter, or microwave oven. The newest thing in the whole room was a fifteen-year-old blender.

I'm good with my hands. I like to repair things.

"This bread is terrific," she said.

I had baked it myself. I watched her mop her plate with a crust, and she asked if she might have seconds.

I understand cleaning one's plate with bread is bad manners. Not that I cared; I do it myself. And other than that, her manners were impeccable. She polished off three helpings of my casserole and when she was done the plate hardly needed washing. I had a sense of a ravenous appetite barely held in check.

She settled back in her chair and I refilled her glass with white wine.

"Are you sure you wouldn't like some more peas?"

"I'd bust." She patted her stomach contentedly. "Thank you so much, Mr. Apfel. I haven't had a home-cooked meal in ages."

"You can call me Victor."

"I just love American food."

"I didn't know there was such a thing. I mean, not like Chinese or . . . you *are* American, aren't you?" She just smiled. "What I meant—"

"I know what you meant, Victor. I'm a citizen, but not native-born. Would you excuse me for a moment? I know it's impolite to jump right up, but with these braces I find I have to brush *instantly* after eating."

I could hear her as I cleared the table. I ran water in the sink and started doing the dishes. Before long she joined me, grabbed a dish towel, and began drying the things in the rack, over my protests.

"You live alone here?" she asked.

"Yes. Have ever since my parents died."

"Ever married? If it's none of my business, just say so."

"That's all right. No, I never married."

"You do pretty good for not having a woman around."

"I've had a lot of practice. Can I ask you a question?"

"Shoot."

"Where are you from? Taiwan?"

"I have a knack for languages. Back home, I spoke pidgin American, but when I got here I cleaned up my act. I also speak rotten French, illiterate Chinese in four or five varieties, gutter Vietnamese, and enough Thai to holler 'Me wanna see American Consul, pretty-damn-quick, you!' "

I laughed. When she said it, her accent was thick.

"I been here eight years now. You figured out where home is?"

"Vietnam?" I ventured.

"The sidewalks of Saigon, fer shure. Or Ho Chi Minh's Shitty, as the pajama-heads renamed it, may their dinks rot off and their butts be filled with jagged punjee sticks. Pardon my French."

She ducked her head in embarrassment. What had started out light had turned hot very quickly. I sensed a hurt at least as deep as my own, and we both backed off from it.

"I took you for a Japanese," I said.

"Yeah, ain't it a pisser? I'll tell you about it someday. Victor, is that a laundry room through that door there? With an electric washer?"

"That's right."

"Would it be too much trouble if I did a load?"

It was no trouble at all. She had seven pairs of faded jeans, some with the legs cut away, and about two dozen T-shirts. It could have been a load of boy's clothing except for the frilly underwear.

We went into the backyard to sit in the last rays of the setting sun, then she had to see my garden. I'm quite proud of it. When I'm well, I spend four or five hours a day working out there, year-round, usually in the morning hours. You can do that in southern California. I have a greenhouse I built myself.

She loved it, though it was not in its best shape. I had spent most of the week in bed or in the tub. As a result, weeds were sprouting here and there.

"We had a garden when I was little," she said. "And I spent two years in a rice paddy."

"That must be a lot different than this."

"Damn straight. Put me off rice for *years*."

She discovered an infestation of aphids, so we squatted down to pick them off. She had that double-jointed Asian peasant's way of sitting that I remembered so well and could never imitate. Her fingers were long and narrow, and soon the tips of them were green from squashed bugs.

We talked about this and that. I don't remember quite how it came up, but I told her I had fought in Korea. I learned she was twenty-five. It turned out we had the same birthday, so some months back I had been exactly twice her age.

The only time Kluge's name came up was when she mentioned how she liked to cook. She hadn't been able to at Kluge's house.

"He has a freezer in the garage full of frozen dinners," she said. "He had one plate, one fork, one spoon, and one glass. He's got the best microwave oven on the market. And that's *it*, man. Ain't nothing else in his kitchen at *all*." She shook her head, and executed an aphid. "He was one weird dude."

When her laundry was done it was late evening, almost dark. She loaded it into my wicker basket and we took it out to the clothesline. It got to be a game. I would shake out a T-shirt and study the picture or message there. Sometimes I got it, and sometimes I didn't. There were pictures of rock groups, a map of Los Angeles, Star Trek tie-ins . . . a little of everything.

"What's the L5 Society?" I asked her.

"Guys that want to build these great big farms in space. I asked 'em if they were gonna grow rice, and they said they didn't think it was the best crop for zero gee, so I bought the shirt."

"How many of these things do you have?"

"Wow, it's gotta be four or five hundred. I usually wear 'em two or three times and then put them away."

I picked up another shirt, and a bra fell out. It wasn't the kind of bra girls wore when I was growing up. It was very sheer, though somehow functional at the same time.

"You like, Yank?" Her accent was very thick. "You oughtta see my sister!"

I glanced at her, and her face fell.

"I'm sorry, Victor," she said. "You don't have to blush." She took the bra from me and clipped it to the line.

She must have misread my face. True, I had been embarrassed, but I was also pleased in some strange way. It had been a long time since anybody had called me anything but Victor or Mr. Apfel.

*   *   *

The next day's mail brought a letter from a law firm in Chicago. It was about the seven hundred thousand dollars. The money had come from a Delaware holding company which had been set up in 1933 to provide for me in my old age. My mother and father were listed as the founders. Certain long-term investments had matured, resulting in my recent windfall. The amount in my bank was *after* taxes.

It was ridiculous on the face of it. My parents had never had that kind of money. I didn't want it. I would have given it back if I could find out who Kluge had stolen it from.

I decided that, if I wasn't in jail this time next year, I'd give it all to some charity. Save the Whales, maybe, or the L5 Society.

I spent the morning in the garden. Later I walked to the market and bought some fresh ground beef and pork. I was feeling good as I pulled my purchases home in my fold-up wire basket. When I passed the silver Ferrari I smiled.

She hadn't come to get her laundry. I took it off the line and folded it, then knocked on Kluge's door.

"It's me. Victor."

"Come on in, Yank."

She was where she had been before, but decently dressed this time. She smiled at me, then hit her forehead when she saw the laundry basket. She hurried to take it from me.

"I'm sorry, Victor. I meant to get this—"

"Don't worry about it," I said. "It was no trouble. And it gave me the chance to ask if you'd like to dine with me again."

Something happened to her face which she covered quickly. Perhaps she didn't like "American" food as much as she professed to. Or maybe it was the cook.

"Sure, Victor, I'd love to. Let me take care of this. And why don't you open those drapes? It's like a tomb in here."

She hurried away. I glanced at the screen she had been using. It was blank, but for one word: intercourse-p. I assumed it was a typo.

I pulled the drapes open in time to see Osborne's car park at the curb. Then Lisa was back, wearing a new T-shirt. This one said A CHANGE OF HOBBIT, and had a picture of a squat, hairy-footed creature. She glanced out the window and saw Osborne coming up the walk.

"I say, Watson," she said. "It's Lestrade of the Yard. Do show him in."

That wasn't nice of her. He gave me a suspicious glance as he entered. I burst out laughing. Lisa sat on the piano bench, poker-faced. She slumped indolently, one arm resting near the keyboard.

"Well, Apfel," Osborne started. "We've finally found out who Kluge really was."

"Patrick William Gavin," Lisa said.

Quite a time went by before Osborne was able to close his mouth. Then he opened it right up again.

"How the hell did you find that out?"

She lazily caressed the keyboard beside her.

"Well, of course I got it when it came into your office this morning. There's a little stoolie program tucked away in your computer that whispers in my ear every time the name Kluge is mentioned. But I didn't need that. I figured it out five days ago."

"Then why the . . . why didn't you tell me?"

"You didn't ask me."

They glared at each other for a while. I had no idea what events had led up to this moment, but it was quite clear they didn't like each other even a little bit. Lisa was on top just now, and seemed to be enjoying it. Then she glanced at her screen, looked surprised, and quickly tapped a key. The word that had been there vanished. She gave me an inscrutable glance, then faced Osborne again.

"If you recall, you brought me in because all your own guys were getting was a lot of crashes. This system was brain-damaged when I got here, practically catatonic. Most of it was down and your guys couldn't get it up." She had to grin at that.

"You decided I couldn't do any worse than your guys were doing. So you asked me to try and break Kluge's codes without frying the system. Well, I did it. All you had to do was come by and interface and I would have downloaded N tons of wallpaper right in your lap."

Osborne listened quietly. Maybe he even knew he had made a mistake.

"What did you get? Can I see it now?"

She nodded, and pressed a few keys. Words started to fill her screen, and one close to Osborne. I got up and read Lisa's terminal.

It was a brief bio of Kluge/Gavin. He was about my age, but while

I was getting shot at in a foreign land, he was cutting a swath through the infant computer industry. He had been there from the ground up, working at many of the top research facilities. It surprised me that it had taken over a week to identify him.

"I compiled this anecdotally," Lisa said, as we read. "The first thing you have to realize about Gavin is that he exists nowhere in any computerized information system. So I called people all over the country—interesting phone system he's got, but the way; it generates a new number for each call, and you can't call back or trace it—and started asking who the top people were in the fifties and sixties. I got a lot of names. After that, it was a matter of finding out who no longer existed in the files. He faked his death in 1967. I located one account of it in a newspaper file. Everybody I talked to who had known him knew of his death. There is a paper birth certificate in Florida. That's the only other evidence I found of him. He was the only guy so many people in the field knew who left no mark on the world. That seemed conclusive to me."

Osborne finished reading, then looked up.

"All right, Ms. Foo. What else have you found out?"

"I've broken some of his codes. I had a piece of luck, getting into a basic rape-and-plunder program he'd written to attack *other* people's programs, and I've managed to use it against a few of his own. I've unlocked a file of passwords with notes on where they came from. And I've learned a few of his tricks. But it's the tip of the iceberg."

She waved a hand at the silent metal brains in the room.

"What I haven't gotten across to anyone is just what this *is*. This is the most devious electronic weapon ever devised. It's armored like a battleship. It has to be; there's a lot of very slick programs out there that grab an invader and hang on like a terrier. If they ever got this far Kluge could deflect them. But usually they never even knew they'd been burgled. Kluge'd come in like a cruise missile, low and fast and twisty. And he'd route his attack through a dozen cut-offs.

"He had a lot of advantages. Big systems these days are heavily protected. People use passwords and very sophisticated codes. But Kluge helped *invent* most of them. You need a damn good lock to keep out a locksmith. He helped install a lot of the major systems. He left informants behind, hidden in the software. If the codes were changed, the computer *itself* would send the information to a safe system that Kluge could tap later. It's like you buy the biggest, meanest, best-trained watchdog you can. And that night, the guy who *trained* the dog comes in, pats him on the head, and robs you blind."

There was a lot more in that vein. I'm afraid that when Lisa began talking about computers, ninety percent of my head shut off.

"I'd like to know something, Osborne," Lisa said.

"What would that be?"

"What is my status here? Am I supposed to be solving your crime for you, or just trying to get this system back to where a competent user can deal with it?"

Osborne thought it over.

"What worries me," she added, "is that I'm poking around in a lot of restricted data banks. I'm worried about somebody knocking on the door and handcuffing me. *You* ought to be worried, too. Some of these agencies wouldn't like a homicide cop looking into their affairs."

Osborne bridled at that. Maybe that's what she intended.

"What do I have to do?" he snarled. "Beg you to stay?"

"No. I just want your authorization. You don't have to put it in writing. Just say you're behind me."

"Look. As far as L.A. County and the State of California are concerned, this house doesn't exist. There is no lot here. It doesn't appear in the tax assessor's records. This place is in a legal limbo. If anybody can authorize you to use this stuff, it's me, because I believe a murder was committed in it. So you just keep doing what you've been doing."

"That's not much of a commitment," she mused.

"It's all you're going to get. Now, what else have you got?"

She turned to her keyboard and typed for a while. Pretty soon a printer started, and Lisa leaned back. I glanced at her screen. It said: osculate posterior-p. I remembered that osculate meant kiss. Well, these people have their own language. Lisa looked up at me and grinned.

"Not you," she said, quietly. *"Him."*

I hadn't the faintest notion of what she was talking about.

Osborne got his printout and was ready to leave. Again, he couldn't resist turning at the door for final orders.

"If you find anything to indicate he didn't commit suicide, let me know."

"Okay. He didn't commit suicide."

Osborne didn't understand for a moment.

"I want proof."

"Well, I have it, but you probably can't use it. He didn't write that ridiculous suicide note."

"How do you know that?"

"I knew my first day here. I had the computer list the program. Then I compared it to Kluge's style. No *way* he could have written it. It's tighter'n a bug's ass. Not a spare line in it. Kluge didn't pick his alias for nothing. You know what it means?"

"Clever," I said.

"Literally. But it means . . . a Rube Goldberg device. Something overly complex. Something that works, but for the wrong reason. You 'kluge around' bugs in a program. It's the hacker's Vaseline."

"So?" Osborne wanted to know.

"So Kluge's programs were really crocked. They were full of bells and whistles he never bothered to clean out. He was a genius, and his programs worked, but you wonder why they did. Routines so bletcherous they'd make your skin crawl. Real crufty bagbiters. But good programming's so rare, even his diddles were better than most people's super-moby hacks."

I suspect Osborne understood about as much of that as I did.

"So you base your opinion on his programming style."

"Yeah. Unfortunately, it's gonna be ten years or so before that's admissible in court, like graphology or fingerprints."

We eventually got rid of him, and I went home to fix the dinner. Lisa joined me when it was ready. Once more she had a huge appetite.

I fixed lemonade and we sat on my small patio and watched evening gather around us.

I woke up in the middle of the night, sweating. I sat up, thinking it out, and I didn't like my conclusions. So I put on my robe and slippers and went over to Kluge's.

The front door was open again. I knocked anyway. Lisa stuck her head around the corner.

"Victor? is something wrong?"

"I'm not sure," I said. "May I come in?"

She gestured, and I followed her into the living room. An open can of Pepsi sat beside her console. Her eyes were red as she sat on her bench.

"What's up?" she said, and yawned.

"You should be asleep, for one thing," I said.

She shrugged, and nodded.

"Yeah. I can't seem to get in the right phase. Just now I'm in day mode. But Victor, I'm used to working odd hours, and long hours, and you didn't come over here to lecture me about that, did you?"

"No. You say Kluge was murdered."

"He didn't write his suicide note. That seems to leave murder."

"I was wondering why someone would kill him. He never left the house, so it was for something he did here with his computers. And now you're . . . well, I don't know *what* you're doing, frankly, but you seem to be poking into the same things. Isn't there a danger the same people will come after you?"

"People?" She raised an eyebrow.

I felt helpless. My fears were not well formed enough to make sense.

"I don't know . . . you mentioned agencies . . ."

"You notice how impressed Osborne was with that? You think there's some kind of conspiracy Kluge tumbled to, or you think the CIA killed him because he found out too much about something, or . . ."

"I don't know, Lisa. But I'm worried the same thing could happen to you."

Surprisingly, she smiled at me.

"Thank you so much, Victor. I wasn't going to admit it to Osborne, but I've been worried about that, too."

"Well, what are you going to do?"

"I want to stay here and keep working. So I gave some thought to what I could do to protect myself. I decided there wasn't anything."

"Surely there's something."

"Well, I got a gun, if that's what you mean. But think about it. Kluge was offed in the middle of the day. Nobody saw anybody enter or leave the house. So I asked myself, who can walk into a house in broad daylight, shoot Kluge, program that suicide note, and walk away, leaving no traces he'd ever been there?"

"Somebody very good."

"Goddamn good. So good there's not much chance one little gook's gonna be able to stop him if he decides to waste her."

She shocked me, both by her words and by her apparent lack of concern for her own fate. But she had said she was worried.

"Then you have to stop this. Get out of here."

"I won't be pushed around that way," she said. There was a tone of finality to it. I thought of things I might say, and rejected them all.

"You could at least . . . lock your front door," I concluded, lamely.

She laughed, and kissed my cheek.

"I'll do that, Yank. And I appreciate your concern. I really do."

I watched her close the door behind me, listened to her lock it, then trudged through the moonlight toward my house. Halfway there I stopped. I could suggest she stay in my spare bedroom. I could offer to stay with her at Kluge's.

No, I decided. She would probably take that the wrong way.

I was back in bed before I realized, with a touch of chagrin and more than a little disgust at myself, that she had every reason to take it the wrong way.

And me exactly twice her age.

I spent the morning in the garden, planning the evening's menu. I have always liked to cook, but dinner with Lisa had rapidly become the high point of my day. Not only that, I was already taking it for granted. So it hit me hard, around noon, when I looked out the front and saw her car gone.

I hurried to Kluge's front door. It was standing open. I made a quick search of the house. I found nothing until the master bedroom, where her clothes were stacked neatly on the floor.

Shivering, I pounded on the Laniers' front door. Betty answered, and immediately saw my agitation.

"The girl at Kluge's house," I said. "I'm afraid something's wrong. Maybe we'd better call the police."

"What happened?" Betty asked, looking over my shoulder. "Did she call you? I see she's not back yet."

"Back?"

"I saw her drive away about an hour ago. That's quite a car she has."

Feeling like a fool, I tried to make nothing of it, but I caught a look in Betty's eye. I think she'd have liked to pat me on the head. It made me furious.

But she'd left her clothes, so surely she was coming back.

I kept telling myself that, then went to run a bath, as hot as I could stand it.

When I answered the door she was standing there with a grocery bag in each arm and her usual blinding smile on her face.

"I wanted to do this yesterday but I forgot until you came over, and I know I should have asked first, but then I wanted to surprise you, so I just went to get one or two items you didn't have in your garden and a couple of things that weren't in your spice rack . . ."

She kept talking as we unloaded the bags in the kitchen. I said nothing. She was wearing a new T-shirt. There was a big V, and under it a picture of a screw, followed by a hyphen and a small-case "p." I thought it over as she babbled on. V, screw-p. I was determined not to ask what it meant.

"Do you like Vietnamese cooking?"

I looked at her, and finally realized she was very nervous.

"I don't know," I said. "I've never had it. But I like Chinese, and Japanese, and Indian. I like to try new things." The last part was a lie, but not as bad as it might have been. I do try new recipes, and my tastes in food are catholic. I didn't expect to have much trouble with southeast Asian cuisine.

"Well, when I get through you *still* won't know," she laughed. "My momma was half-Chinese. So what you're gonna get here is a mongrel meal." She glanced up, saw my face, and laughed.

"I forgot. You've been to Asia. No, Yank, I ain't gonna serve any dog meat."

There was only one intolerable thing, and that was the chopsticks. I used them for as long as I could, then put them aside and got a fork.

"I'm sorry," I said. "Chopsticks happen to be a problem for me."

"You use them very well."

"I had plenty of time to learn how."

It was very good, and I told her so. Each dish was a revelation, not quite like anything I had ever had. Toward the end, I broke down halfway.

"Does the V stand for victory?" I asked.

"Maybe."

"Beethoven? Churchill? World War Two?"

She just smiled.

"Think of it as a challenge, Yank."

"Do I frighten you, Victor?"

"You did at first."

"It's my face, isn't it?"

"It's a generalized phobia of Orientals. I suppose I'm a racist. Not because I want to be."

She nodded slowly, there in the dark. We were on the patio again, but the sun had gone down a long time ago. I can't recall what we had talked about for all those hours. It had kept us busy, anyway.

"I have the same problem," she said.

"Fear of Orientals?" I had meant it as a joke.

"Of Cambodians." She let me take that in for a while, then went on. "I fled to Cambodia when Saigon fell. I walked across it. I'm lucky to be alive really. They had me in labor camps."

"I thought they called it Kampuchea now."

She spat. I'm not even sure she was aware she had done it.

"It's the People's Republic of Syphilitic Dogs. The North Koreans treated you very badly, didn't they, Victor?"

"That's right."

"Koreans are pus suckers." I must have looked surprised, because she chuckled.

"You Americans feel so guilty about racism. As if you had invented it and nobody else—except maybe the South Africans and the Nazis—had ever practiced it as heinously as you. And you can't tell one yellow face from another, so you think of the yellow races as one homogeneous block. When in fact Orientals are among the most racist peoples on the earth. The Vietnamese have hated the Cambodians for a thousand years. The Chinese hate the Japanese. The Koreans hate everybody. And *everybody* hates the 'ethnic Chinese.' The Chinese are the Jews of the East."

"I've heard that."

She nodded, lost in her own thoughts.

"And I hate all Cambodians," she said, at last. "Like you, I don't wish to. Most of the people who suffered in the camps were Cambodians. It was the genocidal leaders, the Pol Pot scum, who I should hate." She looked at me. "But sometimes we don't get a lot of choice about things like that, do we, Yank?"

The next day I visited her at noon. It had cooled down, but was still warm in her dark den. She had not changed her shirt.

She told me a few things about computers. When she let me try some things on the keyboard I quickly got lost. We decided I needn't plan on a career as a computer programmer.

One of the things she showed me was called a telephone modem, whereby she could reach other computers all over the world. She "interfaced" with someone at Stanford whom she had never met, and who she knew only as "Bubble Sorter." They typed things back and forth at each other.

At the end, Bubble Sorter wrote "bye-p." Lisa typed T.

"What's T?" I asked.

"True. Means yes, but yes would be too straightforward for a hacker."

"You told me what a byte is. What's a byep?"

She looked up at me seriously.

"It's a question. Add p to a word, and you make it a question. So bye-p means Bubble Sorter was asking if I wanted to log out. Sign off."

I thought that over.

"So how would you translate 'osculate posterior-p'?"

" 'You wanna kiss my ass?' But remember, that was for Osborne."

I looked at her T-shirt again, then up to her eyes, which were quite serious and serene. She waited, hands folded in her lap.

Intercourse-p.

"Yes," I said. "I would."

She put her glasses on the table and pulled her shirt over her head.

We made love in Kluge's big waterbed.

I had a certain amount of performance anxiety—it had been a long, *long* time. After that, I was so caught up in the touch and smell and taste of her that I went a little crazy. She didn't seem to mind.

At last we were done, and bathed in sweat. She rolled over, stood, and went to the window. She opened it, and a breath of air blew over me. Then she put one knee on the bed, leaned over me, and got a pack of cigarettes from the bedside table. She lit one.

"I hope you're not allergic to smoke," she said.

"No. My father smoked. But I didn't know you did."

"Only afterwards," she said, with a quick smile. She took a deep drag. "Everybody in Saigon smoked, I think." She stretched out on her back beside me and we lay like that, soaking wet, holding hands. She opened her legs so one of her bare feet touched mine. It seemed enough contact. I watched the smoke rise from her right hand.

"I haven't felt warm in thirty years," I said. "I've been hot, but I've never been warm. I feel warm now."

"Tell me about it," she said.

So I did, as much as I could, wondering if it would work this time. At thirty years remove, my story does not sound so horrible. We've seen so much in that time. There were people in jails at that very moment, enduring conditions as bad as any I encountered. The paraphernalia of oppression is still pretty much the same. Nothing physical happened to me that would account for thirty years lived as a recluse.

"I *was* badly injured," I told her. "My skull was fractured. I still have . . . problems from that. Korea can get very cold, and I was never warm enough. But it was the other stuff. What they call brainwashing now.

"We didn't know what it was. We couldn't understand that even after a man had told them all he knew they'd keep on at us. Keeping us awake. Disorienting us. Some guys signed confessions, made up all sorts of stuff, but even that wasn't enough. They'd just keep on at you.

"I never did figure it out. I guess I couldn't understand an evil that big. But when they were sending us back and some of the prisoners wouldn't go . . . they really didn't *want* to go, they really believed . . ."

I had to pause there. Lisa sat up, moved quietly to the end of the bed, and began massaging my feet.

"We got a taste of what the Vietnam guys got, later. Only for us it was reversed. The GI's were heroes, and the prisoners were . . ."

"You didn't break," she said. It wasn't a question.

"No, I didn't."

"That would be worse." ·

I looked at her. She had my foot pressed against her flat belly, holding me by the heel while her other hand massaged my toes.

"The country was shocked," I said. "They didn't understand what brainwashing was. I tried telling people how it was. I thought they were looking at me funny. After a while, I stopped talking about it. And I didn't have anything else to talk about.

"A few years back the army changed its policy. Now they don't expect you to withstand psychological conditioning. It's understood you can say anything or sign anything."

She just looked at me, kept massaging my foot, and nodded slowly. Finally she spoke.

"Cambodia was hot," she said. "I kept telling myself when I finally got to the U.S. I'd live in Maine or someplace, where it snowed. And I did go to Cambridge, but I found out I didn't like snow."

She told me about it. The last I heard, a million people had died over there. It was a whole country frothing at the mouth and snapping at anything that moved. Or like one of those sharks you read about that, when its guts are ripped out, bends in a circle and starts devouring itself.

She told me about being forced to build a pyramid of severed heads. Twenty of them working all day in the hot sun finally got it ten feet high before it collapsed. If any of them stopped working, their own heads were added to the pile.

"It didn't mean anything to me. It was just another job. I was pretty crazy by then. I didn't start to come out of it until I got across the Thai border."

That she had survived it at all seemed a miracle. She had gone through more horror than I could imagine. And she had come through it in much better shape. It made me feel small. When I was her age, I was well on my way to building the prison I have lived in ever since. I told her that.

"Part of it is preparation," she said, wryly. "What you expect out of life, what your life has been so far. You said it yourself. Korea was new to you. I'm not saying I was ready for Cambodia, but my life up to that point hadn't been what you'd call sheltered. I hope you haven't been thinking I made a living in the streets by selling apples."

She kept rubbing my feet, staring off into scenes I could not see.

"How old were you when your mother died?"

"She was killed during Tet, 1968. I was ten."

"By the Viet Cong?"

"Who knows? Lot of bullets flying, lot of grenades being thrown."

She sighed, dropped my foot, and sat there, a scrawny Buddha without a robe.

"You ready to do it again, Yank?"

"I don't think I can, Lisa. I'm an old man."

She moved over me and lowered herself with her chin just below my sternum, settling her breasts in the most delicious place possible.

"We'll see," she said, and giggled. "There's an alternative sex act I'm pretty good at, and I'm pretty sure it would make you a young man again. But I haven't been able to do it for about a year on account of these." She tapped her braces. "It'd be sort of like sticking it in a buzz saw. So now I do this instead. I call it 'touring the silicone valley.'" She started moving her body up and down, just a few inches at a time. She blinked innocently a couple times, then laughed.

"At last, I can see you," she said. "I'm awfully myopic."

I let her do that for a while, then lifted my head.

"Did you say silicone?"

"Uh-huh. You didn't think they were real, did you?"

I confessed that I had.

"I don't think I've ever been so happy with anything I ever bought. Not even the car."

"Why did you?"

"Does it bother you?"

It didn't, and I told her so. But I couldn't conceal my curiosity.

"Because it was safe to. In Saigon I was always angry that I never developed. I could have made a good living as a prostitute, but I was always too tall, too skinny, and too ugly. Then in Cambodia I was lucky. I managed to pass for a boy some of the time. If not for that I'd have been raped a lot more than I was. And in Thailand I knew I'd get to the West one way or another, and when I got there, I'd get the best car there was, eat anything I wanted anytime I wanted to, and purchase the best tits money could buy. You can't imagine what the West looks like from the camps. A place where you can buy tits!"

She looked down between them, then back at my face.

"Looks like it was a good investment," she said.

"They do seem to work okay," I had to admit.

We agreed that she would spend the nights at my house. There were certain things she had to do at Kluge's, involving equipment that had to be physically loaded, but many things she could do with a remote terminal and an armload of software. So we selected one of Kluge's best computers and about a dozen peripherals and installed her at a cafeteria table in my bedroom.

I guess we both knew it wasn't much protection if the people who got Kluge decided to get her. But I know I felt better about it, and I think she did, too.

The second day she was there a delivery van pulled up outside, and two guys started unloading a king-size waterbed. She laughed and laughed when she saw my face.

"Listen, you're not using Kluge's computers to—"

"Relax, Yank. How'd you think I could afford a Ferrari?"

"I've been curious."

"If you're really good at writing software you can make a lot of money. I own my own company. But every hacker picks up tricks here and there. I used to run a few Kluge scams, myself."

"But not anymore?"

She shrugged. "Once a thief, always a thief, Victor. I told you I couldn't make ends meet selling my bod."

Lisa didn't need much sleep.

We got up at seven, and I made breakfast every morning. Then we would spend an hour or two working in the garden. She would go to Kluge's and I'd bring her a sandwich at noon, then drop in on her several times during the day. That was for my own peace of mind; I never stayed more than a minute. Sometime during the afternoon I would shop or do household chores, then at seven one of us would cook dinner. We alternated. I taught her "American" cooking, and she taught me a little of everything. She complained about the lack of vital ingredients in American markets. No dogs, of course, but she claimed to know great ways of preparing monkey, snake, and rat. I never knew how hard she was pulling my leg, and didn't ask.

After dinner she stayed at my house. We would talk, make love, bathe.

She loved my tub. It is about the only alteration I have made in the house, and my only real luxury. I put it in—having to expand the bathroom to do so—in 1975, and never regretted it. We would soak for twenty minutes or an hour, turning the jets and bubblers on and off, washing each other, giggling like kids. Once we used bubble bath and made a mountain of suds four feet high, then destroyed it, splashing water all over the place. Most nights she let me wash her long black hair.

She didn't have any bad habits—or at least none that clashed with mine. She was neat and clean, changing her clothes twice a day and never so much as leaving a dirty glass on the sink. She never left a mess in the bathroom. Two glasses of wine was her limit.

I felt like Lazarus.

Osborne came by three times in the next two weeks. Lisa met him at Kluge's and gave him what she had learned. It was getting to be quite a list.

"Kluge once had an account in a New York bank with nine *trillion* dollars in it," she told me after one of Osborne's visits. "I think he did it just to see if he could. He left it in for one day, took the interest and fed it to a bank in the Bahamas, then destroyed the principal. Which never existed anyway."

In return, Osborne told her what was new on the murder investigation—which was nothing—and on the status of Kluge's property, which was chaotic. Various agencies had sent people out to look the place over. Some FBI men came, wanting to take over the investigation. Lisa, when talking about computers, had the power to cloud men's minds. She did it first by explaining exactly what she was doing, in terms so abstruse that no one could understand her. Sometimes that was enough. If it wasn't, if they started to get tough, she just moved out of the driver's seat and let them try to handle Kluge's contraption. She let them watch in horror as dragons leaped out of nowhere and ate up all the data on a disc, then printed "You Stupid Putz!" on the screen.

"I'm cheating them," she confessed to me. "I'm giving them stuff I *know* they're gonna step in, because I already stepped in it myself. I've lost about forty percent of the data Kluge had stored away. But the others lose a hundred percent. You ought to see their faces when Kluge drops a logic bomb into their work. That second guy threw a three-thousand-dollar printer clear across the room. Then tried to bribe me to be quiet about it."

When some Federal agency sent out an expert from Stanford, and he seemed perfectly content to destroy everything in sight in the firm belief that he was *bound* to get it right sooner or later, Lisa let him get tangled up in the Internal Revenue Service's computer. He couldn't get out, because some sort of watchdog program noticed him. During his struggles, it seemed he had erased all the tax records from the letter S down into the W's. Lisa let him think that for half an hour.

"I thought he was having a heart attack," she told me. "All the blood drained out of his face and he couldn't talk. So I showed him where I had—with my usual foresight—arranged for that data to be recorded, told him how to put it back where he found it, and how to pacify the watchdog. He couldn't get out of that house fast enough. Pretty soon he's gonna realize you *can't* destroy that much information with anything short of dynamite because of the backups and the limits of how much can be running at any one time. But I don't think he'll be back."

"It sounds like a very fancy video game," I said.

"It is, in a way. But it's more like Dungeons and Dragons. It's an endless series of closed rooms with dangers on the other side. You don't dare take it a step at a time. You take it a *hundredth* of a step at a time. Your questions are like, 'Now this isn't a question, but if it entered my mind to *ask* this question—which I'm not about to do—concerning what might happen if I looked at this door here— and I'm not touching it, I'm not even in the next room—what do you suppose you might do?' And the program crunches on that, decides if you fulfilled the conditions for getting a great big cream pie in the face, then either throws it or allows as how it *might* just move from step A to step A Prime. Then you say, 'Well, maybe I *am* looking at that door.' And sometimes the program says 'You looked, you looked, you dirty crook!' And the fireworks start."

Silly as all that sounds, it was very close to the best explanation she was ever able to give me about what she was doing.

"Are you telling him everything, Lisa?" I asked her.

"Well, not *everything*. I didn't mention the four cents."

Four cents? Oh my God.

"Lisa, I didn't want that, I didn't ask for it, I wish he'd never—"

"Calm down, Yank. It's going to be all right."

"He kept records of all that, didn't he?"

"That's what I spend most of my time doing. Decoding his records."

"How long have you known?"

"About the seven hundred thousand dollars? It was in the first disc I cracked."

"I just want to give it back."

She thought that over, and shook her head.

"Victor, it'd be more dangerous to get rid of it now than it would be to keep it. It was imaginary money at first. But now it's got a history. The IRS thinks it knows where it came from. The taxes are paid on it. The State of Delaware is convinced that a legally chartered corporation disbursed it. An Illinois law firm has been paid for handling it. Your bank had been paying interest on it. I'm not saying it would be impossible to go back and wipe all that out, but I wouldn't like to try. I'm good, but I don't have Kluge's touch."

"How could he *do* all that? You say it was imaginary money. That's not the way I thought money worked. He could just pull it out of thin air?"

Lisa patted the top of her computer console, and smiled at me.

"This is money, Yank," she said, and her eyes glittered.

At night she worked by candlelight so she wouldn't disturb me. That turned out to be my downfall. She typed by touch, and needed the candle only to locate software.

So that's how I'd go to sleep every night, looking at her slender body bathed in the glow of the candle. I was always reminded of melting butter dripping down a roasted ear of corn. Golden light on golden skin.

Ugly, she called herself. Skinny. It was true she was thin. I could see her ribs when she sat with her back impossibly straight, her tummy sucked in, her chin up. She worked in the nude these days, sitting in lotus position. For long periods she would not move, her hand lying on her thighs, then she would poise, as if to pound the keys. But her touch was light, almost silent. It looked more like yoga than programming. She said she went into a meditative state for her best work.

I had expected a bony angularity, all sharp elbows and knees. She wasn't like that. I had guessed her weight ten pounds too low, and still didn't know where she put it. But she was soft and rounded, and strong beneath.

No one was ever going to call her face glamorous. Few would even go so far as to call her pretty. The braces did that, I think. They caught the eye and held it, drawing attention to that unsightly jumble.

But her skin was wonderful. She had scars. Not as many as I had expected. She seemed to heal quickly, and well.

I thought she was beautiful.

I had just completed my nightly survey when my eye was caught by the candle. I looked at it, then tried to look away.

Candles do that sometimes. I don't know why. In still air, with the flame perfectly vertical, they begin to flicker. The flame leaps up then squats down, up and down, up and down, brighter and brighter in regular rhythm, two or three beats to the second—

—and I tried to call out to her, wishing the candle would stop its flickering, but already I couldn't speak—

—I could only gasp, and I tried once more, as hard as I could, to yell, to scream, to tell her not to worry, and felt the nausea building . . .

I tasted blood. I took an experimental breath, did not find the smells of vomit, urine, feces. The overhead lights were on.

Lisa was on her hands and knees leaning over me, her face very close. A tear dropped on my forehead. I was on the carpet, on my back.

"Victor, can you hear me?"

I nodded. There was a spoon in my mouth. I spit it out.

"What happened? Are you going to be all right?"

I nodded again, and struggled to speak.

"You just lie there. The ambulance is on its way."

"No. Don't need it."

"Well, it's on its way. You just take it easy and—"

"Help me up."

"Not yet. You're not ready."

She was right. I tried to sit up, and fell back quickly. I took deep breaths for a while. Then the doorbell rang.

She stood up and started to the door. I just managed to get my hand around her ankle. Then she was leaning over me again, her eyes as wide as they would go.

"What is it? What's wrong now?"

"Get some clothes on," I told her. She looked down at herself, surprised.

"Oh. Right."

She got rid of the ambulance crew. Lisa was a lot calmer after she made coffee and we were sitting at the kitchen table. It was one o'clock, and I was still pretty rocky. But it hadn't been a bad one.

I went to the bathroom and got the bottle of Dilantin I'd hidden when she moved in. I let her see me take one.

"I forgot to do this today," I told her.

"It's because you hid them. That was stupid."

"I know." There must have been something else I could have said. It didn't please me to see her look hurt. But she was hurt because I wasn't defending myself against her attack, and that was a bit too complicated for me to dope out just after a grand mal.

"You can move out if you want to," I said. I was in rare form.

So was she. She reached across the table and shook me by the shoulders. She glared at me.

"I won't take a lot more of that kind of shit," she said, and I nodded, and began to cry.

She let me do it. I think that was probably best. She could have babied me, but I do a pretty good job of that myself.

"How long has this been going on?" she finally said. "Is that why you've stayed in your house for thirty years?"

I shrugged. "I guess it's part of it. When I got back they operated, but it just made it worse."

"Okay. I'm mad at you because you didn't tell me about it, so I didn't know what to do. I want to stay, but you'll have to tell me how. Then I won't be mad anymore."

I could have blown the whole thing right there. I'm amazed I didn't. Through the years I've developed very good methods for doing things like that. But I pulled through when I saw her face. She really did want to stay. I didn't know why, but it was enough.

"The spoon was a mistake," I said. "If there's time, and you can do it without risking your fingers, you could jam a piece of cloth in there. Part of a sheet, or something. But nothing hard." I explored my mouth with a finger. "I think I broke a tooth."

"Serves you right," she said. I looked at her, and smiled, then we were both laughing. She came around the table and kissed me, then sat on my knee.

"The biggest danger is drowning. During the first part of the seizure, all my muscles go rigid. That doesn't last long. Then they all start contracting and relaxing at random. It's *very* strong."

"I know. I watched, and I tried to hold you."

"Don't do that. Get me on my side. Stay behind me, and watch out for flailing arms. Get a pillow under my head if you can. Keep me away from things I could injure myself on." I looked her square in the eye. "I want to emphasize this. Just *try* to do all those things. If I'm getting too violent, it's better you stand off to the side. Better for both of us. If I knock you out, you won't be able to help me if I start strangling on vomit."

I kept looking at her eyes. She must have read my mind, because she smiled slightly.

"Sorry, Yank. I am not freaked out. I mean, like, it's totally gross, you know, and it barfs me out to the max, you could—"

"—gag me with a spoon, I know. Okay, right, I know I was dumb. And that's about it. I might bite my tongue or the inside of my cheek. Don't worry about it. There is one more thing."

She waited, and I wondered how much to tell her. There wasn't a lot she could do, but if I died on her I didn't want her to feel it was her fault.

"Sometimes I have to go to the hospital. Sometimes one seizure will follow another. If that keeps up for too long, I won't breathe, and my brain will die of oxygen starvation."

"That only takes about five minutes," she said, alarmed.

"I know. It's only a problem if I start having them frequently, so we could plan for it if I do. But if I don't come out of one, start having another right on the heels of the first, or if you can't detect any breathing for three or four minutes, you'd better call an ambulance."

"Three or four minutes? You'd be dead before they got here."

"It's that or live in a hospital. I don't like hospitals."

"Neither do I."

*   *   *

The next day she took me for a ride in her Ferrari. I was nervous about it, wondering if she was going to do crazy things. If anything, she was too slow. People behind her kept honking. I could tell she hadn't been driving long from the exaggerated attention she put into every movement.

"A Ferrari is wasted on me, I'm afraid," she confessed at one point. "I never drive it faster than fifty-five."

We went to an interior decorator in Beverly Hills and she bought a low-watt gooseneck lamp at an outrageous price.

I had a hard time getting to sleep that night. I suppose I was afraid of having another seizure, though Lisa's new lamp wasn't going to set it off.

Funny about seizures. When I first started having them, everyone called them fits. Then, gradually, it was seizures, until fits began to sound dirty.

I guess it's a sign of growing old, when the language changes on you.

There were rafts of new words. A lot of them were for things that didn't even exist when I was growing up. Like software. I always visualized a limp wrench.

"What got you interested in computers, Lisa?" I asked her.

She didn't move. Her concentration when sitting at the machine was pretty damn good. I rolled onto my back and tried to sleep.

"It's where the power is, Yank." I looked up. She had turned to face me.

"Did you pick it all up since you got to America?"

"I had a head start. I didn't tell you about my captain, did I?"

"I don't think you did."

"He was strange. I knew that. I was about fourteen. He was an American, and he took an interest in me. He got me a nice apartment in Saigon. And he put me in school."

She was studying me, looking for a reaction. I didn't give her one.

"He was surely a pedophile, and probably had homosexual tendencies, since I looked so much like a skinny little boy."

Again the wait. This time she smiled.

"He was good to me. I learned to read well. From there on, anything is possible."

"I didn't actually ask you about your captain. I asked why you got interested in computers."

"That's right. You did."

"Is it just a living?"

"It started that way. It's the future, Victor."

"God knows I've read that enough times."

"It's true. It's already here. It's power, if you know how to use it. You've seen what Kluge was able to do. You can make money with one of these things. I don't mean earn it, I mean *make* it, like if you had a printing press. Remember Osborne mentioned that Kluge's house didn't exist? Did you think what that means?"

"That he wiped it out of the memory banks."

"That was the first step. But the lot exists in the county plat books, wouldn't you think? I mean, this country hasn't *entirely* given up paper."

"So the county really does have a record of the house."

"No. That page was torn out of the records."

"I don't get it. Kluge never left the house."

"Oldest way in the world, friend. Kluge looked through the LAPD files until he found a guy known as Sammy. He sent him a cashier's check for a thousand dollars, along with a letter saying he could earn twice that if he'd go to the hall of records and do something. Sammy didn't bite, and neither did McGee, or Molly Unger. But Little Billy Phipps did, and he got a check just like the letter said, and he and Kluge had a wonderful business relationship for many years. Little Billy drives a new Cadillac now, and hasn't the faintest notion who Kluge was or where he lived. It didn't matter to Kluge how much he spent. He just pulled it out of thin air."

I thought that over for a while. I guess it's true that with enough money you can do just about anything, and Kluge had all the money in the world.

"Did you tell Osborne about Little Billy?"

"I erased that disc, just like I erased your seven hundred thousand. You never know when you might need somebody like Little Billy."

"You're not afraid of getting into trouble over it?"

"Life is risk, Victor. I'm keeping the best stuff for myself. Not because I intend to use it, but because if I ever needed it badly and didn't have it, I'd feel like such a fool."

She cocked her head and narrowed her eyes, which made them practically disappear.

"Tell me something, Yank. Kluge picked you out of all your neighbors because you'd been a boy scout for thirty years. How do you react to what I'm doing?"

"You're cheerfully amoral, and you're a survivor, and you're basically decent. And I pity anybody who gets in your way."

She grinned, stretched, and stood up.

" 'Cheerfully amoral.' I like that." She sat beside me, making a great sloshing in the bed. "You want to be amoral again?"

"In a little bit." She started rubbing my chest. "So you got into computers because they were the wave of the future. Don't you ever worry about them . . . I don't know, I guess it sounds corny . . . do you think they'll take over?"

"Everybody thinks that until they start to use them," she said. "You've got to realize just how stupid they are. Without programming they are good for nothing, literally. Now, what I do believe is that the people who *run* the computers will take over. They already have. That's why I study them."

"I guess that's not what I meant. Maybe I can't say it right."

She frowned. "Kluge was looking into something. He'd been eavesdropping in artificial intelligence labs, and reading a lot of neurological research. I think he was trying to find a common thread."

"Between human brains and computers?"

"Not quite. He was thinking of computers and neurons. Brain cells." She pointed to her computer. "That thing, or any other computer, is light-years away from being a human brain. It can't generalize, or infer, or categorize, or invent. With good programming it can appear to do some of those things, but it's an illusion.

"There's an old speculation about what would happen if we finally built a computer with as many transistors as the brain has neurons. Would there be self-awareness? I think that's baloney. A transistor isn't a neuron, and a quintillion of them aren't any better than a dozen.

"So Kluge—who seems to have felt the same way—started looking into the possible similarities between a neuron and a 16-bit computer. That's why he had all that consumer junk sitting around his house, those Trash-80's and Atari's and TI's and Sinclair's, for chrissake. He was used to *much* more powerful instruments. He ate up the home units like candy."

"What did he find out?"

"Nothing, it looks like. A 16-bit unit is more complex than a neuron, and no computer is in the same galaxy as an organic brain. But see, the words get tricky. I said an Atari is more complex than a neuron, but it's hard to really compare them. It's like comparing a direction with a distance, or a color with a mass. The units are different. Except for one similarity."

"What's that?"

"The connections. Again, it's different, but the concept of networking is the same. A neuron is connected to a lot of others. There are trillions of them, and the way messages pulse through them determines what we are and what we think and what we remember. And with that computer I can reach a million others. It's bigger than the human brain, really, because the information in that network is more than all humanity could cope with in a million years. It reaches from Pioneer Ten, out beyond the orbit of Pluto, right into every living room that has a telephone in it. With that computer you can tap tons of data that have been collected but nobody's even had the time to look at.

"That's what Kluge was interested in. The old 'critical mass computer' idea, the computer that becomes aware, but with a new angle. Maybe it wouldn't be the size of the computer, but the *number* of computers. There used to be thousands of them. Now there's millions. They're putting them in cars. In wristwatches. Every home has several, from the simple timer on a microwave oven up to a video game or home terminal. Kluge was trying to find out if critical mass could be reached that way."

"What did he think?"

"I don't know. He was just getting started." She glanced down at me. "But you know what, Yank? I think you've reached critical mass while I wasn't looking."

"I think you're right." I reached for her.

Lisa liked to cuddle. I didn't, at first, after fifty years of sleeping alone. But I got to like it pretty quickly.

That's what we were doing when we resumed the conversation we had been having. We just lay in each other's arms and talked about things. Nobody had mentioned love yet, but I knew I loved her. I didn't know what to do about it, but I would think of something.

"Critical mass," I said. She nuzzled my neck, and yawned.

"What about it?"

"What would it be like? It seems like it would be such a vast intelligence. So quick, so omniscient. Godlike."

"Could be."

"Wouldn't it . . . run our lives? I guess I'm asking the same questions I started off with. Would it take over?"

She thought about it for a long time.

"I wonder if there would be anything to take over. I mean, why should it care? How could we figure what its concerns would be? Would it want to be worshipped, for instance? I doubt it. Would it want to 'rationalize all human behavior, to eliminate all emotion,' as I'm sure some sci-fi film computer must have told some damsel in distress in the fifties.

"You can use a word like awareness, but what does it mean? An amoeba must be aware. Plants probably are. There may be a level of awareness in a neuron. Even in an integrated circuit chip. We don't even know what our own awareness really is. We've never been able to shine a light on it, dissect it, figure out where it comes from or where it goes when we're dead. To apply human values to a thing like this hypothetical computer-net consciousness would be pretty stupid. But I don't see how it could interact with human awareness at all. It might not even notice us, any more than we notice cells in our bodies, or neutrinos passing through us, or the vibrations of the atoms in the air around us."

So she had to explain what a neutrino was. One thing I always provided her with was an ignorant audience. And after that, I pretty much forgot about our mythical hyper-computer.

"What about your captain?" I asked, much later.

"Do you really want to know, Yank?" she mumbled sleepily.

"I'm not afraid to know."

She sat up and reached for her cigarettes. I had come to know she sometimes smoked them in times of stress. She had told me she smoked after making love, but that first time had been the only time. The lighter flared in the dark. I heard her exhale.

"My major, actually. He got a promotion. Do you want to know his name?"

"Lisa, I don't want to know any of it if you don't want to tell it. But if you do, what I want to know is did he stand by you?"

"He didn't marry me, if that's what you mean. When he knew he had to go, he said he would, but I talked him out of it. Maybe it was the most noble thing I ever did. Maybe it was the most stupid.

"It's no accident I look Japanese. My grandmother was raped in '42 by a Jap soldier of the occupation. She was Chinese, living in Hanoi. My mother was born there. They went south after Dien Bien Phu. My grandmother died. My mother had it hard. Being Chinese was tough enough, but being half Chinese and half Japanese was worse. My father was half French and half Annamese. Another bad combination. I never knew him. But I'm sort of a capsule history of Vietnam."

The end of her cigarette glowed brighter once more.

"I've got one grandfather's face and the other grandfather's height. With tits by Goodyear. About all I missed was some American genes, but I was working on that for my children.

"When Saigon was falling I tried to get to the American Embassy. Didn't make it. You know the rest, until I got to Thailand, and when I finally got Americans to notice me, it turned out my major was still looking for me. He sponsored me over here, and I made it in time to watch him die of cancer. Two months I had with him, all of it in the hospital."

"My God." I had a horrible thought. "That wasn't the war, too, was it? I mean, the story of your life—"

"—is the rape of Asia. No, Victor. Not that war, anyway. But he was one of those guys who got to see atom bombs up close, out in Nevada. He was too regular army to complain about it, but I think he knew that's what killed him."

"Did you love him?"

"What do you want me to say? He got me out of hell."

Again the cigarette flared, and I saw her stub it out.

"No," she said. "I didn't love him. He knew that. I've never loved anybody. He was very dear, very special to me. I would have done almost anything for him. He was fatherly to me." I felt her looking at me in the dark. "Aren't you going to ask how old he was?"

"Fiftyish," I said.

"On the nose. Can I ask you something?"

"I guess it's your turn."

"How many girls have you had since you got back from Korea?"

I held up my hand and pretended to count on my fingers.

"One," I said, at last.

"How many before you went?"

"One. We broke up before I left for the war."

"How many in Korea?"

"Nine. All at Madam Park's jolly little whorehouse in Pusan."

"So you've made love to one white and ten Asians. I bet none of the others were as tall as me."

"Korean girls have fatter cheeks too. But they all had your eyes."

She nuzzled against my chest, took a deep breath, and sighed.

"We're a hell of a pair, aren't we?"

I hugged her, and her breath came again, hot on my chest. I wondered how I'd lived so long without such a simple miracle as that.

"Yes. I think we really are."

Osborne came by again about a week later. He seemed subdued. He listened to the things Lisa had decided to give him without much interest. He took the printout she handed him, and promised to turn it over to the departments that handled those things. But he didn't get up to leave.

"I thought I ought to tell you, Apfel," he said, at last. "The Gavin case has been closed."

I had to think a moment to remember Kluge's real name had been Gavin.

"The coroner ruled suicide a long time ago. I was able to keep the case open quite a while on the strength of my suspicions." He nodded toward Lisa. "And on what she said about the suicide note. But there was just no evidence at all."

"It probably happened quickly," Lisa said. "Somebody caught him, tracked him back—it can be done; Kluge was lucky for a long time—and did him the same day."

"You don't think it was suicide?" I asked Osborne.

"No. But whoever did it is home free unless something new turns up."

"I'll tell you if it does," Lisa said.

"That's something else," Osborne said. "I can't authorize you to work over there anymore. The county's taken possession of house and contents."

"Don't worry about it," Lisa said, softly.

There was a short silence as she leaned over to shake a cigarette from the pack on the coffee table. She lit it, exhaled, and leaned back beside me, giving Osborne her most inscrutable look. He sighed.

"I'd hate to play poker with you, lady," he said. "What do you mean, 'Don't worry about it'?"

"I bought the house four days ago. And its contents. If anything turns up that would help you reopen the murder investigation, I will let you know."

Osborne was too defeated to get angry. He studied her quietly for a while.

"I'd like to know how you swung that."

"I did nothing illegal. You're free to check it out. I paid good cash money for it. The house came onto the market. I got a good price at the sheriff's sale."

"How'd you like it if I put my best men on the transaction? See if they can dig up some funny money? Maybe fraud. How about I get the FBI in to look it all over?"

She gave him a cool look.

"You're welcome to. Frankly, Detective Osborne, I could have stolen that house, Griffith Park, and the Harbor Freeway and I don't think you could have caught me."

"So where does that leave me?"

"Just where you were. With a closed case, and a promise from me."

"I don't like you having all that stuff, if it can do the things you say it can do."

"I didn't expect you would. But that's not your department, is it? The county owned it for a while, through simple confiscation. They didn't know what they had, and they let it go."

"Maybe I can get the Fraud detail out here to confiscate your software. There's criminal evidence on it."

"You could try that," she agreed.

They stared at each other for a while. Lisa won. Osborne rubbed his eyes and nodded. Then he heaved himself to his feet and slumped to the door.

Lisa stubbed out her cigarette. We listened to him going down the walk.

"I'm surprised he gave up so easy," I said. "Or did he? Do you think he'll try a raid?"

"It's not likely. He knows the score."

"Maybe you could tell it to me."

"For one thing, it's not his department, and he knows it."

"Why did you buy the house?"

"You ought to ask *how*."

I looked at her closely. There was a gleam of amusement behind the poker face.

"Lisa. What did you do?"

"That's what Osborne asked himself. He got the right answer, because he understands Kluge's machines. And he knows how things get done. It was no accident that house going on the market, and no accident I was the only bidder. I used one of Kluge's pet councilmen."

"You bribed him?"

She laughed, and kissed me.

"I think I finally managed to shock you, Yank. That's gotta be the biggest difference between me and a native-born American. Average citizens don't spend much on bribes over here. In Saigon, everybody bribes."

"Did you bribe him?"

"Nothing so indelicate. One has to go in the back door over here. Several entirely legal campaign contributions appeared in the accounts of a state senator, who mentioned a certain situation to someone, who happened to be in the position to do legally what I happened to want done." She looked at me askance. "Of *course* I bribed him, Victor. You'd be amazed to know how cheaply. Does that bother you?"

"Yes," I admitted. "I don't like bribery."

"I'm indifferent to it. It happens, like gravity. It may not be admirable, but it gets things done."

"I assume you covered yourself."

"Reasonably well. You're never entirely covered with a bribe, because of the human element. The councilman might geek if they got him in front of a grand jury. But they won't, because Osborne won't pursue it. That's the second reason he walked out of here without a fight. *He* knows how the world wobbles, he knows what kind of force I now possess, and he knows he can't fight it."

There was a long silence after that. I had a lot to think about, and I didn't feel good about most of it. At one point Lisa reached for the pack of cigarettes, then changed her mind. She waited for me to work it out.

"It is a terrific force, isn't it," I finally said.

"It's frightening," she agreed. "Don't think it doesn't scare me. Don't think I haven't had fantasies of being superwoman. Power is an awful temptation, and it's not easy to reject. There's so much I could do."

"Will you?"

"I'm not talking about stealing things, or getting rich."

"I didn't think you were."

"This is political power. But I don't know how to wield it . . . it sounds corny, but to use it for good. I've seen so much evil come from good intentions. I don't think I'm wise enough to do any good. And the chances of getting torn up like Kluge did are large. But I'm not wise enough to walk away from it. I'm still a street urchin from Saigon, Yank. I'm smart enough not to use it unless I have to. But I can't give it away, and I can't destroy it. Is that stupid?"

I didn't have a good answer for that one. But I had a bad feeling.

My doubts had another week to work on me. I didn't come to any great moral conclusions. Lisa knew of some crimes, and she wasn't reporting them to the authorities. That didn't bother me much. She had at her fingertips the means to commit more crimes, and that bothered me a lot. Yet I really didn't think she planned to do anything. She was smart enough to use the things she had only in a defensive way—but with Lisa that could cover a lot of ground.

When she didn't show up for dinner one evening, I went over to Kluge's and found her busy in the living room. A nine-foot section of shelving had been cleared. The discs and tapes were stacked on a table. She had a big plastic garbage can and a magnet the size of a softball. I watched her wave a tape near the magnet, then toss it in the garbage can, which was almost full. She glanced up, did the same operation with a handful of discs, then took off her glasses and wiped her eyes.

"Feel any better now, Victor?" she asked.

"What do you mean? I feel fine."

"No you don't. And I haven't felt right, either. It hurts me to do it, but I have to. You want to go get the other trash can?"

I did, and helped her pull more software from the shelves.

"You're not going to wipe it all, are you?"

"No. I'm wiping records, and . . . something else."

"Are you going to tell me what?"

"There are things it's better not to know," she said, darkly.

I finally managed to convince her to talk over dinner. She had said little, just eating and shaking her head. But she gave in.

"Rather dreary, actually," she said. "I've been probing around some delicate places the last couple days. These are places Kluge visited at will, but they scare the hell out of me. Dirty places. Places where they know things I thought I'd like to find out."

She shivered, and seemed reluctant to go on.

"Are you talking about military computers? The CIA?"

"The CIA is where it starts. It's the easiest. I've looked around at NORAD—that's the guys who get to fight the next war. It makes me shiver to see how easy Kluge got in there. He cobbled up a way to start Word War Three, just as an exercise. That's one of the things we just erased. The last two days I was nibbling around the edges of the big boys. The Defense Intelligence Agency and the National Security . . . something. DIA and NSA. Each of them is bigger than the CIA. Something knew I was there. Some watchdog program. As soon as I realized that I got out quick, and I've spent the last five hours being sure it didn't follow me. And now I'm sure, and I've destroyed all that, too."

"You think they're the one who killed Kluge?"

"They're surely the best candidates. He had tons of their stuff. I know he helped design the biggest installations at NSA, and he'd been poking around in there for years. One false step is all it would take."

"Did you get it all? I mean are you sure?"

"I'm sure they didn't track me. I'm not sure I've destroyed all the records. I'm going back now to take a last look."

"I'll go with you."

* * *

We worked until well after midnight. Lisa would review a tape or a disc, and if she was in any doubt, toss it to me for the magnetic treatment. At one point, simply because she was unsure, she took the magnet and passed it in front of an entire shelf of software.

It was amazing to think about it. With that one wipe she had randomized billions of bits of information. Some of it might not exist anywhere else in the world. I found myself confronted by even harder questions. Did she have the right to do it? Didn't knowledge exist for everyone? But I confess I had little trouble quelling my protests. Mostly I was happy to see it go. The old reactionary in me found it easier to believe There Are Things We Are Not Meant To Know.

We were almost through when her monitor screen began to malfunction. It actually gave off a few hisses and pops, so Lisa stood back from it for a moment, then the screen started to flicker. I stared at it for a while. It seemed to me there was an image trying to form in the screen. Something three-dimensional. Just as I was starting to get a picture of it I happened to glance at Lisa, and she was looking at me. Her face was flickering. She came to me and put her hands over my eyes.

"Victor, you shouldn't look at that."

"It's okay," I told her. And when I said it, it was, but as soon as I had the words out I knew it wasn't. And that is the last thing I remembered for a long time.

I'm told it was a very bad two weeks. I remember very little of it. I was kept under high dosages of drugs, and my few lucid periods were always followed by a fresh seizure.

The first thing I recall clearly was looking up at Dr. Stuart's face. I was in a hospital bed. I later learned it was in Cedars-Sinai, not the Veteran's Hospital. Lisa had paid for a private room.

Stuart put me through the usual questions. I was able to answer them, though I was very tired. When he was satisfied as to my condition he finally began to answer some of my questions. I learned how long I had been there, and how it had happened.

"You went into consecutive seizures," he confirmed. "I don't know why, frankly. You haven't been prone to them for a decade. I was thinking you were well under control. But nothing is ever really stable, I guess."

"So Lisa got me here in time."

"She did more than that. She didn't want to level with me at first.
It seems that after the first seizure she witnessed she read everything
she could find. From that day, she had a syringe and a solution of
Valium handy. When she saw you couldn't breathe she injected
you, and there's no doubt it saved your life."

Stuart and I had known each other a long time. He knew I had no
prescription for Valium, though we had talked about it the last time
I was hospitalized. Since I lived alone, there would be no one to
inject me if I got in trouble.

He was more interested in results than anything else, and what
Lisa did had the desired result. I was still alive.

He wouldn't let me have any visitors that day. I protested, but soon
was asleep. The next day she came. She wore a new T-shirt. This one
had a picture of a robot wearing a gown and mortarboard, and said
CLASS of 11111000000. It turns out that was 1984 in binary notation.

She had a big smile and said "Hi, Yank!" and as she sat on the bed
I started to shake. She looked alarmed and asked if she should call
the doctor.

"It's not that," I managed to say. "I'd like it if you just held me."

She took off her shoes and got under the covers with me. She held
me tightly. At some point a nurse came in and tried to shoo her out.
Lisa gave her profanities in Vietnamese, Chinese, and a few startling
ones in English, and the nurse left. I saw Dr. Stuart glance in later.

I felt much better when I finally stopped crying. Lisa's eyes were
wet, too.

"I've been here every day," she said. "You look awful, Victor."

"I feel a lot better."

"Well, you look better than you did. But your doctor says you'd
better stick around another couple of days, just to make sure."

"I think he's right."

"I'm planning a big dinner for when you get back. You think we
should invite the neighbors?"

I didn't say anything for a while. There were so many things we
hadn't faced. Just how long could it go on between us? How long
before I got sour about being so useless? How long before she got
tired of being with an old man? I don't know just when I had started

to think of Lisa as a permanent part of my life. And I wondered how I could have thought that.

"Do you want to spend more years waiting in hospitals for a man to die?"

"What do you want, Victor? I'll marry you if you want me to. Or I'll live with you in sin. I prefer sin, myself, but if it'll make you happy—"

"I don't know why you want to saddle yourself with an epileptic old fart."

"Because I love you."

It was the first time she had said it. I could have gone on questioning—bringing up her major again, for instance—but I had no urge to. I'm very glad I didn't. So I changed the subject.

"Did you get the job finished?"

She knew which job I was talking about. She lowered her voice and put her mouth close to my ear.

"Let's don't be specific about it here, Victor. I don't trust any place I haven't swept for bugs. But, to put your mind at ease, I did finish, and it's been a quiet couple of weeks. No one is any wiser, and I'll never meddle in things like that again."

I felt a lot better. I was also exhausted. I tried to conceal my yawns, but she sensed it was time to go. She gave me one more kiss, promising many more to come, and left me.

It was the last time I ever saw her.

At about ten o'clock that evening Lisa went into Kluge's kitchen with a screwdriver and some other tools and got to work on the microwave oven.

The manufacturers of those appliances are very careful to insure they can't be turned on with the door open, as they emit lethal radiation. But with simple tools and a good brain it is possible to circumvent the safety interlocks. Lisa had no trouble with them. About ten minutes after she entered the kitchen she put her head in the oven and turned it on.

It is impossible to say how long she held her head in there. It was long enough to turn her eyeballs to the consistency of boiled eggs. At some point she lost voluntary muscle control and fell to the floor, pulling the microwave down with her. It shorted out, and a fire started.

The fire set off the sophisticated burglar alarm she had installed a month before. Betty Lanier saw the flames and called the fire department as Hal ran across the street and into the burning kitchen. He dragged what was left of Lisa out onto the grass. When he saw what the fire had done to her upper body, and in particular her breasts, he threw up.

She was rushed to the hospital. The doctors there amputated one arm and cut away the frightful masses of vulcanized silicone, pulled all her teeth, and didn't know what to do about the eyes. They put her on a respirator.

It was an orderly who first noticed the blackened and bloody T-shirt they had cut from her. Some of the message was unreadable, but it began, "I can't go on this way anymore . . ."

There is no other way I could have told all that. I discovered it piecemeal, starting with the disturbed look on Dr. Stuart's face when Lisa didn't show up the next day. He wouldn't tell me anything, and I had another seizure shortly after.

The next week is a blur. Betty was very good to me. They gave me a tranquilizer called Tranxene, and it was even better. I ate them like candy. I wandered in a drugged haze, eating only when Betty insisted, sleeping sitting up in my chair, coming awake not knowing where or who I was. I returned to the prison camp many times. Once I recall helping Lisa stack severed heads.

When I saw myself in the mirror, there was a vague smile on my face. It was Tranxene, caressing my frontal lobes. I knew that if I was to live much longer, me and Tranxene would have to become very good friends.

I eventually became capable of something that passed for rational thought. I was helped along somewhat by a visit from Osborne. I was trying at that time, to find reasons to live, and wondered if he had any.

"I'm very sorry," he started off. I said nothing. "This is on my own time," he went on. "The department doesn't know I'm here."

"Was it suicide?" I asked him.

"I brought along a copy of the . . . the note. She ordered it from a shirt company in Westwood, three days before the . . . accident."

He handed it to me, and I read it. I was mentioned, though not by name. I was "the man I love." She said she couldn't cope with my problems. It was a short note. You can't get too much on a T-shirt. I read it through five times, then handed it back to him.

"She told you Kluge didn't write his note. I tell you she didn't write this."

He nodded reluctantly. I felt a vast calm, with a howling nightmare just below it. Praise Tranxene.

"Can you back that up?"

"She saw me in the hospital shortly before the . . . accident. She was full of life and hope. You say she ordered the shirt three days before. I would have felt that. And that note is pathetic. Lisa was never pathetic."

He nodded again.

"Some things I want to tell you. There were no signs of a struggle. Mrs. Lanier is sure no one came in the front. The crime lab went over the whole place and we're sure no one was in there with her. I'd stake my life on the fact that no one entered or left that house. Now, I don't believe it was suicide, either, but do you have any suggestions?"

"The NSA," I said.

I explained about the last things she had done while I was still there. I told him of her fear of the government spy agencies. That was all I had.

"Well, I guess they're the ones who could do a thing like that, if anyone could. But I'll tell you, I have a hard time swallowing it. I don't know why, for one thing. Maybe you believe those people kill like you and I'd swat a fly." His look made it into a question.

"I don't know what I believe."

"I'm not saying they wouldn't kill for national security, or some such shit. But they'd have taken the computers, too. They wouldn't have left her alone, they wouldn't even have let her *near* that stuff after they killed Kluge."

"What you're saying makes sense."

He muttered on about it for quite some time. Eventually I offered him some wine. He accepted thankfully. I considered joining him— it would be a quick way to die—but did not. He drank the whole bottle, and was comfortably drunk when he suggested we go next door and look it over one more time. I was planning on visiting Lisa the next day, and knew I had to start somewhere building myself up for that, so I agreed to go with him.

We inspected the kitchen. The fire had blackened the counters and melted some linoleum, but not much else. Water had made a mess of the place. There was a brown stain on the floor which I was able to look at with no emotion.

So we went back to the living room, and one of the computers was turned on. There was a short message on the screen.

```
IF YOU WISH TO KNOW MORE

PRESS ENTER ■
```

"Don't do it," I told him. But he did. He stood, blinking solemnly, as the words wiped themselves out and a new message appeared.

```
YOU LOOKED
```

The screen started to flicker and I was in my car, in darkness, with a pill in my mouth and another in my hand. I spit out the pill, and sat for a moment, listening to the old engine ticking over. In my hand was the plastic pill bottle. I felt very tired, but opened the car door and shut off the engine. I felt my way to the garage door and opened it. The air outside was fresh and sweet. I looked down at the pill bottle and hurried into the bathroom.

When I got through what had to be done there were a dozen pills floating in the toilet that hadn't even dissolved. There were the wasted shells of many more, and a lot of other stuff I won't bother to describe. I counted the pills in the bottle, remembered how many there had been, and wondered if I would make it.

I went over to Kluge's house and could not find Osborne. I was getting tired, but I made it back to my house and stretched out on the couch to see if I would live or die.

The next day I found the story in the paper. Osborne had gone home and blown out the back of his head with his revolver. It was not a big story. It happens to cops all the time. He didn't leave a note.

I got on the bus and rode out to the hospital and spent three hours trying to get in to see Lisa. I wasn't able to do it. I was not a relative and the doctors were quite firm about her having no visitors. When I got angry they were as gentle as possible. It was then I learned the extent of her injuries. Hal had kept the worst from me. None of it would have mattered, but the doctors swore there was nothing left in her head. So I went home.

She died two days later.

She had left a will, to my surprise. I got the house and contents. I picked up the phone as soon as I learned of it, and called a garbage company. While they were on the way over I went for the last time into Kluge's house.

The same computer was still on, and it gave the same message.

    PRESS ENTER ▇

I cautiously located the power switch, and turned it off. I had the garbage people strip the place to the bare walls.

I went over my own house very carefully, looking for anything that was even the first cousin to a computer. I threw out the radio. I sold the car, and the refrigerator, and the stove, and the blender, and the electric clock. I drained the waterbed and threw out the heater.

Then I bought the best propane stove on the market, and hunted a long time before I found an old icebox. I had the garage stacked to the ceiling with firewood. I had the chimney cleaned. It would be getting cold soon.

One day I took the bus to Pasadena and established the Lisa Foo Memorial Scholarship fund for Vietnamese refugees and their children. I endowed it with seven hundred thousand eighty-three dollars and four cents. I told them it could be used for any field of study except computer science. I could tell they thought me eccentric.

And I really thought I was safe, until the phone rang.

I thought it over for a long time before answering it. In the end, I knew it would just keep on going until I did. So I picked it up.

For a few seconds there was a dial tone, but I was not fooled. I kept holding it to my ear, and finally the tone turned off. There was just silence. I listened intently. I heard some of those far-off musical tones that live in phone wires. Echoes of conversations taking place a thousand miles away. And something infinitely more distant and cool.

I do not know what they have incubated out there at the NSA. I don't know if they did it on purpose, or if it just happened, or if it even has anything to do with them, in the end. But I know it's out there, because I heard its soul breathing on the wires. I spoke very carefully.

"I do not wish to know any more," I said. "I won't tell anyone anything. Kluge, Lisa, and Osborne all committed suicide. I am just a lonely man, and I won't cause you any trouble."

There was a click, and a dial tone.

Getting the phone taken out was easy. Getting them to remove all the wires was a little harder, since once a place is wired they expect it to be wired forever. They grumbled, but when I started pulling them out myself, they relented, though they warned me it was going to cost.

PG&E was harder. They actually seemed to believe there was a regulation requiring each house to be hooked up to the grid. They were willing to shut off my power—though hardly pleased about it—but they just weren't going to take the wires away from my house. I went up on the roof with an axe and demolished four feet of eaves as they gaped at me. Then they coiled up their wires and went home.

I threw out all my lamps, all things electrical. With hammer, chisel, and handsaw I went to work on the drywall just above the baseboards.

As I stripped the house of wiring I wondered many times why I was doing it. Why was it worth it? I couldn't have very many more years before a final seizure finished me off. Those years were not going to be a lot of fun.

Lisa had been a survivor. She would have known why I was doing this. She had once said I was a survivor, too. I survived the camp. I survived the death of my mother and father and managed to fashion a solitary life. Lisa survived the death of just about everything. No survivor expects to live through it all. But while she was alive, she would have worked to stay alive.

And that's what I did. I got all the wires out of the walls, went over the house with a magnet to see if I had missed any metal, then spent a week cleaning up, fixing the holes I had knocked in the walls, ceiling, and attic. I was amused trying to picture the real-estate agent selling this place after I was gone.

It's a great little house, folks. No electricity . . .

Now I live quietly, as before.

I work in my garden during most of the daylight hours. I've expanded it considerably, and even have things growing in the front yard now.

I live by candlelight, and kerosene lamp. I grow most of what I eat.

It took a long time to taper off the Tranxene and the Dilantin, but I did it, and now take the seizures as they come. I've usually got bruises to show for it.

In the middle of a vast city I have cut myself off. I am not part of the network growing faster than I can conceive. I don't even know if it's dangerous to ordinary people. It noticed me, and Kluge, and Osborne. And Lisa. It brushed against our minds like I would brush away a mosquito, never noticing I had crushed it. Only I survived.

But I wonder.

It would be very hard . . . Lisa told me how it can get in through the wiring. There's something called a carrier wave that can move over wires carrying household current. That's why the electricity had to go.

I need water for my garden. There's just not enough rain here in southern California, and I don't know how else I could get the water.

Do you think it could come through the pipes?

Octavia Butler appears here for the second time in this volume. This story is taken from a collection for which the blurb reads, in part, "Here is a story that might be a bit strong for those with weak stomachs . . ."

Does that include me? Well, yes and no.

I don't have a weak stomach literally, for I was brought up under conditions in which food had to be prepared rapidly and eaten quickly, so that I had two choices — to die of heartburn, or to develop an alimentary canal that could digest anything. Fortunately, it was the latter, in my case.

However, I think the blurb-writer was speaking of weak stomachs in the figurative sense, and there they have me. Anything unpleasant, anything harmful, anything painful, and I blanch. I have any number of friends who solicitously guide me away from certain movies. "Don't watch, Isaac," they'll say. "It's too violent."

When duty calls, however, things are different. I once wrote a book called The Human Body. *In it, it was necessary for me to describe all sorts of unpleasant diseases and disabilities, and I did it cold-bloodedly and without a tremor. After all, I was writing a book, and that takes precedence over my sense of queasiness.*

Ordinarily, had I been warned off a story by a blurb like that, I would have sighed and passed on to the next story at once. However, since I am preparing an anthology, and this story must be included, I must therefore read it in order to prepare a headnote.

So I read it. And I endured it easily for the sake of the excellence with which it is done. It puts into human terms a way of life that goes on right here on earth among certain insect species. Life, after all, is not necessarily pleasant, and the law that directs a species to "Survive!" does not say that it must not be done at the expense of other species.

We ourselves kill in order to eat. Even if we are vegetarians—plants are also living things.

—Isaac Asimov

Bloodchild

by Octavia E. Butler

My last night of childhood began with a visit home. T'Gatoi's sister had given us two sterile eggs. T'Gatoi gave one to my mother, brother, and sisters. She insisted that I eat the other one alone. It didn't matter. There was still enough to leave everyone feeling good. Almost everyone. My mother wouldn't take any. She sat, watching everyone drifting and dreaming without her. Most of the time she watched me.

I lay against T'Gatoi's long, velvet underside, sipping from my egg now and then, wondering why my mother denied herself such a harmless pleasure. Less of her hair would be gray if she indulged now and then. The eggs prolonged life, prolonged vigor. My father, who had never refused one in his life, had lived more than twice as long as he should have. And toward the end of his life, when he should have been slowing down, he had married my mother and fathered four children.

But my mother seemed content to age before she had to. I saw her turn away as several of T'Gatoi's limbs secured me closer. T'Gatoi liked our body heat, and took advantage of it whenever she could. When I was little and at home more, my mother used to try to tell me how to behave with T'Gatoi—how to be respectful and always obedient because T'Gatoi was the Tlic government official in charge of the Preserve, and thus the most important of her kind to deal directly with Terrans. It was an honor, my mother said, that such a person had chosen to come into the family. My mother was at her most formal and severe when she was lying.

I had no idea why she was lying, or even what she was lying about. It *was* an honor to have T'Gatoi in the family, but it was hardly a novelty. T'Gatoi and my mother had been friends all my mother's life, and T'Gatoi was not interested in being honored in the house she considered her second home. She simply came in, climbed onto one of her special couches and called me over to keep her warm. It was impossible to be formal with her while lying against her and hearing her complain as usual that I was too skinny.

278

"You're better," she said this time, probing me with six or seven of her limbs. "You're gaining weight finally. Thinness is dangerous." The probing changed subtly, became a series of caresses.

"He's still too thin," my mother said sharply.

T'Gatoi lifted her head and perhaps a meter of her body off the couch as though she were setting up. She looked at my mother, and my mother, her face lined and old-looking, turned away.

"Lien, I would like you to have what's left of Gan's egg."

"The eggs are for the children," my mother said.

"They are for the family. Please take it."

Unwillingly obedient, my mother took it from me and put it to her mouth. There were only a few drops left in the now-shrunken, elastic shell, but she squeezed them out, swallowed them, and after a few moments some of the lines of tension began to smooth from her face.

"It's good," she whispered. "Sometimes I forget how good it is."

"You should take more," T'Gatoi said. "Why are you in such a hurry to be old?"

My mother said nothing.

"I like being able to come here," T'Gatoi said. "This place is a refuge because of you, yet you won't take care of yourself."

T'Gatoi was hounded on the outside. Her people wanted more of us made available. Only she and her political faction stood between us and the hordes who did not understand why there was a Preserve—why any Terran could not be courted, paid, drafted, in some way made available to them. Or they did understand, but in their desperation, they did not care. She parceled us out to the desperate and sold us to the rich and powerful for their political support. Thus, we were necessities, status symbols, and an independent people. She oversaw the joining of families, putting an end to the final remnants of the earlier system of breaking up Terran families to suit impatient Tlic. I had lived outside with her. I had seen the desperate eagerness in the way some people looked at me. It was a little frightening to know that only she stood between us and that desperation that could so easily swallow us. My mother would look at her sometimes and say to me, "Take care of her." And I would remember that she too had been outside, had seen.

Now T'Gatoi used four of her limbs to push me away from her onto the floor. "Go on, Gan," she said. "Sit down there with your sisters and enjoy not being sober. You had most of the egg. Lien, come warm me."

My mother hesitated for no reason that I could see. One of my earliest memories is of my mother stretched alongside T'Gatoi, talking about things I could not understand, picking me up from the floor and laughing as she sat me on one of T'Gatoi's segments. She ate her share of eggs then. I wondered when she had stopped, and why.

She lay down now against T'Gatoi, and the whole left row of T'Gatoi's limbs closed around her, holding her loosely, but securely. I had always found it comfortable to lie that way, but except for my older sister, no one else in the family liked it. They said it made them feel caged.

T'Gatoi meant to cage my mother. Once she had, she moved her tail slightly, then spoke. "Not enough egg, Lien. You should have taken it when it was passed to you. You need it badly now."

T'Gatoi's tail moved once more, its whip motion so swift I wouldn't have seen it if I hadn't been watching for it. Her sting drew only a single drop of blood from my mother's bare leg.

My mother cried out—probably in surprise. Being stung doesn't hurt. Then she sighed and I could see her body relax. She moved languidly into a more comfortable position within the cage of T'Gatoi's limbs. "Why did you do that?" she asked, sounding half asleep.

"I could not watch you sitting and suffering any longer."

My mother managed to move her shoulders in a small shrug. "Tomorrow," she said.

"Yes. Tomorrow you will resume your suffering—if you must. But just now, just for now, lie here and warm me and let me ease your way a little."

"He's still mine, you know," my mother said suddenly.

"Nothing can buy him from me." Sober, she would not have permitted herself to refer to such things.

"Nothing," T'Gatoi agreed, humoring her.

"Did you think I would sell him for eggs? for long life? My son?"

"Not for anything," T'Gatoi said, stroking my mother's shoulders, toying with her long, graying hair.

I would like to have touched my mother, shared that moment with her. She would take my hand if I touched her now. Freed by the egg and the sting, she would smile and perhaps say things long held in.

But tomorrow, she would remember all this as a humiliation. I did not want to be part of a remembered humiliation. Best just be still and know she loved me under all the duty and pride and pain.

"Xuan Hoa, take off her shoes," T'Gatoi said. "In a little while I'll sting her again and she can sleep."

My older sister obeyed, swaying drunkenly as she stood up. When she had finished, she sat down beside me and took my hand. We had always been a unit, she and I.

My mother put the back of her head against T'Gatoi's underside and tried from that impossible angle to look up into the broad, round face. "You're going to sting me again?"

"Yes, Lien."

"I'll sleep until tomorrow noon."

"Good. You need it. When did you sleep last?"

My mother made a wordless sound of annoyance. "I should have stepped on you when you were small enough," she muttered.

It was an old joke between them. They had grown up together, sort of, though T'Gatoi had not, in my mother's lifetime, been small enough for any Terran to step on. She was nearly three times my mother's present age, yet would still be young when my mother died of age. But T'Gatoi and my mother had met as T'Gatoi was coming into a period of rapid development—a kind of Tlic adolescence. My mother was only a child, but for a while they developed at the same rate and had no better friends than each other.

T'Gatoi had even introduced my mother to the man who became my father. My parents, pleased with each other in spite of their different ages, married as T'Gatoi was going into her family's business—politics. She and my mother saw each other less. But sometime before my older sister was born, my mother promised T'Gatoi one of her children. She would have to give one of us to someone, and she preferred T'Gatoi to some stranger.

Years passed. T'Gatoi traveled and increased her influence. The Preserve was hers by the time she came back to my mother to collect what she probably saw as her just reward for her hard work. My older sister took an instant liking to her and wanted to be chosen, but my mother was just coming to term with me and T'Gatoi liked the idea of choosing an infant and watching and taking part in all the phases of development. I'm told I was first caged within T'Gatoi's many limbs only three minutes after my birth. A few days later, I was given my first taste of egg. I tell Terrans that when they ask whether I was ever afraid of her. And I tell it to Tlic when T'Gatoi suggests a young Terran child for them and they, anxious and ignorant, demand an adolescent. Even my brother who had somehow grown up to fear and distrust the Tlic could probably have gone smoothly into one of their families if he had been adopted early enough. Sometimes, I think for his sake he should have been. I looked at him, stretched out on the floor across the room, his eyes open, but glazed as he dreamed his egg dream. No matter what he felt toward the Tlic, he always demanded his share of egg.

"Lien, can you stand up?" T'Gatoi asked suddenly.

"Stand?" my mother said. "I thought I was going to sleep."

"Later. Something sounds wrong outside." The cage was abruptly gone.

"What?"

"Up, Lien!"

My mother recognized her tone and got up just in time to avoid being dumped on the floor. T'Gatoi whipped her three meters of body off her couch, toward the door, and out at full speed. She had bones—ribs, a long spine, a skull, four sets of limb bones per segment. But when she moved that way, twisting, hurling herself into controlled falls, landing running, she seemed not only boneless, but aquatic—something swimming through the air as though it were water. I loved watching her move.

I left my sister and started to follow her out the door, though I wasn't very steady on my own feet. It would have been better to sit and dream, better yet to find a girl and share a waking dream with her. Back when the Tlic saw us as not much more than convenient big warm-blooded animals, they would pen several of us together, male and female, and feed us only eggs. That way they could be sure of getting another generation of us no matter how we tried to hold out. We were lucky that didn't go on long. A few generations of it and we would have *been* little more than convenient big animals.

"Hold the door open, Gan," T'Gatoi said. "And tell the family to stay back."

"What is it?" I asked.

"N'Tlic."

I shrank back against the door. "Here? Alone?"

"He was trying to reach a call box, I suppose." She carried the man past me, unconscious, folded like a coat over some of her limbs. He looked young—my brother's age perhaps—and he was thinner than he should have been. What T'Gatoi would have called dangerously thin.

"Gan, go to the call box," she said. She put the man on the floor and began stripping off his clothing.

I did not move.

After a moment, she looked up at me, her sudden stillness a sign of deep impatience.

"Send Qui," I told her. "I'll stay here. Maybe I can help."

She let her limbs begin to move again, lifting the man and pulling his shirt over his head. "You don't want to see this," she said. "It will be hard. I can't help this man the way his Tlic could."

"I know. But send Qui. He won't want to be of any help here. I'm at least willing to try."

She looked at my brother—older, bigger, stronger, certainly more able to help her here. He was sitting up now, braced against the wall, staring at the man on the floor with undisguised fear and revulsion. Even she could see that he would be useless.

"Qui, go!" she said.

He didn't argue. He stood up, swayed briefly, then steadied, frightened sober.

"This man's name is Bram Lomas," she told him, reading from the man's armband. I fingered my own arm band in sympathy. "He needs T'Khotgif Teh. Do you hear?"

"Bram Lomas, T'Khotgif Teh," my brother said. "I'm going." He edged around Lomas and ran out the door.

Lomas began to regain consciousness. He only moaned at first and clutched spasmodically at a pair of T'Gatoi's limbs. My younger sister, finally awake from her egg dream, came close to look at him, until my mother pulled her back.

T'Gatoi removed the man's shoes, then his pants, all the while leaving him two of her limbs to grip. Except for the final few, all her limbs were equally dexterous. "I want no argument from you this time, Gan," she said.

I straightened. "What shall I do?"

"Go out and slaughter an animal that is at least half your size."

"Slaughter? But I've never—"

She knocked me across the room. Her tail was an efficient weapon whether she exposed the sting or not.

I got up, feeling stupid for having ignored her warning, and went into the kitchen. Maybe I could kill something with a knife or an ax. My mother raised a few Terran animals for the table and several thousand local ones for their fur. T'Gatoi would probably prefer something local. An achti, perhaps. Some of those were the right size, though they had about three times as many teeth as I did and a real love of using them. My mother, Hoa, and Qui could kill them with knives. I had never killed one at all, had never slaughtered any animal. I had spent most of my time with T'Gatoi while my brother and sisters were learning the family business. T'Gatoi had been right. I should have been the one to go to the call box. At least I could do that.

I went to the corner cabinet where my mother kept her large house and garden tools. At the back of the cabinet there was a pipe that carried off waste water from the kitchen—except that it didn't anymore. My father had rerouted the waste water below before I was born. Now the pipe could be turned so that one half slid around the other and a rifle could be stored inside. This wasn't our only gun, but it was our most easily accessible one. I would have to use it to shoot one of the biggest of the achti. Then T'Gatoi would probably confiscate it. Firearms were illegal in the Preserve. There had been incidents right after the Preserve was established—Terrans shooting Tlic, shooting N'Tlic. This was before the joining of families began, before everyone had a personal stake in keeping the peace. No one had shot a Tlic in my lifetime or my mother's, but the law still stood—for our protection, we were told. There were stories of whole Terran families wiped out in reprisal back during the assassinations.

I went out to the cages and shot the biggest achti I could find. It was a handsome breeding male and my mother would not be pleased to see me bring it in. But it was the right size, and I was in a hurry.

I put the achti's long, warm body over my shoulder—glad that some of the weight I'd gained was muscle—and took it to the kitchen. There, I put the gun back in its hiding place. If T'Gatoi noticed the achti's wounds and demanded the gun, I would give it to her. Otherwise, let it stay where my father wanted it.

I turned to take the achti to her, then hesitated. For several seconds, I stood in front of the closed door wondering why I was suddenly afraid. I knew what was going to happen. I hadn't seen it before but T'Gatoi had shown me diagrams, and drawings. She had made sure I knew the truth as soon as I was old enough to understand it.

Yet I did not want to go into that room. I wasted a little time choosing a knife from the carved, wooden box in which my mother kept them. T'Gatoi might want one, I told myself, for the tough, heavily furred hide of the Achti.

"Gan!" T'Gatoi called, her voice harsh with urgency.

I swallowed. I had not imagined a single moving of the feet could be so difficult. I realized I was trembling and that shamed me. Shame impelled me through the door.

I put the achti down near T'Gatoi and saw that Lomas was unconscious again. She, Lomas, and I were alone in the room, my mother and sisters probably sent out so they would not have to watch. I envied them.

But my mother came back into the room as T'Gatoi seized the achti. Ignoring the knife I offered her, she extended claws from several of her limbs and slit the achti from throat to anus. She looked at me, her yellow eyes intent. "Hold this man's shoulders, Gan."

I stared at Lomas in panic, realizing that I did not want to touch him, let alone hold him. This would not be like shooting an animal. Not as quick, not as merciful, and, I hoped, not as final, but there was nothing I wanted less than to be part of it.

My mother came forward. "Gan, you hold his right side," she said. "I'll hold his left." And if he came to, he would throw her off without realizing he had done it. She was a tiny woman. She often wondered aloud how she had produced, as she said, such "huge" children.

"Never mind," I told her, taking the man's shoulders. "I'll do it." She hovered nearby.

"Don't worry," I said. "I won't shame you. You don't have to stay and watch."

She looked at me uncertainly, then touched my face in a rare caress. Finally, she went back to her bedroom.

T'Gatoi lowered her head in relief. "Thank you, Gan," she said with courtesy more Terran than Tlic. "That one . . . she is always finding new ways for me to make her suffer."

Lomas began to groan and make choked sounds. I had hoped he would stay unconscious. T'Gatoi put her face near his so that he focused on her.

"I've stung you as much as I dare for now," she told him. "When this is over, I'll sting you to sleep and you won't hurt anymore."

"Please," the man begged. "Wait . . ."

"There's no more time, Bram. I'll sting you as soon as it's over. When T'Khotgif arrives she'll give you eggs to help you heal. It will be over soon."

"T'Khotgif!" the man shouted, straining against my hands.

"Soon, Bram." T'Gatoi glanced at me, then placed a claw against his abdomen slightly to the right of the middle, just below the left rib. There was movement on the right side—tiny, seemingly random pulsations moving his brown flesh, creating a concavity there, a convexity there, over and over until I could see the rhythm of it and knew where the next pulse would be.

Lomas's entire body stiffened under T'Gatoi's claw, though she merely rested it against him as she wound the rear section of her body around his legs. He might break my grip, but he would not break hers. He wept helplessly as she used his pants to tie his hands, then pushed his hands above his head so that I could kneel on the cloth between them and pin them in place. She rolled up his shirt and gave it to him to bite down on.

And she opened him.

His body convulsed with the first cut. He almost tore himself away from me. The sounds he made . . . I had never heard such sounds come from anything human. T'Gatoi seemed to pay no attention as she lengthened and deepened the cut, now and then pausing to lick away blood. His blood vessels contracted, reacting to the chemistry of her saliva, and the bleeding slowed.

I felt as though I were helping her torture him, helping her consume him. I knew I would vomit soon, didn't know why I hadn't already. I couldn't possibly last until she was finished.

She found the first grub. It was fat and deep red with his blood—both inside and out. It had already eaten its own egg case, but apparently had not yet begun to eat its host. At this stage, it would eat any flesh except its mother's. Let alone, it would have gone on excreting the poisons that had both sickened and alerted Lomas. Eventually it would have begun to eat. By the time it ate its way out of Lomas's flesh, Lomas would be dead or dying—and unable to take revenge on the thing that was killing him. There was always a grace period between the time the host sickened and the time the grubs began to eat him.

T'Gatoi picked up the writhing grub carefully, and looked at it, somehow ignoring the terrible groans of the man.

Abruptly, the man lost consciousness.

"Good," T'Gatoi looked down at him. "I wish you Terrans could do that at will." She felt nothing. And the thing she held . . .

It was limbless and boneless at this stage, perhaps fifteen centimeters long and two thick, blind and slimy with blood. It was like a large worm. T'Gatoi put it into the belly of the achti, and it began at once to burrow. It would stay there and eat as long as there was anything to eat.

Probing through Lomas's flesh, she found two more, one of them smaller and more vigorous. "A male!" she said happily. He would be dead before I would. He would be through his metamorphosis and screwing everything that would hold still before his sisters even had limbs. He was the only one to make a serious effort to bite T'Gatoi as she placed him in the achti.

Paler worms oozed to visibility in Lomas's flesh. I closed my eyes. It was worse than finding something dead, rotting, and filled with tiny animal grubs. And it was far worse than any drawing or diagram.

"Ah, there are more," T'Gatoi said, plucking out two long, thick grubs. You may have to kill another animal, Gan. Everything lives inside you Terrans."

I had been told all my life that this was a good and necessary thing Tlic and Terran did together—a kind of birth. I had believed it until now. I knew birth was painful and bloody, no matter what. But this was something else, something worse. And I wasn't ready to see it. Maybe I never would be. Yet I couldn't *not* see it. Closing my eyes didn't help.

T'Gatoi found a grub still eating its egg case. The remains of the case were still wired into a blood vessel by their own little tube or hook or whatever. That was the way the grubs were anchored and the way they fed. They took only blood until they were ready to emerge. Then they ate their stretched, elastic egg cases. Then they ate their hosts.

T'Gatoi bit away the egg case, licked away the blood. Did she like the taste? Did childhood habits die hard—or not die at all?

The whole procedure was wrong, alien. I wouldn't have thought anything about her could seem alien to me.

"One more, I think," she said. "Perhaps two. A good family. In a host animal these days, we would be happy to find one or two alive." She glanced at me. "Go outside, Gan, and empty your stomach. Go now while the man is unconscious."

I staggered out, barely made it. Beneath the tree just beyond the front door, I vomited until there was nothing left to bring up. Finally, I stood shaking, tears streaming down my face. I did not know why I was crying, but I could not stop. I went further from the house to avoid being seen. Every time I closed my eyes I saw red worms crawling over redder human flesh.

There was a car coming toward the house. Since Terrans were forbidden motorized vehicles except for certain farm equipment, I knew this must be Lomas's Tlic with Qui and perhaps a Terran doctor. I wiped my face on my shirt, struggled for control.

"Gan," Qui called as the car stopped. "What happened?" He crawled out of the low, round, Tlic-convenient car door. Another Terran crawled out the other side and went into the house without speaking to me. The doctor. With his help and a few eggs, Lomas might make it.

"T'Khotgif Teh?" I said.

The Tlic driver surged out of her car, reared up half her length before me. She was paler and smaller than T'Gatoi—probably born from the body of an animal. Tlic from Terran bodies were always larger as well as more numerous.

"Six young," I told her. "Maybe seven, all alive. At least one male."

"Lomas?" she said harshly. I liked her for the question and the concern in her voice when she asked it. The last coherent thing he had said was her name.

"He's alive," I said.

She surged away to the house without another word.

"She's been sick," my brother said, watching her go. "When I called, I could hear people telling her she wasn't well enough to go out even for this."

I said nothing. I had extended courtesy to the Tlic. Now I didn't want to talk to anyone. I hoped he would go in—out of curiosity if nothing else.

"Finally found out more than you wanted to know, eh?"

I looked at him.

"Don't give me one of *her* looks," he said. "You're not her. You're just her property."

One of her looks. Had I picked up even an ability to imitate her expressions?

"What'd you do, puke?" He sniffed the air. "So now you know what you're in for."

I walked away from him. He and I had been close when we were kids. He would let me follow him around when I was home and sometimes T'Gatoi would let me bring him along when she took me into the city. But something had happened when he reached adolescence. I never knew what. He began keeping out of T'Gatoi's way. Then he began running away—until he realized there was no "away." Not in the Preserve. Certainly not outside. After that he concentrated on getting his share of every egg that came into the house, and on looking out for me in a way that made me all but hate him—a way that clearly said, as long as I was all right, he was safe from the Tlic.

"How was it, really?" he demanded, following me.

"I killed an achti. The young ate it."

"You didn't run out of the house and puke because they ate an achti."

"I had . . . never seen a person cut open before." That was true, and enough for him to know. I couldn't talk about the other. Not with him.

"Oh," he said. He glanced at me as though he wanted to say more, but he kept quiet.

We walked, not really headed anywhere. Toward the back, toward the cages, toward the fields.

"Did he say anything?" Qui asked. "Lomas, I mean."

Who else would he mean? "He said 'T'Khotgif.' "

Qui shuddered. "If she had done that to me, she'd be the last person I'd call for."

"You'd call for her. Her sting would ease your pain without killing the grubs in you."

"You think I'd care if they died?"

No. Of course he wouldn't. Would I?

"Shit!" He drew a deep breath. "I've seen what they do. You think this thing with Lomas was bad? It was nothing."

I didn't argue. He didn't know what he was talking about.

"I saw them eat a man," he said.

I turned to face him. "You're lying!"

"*I saw them eat a man.*" He paused. "It was when I was little. I had been to the Hartmund house and I was on my way home. Halfway here, I saw a man and a Tlic and the man was N'Tlic. The ground was hilly. I was able to hide from them and watch. The Tlic wouldn't open the man because she had nothing to feed the grubs. The man couldn't go any further and there were no houses around. He was in so much pain he told her to kill him. He begged her to kill him. Finally, she did. She cut his throat. One swipe of one claw. I saw the grubs eat their way out, then burrow in again, still eating."

His words made me see Lomas's flesh again, parasitized, crawling. "Why didn't you tell me that?" I whispered.

He looked startled as though he'd forgotten I was listening. "I don't know."

"You started to run away not long after that, didn't you?"

"Yeah. Stupid. Running inside the Preserve. Running in a cage."

I shook my head, said what I should have said to him long ago. "She wouldn't take you, Qui. You don't have to worry."

"She would . . . if anything happened to you."

"No. She'd take Xuan Hoa. Hoa . . . wants it." She wouldn't if she had stayed to watch Lomas.

"They don't take women," he said with contempt.

"They do sometimes." I glanced at him. "Actually, they prefer women. You should be around them when they talk among themselves. They say women have more body fat to protect the grubs. But they usually take men to leave the women free to bear their own young."

"To provide the next generation of host animals." he said, switching from contempt to bitterness.

"It's more than that!" I countered. Was it?

"If it were going to happen to me, I'd want to believe it was more, too."

"It *is* more!" I felt like a kid. Stupid argument.

"Did you think so while T'Gatoi was picking worms out of that guy's guts?"

"It's not supposed to happen that way."

"Sure it is. You weren't supposed to see it, that's all. And his Tlic was supposed to do it. She could sting him unconscious and the operation wouldn't have been as painful. But she'd still open him, pick out the grubs, and if she missed even one, it would poison him and eat him from the inside out."

There was actually a time when my mother told me to show respect for Qui because he was my older brother. I walked away, hating him. In his way, he was gloating. He was safe and I wasn't. I could have hit him, but I didn't think I would be able to stand it when he refused to hit back, when he looked at me with contempt and pity.

He wouldn't let me get away. Longer-legged, he swung ahead of me and made me feel as though I were following him.

"I'm sorry," he said.

I strode on, sick and furious.

"Look, it probably won't be that bad with you. T'Gatoi likes you. She'll be careful."

I turned back toward the house, almost running from him.

"Has she done it to you yet?" he asked, keeping up easily. "I mean, you're about the right age for implantation. Has she—"

I hit him. I didn't know I was going to do it, but I think I meant to kill him. If he hadn't been bigger and stronger, I think I would have.

He tried to hold me off, but in the end, had to defend himself. He only hit me a couple of times. That was plenty. I don't remember going down, but when I came to, he was gone. It was worth the pain to be rid of him.

I got up and walked slowly toward the house. The back was dark. No one was in the kitchen. My mother and sisters were sleeping in their bedrooms—or pretending to.

Once I was in the kitchen, I could hear voices—Tlic and Terran from the next room. I couldn't make out what they were saying—didn't want to make it out.

I sat down at my mother's table, waiting for quiet. The table was smooth and worn, heavy and well crafted. My father had made it for her just before he died. I remembered hanging around underfoot when he built it. He didn't mind. Now I sat leaning on it, missing him. I could have talked to him. He had done it three times in his long life. Three clutches of eggs, three times being opened up and sewed up. How had he done it? How did anyone do it?

I got up, took the rifle from its hiding place, and sat down again with it. It needed cleaning, oiling.

All I did was load it.

"Gan?"

She made a lot of little clicking sounds when she walked on bare floor, each limb clicking in succession as it touched down. Waves of little clicks.

She came to the table, raised the front half of her body above it, and surged onto it. Sometimes she moved so smoothly she seemed to flow like water itself. She coiled herself into a small hill in the middle of the table and looked at me.

"That was bad," she said softly. "You should not have seen it. It need not be that way."

"I know."

"T'Khotgif—Ch'Khotgif now—she will die of her disease. She will not live to raise her children. But her sister will provide for them, and for Bram Lomas." Sterile sister. One fertile female in every lot. One to keep the family going. That sister owed Lomas more than she could ever repay.

"He'll live then?"

"Yes."

"I wonder if he would do it again."

"No one would ask him to do that again."

I looked into the yellow eyes, wondering how much I saw and understood there, and how much I only imagined. "No one ever asks us, " I said. "You never asked me."

She moved her head slightly. "What's the matter with your face?"

"Nothing. Nothing important." Human eyes probably wouldn't have noticed the swelling in the darkness. The only light was from one of the moons, shining through a window across the room.

"Did you use the rifle to shoot the achti?"

"Yes."

"And do you mean to use it to shoot me?"

I stared at her, outlined in the moonlight—coiled, graceful body. "What does Terran blood taste like to you?"

She said nothing.

"What are you?" I whispered. "What are we to you?"

She lay still, rested her head on her topmost coil. "You know me as no other does," she said softly. "You must decide."

"That's what happened to my face," I told her.

"What?"

"Qui goaded me into deciding to do something. It didn't turn out very well." I moved the gun slightly, brought the barrel up diagonally under my own chin. "At least it was a decision I made."

"As this will be."

"Ask me, Gatoi."

"For my children's lives?"

She would say something like that. She knew how to manipulate people, Terran and Tlic. But not this time.

"I don't want to be a host animal," I said. "Not even yours."

It took her a long time to answer. "We use almost no host animals these days," she said. "You know that."

"You use us."

"We do. We wait long years for you and teach you and join our families to yours." She moved restlessly. "You know you aren't animals to us."

I stared at her, saying nothing.

"The animals we once used began killing most of our eggs after implantation long before your ancestors arrived," she said softly. "You know these things, Gan. Because your people arrived, we are relearning what it means to be a healthy, thriving people. And your ancestors, fleeing from their homeworld, from their own kind who would have killed or enslaved them—they survived because of us. We saw them as people and gave them the Preserve when they still tried to kill us as worms.

At the word "worms" I jumped. I couldn't help it, and she couldn't help noticing it.

"I see," she said quietly. "Would you really rather die than bear my young, Gan?"

I didn't answer.

"Shall I go to Xuan Hoa?"

"Yes!" Hoa wanted it. Let her have it. She hadn't had to watch Lomas. She'd be proud. . . . Not terrified.

T'Gatoi flowed off the table onto the floor, startling me almost too much.

"I'll sleep in Hoa's room tonight," she said. "And sometime tonight or in the morning, I'll tell her."

This was going too fast. My sister Hoa had had almost as much to do with raising me as my mother. I was still close to her—not like Qui. She could want T'Gatoi and still love me.

"Wait! Gatoi!"

She looked back, then raised nearly half her length off the floor and turned it to face me. "These are adult things, Gan. This is my life, my family!"

"But she's . . . my sister."

"I have done what you demanded. I have asked you!"

"But—"

"It will be easier for Hoa. She has always expected to carry other lives inside her."

Human lives. Human young who should someday drink at her breasts, not at her veins.

I shook my head. "Don't do it to her, Gatoi." I was not Qui. It seemed I could become him, though, with no effort at all. I could make Xuan Hoa my shield. Would it be easier to know that red worms were growing in her flesh instead of mine?

"Don't do it to Hoa," I repeated.

She stared at me, utterly still.

I looked away, then back at her. "Do it to me."

I lowered the gun from my throat and she leaned forward to take it.

"No," I told her.

"It's the law," she said.

"Leave it for the family. One of them might use it to save my life someday."

She grasped the rifle barrel, but I wouldn't let go. I was pulled into a standing position over her.

"Leave it here!" I repeated. "If we're not your animals, if these are adult things, accept the risk. There is risk, Gatoi, in dealing with a partner."

It was clearly hard for her to let go of the rifle. A shudder went through her and she made a hissing sound of distress. It occurred to me that she was afraid. She was old enough to have seen what guns could do to people. Now her young and this gun would be together in the same house. She did not know about the other guns. In this dispute, they did not matter.

"I will implant the first egg tonight," she said as I put the gun away. "Do you hear, Gan?"

Why else had I been given a whole egg to eat while the rest of the family was left to share one? Why else had my mother kept looking at me as though I were going away from her, going where she could not follow? Did T'Gatoi imagine I hadn't known?

"I hear."

"Now!" I let her push me out of the kitchen, then walked ahead of her toward my bedroom. The sudden urgency in her voice sounded real. "You would have done it to Hoa tonight!" I accused.

"I must do it to someone tonight."

I stopped in spite of her urgency and stood in her way. "Don't you care who?"

She flowed around me and into my bedroom. I found her waiting on the couch we shared. There was nothing in Hoa's room that she could have used. She would have done it to Hoa on the floor. The thought of her doing it to Hoa at all disturbed me in a different way now, and I was suddenly angry.

Yet I undressed and lay down beside her. I knew what to do, what to expect. I had been told all my life. I felt the familiar sting, narcotic, mildly pleasant. Then the blind probing of her ovipositor. The puncture was painless, easy. So easy going in. She undulated slowly against me, her muscles forcing the egg from her body into mine. I held on to a pair of her limbs until I remembered Lomas holding her that way. Then I let go, moved inadvertently, and hurt her. She gave a low cry of pain and I expected to be caged at once within her limbs. When I wasn't, I held on to her again, feeling oddly ashamed.

"I'm sorry," I whispered.

She rubbed my shoulders with four of her limbs.

"Do you care?" I asked. "Do you care that it's me?"

She did not answer for some time. Finally, "You were the one making the choices tonight, Gan. I made mine long ago."

"Would you have gone to Hoa?"

"Yes. How could I put my children into the care of one who hates them?"

"It wasn't . . . hate."

"I know what it was."

"I was afraid."

Silence.

"I still am." I could admit it to her here, now.

"But you came to me . . . to save Hoa."

"Yes." I leaned my forehead against her. She was cool velvet, deceptively soft. "And to keep you for myself," I said. It was so. I didn't understand it, but it was so.

She made a soft hum of contentment. "I couldn't believe I had made such a mistake with you," she said. "I chose you. I believed you had grown to choose me."

"I had, but . . ."

"Lomas."

"Yes."

"I had never known a Terran to see a birth and take it well. Qui has seen one, hasn't he?"

"Yes."

"Terrans should be protected from seeing."

I didn't like the sound of that—and I doubted that it was possible. "Not protected," I said. "Shown. Shown when we're young kids, and shown more than once. Gatoi, no Terran ever sees a birth that goes right. All we see is N'Tlic—pain and terror and maybe death."

She looked down at me. "It is a private thing. It has always been a private thing."

Her tone kept me from insisting—that and the knowledge that if she changed her mind, I might be the first public example. But I had planted the thought in her mind. Chances were it would grow, and eventually she would experiment.

"You won't see it again," she said. "I don't want you thinking any more about shooting me."

The small amount of fluid that came into me with her egg relaxed me as completely as a sterile egg would have, so that I could remember the rifle in my hands and my feelings of fear and revulsion, anger and despair. I could remember the feelings without reviving them. I could talk about them.

"I wouldn't have shot you," I said. "Not you." She had been taken from my father's flesh when he was my age.

"You could have," she insisted.

"Not you." She stood between us and her own people, protecting, interweaving.

"Would you have destroyed yourself?"

I moved carefully, uncomfortable. "I could have done that. I nearly did. That's Qui's 'away.' I wonder if he knows."

"What?"

I did not answer.

"You will live now."

"Yes." *Take care of her*, my mother used to say. Yes.

"I'm healthy and young," she said. "I won't leave you as Lomas was left—alone, N'Tlic. I'll take care of you."

I think it was David Brin who, at a banquet I attended in 1987, said that writing a novel was like starting in Vladivostok and walking to Paris on your knees. When you reach Paris (having completed the novel), you stand up and celebrate with a wild champagne dinner and go to sleep—and wake up in Vladivostok on your knees.

I feel exactly that way about it but have never been clever enough to put it into the proper words. Thank you, David.

Now let me tell you something that "The Crystal Spheres" make me think of.

Sitting around with a group of other writers once, one of us (maybe it was Lester del Rey, but I don't remember) suggested that we all write first-trip-to-the-moon stories, even though the first trip to the moon was now history. The idea was that we could all think of ways of getting around the fact that men had already visited the moon.

For instance, (1) You could visit a well-settled moon, and in some valley untouched as yet by human beings, you come across the record of a human being who reached the moon in 1852.

Or (2) You live in an alternate world in which the moon was never reached, even though Mars and other worlds have been, and you have to explain why—and how the taboo was broken.

Or (3) The whole Apollo program was faked, and now it must be done right.

As far as I know, no one then present actually followed (3), but suppose a different idea of the kind had been suggested.

The Greeks felt that each of the seven planets was embedded in a crystal (i.e., "transparent") sphere, and each sphere moved at its own speed and in its own way. Even Johannes Kepler, in 1600 or so, played with that two-thousand-year-old idea. But then, in 1609, Kepler demonstrated the elliptical nature of the planetary orbits, and the crystal spheres disappeared forever.

So why don't we science fiction writers compose a story in which the astronomers from Plato to the young Kepler were right and there were crystal spheres? Naturally, it would have to fit in somewhat with what we know about astronomy today, but don't bother . . .

David Brin wrote the story, as you can tell from its very title, and here it is. And read what he does with it, too, and remember Fermi's famous question, which I mentioned in an earlier headnote.

—Isaac Asimov

The Crystal Spheres

by David Brin

1

It was just a luckychance that I had been defrosted when I was—the very year that farprobe 992573-aa4 reported back that it had found a goodstar with a shattered crystalsphere. I was one of only twelve deepspacers alivewarm at the time, so naturally I got to take part in the adventure.

At first I knew nothing about it. When the flivver came, I was climbing the flanks of the Sicilian plateau, in the great valley a recent ice age had made of the Mediterranean Sea I had once known. I and five other newly awakened Sleepers had come to camp and tramp through this wonder while we acclimated to the times.

We were a motley assortment from various eras, though none was older than I. We had just finished a visit to the once-sunken ruins of Atlantis, and were hiking out on a forest trail under the evening glow of the ringcity high overhead. In the centuries since I had last deepslept, the gleaming, flexisolid belt of habitindustry around our world had grown. In the middle latitudes, night was now a pale thing. Nearer the equator, there was little to distinguish it from day, so glorious was the lightribbon in the sky.

Not that night could ever be the same as it had been when my grandfather was a child, even if every work of man were removed. For ever since the twenty-second century there had been the Shards, casting colors out where once there had been but galaxies and stars.

No wonder no one had objected to the banishment of night from Earthsurface. Humanity out on the smallbodies might have to look upon the Shards, but Earthdwellers had no particular desire to gaze out upon those unpleasant reminders.

Being only a year thawed, I wasn't ready yet to even ask what century it was, let alone begin finding some passable profession for this life. Reawakened sleepers were generally given a decade or so to enjoy and explore the differences that had grown in the Earth and in the solar system before having to make any choices.

This was especially true in deepspacers like me. The State—more ageless than any of its nearly immortal members—had a nostalgic affection for us strange ones, officers of a near-extinct service. When a deepspacer awakened, he or she was encouraged to go about the altered Terra without interference, seeking strangeness. He might even dream he was exploring another goodworld, where no man had ever trod, instead of breathing the same air that had been in his own lungs so many times, during so many ages past.

I had expected to go my rebirthtrek unbothered. So it was with amazement, that evening on the forestflank of Sicily, that I saw a creamy-colored Sol-Gov flivver drop out of a bank of lacy clouds and drift toward the campsite, where my group of timecast wanderers had settled to doze and aimlessly gossip about the events of the day.

We all stood and watched it come. The other campers looked at one another suspiciously as the flivver fell toward us. They wondered who was important enough to compel the ever-polite Worldcomps to break into our privacy, sending this teardrop down below the Palermo heights to parklands where it didn't belong.

I kept my secret feeling to myself. The thing had come for me. I knew it. Don't ask me how. A deepspacer *knows* things. That is all.

We who have been out beyond the shattered Shards of Sol's broken crystalsphere, and have peered from the outside to see living worlds within faraway shells . . . We are the ones who have pressed our faces against the glass at the candy store, staring in at what we could not have. We are the ones who understand the depth of our deprivation, and the joke the Universe has played on us.

The billions of our fellow humans—those who have never left Sol's soft, yellow kindness—need psychists even to tell of the irreparable trauma they endure. Most people drift through their lives suffering only occasional bouts of greatdepression, easily treated, or ended with finalsleep.

But we deepspacers have rattled the bars of our cage. We *know* our neuroses arise out of the Universe's great jest.

I stepped forward toward the clearing where the Sol-Gov flivver was settling. It gave my campmates someone to blame for the interruption. I could feel their burning stares.

The beige teardrop opened, and out stepped a tall woman. She possessed a type of statuesque, austere beauty that had not been in fashion on Earth during any of my last four lives. Clearly she had never indulged in biosculpting.

I admit freely that in that first instant I did not recognize her, though we had thrice been married over the slow waityears.

The first thing I knew, the very first thing of all, was that she wore our uniform . . . the uniform of a Service that had been "moth-balled" (O quaint term!) thousands of years ago.

Silver against dark blue, and eyes that matched . . . "Alice," I breathed after a long moment. "Is it true at last?"

She came forward and took my hand. She must have known how weak and tense I felt.

"Yes, Joshua. One of the probes has found another cracked shell."

"There is no mistake? It's a goodstar?"

She nodded her head, saying yes with her eyes. Black ringlets framed her face, shimmering like the trail of a rocket.

"The probe called a class-A alert." She grinned. "There are Shards all around the star, shattered and glimmering like the Oort-sky of Sol. And the probe reports that there is a *world* within! One that we can touch!"

I laughed out loud and pulled her to me. I could tell the campers behind me came from times when one did not do such things, for they muttered in consternation.

"When? When did the news come?"

"We found out months ago, just after you thawed. Worldcomp still said that we had to give you a year of wakeup, but I came the instant it was over. We have waited long enough, Joshua. Moishe Bok is taking out every deepspacer nowalive.

"Joshua, we want you to come. We need you. Our expedition leaves in three days. Will you join us?"

She need not have asked. We embraced again. And this time I had to blink back tears.

Of recent weeks, as I wandered, I had pondered what profession I would pursue in this life. But joy of joys, it never occurred to me I would be a deepspacer again! I would wear the uniform once more, and fartravel to the stars!

2

The project was under a total news blackout. The Sol-Gov psy-chists were of the opinion that the race could not stand another disappointment. They feared an epidemic of greatdepression, and a few of them even tried to stop us from mounting the expedition.

Fortunately, the Worldcomps remembered their ancient promise. We deepspacers long ago agreed to stop exploring, and raising people's hopes with our efforts. In return, the billion robot farprobes were sent out, and we would be allowed to go investigate any report they sent back of a cracked shell.

By the time Alice and I arrived at Charon, the others had almost finished recommissioning the ship we were to take. I had hoped we would be using the *Robert Rodgers,* or *Ponce de León*, two ships I had once commanded. But they had chosen instead to use the old *Pelenor.* She would be big enough for the purposes we had in mind, without being unwieldy.

Sol-Gov tugs were loading about ten thousand corpsicles even as the shuttle carrying Alice and me passed Pluto and began rendezvous maneuvers. Out here, ten percent of the way to the Edge, the Shards glimmered with a brightsheen of indescribable colors. I let Alice do the piloting, and stared out at the glowing fragments of Sol's shattered crystalsphere.

When my grandfather was a boy, Charon had been a site of similar activity. Thousands of excited men and women had clustered around an asteroid ship half the size of the little moon itself, taking aboard a virtual ark of hopeful would-be colonists, their animals, and their goods.

Those early explorers knew they would never see their final destination. But they were not sad. They suffered from no greatdepression. Those people launched forth in their so-primitive first starship full of hope for their great-grandchildren—and for the world which their sensitive telescopes had proved circled, green and pleasant, around the star Tau Ceti.

Ten thousand waityears later, I looked out at the mammoth Yards of Charon as we passed overhead. Rank on serried rank of starships lay berthed below. Over the millennia, thousands had been built, from generation ships and hiberna-barges to ram-shippers and greatstrutted wormhole-divers.

They all lay below, all except the few that were destroyed in accidents, or whose crews killed themselves in despair. They had all come back to Charon, failures.

I looked at the most ancient hulks, the generation ships, and thought about the day of my grandfather's youth, when the *Seeker* cruised blithely over the Edge, and collided at one percent of light speed with the inner face of Sol's crystalsphere.

They never knew what hit them, that firstcrew.

They had begun to pass through the outermost shoals of the solar system . . . the Oort Cloud, where billions of comets drifted like puffs of snow in the sun's weakened grasp.

Seeker's instruments sought through the sparse cloud, touching isolated, drifting balls of ice. The would-be colonists planned to keep busy doing science throughout the long passage. Among the questions they wanted to solve on their way was the mystery of the comets' mass.

Why was it, astronomers had asked for centuries, that virtually all of these icy bodies were nearly the same size—a few miles across?

Seeker's instruments ploughed for knowledge. Little did her pilots know she would reap the Joke of the Gods.

When she collided with the crystalsphere, it bowed outward with her over a span of lightminutes. *Seeker* had time for a frantic lasercast back to Earth. They only knew that something strange was happening. Something had begun tearing them apart, even as the fabric of space itself seemed to rend!

Then the crystalsphere shattered.

And where there had once been ten billion comets, now there were ten quadrillion.

Nobody ever found the wreckage of *Seeker*. Perhaps she had vaporized. Almost half the human race died in the battle against the comets, and by the time the planets were safe again, centuries later, *Seeker* was long gone.

We never did find out how, by what accident, she managed to crack the shell. There are still those who contend that it was the crew's ignorance that crystalspheres even *existed* that enabled them to achieve what had forever since seemed so impossible.

Now the Shards illuminate the sky. Sol shines within a halo of light, reflected by the ten quadrillion comets . . . the mark of the only goodstar accessible to man.

"We're coming in," Alice told me. I sat up in my seat and watched her nimble hands dance across the panel. Then *Pelenor* drifted into view.

The great globe shone dully in the light from the Shards. Already the nimbus of her drives caused space around her to shimmer.

The Sol-Gov tugs had finished loading the colonists abroad, and were departing. The ten thousand corpsicles would require little tending during our mission, so we dozen deepspacers would be free to explore. But if the goodstar did, indeed, shine into an accessible goodworld, we would awaken the men and women from frozensleep and deliver them to their new home.

No doubt the Worldcomps chose well these sleepers to be potential colonists. Still, we were under orders that none of them should be awakened unless a colony was possible. Perhaps this trip would turn out to be just another disappointment, in which case the corpsicles were never to know that they had been on a journey twenty thousand parsecs and back.

"Let's dock," I said eagerly. "I want to get going."

Alice smiled. "Always the impatient one. The deepspacer's deepspacer. Give it a day or two, Joshua. We'll be winging out of the nest soon enough."

There was no point in reminding her that I had been latewaiting longer than she—indeed, longer than nearly any other human left alive. I kept my restlessness within and listened, in my head, to the music of the spheres.

3

In my time there were four ways known to cheat Einstein, and two ways to flat-out fool him. On our journey *Pelenor* used all of them. Our route was circuitous, from wormhole to quantumpoint to collapsar. By the time we arrived, I wondered how the deepprobe had ever gotten so far, let alone back, with its news.

The find was in the nearby minor galaxy, Sculptor. It took us twelve years, shiptime, to get there.

On the way we passed close to at least two hundred goodstars, glowing hotyellow, stable, and solitary. In every case there were signs of planets circling around. Several times we swept by close enough to catch glimpses, in our superscopes, of bright blue waterworlds, circling invitingly like temptresses, forever out of reach.

In the old days we would have mapped these places, excitedly standing off just outside the dangerzone, studying the Earth-like worlds with our instruments. We would have charted them carefully, against the day when mankind finally learned how to do on purpose what *Seeker* had accomplished in ignorance.

Once we did stop, and lingered two lightdays away from a certain goodstar—just outside of its crystalsphere. Perhaps we were foolish to come so close, but we couldn't help it. For there were modulated radio waves coming from the waterworld within!

It was only the fourth time technological civilization had been found. We spent an excited year setting up robot watchers and recorders to study the phenomenon.

But we did not bother trying to communicate. We knew, by now, what would happen. Any probe we sent in would collide with the crystalsphere around this goodstar. It would be crushed, ice precipitating upon it from all directions until it was destroyed and hidden under megatons of water—a newborn comet.

Any focused beams we cast inward would cause a similar reaction, creating a reflecting mirror that blocked all efforts to communicate with the locals.

Still, we could listen to *their* traffic. The crystalsphere was a one-way barrier to modulated light and radio, and intelligence of any form. But it let the noise the locals made escape.

In this case, we soon concluded that it was another hive-race. The creatures had no interest in, or even conception of, spacetravel. Disappointed, we left our watchers in place and hurried on.

Our target was obvious as soon as we arrived within a few lightweeks of the goal. Our excitement rose as we found that the probe had not lied. It *was* a goodstar—stable, old, companionless—and its friendly yellow glow diffracted through a pale, shimmering aura of ten quadrillion snowflakes . . . its shattered crystalsphere.

"There's a complete suite of planets," announced Yen Ching, our cosmophysicist. His hands groped about in his holistank, touching in its murk what the ship's instruments were able to decipher from this distance.

"I can feel three gasgiants, about two million asteroid smallbodies, and"—he made us wait, while he felt carefully to make sure—"three littleworlds!"

We cheered. With numbers like those, odds were that at least one of the rocky planets circled within the Lifezone.

"Let me see . . . there's one littleworld here that has—" Yen pulled his hand from the tank. He popped a finger in his mouth and tasted for a moment, rolling his eyes like a connoisseur savoring fine wine.

"Water." He smacked thoughtfully. "Yes! Plenty of water. I can taste life, too. Standard adenine-based carbolife. Hmmm. In fact, it's chlorophyllic and left-handed!"

In the excited, happy babble that followed, Moishe Bok, our captain, had to shout to be heard.

"All right! People! Look, it's clear none of us are going to get any sleep soon. Lifesciencer Taiga, have you prepared a list of corpsicles to thaw, in case we have found a goodworld?"

Alice drew the list from her pocket. "Ready, Moishe. I have biologists, technicians, planetologists, crystallographers . . ."

"You'd also better awaken a few archaeologists and Contacters," Yen added dryly.

We turned and saw that his hands were back in the holistank. His face bore a dreamy expression.

"It took our civilization three thousand years to herd our asteroids into optimum orbits for space colonies. But compared with this system, we're amateurs. Every smallbody orbiting this star has been transformed. They march around like ancient soldiers on a drillfield. I have never even imagined engineering on this scale."

Moishe's gaze flickered to me. As executive officer, it would be my job to fight for the ship, if *Pelenor* found herself in trouble . . . and to destroy her if capture were inevitable.

Long ago we had reached one conclusion. If goodstars without crystalspheres were rare, and dreamt of by a frustrated mankind, the same might hold for some *other* star-traveling race. If some other people had managed to break out of its shell, and now wandered about, like us, in search of another open goodstar, what would such a race think, upon detecting our ship?

I know what *we* would think. We would think that the intruder had to *come* from somewhere . . . an open goodstar.

My job was to make sure nobody ever followed *Pelenor* back to Earth.

I nodded to my assistant, Yoko Murukami, who followed me to

the armsglobe. We unfolded the firing panel and waited while Moishe ordered *Pelenor* piloted cautiously closer.

Yoko looked at the panel dubiously. She obviously doubted the efficacy of even a mega-terawatt laser against technology of the scale described by Yen.

I shrugged. We would find out soon. My duty was done the moment I flicked the arming switch and took hold of our deadman autodestruct. In the hours that passed, I watched the developments carefully, but could not help deepremembering.

4

Back in the days before starships—before *Seeker* broke Sol's egg-shell and precipitated the two-century CometWar —mankind had awakened to a quandary that caused the thinkers of those early days many sleepless nights.

As telescopes improved, as biologists began to understand, and even tailormake life, more and more people began to look up at the sky and ask, "Where the hell *is* everybody?"

The great lunar-based cameras tracked planets around nearby yellow suns. There were telltale traces of life even in those faint twenty-first-century spectra. Philosophers case nervous calculations to show that the galaxies must teem with living worlds.

And as they prepared our first starships, the deepthinkers began to wonder. If travel between the stars was as easy as it appeared to be, why hadn't the fertile stars already been settled by somebody else?

After all, we were getting ready to head out and colonize. By even modest estimates of expansion rates, we seemed sure to fill the entire galaxy with human settlements within a few million years.

So why hadn't this already *happened*? Why was there no sign of traffic among the stars? Why had the predicted galactic radio network of communications never been detected?

Even more puzzling . . . why was there absolutely *no* evidence that Earth had ever been colonized in the past? We were by then quite certain that our world had never hosted visitors from other worlds.

For one thing, there was the history of the Precambrian to consider.

Before the age of reptiles, before fish or trilobites or even amoebae, there was, on Earth, a two-billion-year epoch in which the only lifeforms were crude single-celled organisms without nuclei—the prokaryotes—struggling slowly to invent the basic structure of life.

No alien colonists ever came to Earth during all that time. We knew that for certain, for if they had, the very garbage they buried would have changed the history of life on our planet. A single leaky latrine would have filled the oceans with superior lifeforms that would have overwhelmed our crude little ancestors.

Two billion years without being colonized . . . and then the silent emptiness of the radioways . . . the philosophers of the twenty-first century called it the Great Silence. They hoped the starships would find the answer.

Then the very first ship, *Seeker*, somehow smashed the crystalsphere we hadn't even known existed, and inadvertently explained the mystery for us.

During the ensuing CometWar, we had little time for philosophical musings. I was born into that battle, and spent my first hundred years in harsh screaming littleships, blasting and herding iceballs that, left alone, would have fallen upon and crushed our fragile worlds.

We might have let Earth fall then. After all, more than half of humanity at that time lived in space colonies, which could be protected more easily than any sittingduck planet.

That might have been logical. But mankind went a little crazy when Earthmother was threatened. Belters herded cities of millions into the paths of hurling iceballs, just to save a heavy world they had only known from books and a faint blue twinkle in the blackness. The psychists took a long time to understand why. At the time it seemed like some sort of divine madness.

Finally the war was won. The comets were tamed and we started looking outward again. New starships were built, better than before.

I had to wait for a berth on the twelfth ship, and the wait saved my life.

The first seven ships were lost. As they beamed back their jubilant reports, spiraling closer to the beautiful green worlds they had found, they plowed into unseen crystalspheres and were destroyed.

And, unlike *Seeker*, they did not accomplish anything by dying. The crystalspheres remained after the ships had been icecrushed into comets.

We had all had such hopes . . . though those who remembered *Seeker* had worried quietly. Humanity seemed about to breathe free, at last! We were going to spread our eggs to other baskets, and be safe for the first time. No more would we fear overpopulation, crowding, or stagnation.

And all at once the hopes were smashed—dashed against those unseen, deadly spheres.

It took centuries even to learn how to *detect* the deadzones! *How*, we asked. How could the universe be so perverse? Was it all some great practical joke? What *were* these monstrous barriers that defied all the physics we knew, and kept us away from the beautiful littleworlds we so desired?

For three centuries, humanity went a little crazy.

I missed the worst years of the greatdepression. I was with a group trying to study the sphere around Tau Ceti. By the time I got back, some degree of order had been restored.

But I returned to a solar system that had clearly lost a piece of its heart. It was a long time before I heard true laughter again, on Earth or on her smallbodies.

I too went to bed and pulled the covers over my head for a couple of hundred years.

5

The entire crew breathed a reliefsigh when Captain Bok ordered me to put the safeties back on. I finally let go of my deadman switch and got up. The tension seeped away into a chain of shivers, and Alice had to hold me until I could stand again on my own.

Moishe had ordered us off alert because the goodsun's system was empty.

To be accurate, the system *teemed* with life, but none of it was intelligent.

The greater asteroids held marvelous, self-sustaining ecosystems, absorbing sunlight under great windows. Twenty moons sheltered huge forests beneath tremendous domes. But there was no traffic, no radio or light messages. Yen's detectors revealed no machine activity, nor the thought-touch of analytical beings.

It felt eerie to poke our way through those civilized lanes in the smallbody ways. For so long we had only performed such maneuvers in the well-known spaces of Solsystem.

During those first centuries after the crystal crisis, some men and women still thought it would be possible to live among the stars. Belters mostly, they claimed aloud that planets were nasty, heavy places anyway. So who needed them?

They went out to the *badstars*—red giants and tiny red dwarves, tight binaries and unstable suns. The badstars were protected by no crystalspheres. The would-be colonists found drifting clots of matter near the suns, and set up smallbody cities as they had at home.

Every one of the attempts failed within a few generations. The colonists simply lost interest in procreation.

The psychists finally decided the cause was related to the divine madness that had enabled us to win the CometWar.

Simply put, men and women could live on asteroids, but they needed to *know* that there was as blue world nearby—to see it in their sky. It's a flaw in our character, no doubt, but we cannot go out and live in space all alone.

We have to have waterworlds, if the universe is ever to be ours.

This system's waterworld we named Quest, after the beast so long sought by King Pelenor, our ship's namesake. It shone blue and brown, under a clean whiteswaddling of clouds. For hours we circled above it, and simply cried.

Alice awakened ten corpsicles—prominent scientists who, the Worldcomps had promised, would not fall apart on the reawakening of hope.

We watched them take their turn at the viewport, joytears streaming down their faces, and we joined them to weep freely once again.

6

Pelenor was hardly up to the task of exploring this system by herself. We spent a year recovering and modifying several of the ancient ships we found drifting over our planet, so that teams could spread out, investigating every farcorner of this system.

By our second anniversary, a hundred biologists were quickscampering over the surface of Quest. They genescanned the local flora and fauna excitedly, and already were modifying Earthplants to fit into the ecosystem without causing imbalance. Soon they would start on animals from our genetanks.

Engineers exploring the smallbodies excitedly declared that they could get the lifemachines left behind by the prior race to work. There was room for a billion colonists out there, straight from the start.

But the archaeologists were the ones whose report we awaited most anxiously. Between my ferrying runs, they were the ones I helped. I joined them in the dusty ruins of Oldcity, at the edge of Longvalley, putting together piles of artifacts to be catalogued and slowly analyzed.

We learned that the inhabitants had called themselves the Nataral. They were about as similar to us as we might have expected—bipedal, ninefingered, weirdlooking.

Still, one got used to their faces after staring at their statues and pictures long enough. I even began to perceive subtle facial cues, and delicate, sensitive nuances of expression. When the language was cracked, we learned their race name and some of their story.

Unlike the few other alien intelligences we had observed from afar, the Natarals were individuals, and explorers. They too had spread into their planetary system after a worldbound history fully as colorful and goodbad as our own.

Like us, they had two conflicting dreams. They longed for the stars, for room to grow. And they also wished for other faces, for neighbors.

By the time they built a starship—their first—they had given up on the idea of neighbors. There was no sign anybody had ever visited their world. They heard nothing but silence from the stars.

Still, when they were ready, they launched their firstship toward their other dream—Room.

And within weeks of the launching, their sun's crystalsphere shattered.

*   *   *

For two weeks we double-checked the translations. We triple-checked.

For millennia we had been searching for a way to destroy these deadly barriers around goodstars . . . trying to duplicate on purpose what *Seeker* had accomplished by accident. And now we had the answer

The Nataral, like us, had managed to destroy one and only one crystalsphere. Their own. And the pattern was exactly the same, down to the CometWar that subsequently almost wrecked their high civilization.

The conclusion was obvious. The deathbarriers were destructible, but *only from the inside!*

And just when that idea was starting to sink in, the archaeologists dug up the Obelisk.

7

Our top linguist, Garcia Cardenas, had a flair for the dramatic. When Alice and I visited him in his encampment at the base of the newly excavated monument, he insisted on putting off all discussion of his discovery until the next day. He and his partner instead prepared a special meal for us, and raised their glasses to toast Alice.

She stood and accepted their accolades with dry wit, and then sat down to continue nursing our baby.

Old habits break hard, and only a few of the women had managed yet to break centuries of biofeedback conditioning not to breed. Alice was among the first to reactivate her ovaries and bring a child to our new world.

It wasn't that I was jealous. After all, I basked in the only slightly lesser glory of fatherhood. But I was getting impatient with all of this ballyhoo. Except for Moishe Bok, I was perhaps the oldest human here—old enough to remember when people had children as a matter of course, and therefore made time for *other* matters, when something important was up!

Finally, when the celebration had wound down, Garcia Cardenas nodded to me, and led me out the back flap of the tent. We followed a dim path down a sloping trail to the digs, by the light of the ring of bright smallbodies the Nataral had left permanently in place over the equatorial sky of Quest.

We finally arrived at a bright alloy wall that towered high above our heads. It was made of a material our techs had barely begun to analyze, and was nearly impervious to the effects of time. On it were inscribed hardpatterns bearing the tale of the last days of the Nataral.

A lot of that story we knew from other translated records. But the end itself was still a mystery, and no small cause of nervousness. Had it been some terrible plague? Did the intelligent machines, on which both their civilization and ours relied, rebel and slaughter their masters? Did their sophisticated bioengineering technology get out of their control?

What we *did* know was that the Nataral had suffered. Like humans, they had gone out and found the universe closed to them. Both of their great dreams—of goodplaces to spreadsettle, and of other minds to meet—had been shattered like the deathsphere around their own star. Like humans, they spent quite a long time not entirely sane.

In the darkness deep within the dig, Cardenas had promised I would find answers.

As he prepared his instruments I listened to the sounds of the surrounding forestjungle. Life abounded on this world. There were lovely, complicated creatures, some clearly natural, and some just as clearly the result of clever biosculpting. In their creatures, in their art and architecture, in the very reasons they had almost despaired, I felt a powerful closeness to the Nataral. I would have liked them, I imagined.

I was glad to take this world for humanity, for it might mean salvation for my species. Still, I regretted that the other race was gone.

Cardenas motioned me over to a holistank he had set up at the base of the Obelisk. As we put our hands into the blackness, a light appeared on the face of the monolith. Where the light traveled, we would touch, and feel the passion of those final days of the Nataral.

I stroked the finetuned, softresonant surface. Cardenas led me, and I felt the Endingtime as the Nataral meant it to be felt.

*   *   *

Like us, the Nataral had passed through a long period of bitterness, even longer than we had endured until now. To them, indeed, it seemed as if the universe was a great, sick joke.

Life was found everywhere among the stars. But intelligence arose only slowly and rarely, with many false starts. Where it did occur, it was often in a form that did not happen to covet space or other planets.

But if the crystalspheres had not existed, the rare sites where starfaring developed would spread outward. Species like us would expand, and eventually make contact with one another, instead of searching forever among sandgrains. An elder race might arrive where another was just getting started, and help it over some of its crises.

If the crystalspheres had not existed . . .

But that was not to be. Starfarers could not spread, because crystalspheres could only be broken from the inside! What a cruel universe it was!

Or so the Nataral had thought.

But they persevered. And after ages spent hunting for the miraculous goodstar, their farprobes found five water-worlds unprotected by deathbarriers.

My touchhand trembled as I stroked the coordinates of these accessible planets. My throat caught at the magnitude of the gift that had been given us on this obelisk. No *wonder* Cardenas had made me wait! I, too, would linger when I showed it to Alice.

But then, I wondered, where had the Nataral gone? And why? With six worlds, surely their morale would have lifted!

There was a confusing place on the Obelisk . . . talk of black holes and of *time*. I touched the spot again and again, while Cardenas watched my reaction. Finally, I understood.

"Great Egg!" I cried. The revelation of what had happened made the discovery of the five goodworlds pale into insignificance.

"Is *that* what the crystalspheres are for?"

I couldn't believe it.

Cardenas smiled. "Watch out for teleology, Joshua. It is true that the barriers would seem to show the hand of the creator at work. But it might be simply circumstance, rather than some grand design.

"All that we do know is this. Without the crystalspheres, we ourselves would not exist. Intelligence would be more rare than it already is. And the stars would be almost barren of life.

"We have cursed the crystalspheres for ten thousand years," Cardenas sighed. "The Nataral did so for far longer—until they at last understood."

8

If the crystalspheres had not existed . . .

I thought about it that night, as I stared up at the shimmering, pale light from the drifting Shards, through which the brighter stars still shone.

If the crystalspheres had not existed, then there would come to each galaxy a first race of star-treaders. Even if most intelligences were stay-at-homes, the coming of an aggressive, colonizing species was inevitable, sooner or later.

If the crystalspheres had not existed, the first such star-treaders would have gone out and taken all the worlds they found. They would have settled all the waterworlds, and civilized the smallbodies around every single goodstar.

Two centuries before we discovered our crystalsphere, we humans had already started wondering why this had never happened to Earth. Why, during the three billion years that Earth was "choice real estate," had no race like us come along and colonized it?

We found out it was because of the deathbarrier surrounding Sol, which kept our crude little ancestors safe from interference from the outside . . . which let our nursery world nurture us in peace and isolation.

If the crystalspheres had not been, then the first star-treaders would have filled the galaxy, perhaps the universe. It is what *we* would have done, had the barriers not been there. The histories of those worlds would be forever changed. And there is no way to imagine the death-of-possibility that would have resulted.

So, the barriers protected worlds until they developed life capable of cracking the shells from within.

But what was the point? What benefit was there in protecting some young thing, only for it to grow up into bitter, cramped loneliness in adulthood?

Imagine what it must have been like for the very first race of star-treaders. Never, were they patient as Job, would they find another goodstar to possess. Not until the next egg cracked would they have neighbors to talk to.

No doubt they despaired long before that.

Now we, humanity, had been gifted of six beautiful worlds. And if we could not meet the Nataral, we could, at least, read their books and come to know them. And from their careful records we could learn about the still earlier races which had emerged from each of the other five goodworlds, each into a lonely universe.

Perhaps in another billion years the universe will more closely resemble the sciencefictional schemes of my grandfather's day. Maybe then commerce will plow the starlanes between busy, talky worlds.

But we, like the Nataral, came too early for that. We are cursed, if we hang around until that day, to be an Elder Race.

I looked one more time toward the constellation we named Phoenix, whither the Nataral had departed millions of our years ago. I could not see the dark star where they had gone. But I knew exactly where it lay. They had left explicit instructions.

Then I turned and entered the tent that I shared with Alice and our child, leaving the stars and shards behind me.

Tomorrow would be a busy day. I had promised Alice that we might begin building a house on a hillside not far from Oldcity.

She muttered some dreamtalk and cuddled close as I slipped into bed beside her. The baby slept quietly in her cradle a few feet away. I held Alice, and breathed slowly.

But sleep came only gradually. I kept thinking about what the Nataral had given us.

Correction . . . what they had *lent* us.

We could use their six worlds, on the condition we were kind to them. Those were the same conditions they had accepted when they took the four worlds long abandoned by the Lap-Klenno, their predecessors on the lonely starlanes . . . and that the Lap-Klenno had agreed to on inheriting the three Thwoozoon suns . . .

So long as the urge to spreadsettle was primary in us, the worlds were ours, and any others we happened upon.

But someday our priorities would change. Elbowroom would no

longer be our chief fixation. More and more, the Nataral had understood, we would begin to think instead about loneliness.

I knew they were right. Someday my great-to-the-nth descendants would find that they could no longer bear a universe without other voices in it. They would tire of these beautiful worlds, and pack up the entire tribe to head for a darkstar.

There, within the event horizon of a great black hole, they would find the Nataral, and the Lap-Klenno, and the Thwoozoon, waiting in a cup of suspended time.

I listened to the wind gentleflapping the tent, and envied my great-nth grandchildren. I, at least, would like to meet the other star-treaders, so very much like us.

Oh, we could wait around for a few billion years, till that distant time when most of the shells have cracked, and the universe bustles with activity. But by then we would have changed. By necessity we would indeed have become an ElderRace . . .

But what species in its right mind would choose such a fate? Better, by far, to stay young until the universe finally becomes a fun place to enjoy!

To wait for that day, the races who came before us sleep at the edge of their timestretched black hole. Within, they abide to welcome us; and we shall sit out, together, the barren early years of the galaxies.

I felt the last shreds of the old greatdepression dissipate as I contemplated the elegant solution of the Nataral. For so long we had feared that the Universe was a practical joker, and that our place in it was to be victims—patsies. But now, at last, my darkthoughts shattered like an eggshell . . . like the walls of a crystalcage.

I held my woman close. She sighed something said in dreamthought. As sleep finally came, I felt better than I had in a thousand years. I felt so very, very young.

APPENDIX
THE HUGO AWARDS

1953–1961 inclusive—See Volume One.
1962–1970 inclusive—See Volume Two.
1971–1975 inclusive—See Volume Three.

1976: 34th Convention—Kansas City
NOVEL—*The Forever War*, by Joe Haldeman
NOVELLA—"Home Is the Hangman," by Roger Zelazny
NOVELETTE—"The Borderland of Sol," by Larry Niven
SHORT STORY—"Catch That Zeppelin!" by Fritz Leiber
PROFESSIONAL EDITOR—Ben Bova
DRAMATIC PRESENTATION—*A Boy and His Dog*
PROFESSIONAL ARTIST—Frank Kelly Freas
FANZINE—*Locus*, Charles and Dena Brown
FAN WRITER—Richard E. Geis
FAN ARTIST—Tim Kirk
GRAND MASTER OF FANTASY AWARD—L. Sprague de Camp
JOHN W. CAMPBELL AWARD—Tom Reamy
SPECIAL COMMITTEE AWARD—James E. Gunn

1977: 35th Convention—Miami Beach
NOVEL—*Where Late the Sweet Birds Sang*, by Kate Wilhelm
NOVELLA—"Houston, Houston, Do You Read?" by James Tiptree, Jr., and "By Any Other Name," by Spider Robinson
NOVELETTE—"The Bicentennial Man," by Isaac Asimov
SHORT STORY—"Tricentennial," by Joe Haldeman
PROFESSIONAL EDITOR—Ben Bova
DRAMATIC PRESENTATION—No Award
PROFESSIONAL ARTIST—Rick Sternbach
FAN WRITER—Richard E. Geis and Susan Wood
FANZINE—*Science Fiction Review*, Richard E. Geis
FAN ARTIST—Phil Foglio
GRAND MASTER OF FANTASY AWARD—Andre Norton
JOHN W. CAMPBELL AWARD—C. J. Cherryh
SPECIAL COMMITTEE AWARD—George Lucas

1978: 36th Convention—Phoenix
NOVEL—*Gateway*, by Frederick Pohl
NOVELLA—"Stardance," by Spider Robinson
NOVELETTE—"Eyes of Amber," by Joan D. Vinge
SHORT STORY—"Jeffty Is Five," by Harlan Ellison
PROFESSIONAL EDITOR—George Scithers
DRAMATIC PRESENTATION—*Star Wars*
PROFESSIONAL ARTIST—Rick Sternbach
FAN WRITER—Richard E. Geis
FANZINE—*Locus*, Charles and Dena Brown
FAN ARTIST—Phil Foglio
GRAND MASTER OF FANTASY AWARD—Poul Anderson

BOOKLENGTH FANTASY—*The Silmarillion*, by J. R. R. Tolkien
JOHN W. CAMPBELL AWARD—Orson Scott Card

1979: 37th Convention—Brighton, United Kingdom
NOVEL—*Dreamsnake*, by Vonda McIntyre
NOVELLA—"The Persistence of Vision," by John Varley
NOVELETTE—"Hunter's Moon," by Poul Anderson
SHORT STORY—"Cassandra," by C. J. Cherryh
PROFESSIONAL EDITOR—Ben Bova
DRAMATIC PRESENTATION—*Superman*
PROFESSIONAL ARTIST—Vincent DiFate
FAN WRITER—Bob Shaw
FANZINE—*Science Fiction Review*, Richard E. Geis
FAN ARTIST—Bill Rotsler
GRAND MASTER OF FANTASY AWARD—Ursula K. Le Guin
BOOKLENGTH FANTASY—*The White Dragon*, by Anne McCaffrey
JOHN W. CAMPBELL AWARD—Stephen R. Donaldson

1980: 38th Convention—Boston
NOVEL—*The Fountains of Paradise*, by Arthur C. Clarke
NOVELLA—"Enemy Mine," by Barry Longyear
NOVELETTE—"Sandkings," by George R. R. Martin
SHORT STORY—"The Way of Cross and Dragon," by George R. R. Martin
NONFICTION BOOK—*The Science Fiction Encyclopedia*, Peter Nicholls
PROFESSIONAL EDITOR—George Scithers
DRAMATIC PRESENTATION—*Alien*
PROFESSIONAL ARTIST—Michael Whelan
FANZINE—*Locus*, Charles N. Brown
FAN WRITER—Bob Shaw
FAN ARTIST—Alexis Gilliland
GRAND MASTER OF FANTASY—Ray Bradbury
JOHN W. CAMPBELL AWARD—Barry Longyear

1981: 39th Convention—Denver
NOVEL—*The Snow Queen*, by Joan D. Vinge
NOVELLA—"Lost Dorsai," by Gordon R. Dickson
NOVELETTE—"The Cloak and the Staff," by Gordon R. Dickson
SHORT STORY—"Grotto of the Dancing Bear," by Clifford D. Simak
NONFICTION BOOK—*Cosmos*, by Carl Sagan
PROFESSIONAL EDITOR—Ed Ferman
DRAMATIC PRESENTATION—*The Empire Strikes Back*
PROFESSIONAL ARTIST—Michael Whelan
FANZINE—*Locus*, Charles N. Brown
FAN WRITER—Susan Wood
FAN ARTIST—Victoria Poyser
JOHN W. CAMPBELL AWARD—Somtow Sucharitkul

1982—40th Convention—Chicago
NOVEL—*Downbelow Station*, by C. J. Cherryh
NOVELLA—"The Saturn Game," by Poul Anderson
NOVELETTE—"Unicorn Variation," by Roger Zelazny
SHORT STORY—"The Pusher," by John Varley
NONFICTION BOOK—*Danse Macabre*, by Stephen King
PROFESSIONAL EDITOR—Ed Ferman
DRAMATIC PRESENTATION—*Raiders of the Lost Ark*
PROFESSIONAL ARTIST—Michael Whelan

FANZINE—*Locus*, Charles N. Brown
FAN WRITER—Richard E. Geis
FAN ARTIST—Victoria Poyser
JOHN W. CAMPBELL AWARD—Alexis Gilliland

1983—41st Convention—Baltimore
NOVEL—*Foundation's Edge*, by Isaac Asimov
NOVELLA—"Souls," by Joanna Russ
NOVELETTE—"Fire Watch," by Connie Willis
SHORT STORY—"Melancholy Elephants," by Spider Robinson
NONFICTION BOOK—*Isaac Asimov: The Foundations of Science Fiction*, by James E. Gunn
PROFESSIONAL EDITOR—Ed Ferman
DRAMATIC PRESENTATION—*Blade Runner*
PROFESSIONAL ARTIST—Michael Whelan
FANZINE—*Locus*, Charles N. Brown
FAN WRITER—Richard E. Geis
FAN ARTIST—Alexis Gilliland
JOHN W. CAMPBELL AWARD—Paul O. Williams

1984—42nd Convention—Anaheim
NOVEL—*Startide Rising*, by David Brin
NOVELLA—"Cascade Point," by Timothy Zahn
NOVELETTE—"Blood Music," by Greg Bear
SHORT STORY—"Speech Sounds," by Octavia E. Butler
NONFICTION BOOK—*The Encyclopedia of Science Fiction and Fantasy*, Vol. 3, Donald H. Tuck
PROFESSIONAL EDITOR—Shawna McCarthy
DRAMATIC PRESENTATION—*Return of the Jedi*
PROFESSIONAL ARTIST—Michael Whelan
SEMI-PROFESSIONAL MAGAZINE—*Locus*, Charles N. Brown
FANZINE—*File 770*, Michael Glyer
FAN WRITER—Michael Glyer
FAN ARTIST—Alexis Gilliland
JOHN W. CAMPBELL AWARD—R. A. MacAvoy
SPECIAL COMMITTEE AWARD—Larry T. Shaw and Robert Bloch

1985—43rd Convention—Melbourne, Australia
NOVEL—*Neuromancer*, by William Gibson
NOVELLA—"Press Enter," by John Varley
NOVELETTE—"Bloodchild," by Octavia E. Butler
SHORT STORY—"The Crystal Spheres," by David Brin
NONFICTION BOOK—*Wonder's Child: My Life in Science Fiction*, by Jack Williamson
PROFESSIONAL EDITOR—Terry Carr
DRAMATIC PRESENTATION—*2010*
PROFESSIONAL ARTIST—Michael Whelan
SEMI-PROFESSIONAL MAGAZINE—*Locus*, Charles N. Brown
FANZINE—*File 770*, Michael Glyer
FAN WRITER—David Langford
FAN ARTIST—Alexis Gilliland
JOHN W. CAMPBELL AWARD—Lucius Shepard